TRENCH

N

W

S

Kenton Hill

Hoaklin

Trent

Dorser

Dunnitch

Scurry

Hesson

Lavnonshire

A FORSAKEN PROPHECY

BY STACEY McEWAN

THE ARTISAN TRILOGY

A Forbidden Alchemy

A Forsaken Prophecy

THE GLACIAN TRILOGY

Ledge

Chasm

Valley

A FORSAKEN PROPHECY

THE ARTISAN BOOK 2

STACEY McEWAN

London · New York · Amsterdam/Antwerp · Sydney/Melbourne · Toronto · New Delhi

First published in the United States of America by Saga Press, an imprint of Simon & Schuster, LLC, 2026
First published in Great Britain by Solstice Books, an imprint of Simon & Schuster UK Ltd, 2026

1 3 5 7 9 10 8 6 4 2

Simon & Schuster UK Ltd, 7th Floor,
199 Bishopsgate, London, EC2M 3TY

Simon & Schuster Australia, Sydney
Simon & Schuster India, New Delhi

www.simonandschuster.co.uk
www.simonandschuster.com.au
www.simonandschuster.co.in

The authorised representative in the EEA is Simon & Schuster Netherlands BV, Herculesplein 96, 3584 AA Utrecht, Netherlands. info@simonandschuster.nl

A CIP catalogue record for this book
is available from the British Library

Hardback ISBN: 978-1-3985-3733-0
Paperback ISBN: 978-1-3985-3736-1
eBook ISBN: 978-1-3985-3734-7
Audio ISBN: 978-1-3985-3735-4

Cover design by James Fenner
Interior design by Erika R. Genova
Internal illustration by Lila Raymond

Printed and Bound in the UK using 100% Renewable Electricity at CPI Group (UK) Ltd

For my sisters, Alycia and Teagan,
and the magic between us.

But one man loved the pilgrim soul in you,
And loved the sorrows of your changing face
—William Butler Yeats

PROLOGUE

NINA
seventeen years previous

Ma and I were the only ones in church with the coming of winter. I hated her for it.

The walk was slushy, the building jarringly cold, the pews merciless. I wriggled my backside against it and whined to holy hell.

"I want to leave."

"I know you do." My mother's voice was distant. She looked to the altar as though she saw something else entirely. She only ever wore her best clothes here; a white dress turned yellow at the armpits and hem, a woolen hat low over her ears, earrings her own mother had given her on her wedding day.

There was no one in the parish more religious than my mother, it seemed. Not even the pastor rose on Sundays while snow was falling. No one but her and I to light the candles and converse with Idia, or pretend to. In Scurry, there was not much religion to be had at all. I knew for a fact that Pastor David liked to take God's name in vain. I heard it through the walls of our apartment when he visited Mrs. Flamshank in the night.

The other children of Scurry were not freezing on hard wood benches every week. They were under blankets in their beds, staving off the morning chill. They wouldn't be back in church until the snow had melted and the Scurry ground was full of widow's lace and wildflower.

"It's cold."

"Just a little longer." She scooted me closer to her, so I was tucked under her arm. I went reluctantly, wanting to reproach her, but gravitating toward the warmth. "It's important we come, even when we don't want to."

"But why?"

"Because it takes sufferin' to have your wishes answered," she said. "That's what God wants. He wants to know we've earned it."

"Is that why the seats hurt so bloody much?"

"Yeah. Don't swear."

I frowned at the little statue on the altar. Shorter than me, hollow-eyed, bone-white. Idia, frozen in her suffering. How much had she had to endure before God was finally satisfied?

"What do you wish for?" I asked Ma now. Whatever it was, she wanted it badly. Badly enough to wake me at dawn every week. Badly enough that tears filmed her eyes when she prayed to that ugly statue.

Her smile was as weak as they came. "When God grants it, I'll tell you." She kissed my curls, the same as her own: golden in sunlight, dull there in the nave.

"Pastor David says that God loves us all, even if we don't come to church."

"Well, Pastor David is a pig."

We sat in silence for a moment. Me fidgeting, Ma reveling in whatever evangelical reassurance she found in a place that smelled of tobacco and damp wood.

"Wishes ain't real," I said eventually, and only because I wanted to poke a hole in her peace. The bones of my backside pulverized further.

"I wished for *you*, and here you are. What say you to that?"

"All the women have babies, even the ones that don't want 'em. That ain't a real wish."

She scoffed. "And if you could wish for anythin', Nina, what would *you* wish for?"

What a question to lob at an eight-year-old. I wanted for more things than I knew how to voice. All that wanting had become an unrelenting ache in my fingers. Sometimes it was hard to tell exactly what it was I longed for.

Desserts? Toys? A big house with twelve rooms? Or was it tied more closely to the things I was afraid of? Vacant eyes. The tremor in Dad's fingers. The shake of Ma's frame when she lay aside me in bed.

"I'd wish for magic," I said. It seemed the only answer to encompass the whole lot.

She nodded, looked back to that sorry statue. "Me own Ma used to tell me a story about wishes. Do you want to hear it?"

I nodded.

She licked her cracked lips in readiness. "Let's see now. God bestowed three daughters to Earth—"

"God only had one daughter," I interrupted haughtily. "Idia."

"But in this story, there're *three*," she winked at me. "Idia, Joan, and Dione. The three daughters were sent to Earth with powerful gifts. In their blood was a magic no man or woman had ever seen. They could bend rivers, plunder the earth, levitate any matter they set their mind to. They held the world in the palm of their hands, and the humans, those greedy blighters, they wanted that power for themselves, didn't they?"

I leaned closer, captivated despite myself.

"Soon, people from foreign lands learned of their magic and came to take it from them. But the three daughters had grown and worked on this land, and their neighbors had come to love them. They vowed to protect the daughters—to hide them. These men and women called themselves 'the Stewards.'"

My ears pricked. A word I'd heard before. The ramblings of a street corner preacher on Pewter Lane who spoke of Stewards. There was a song they sang in the schoolyard:

Hide, hide the witch,
The stewards, they hid three.
Two in the parish,
One by the sea.
Catch, catch the witch,

Never let her flee.
Put her to the post,
The devil's slave, is she.

Ma continued. "But the enemy were relentless, and so of course, eventually the daughters were found, and their magic was stolen."

I saw it in my mind, those daughters holding their magic against their chests, kicking the shins of those who wanted to take it.

"Why didn't God help 'em?" I asked. But if my mother had an answer, it was stuck between her lips. She pressed them together tightly.

"Perhaps it was their turn to suffer," she said.

I looked to my shoelaces and pondered a God that would give his daughters magic, then punish them for it.

"They say if you visit their graves and make a wish, the three daughters will grant it," Ma said now, bumping her shoulder against mine.

"Have you seen 'em?" I frowned. "Their graves."

Ma looked to the ceiling. "No. But one day we both will."

"And we'll make a wish?"

"We'll make as many wishes as we can manage," she said.

Warmth gathered in. I mashed my nose into the sides of her ribs. "And Dad as well?"

She sighed, all the breath in her lungs escaping. "No, darlin'. That's a trip meant for you and me."

And she turned enough that I could see the bruise shadowing the left side of her face, creeping in from her hairline, swelling her eye near closed, and I thought it was just as well that we left him behind.

Those three daughters had seen enough suffering. Hadn't they?

CHAPTER ONE

PATRICK

Kenton Hill miners were made of songs, one sung most often.

This was saved for the weary hours just before the whistle sounded and the men were hauled back up the shaft. In Patrick's first years below-ground, his father would whisper it to him when Patrick's knees buckled, when his bones protested, when mud weighed him down.

Till the light comes, Patty, he'd say. *Till the lights come on up top, down we go.*

On the days when the second-shift miners were deathly tired, the song became just one murmured verse, repeated like a vow. *Till the light comes.*

It moved their feet to the end of each shift, tempted unwilling bodies into the shafts, and indeed, light found them. Morning breaking. They spilled out into the day.

Now, the song seemed like a threat. He rather hoped light never found him again.

In Margarite's tunnel, Patrick's shoulder beat its own pulse. His legs had begun to quake—from the blood loss, he suspected.

The bleeding had stopped, but the bullet remained buried somewhere in the sinew, and every so often he found his focus drifting, his view slipping sideways.

The tunnel in each direction was filled with soldiers wearing Artisan navy. The Lords' infantry. They staggered along with their own weeping sores. The soldier at Patrick's elbow was trying valiantly to hold his own brow together, but it was intent on streaming like a geyser.

All around them, the tunnel groaned.

This seemed of no consequence to anyone but Patrick. The soldiers continued onward, following the bobbing lanterns held aloft on the ends of bayonets. They journeyed farther and farther from Kenton Hill, water seeping from weep holes, insects and rats skittering between their feet, fathoms of earth suspended above them, speaking to them.

It was clear none of these men had spent much time beneath ground. If they had, their eyes would flit from wall to wall. They'd swallow dryly. Their balls would lodge in their stomachs and take all their valor with it.

Instead, they marched, carrying Patrick in tow, onward until the light came, unlettered to the language of tunnels.

Patrick sorely hoped the light never found them. He hoped they'd all be crushed under tons of dirt, hoped Belavere Trench would be left with one less army, one less Alchemist.

Should've put a bullet in your head when you had the chance, Patrick told himself.

The tunnel seemed to turn sideways again, his legs gave way, and the soldier at his arm grunted and cursed.

Patrick became vaguely aware of earth against his nostrils, soft mud cradling him on all sides.

"*Patrick?*" came a familiar voice. There were hands at his face, then on his shoulder. He winced. "Patrick, you have to get up!"

It was a voice both ugly and beautiful to him. Pain invaded again.

"Watch yourself, Charmer. Get away from him."

"*Patrick?* Open your eyes."

He wished he hadn't. He wanted very much to never glimpse her again. But a soldier crouched nearby with a lantern, and it haloed around her face as she hovered over him, her brow pinched and lined, the hazel of her eyes still prominent even shot through with blood. Her hair had pulled free and turned wild, long tangled curls falling into her face. Her muddy fingers were coursing up his neck, settling warmly against his jaw.

He detested the blood racing beneath her touch.

"Patrick?" she said again, relief blooming across her face.

"Sink . . . it," he grunted. *"Please."*

Tears drowned the hazel. "I can't," she whispered, her desperation nearly tangible.

But it was not for him, he now knew. Not for Kenton. Just for herself.

"Then get away from me." He turned his head out of her grasp, managed to roll onto his stomach. Two soldiers took him beneath his arms and hauled him to standing. He cried out in pain.

After that, he couldn't discern if his feet moved of his own accord or if he was being dragged by the men flanking him. The tunnel Nina had carved stretched onward, the dead end looming closer, and he listened to the sounds of her labored breath behind him, the earth's taunts, the grunting of the soldiers. He watched the images that plagued his mind of crumbling rooftops and screaming children. Whistling bullets and living fire, bouncing from house to house.

He pictured Kenton Hill, smoldering until the light came and then long after.

And he refused to ever picture Nina Harrow again.

CHAPTER TWO

NINA

Patrick's eyes had long been a danger to me.

How practiced I had become at avoiding them. One glance, and I was swallowed.

"Sink . . . it," he'd begged me. "Please."

He was slumped in the mud, his shirt painted to his chest with blood. Slow-blinking, arms limp, his teeth chattered with cold. Worse still, the blue in his eyes, not yet deadened by the dark. Still hoping.

A soldier kicked the sole of Patrick's boot and shouted at him to stand. He barely seemed to notice.

His eyes were drowning me.

Behind us, his town and his people were patching up bullet holes and stitching gashes. The dead were awaiting their graves. The runaways were likely rising from the tunnels and being greeted by the barrels of more guns, more soldiers. The Artisans had taken everything they needed from Kenton Hill. They had the last Alchemist. They had the earth Charmer.

And Patrick had no one but me.

I held him as though he were a sinking raft. I gritted my teeth. "I can't."

Blue turned to ice—his one remaining hope, snuffed out. He pivoted sharply out of my grasp.

But not before I saw the agony.

"Then get away from me."

And a tether between me and him snapped. Perhaps the final one. I felt the ricochet down to my core.

Someone grasped my shoulders and pulled me back, and in the mess of my breaking heart I flung wildly, turning to push them away, to fight and scratch and claw. To me, every one of these navy blue uniforms was Lord Tanner, the leader of the House himself. All this was his doing. *His* fault.

But the person who handled me spoke softly. He gripped my wrists to keep me from tearing out his eyes. "Shhh, Nina! Stop! *Stop!*" Theo's face hovered in the gloom, one eye swollen shut, the other pleading. "They'll knock you out, Nina. Please." His eyes flittered to the soldiers standing on every side, grappling for sense in the dark.

"Tie her up!" one shouted. "She's rabid. Get me some fucking rope!"

Theo gripped the sides of my face harder than he ever had. He pierced me with a stare so forceful that I had no choice but to focus on the edges of him, expanding and retracting in the glow. He spoke clearly, an anchor in his voice. "We'll figure it all out," he told me. "I promise you, we'll find a way."

And then we were wrenched apart again, and a sack was pulled over my face, my hands were tied, and several shouts echoed. Shoving. Grunting. The toes of boots glancing my heels.

The walls groaned their reproach. My fingers itched with the urge to pull them inward, to bury all of us.

But especially me.

Yes. Especially me.

The tunnel ended somewhere under Gilmore.

The infantry had dug themselves a crude hole all the way down to reach it, rope ladders dangling freely on every side, and I was permitted my sight to climb to the surface.

"Go on," said a soldier with an overflowing neck. He smacked my arse before my foot could find the first rung. "Up you go."

I spat at his boots, and he jumped back in disgust.

I was sure I would slip and fall at every rung. My limbs felt too feeble for climbing. Each time I blinked upward, the surface seemed impossibly far away.

I was dragged out by more unwanted hands, my front hauled over pebble and dirt, and I stumbled to my feet, immediately looking around for Patrick or Theo before someone thought to blindfold me again.

I saw neither among all the navy. Two soldiers gripped either arm, the heavy-necked one and another, and I was frog-marched into the sea of soldiers, some of them trading canisters, others finding damp cigarettes in their pockets and trying to light them in vain.

"She's a pretty one," said the toad. I feared from his position he could see down my blouse. "Ain't she?"

"Shut up, Luderman," said his comrade, repositioning his grip on my arm. "She's the earth Charmer. It don't matter what else she is."

And yet, the toad's eyes remained on the split buttons below my neck.

We climbed knolls of no discerning marks until a steam train loomed ahead, on tracks bracketed by hills. The swarm of navy blue cascaded down the slopes toward it.

I was loaded into a carriage with no seats, no benches. Just rotting wooden walls and floors, a bucket in the corner that smelled strongly of urine. Theo and Patrick were loaded in after me, the latter dragged, the three of us made to sit at different corners of the carriage, our hands tied by rope and looped through cattle rings.

There was no telling how much blood Patrick had lost or how dire his condition. It had been impossible to gauge in the tunnel. Luderman was blocking my view of Patrick as he fastened my bindings, and I tried desperately to lean around him.

The soldier chuckled knowingly. It sent ripples down his neck. "That your beau, is it?" he asked, one eyebrow raised. "Don't seem to like you too much."

Patrick's eyelids had peeled back, consciousness finding him. And indeed, he groaned at the sight of me.

Luderman barked a laugh at that, then grasped my jaw hard enough to send bolts of warning down my spine. "Perhaps you're in the market for someone friendlier," he said. Then, horrifyingly, he descended to mash his mouth against mine.

And I tasted spit and decay. I bit down hard on the soldier's lip, driven by panic more than bravery, and felt it split. I could hear the clink and rattle of thrown chain bindings, the pounding of my own blood. Beyond that, a roar. I reared my leg back then kicked without particular aim.

Luderman toppled to the floor, clutching his groin. He sprayed a litany of curses through the blood trickling from his lip, eyes bulging. "You fuckin' bitch!" he yelled, the other soldiers laughing as he rolled onto his back, hands between his legs.

"Not bad for a city girl," one of them said, grinning and passing a lighter to his comrade.

"Scurry" came a voice. Patrick spoke with eyes so maddened he looked possessed. "She's from Scurry."

He did not look at me, or the soldiers, but right at that panting, bleeding Luderman.

The soldiers chuckled and nodded, retreating to the end of the carriage as the train coughed to life.

But Luderman regained his footing, albeit with some difficulty. He spat blood and staggered in my direction, twitching with rage.

"Wait!" Theo called out, pulling at his bindings. "Stop—"

My heart sprinted. Instinctively, I curled up. The soldier's boots stopped in front of me, and I waited for the blow.

"There's one hundred pounds in my pocket" came Patrick's voice, and I looked out from the crevice between my strung arms.

He stared back at me, his jaw tightened, his wrists ghost-white against the ropes. "It's all yours if you leave the lady be."

A moment of hesitancy, of silence. I peered up at Luderman to see a slow grin spread over his cheeks. "Not really in a position to be makin' deals, are you, Colson?" he said, and yet the soldier swung his large form in Patrick's direction, already scanning his clothing. "But I might as well have me way with both of you, since you offered."

Luderman looked back at me once, winked. "Won't be a moment," he promised, flashing his yellow teeth. He bent down to a waiting Patrick, fossicking through one of his trouser pockets, and then the other. "Ain't nothin' there," he grunted, brow pinched.

Then Patrick threw his forehead so hard into the bridge of the man's nose, the crack reverberated around the carriage.

The soldier's head snapped back on his neck, and for a second time, he toppled sideways.

Patrick gave a loud groan. "Fuck," he said, cinching his eyes shut.

"Patrick?"

He blinked rapidly, only to find the other soldiers converging in front of him, Luderman slumped lifeless at their feet.

"Hello, boys," Patrick said warily, resting his head with a grimace against the wall. "Don't suppose any of you want a hundred pounds?"

"Knock him out for the journey," said the shorter of the two men. He lifted his bayonet until it was level with Patrick's face, and the barrel shook. "Quickly," he uttered, eyeing his unconscious comrade.

Patrick looked resigned, but as the taller soldier stalked toward him, I reared upward. "No," I uttered without thinking. "Wait, please!"

"Gentlemen," said Theo, his face and clothes as dirty as my own, but his voice far more polished. "This man is the very last Alchemist on the continent. Think about that for a moment. Far from me to tell you how to do your job." Here, Theo paused, watching the soldier's gun wobble dangerously close to Patrick's eye. "But if you were to injure Lord Tanner's most wanted man with any permanence, I doubt they'd let you wear that uniform to the gallows."

The soldiers, both tall and short, hesitated. They looked to each other with matched indecision. Then the shorter one cursed and lowered his bayonet. "If you get clever," he said, jutting a finger at Patrick. "I'll shoot you."

"Will you?" Theo asked skeptically.

The soldier grimaced. "I'll knock you witless, then."

"Fair," Theo consented, as though the business were concluded.

The soldiers eyed Patrick wearily, then left Luderman where he lay, retreating back to their far corner, less jovial than before.

I exhaled in a gust, then manically wiped my mouth as best I could on my sleeve, nausea broiling.

"Are you all right?" Theo asked. His brow was creased, the coolness he'd exuded before now gone. He turned his body to better see me in a way that looked painful.

"Fine," I uttered.

Patrick had closed his eyes again, his pallor gray.

"You'd be wise not to sleep, Colson," Theo told him. "You're likely concussed."

"Leave him be," I said. It hissed past my teeth unexpectedly. "He's lost blood. He needs to rest."

"And slip into a coma?"

"What I need," Patrick murmured, eyelids sealed tightly, "is for the both of you to shut up."

And we did. Theo with a shrug, me with my lip between my teeth.

"Unless you feel inspired to derail this train, Nina." Patrick's back slumped farther down the wall. "I wouldn't say no to an earthquake."

I eyed his injuries once more, the rope looping through the cattle rings. I shook my head. "I can't."

His eyes snapped open then, colder than I'd ever seen them. "Don't lie to me," he said, so darkly it crawled over my flesh. "I've seen you move hills. It ain't a matter of *can't*, is it? It's a matter of *won't*." He held my gaze. "I never had your loyalty, did I?"

And there it was. That gun of his pointed between my eyes, finally firing.

I think he saw it—the way my mind folded in, they way my heart stuttered. "Patrick, I—"

"Tell me," he said, his tone banal to anyone but me. "Say it exactly as it is, Nina. You work for the House, and I'm a fool."

I saw, for that brief moment, all the way through him. Irreparable wounds. Punctures and shattered bones, tendons unmoored and swinging, spirals of slackened gut and a gasping heart.

And I was desperate to tell him everything. Every wretched thing I'd done, every wretched thing done to me. But the list of confessions was overwhelming. How could I tell him that I was every bit as terrible as he feared and still have him love me in the end?

"The House has my mother," I said, the words barely breaching my lips. "And Tanner promised to kill her unless I . . . unless I helped him."

Patrick's eyes rolled back and closed once more. For a moment, I thought him asleep. "So, you helped him," he whispered—to himself, it seemed. "You found the last Alchemist for him."

"No," I said, louder than before. "No, I changed my mi—"

"And why did Tanner need the earth Charmer to do it?" Patrick interrupted. "What else did he ask you to do, Nina? After you'd found me?"

I lowered my head and closed my eyes. "Patrick—"

"Did he ask you to bury us all in the mud?" he pressed. "Was that the grand plan?"

Theo scoffed darkly. "I assure you, Colson, if she wanted to bury Kenton Hill, the whole place would be fifty feet under." His cheeks had turned ruddy. He leaned his head dejectedly against the wall. "Her grand plan was to seduce you," he said, the veins in his hands growing more prominent as he said it. "In the hopes you'd reveal where you were keeping Domelius Becker."

I sucked in a breath.

Patrick's jaw went rigid. I watched his throat bob once, twice. He did not look at me again. "Then you can tell your boss she was successful." His eyes closed. "A better actress, I've never seen."

I felt myself crack and splinter.

"So, I told you my secrets," Patrick said, quieter now. "You took them straight to Polly. And she scribbled it all to Tanner." His eyelids fluttered, strength failing him. "You even paved him a road right into Kenton, and had me believe you were paving it for *me*." He sounded begrudgingly impressed.

And there were waves of guilt in me, yes, but there was irritation, too. Defiance.

An actress, he'd called me. They both had. But I could bring to mind every instance of Patrick's eyes pinning me to a wall, his fingers whispering over mine, and always it seemed something was perched on the edge of his lips when I was near, seconds from tumbling free.

He had seduced *me*.

I set my eyes on Theo first, tongue pulsing. "You told me that you came to Kenton Hill as a trade. In return, Lord Tanner would resume his search for me."

Theo's eyes became confused, guarded. He nodded slowly. "Yes."

"And then I turned up alive, and you were surprised to find that I wasn't still eighteen years old and fawning over you."

His lips pressed together tightly. "That's not—"

"And it hurt your feelings that I no longer needed you. Angered you. It makes you mad still, to know I chose someone else."

He couldn't seem to conjure a denial. Instead, he glowered.

"And *you*," I continued, turning on Patrick. I found him watching me closely. "Who brought me into his parish with my wrists tied and a sack over my head. Can you honestly meet my eye and claim that I *tricked* you into . . . into . . ."

"Lovin' you?" Patrick asked, his voice deep, rebounding in my chest. I hadn't unbalanced him at all. Hadn't made a dent. "In truth, Nina, I don't have it in me to unravel that question."

He turned his head away as though he couldn't stand the sight of me.

I blanched. But I had to tell him all of it now, while he was still close enough to hear it. "I lied to you," I admitted. "About Tanner, about what he'd demanded of me, but not the rest. I didn't reveal your secret to anyone. Not even Polly. I didn't bring soldiers into Kenton Hill."

"I wish I could believe that," Patrick said, wincing. "But even if you weren't lyin' to me right now, it wouldn't count for much, would it? We've both of us made a few too many missteps." He didn't seem to need my response. "Mine was lettin' swanks into Kenton Hill in the first place."

I fumed. "I didn't give you up."

"So you say."

"Yeah." I tugged at the ropes around my wrists. "So I say."

"Yet there's the matter of timin'," said Patrick, "and the scant few who knew what I was."

"Patrick, you *know* me!"

He chuckled grimly, wiping his brow against his sleeve, and looked resolutely at nothing at all. "It felt that way, didn't it?" he said. "Like we knew each other." He closed his eyes and leaned back into the wall of the carriage. "But when I think about it, Nina, you're a stranger to me." He nodded to himself as though confirming something. His eyes closed. "A stranger with all my secrets."

A tear slipped free and sprinted for my chin. My heart thrashed, and I did nothing to quell it. I watched Patrick close off in increments until his entire body was angled away from mine, and I could see nothing but the flushed skin at the back of his neck, the jumping pulse beneath his ear.

Theo cleared his throat. When I spared him a withering glance, his jaw softened. "For what it's worth, Pat," he said, seemingly with great effort, "it can't have been Nina who brought this army to your doorstep."

"Your word's worth nothin' to me," Patrick said with finality. A few moments later, he lost consciousness.

The train rattled on, and the three of us swayed like slaughtered pigs on hooks. Night crept in and made breathing easier. It was more difficult to see the blood across Patrick's chest, easier to avoid Theodore's insistent gaze. I couldn't be sure how long I had gone without sleeping. Without eating. I ignored my screaming bladder.

Anger kept me awake. The more my mind churned, the more that rage grew.

For Theodore, who thought I was his, no matter my own feelings; for Patrick, blinded by his own hate; for Polly, who was damningly absent; for Lord Tanner; and Luderman; and all men, suddenly. How quick they were to use and discard me.

But then that anger turned inward, and I found myself wanting to claw at my chest, take my own heart in my hands and wring it. This was my doing. My cowardice. I'd waited too long to tell Patrick the truth. I'd had power and squandered it, hadn't done a thing to help another with it. I'd hidden behind years of neutrality, running and running until the consequences caught up to me.

Loathing like I'd never felt before made its home under my skin.

I let it sink in. A penance.

The train clattered on.

Luderman awoke as the train whistled its arrival. He'd snored for more than half the journey and came up bleary eyed, his nose off-center, his lips sealed in dried blood. He took one glance in my direction and glared but did not advance.

While the soldiers stretched and yawned and gathered their bayonets, Patrick spoke. It was soft. Reluctant.

But he spoke for me, in a quiet aside, as though he couldn't bear not to say it. "You have something the House needs," he told me. "It gives you power. You understand?"

I stared at him, nodded. He was looking dead ahead at the forthcoming soldiers. "They can't take that from you," he said. "Whatever else they might take, they can't take who you are."

I remembered what he'd said to me once, when we were twelve.

You've got a mind of your own. Don't let those fuckers take it.

I shivered.

I meant to say something more to Patrick, or to Theo. I felt suddenly, frighteningly, as though it might be my last opportunity.

But any words, all words, now seemed futile. What could possibly be said in these last few seconds to dispel the rot?

We prisoners were blindfolded again, our hands retied, threats spat in our ears about being belted senseless if we tried to magic our way out of capture, but with hundreds of soldiers surrounding us on all sides, that promise seemed extraneous.

I could do nothing but listen. I listened to the train cranks settle and the steam chest let out a final sigh.

Hundreds of feet and voices rent the cold air. Some were gleeful, wives and fathers and children fishing their soldier from the trough, delighted they weren't dead. Some cried, their soldier not among the school. I was shoved and herded onward until the sound dwindled, and the music of the city rose up, though not as I remembered it.

I tried to bring to mind the National House, the citadel and its domed roof, the clock tower, the steepled rooftops, the thin channels of fresh water running street side, the horseless wagons and red bricks.

I wondered if it looked as different as it sounded—subdued. On edge.

I noticed the change underfoot when we entered the courtyard of the National House. Cobblestone became dirt, then steps, then mosaic, until the city was muted. Heavy doors closed. I heard Theodore arguing to have his blindfold lifted, Patrick breathing heavily. I wondered how long it would take for his wound to foul.

I had spent enough time in the House to know where we were heading. Up the grand winding stairs, down one corridor and another, into a vast, sparkling room normally occupied by—

"Lord Tanner," said a soldier. It sounded like the general, the very same one who had taken us hostage. The one who had run Gunner through with a knife. "I apologize for the hour. You said to bring them straight to you."

"And so you have."

The blindfold lifted away, and before me, Lord Tanner clacked his teeth together and stood from an oversize desk. He looked older. Gaunt. There were even fewer hairs on his head. His jowls didn't quiver as much as I remembered. It all served to make him seem more severe, and no less frightening.

"Miss Clarke," he said to me. "Well done."

My throat closed over. I did not have the courage to look to my left at Patrick. I felt Theo's stare burning into me, willing me to stay quiet, to be clever.

I knew I ought to smile and bow my head and let my charade of loyalty to the House continue, but I was done playing their games. I was bone-tired and burning with anger. "Where is my mother?" I bit out.

Tanner's slippery grin wavered. He turned to Theo, who looked, by all accounts, haggard, his eye swollen nearly shut and his shirt torn at the sleeve.

"Mr. Shop," Tanner continued. "I wish I could offer you the same praise." He then pulled a scribble from his pocket, an eyeglass from his robe, and poised it over the bridge of his nose. He read aloud.

"*To the right honorable Lord Tanner . . .* Where is it?" his eyes skimmed the page. "Ah, here . . . *three fire Charmers found dead in the canals . . . the former Lord Theodore Shop found deserting at Kenton Hill and resisted detainment . . .* My, my." Tanner quickly folded the parchment again, then walked to his desk to discard it. "I cannot say I blame you, boy. You've come up rather short these past years." He clasped his hands before him. The words were mild, but I sensed a spiking fury behind them. Tanner's eyes flashed. "Two years, the Alchemist eluded you, and he was under your nose the whole time." He tsked, and again the noise was too clipped, too overzealous. "And now I come to find you tried to abandon your post. The very one *you* volunteered for. Am I to believe that you've turned to the side of the rebels?"

Theodore straightened, though I saw the slight flinch. "No, my lord," and he said, glancing once at me. "I only meant to escape the Union's recapture. It wasn't my intention to flee the Lords' Army. I . . . I suppose I lost my wits for a moment."

Tanner regarded him as though he were a lowly insect. "Your father will be much relieved to hear it," he said. "I, however, remain unconvinced." He nodded once to the soldier at Theodore's side, and there was a flurry of movement.

One soldier pulled a switchblade from his belt.

Another seized Theodore's tied wrists, ripped his shirtsleeve to the crook of his elbow.

Theodore struggled. "What are you doing?"

And the blade sank into his Artisan brand, brilliant red pooling and then flowing freely over Theo's forearm. Theo shouted in pain, the blood spilling quickly. His knees sank down to the tile, black-and-white checkers now slickened.

"Just a precaution," Tanner said, grimacing at the mess. "While I make up my mind."

I realized I was straining against the hold of a soldier, who cursed and yanked at my arm. "Theo?" I called.

But Theo was bent over his wrist, his breaths ragged, one side of his shirt turning crimson.

"You'll kill him!" I shouted at Tanner, trying to wrench my arm free.

The lord turned to the soldier at my side and nodded in kind.

Hands clamped over my forearm, shunting my sleeve up.

The mottled skin where Idia once resided bore up. A blade flashed down, and in it sank, all the way to the bone.

I screamed and wrenched myself free, falling to the floor. Somewhere above, a voice thundered. A shout of pain. More feet smattered across the tiles. I looked up wearily to see Patrick with his arms looped over a soldier's neck, his roped hands pressing tightly against the man's throat.

Patrick's eyes were on me, bulging desperately.

A huddle of soldiers grasped Patrick from every side, but Patrick was bigger, far stronger, and the soldier in his grasp flailed.

One soldier held a pistol to Patrick's temple.

"STOP!" Tanner bellowed. It rebounded into the vaulted ceiling. "I SAID, STOP!"

The soldiers froze, confused.

They doubled in my vision, tripled. I blinked rapidly.

"*Enough*," Tanner growled, the cords of his neck pulsating. "Remove your hands from the Alchemist. *Now.*"

One by one, they did. They stepped back reluctantly, leaving Patrick to stand as he was, the rope of his restraints sitting firmly against the windpipe of his captive.

The soldier's face was puce. His fingers dug desperately at Patrick's hold.

"Help her," Patrick said. Not to me, but to Tanner. His hands shook, and his shoulder was bleeding again, the ropes of muscle in his arms flexed. *"Now."*

My eyes closed of their own accord, and I forgot how to open them. When I did, all I saw was blood pooling in the cradle of my hands. It rushed from the wound, eager to escape. Nausea descended.

"HELP HER!"

"Calm yourself," Tanner commanded, his expression livid. "Once enough idium has drained away, they'll be treated with bluff to keep them from bleeding out. They'll recover. Precautions must be taken while I ascertain which side you've aligned with, Miss Clarke, Mr. Shop. Until then, I'm afraid I can't have you wielding your mediums, now, can I?" Tanner peered at the soldier in Patrick's grasp, whose eyes were beginning to roll back. "If you plan to kill the man, then do it quickly, Mr. Colson, for Idia's sake. The hour is late."

Theodore fell sideways, his eyes closing. The wound at his wrist continued to flow.

"*Fuck*," Patrick spat, and he released the man, who promptly collapsed. Patrick staggered and groaned, his hands rising to grip the bullet wound on his shoulder. "You have me," he said, panting painfully. "You got what you wanted because of *her*," he righted himself, hissing another curse. "You've no reason to punish her. She followed *your fucking orders*."

"She did," Tanner agreed. "For the most part. Though I'm not a fool. She's a slippery, defiant little thing. She developed a rather obnoxious habit of being a traitor when she was young."

I thought perhaps I'd fallen sideways, too. Something hot and slick puddled against my cheek.

"You and I have business to discuss, Mr. Colson."

"Get her a doctor, or there'll be no business."

The ceiling seemed to be rising, lifting away into the night. And I was sinking, sinking. Warmth escaped me, and it took with it all the light, the color.

"Don't worry yourself, Mr. Colson," Lord Tanner's voice said, as though it were whispering into my ear. "There's a greater purpose at hand. One in which I'd very much like the both of you to remain alive for."

THE TRENCH TRIBUNE

REBEL ALCHEMIST UNCOVERED

From the last remaining print house in Belavere City, this journalist receives official scribble from the House of Lords that their raids in the Northeast have proven fruitful.

Lord Tanner named Kenton Hill, a little-known collier town, as the home of the elusive Miners Union command—a confounding statement of which this reporter remains skeptical.

Moreover, the Right Honorable Lord has proclaimed that the rebel chairman, a PATRICK COLSON, has been arrested and transported to Belavere City.

Inside sources add to these startling revelations that the House recognizes Colson as none other than a hidden Alchemist.

There has been no word as to the welfare of former House Alchemist Domelius Becker.

CHAPTER THREE

PATRICK

The year he turned thirteen, Patrick and his brothers came close to death.

It was a dead winter, the most ravenous anyone could remember. The coal ran low before frost stuck to the ground. Influenza spread. Bluff prices rocketed. There were many families in Kenton Hill who simply awaited death from their beds, bellies hollow, throats aflame, burning schoolbooks in the hearth to keep children warm in their final hours.

Many did not make it to spring, and there were fraught moments in which Patrick was certain he was slipping away.

Donny caught the fever first. He slowly boiled before their eyes. Their mother spooned soup past his cracked lips.

The next morning, Patrick awoke sweating, panting, barely aware of Tess Colson mopping his brow. Gunner quickly followed, all three of them abed while their mother changed their pajamas, their sheets, collected their vomit, prayed.

Patrick remembered it only in fragments—a shutter of frames. His mother counting farthings on a wooden table, eyes tightening. Donny's wails. Gunner sleeping interminably, as though he were already dead. He remembered his own body convulsing, seizing, squeezing the very last vestiges of his strength.

Patrick did not remember his father in this reel of memory. As he recalled, John Colson had gone away to Dorser by train that winter. The Miners Union had been in its infancy then, the support not yet far-reaching. He traveled often in the beginning, amassing members with his speeches, establishing connections. Always, he returned a little more invigorated than when he left, while his wife slowly iced over.

Patrick's mother did not cry that winter, but she apologized often—every time her sons moaned, cried, vomited. "Bluff," he remembers begging her. And her forehead would crease so deeply it seemed it was splitting, and she'd return to those coins on the table, counting them over and over, then swearing and knocking them to the floor.

And then when it seemed Donny was at his worst, when he hadn't woken for more than two days, hadn't eaten for even longer, Tess Colson left them alone. Patrick heard the kitchen door collide violently with its frame.

Gunner might have held his hand, Patrick thought. There was an image in his mind, his big brother reaching out across his cot, fingers hot and limp. Patrick thought perhaps he himself cried, that he begged for their father.

His next memory was a lick of heat in his veins. Patrick had come awake with a clearer mind, to the sight of his mother leaning over him, cheeks ruddy red with the cold, a spoonful of black solution poised at his lips. "Drink, son," she had said calmly.

The clarity of age led Patrick to surmise his mother stole the bluff, having found herself short of coin. From what household, he did not wish to know.

The Colson brothers recovered as the bottle of bluff ran dry, in time for their father to return, in time for Tess Colson to yield to her own rampant fever.

The influenza of that dead winter was later named gray fever. It turned one's skin red first, then purple, then ashen near the end. Of all the Colsons struck down that season, it was Tess who came closest to death. She was the color of storm clouds when John Colson walked back through the door, his smile wide and beard heavy with snow. Gunner had whaled his fists against John's chest for staying away so long. Donny had cried. Patrick had wrapped his arms around his father's middle, despite not having hugged his father that way since he was small. Tess had coughed in a way that invoked death.

John Colson's timely return, Patrick knew, was the only reason his mother still lived. After that, even when Tess Colson seemed at her worst, Patrick had not worried for her. He knew his father had everything in hand. His father could fix it, could fix anything. He'd come back with pockets full of money and vials.

It took two days for the bluff to win the battle. Two days of Patrick and Gunner and Donny hovering uselessly by her bed, watching their mother snatch in each breath. They held on to her bedsheets as though they could anchor her there. "Patience, boys," John told them. "She's as tough as they come. Tougher than me, even."

He was right, as he always was. Her color returned, the coughing thinned. She rose from her sick bed and yelled at Donny for running through the kitchen. But Tess Colson was never quite the same. Her lungs seemed to hoard remnants of the fever, and no amount of bluff ever snuffed it for good.

Soon after Tess recovered, John Colson hauled a sack into the kitchen and dumped its contents onto the floor. Terranium ore spilled out, blue-black and glistening.

He'd pointed one calloused finger at it. "Siphon these rocks," he'd said to Patrick. "And your mother'll never again lay sick in bed."

And he had. Eventually.

It took weeks to make any progress. The idium he'd stolen from the National House had long since begun to wane. The magic that remained in him was weak. Reluctant. Most of those terranium rocks had crumbled, splitting unevenly, the bluff inside made unusable. To this day, there are two holes in the plaster of the Colson's kitchen, where Patrick had launched the ruined ore away in frustration.

"Easy, son," his dad had said, over and over. "Easy does it. Be patient with it. Feel the hollow? That's where the ink is hiding. Split it right down the middle."

But the ore was delicate. It shattered at the slightest disruption, contaminating that which it fiercely guarded.

"Gentle with it," John Colson had told him. "Learn control. Learn composure. Composed men do far better than the bulls."

Patrick heard his father's voice echoing off the stained glass windows and barren walls of the swanks' National House.

He'd been confined alone to a strange room. The floors here were checkered white and black, so starkly contrasting they seemed to morph, tricking him. He thought it was likely once a small laboratory. There was a large bench with a basin. Oak shelves and cupboards built into the walls, floor to ceiling. Every one of them was emptied of anything but dust. The hearth was cobwebbed. The window depicted a nude image of a man he assumed was God almighty, though he could not, for the life of him, understand why an all-powerful being would be in possession of such a small cock.

He felt much the way he had felt that dead winter when he was thirteen. He hadn't eaten, hadn't slept. His head pulsed as though breaching his skull.

He sat on the floor, his back against the shelves, clothed in the same sorry attire he'd arrived in. Several feet away, a sack of terranium ore awaited him, just as it had in his mother's kitchen.

He had yet to open it, to see its contents, and yet he knew what it was. Terranium had a certain beat, a vibration. He felt it from where he sat. They used to send Alchemists into the mines to feel out the deposits of ore, to tell the diggers what to aim for, back when Alchemists were a dime a dozen and it didn't much matter if they were blown to pieces or buried under.

The door hadn't opened in some time. In a moment of useless ire, he'd thrown his shoulder into it to no avail, forgetting the bullet buried in the tissue.

Tanner was due to visit any moment, Patrick thought. He'd returned regularly these past two days, flanked by guards. The most recent had been his longest stay yet.

"You worsen by the hour," he'd said. Patrick hadn't risen from his place on the tiles, and Tanner hadn't ventured past the doorway. He'd nodded to the sack that remained untouched. "I'm sure some of that ore holds the bluff you need."

A bubble of laughter climbed up Patrick's throat, more menacing than mirthful. "And what makes you believe I intend to recover?" he murmured. The tiles distended again. He pinched his eyes shut.

"I'm afraid death is not an option, Mr. Colson. In fact, I've brought a gift."

And from behind him came a middle-aged woman in Artisan blue robes with wide, fearful eyes. She stepped around Tanner hesitantly, looking back at the lord for approval.

"Letty is a Smith of lead," Tanner explained to Patrick. "She's here to pull that bullet from your shoulder. It may be wise to bite down on something."

But there was no time. The woman named Letty raised a shaky hand in the direction of Patrick's shoulder, and he immediately felt the sensation of something twisting, pulling. He hissed, cursed, his hand flying to his arm.

Bit by bit the bullet wheedled free, finally flying into Letty's hand. The woman's pallor turned abruptly green, and she dropped the bullet onto the floor, her hand now covered in gore. She trembled delicately at the sight of it.

"Thank you, Letty. You may go."

Letty's shoes clacked off the tiles as she hurried out.

Patrick's breaths had turned rapid. He closed his eyes and waited for the throb of his arm to slow.

"You might like to know that Nina Clarke is well. All that blood was . . . unseemly, I know." His nose crinkled. "But if you and Miss Clarke do as is required, there won't be a need for any more bad business."

"Harrow," Patrick grunted. "Not Clarke."

Tanner regarded him curiously. "I'm surprised you should care for her at all."

And to that, Patrick had no argument.

"She was a fair actress in her schooling years, according to her professors," Tanner ruminated. "I suppose she must have been rather convincing. She *is* uniquely beautiful, I can admit. There is an . . . allure there."

Patrick tasted something horribly metallic. His jaw rolled.

"Still," Tanner continued. "I did not imagine the feats she'd be capable of. She found her way right under your skin, didn't she?"

Patrick pictured himself on a meat hook, his torso flayed.

"Yes," Tanner nodded, as though he could see right through to Patrick's skeleton, every nick and fracture there. Every weakness.

"Women have long been man's ruin."

Patrick slid sideways, unable to hold his spine straight another moment. His temple sought the cold tile.

"I need an Alchemist, Mr. Colson. Quite badly." He went to nudge the sack of terranium with his shoe. "You have the burden of being the only living man who might be able to siphon idium from whatever sad stores of rock remain."

"And if I don't?" Patrick murmured. He could not be sure the words did not blend.

Tanner's footsteps gathered in his ears. He was suddenly close enough for Patrick to spit on. "Then hundreds of years of Artisan tradition will be no longer."

"Never cared much for swank traditions."

"Those born in the brink rarely do. But they care a great deal about bluff, do they not?"

Patrick felt as though his head were being incised, but his eyes opened, and he peered at Tanner, now leering somewhere above.

Tanner clicked his tongue. "My commander relayed all manner of information about the Kenton Hill raids. My men found your guns, your grenades. They even found your family's inn, Mr. Colson, its kitchen filled with shelves of bluff. Quite a trove."

Patrick's eyes flashed. Burning bile coursed his throat.

"It is all now in my possession, of course," Tanner continued. "The bluff will be meted out fairly, to those in dire need of it here in the city. As for those wounded members of your Union . . . well, I imagine they will not fare well if you decide to be selfish in this time of need."

"Fuck you," Patrick said.

"Would you deny the continent hope, Mr. Colson? All those sick children and elders? Would you see your own kin without any bluff to heal them from their battle injuries?"

The Tess Colson of the past roared to mind, coughing and spitting and failing on her bed, his father tipping vial after vial past her lips.

"Your reluctance will kill them," Tanner said. "There is no escaping what now must be accepted. Your revolution has failed, Mr. Colson." Tanner paced with his hands behind his back. "The Miners Union has scattered, and your hometown is abandoned. If you continue to resist, more people will suffer. Meanwhile, I'll be forced to take more unsavory measures. It shouldn't be hard to find a blind man—Donny, is that his name? And the brother who was gravely wounded . . . Gunner, I believe. Perhaps I could bring them here—"

"I bet your Artisans turn to water when you threaten their families," Patrick said, weariness beginning to overcome him. "Bet you love to see 'em cower at your feet, eh? Cryin' and pissin' themselves?"

Tanner's eyes narrowed, his hands opened and closed.

"Yeah," Patrick murmured, coughing painfully. "It's made you lazy. Uncreative." Tanner's eyes flashed, a nerve plucked. "You go ahead and bring my brothers here," Patrick smiled at the thought. "Though I'll warn you, you ought to double your guard. Craftsmen don't bother quiverin' when you threaten 'em. They just go about cuttin'. Savages, the lot of 'em."

Tanner turned quickly purple, a vein in his temple thickening. After a few beats of silence, he said, as though he were spitting rocks, "And if I was to be more creative with our earth Charmer?"

Patrick's humor vanished.

"Perhaps I could take a leaf from your book, Colson. What would a gangster do? Pull teeth? Take fingers? Would you be persuaded then?"

The sack on the floor quivered. Patrick willed his mind to grasp the rocks within, to pulverize Tanner's brain with them. But his mind was a sieve. The sack fell still quickly.

"I'll take that as a yes," Tanner said, his eyes sticking to the sack. "But fear not, Mr. Colson. There are others with whom I might find my creative release."

And through the film of fatigue, Patrick saw the guards step aside, and over the threshold came a man with his hands bound behind him, chestnut hair silver-streaked and receding at the temples. He had sun-damaged skin, yellow teeth, an overgrown beard, and the same muddy brown eyes as Gunner Colson.

"Dad," Patrick said, and it came out in an exhale, a gust.

John Colson's eyes watered, his lips mashed together as though to pinch off sensation.

A guard raised a long, polished baton, and it cracked soundly over the back of John Colson's head.

They left him there on the floor, his legs kicked aside as the guards closed him in.

Some part of Patrick's mind noted it was clever indeed, to have his father's skull bleed rivers onto the tiles while he sat idle by a bag of terranium. What better way to force his hand?

Patrick turned over his father, grasped his slack face in his hand, somehow here, somehow warm and alive, after everything.

"*Dad*," he called, shook him, pressed his fingertips to his neck, cupped the gash at his crown as though it might stem the tide.

John Colson's eyes rolled beneath the lids. He gasped a few times. It was frighteningly shallow. Horribly infrequent.

And there was really no question, then, about what should be done. It would only need to be just enough bluff. For his father, not for Tanner. It wasn't surrender. John Colson would never forgive him for that.

With the last vestiges of his strength, Patrick pulled a jagged piece of black ore from the sack and inspected it against the light, squinting, seeing double. He held it up to the window, compared it with another, then another, until he found one without the blueish hue at its center—black as hell, all the way through.

He found the fissure in the rock that would split it in two. The point of separation had to be precise, or the bluff within was ruined. He went to those leering shelves, pulled down a single vial, then held the lump of ore over it. He felt along its ridges with his calloused fingertips, then closed his eyes.

When terranium was split correctly, it was musical, like glass—a high-pitched crack. It sang now as Patrick separated two perfect pieces, no shards or fragments coming free.

The ink spilled out, untainted, dripping into the vial, onto the lip of the counter, onto his shoes. Just enough. That was all he needed.

He felt consciousness leave him the moment he tipped the vial to John Colson's gaping mouth.

Then there was only fire in his shoulder, ink on his hands, a ringing in his mind like a cathedral bell, swinging back and forth.

He dreamed of his kid brothers screaming down a yellow hill, lit firecrackers in their hands, grass stalks sighing, their father pointing at the clouds marching across the heavens, promising something existed beyond them.

CHAPTER FOUR

NINA

I was confined to a servants' quarters, with yellow walls, a cot, and a neatly folded blanket. If there was ever any other furniture in the room, it had since been removed.

I stared for long hours at a map of Belavere Trench—all the provinces stitched together in a great tapestry. I wondered how long it had taken the Artisan to weave it, all for it to lay on this floor like any common rug, in a room that seemed a wardrobe.

The Gyser River ran down the map's middle from wall to wall, splitting the richer provinces from the rest like Idia herself had meant it a blockade. I raised my hand, the wound along my forearm now heavily bandaged, and traced in midair the path from Scurry to the city. Down the belly of the Trench where I thought the train line went, around the farming towns, the black-brick factories, across the Gyser, and into pasture.

I did not look to Kenton Hill, a pinprick in the far northeast corner of the brink.

The door to the room was locked twice on the outside and opened three times a day for the purposes of keeping me fed, and, I presume, to ascertain I had not found a way to jump four stories to the courtyard below.

I counted three days since I'd arrived. I did not feel a scratch of idium left in my veins. Every so often I pounded on the door, frustration spilling over. Was it truly their intention to keep me locked away in this room until they had use of me?

I thought of Ma and Patrick and Gunner and Theo and Polly as though they spun on a carousel, blurring into soup. Sleep was no remedy—their faces hounded me there, too.

Where was my mother? What was Patrick doing this very moment? What of Theo? Had Gunner survived that knife between his ribs?

Where was Polly? For surely it was her who'd given away Margarite's tunnel.

My finger was tracing the outskirts of Sommerland when the door rattled again, someone on the other side snicking the locks. The timber resisted as it opened.

This time, there was no maid or guard with a dish.

It was Theo.

There was a soldier behind him, baton already in hand, knees prepped as though he might lunge. Theo, contrastingly, looked ready to make a quick retreat.

I sat upright, not bothering to straighten my blouse or flatten my hair. I noted that there were no more binds around Theo's wrists, that the guard's eyes were trained on me and not him. I noted the Artisan blue Theo wore, the lapels as sharp as ever. His hair looked clean and freshly combed.

And I think he sensed my blood lashing hot. He stalked in, eyes averted.

"Hello," he said, and then, in a ramble, "I came to see you yesterday, but you were sleeping." He gestured to the bandage around my forearm, as though wishing to grasp at any topic to stave the silence. "Have they changed your bandages today? Mine were redressed when I woke, but if no one has come yet—"

On he continued, hands clenched behind his back and voice warbling. I barely heard what he said, too absorbed I was by the high shine of his shoes, the crisp whiteness of his shirt, the emblem on his navy breast.

"—they haven't much bluff on hand, but I could send for a tonic if—"

"You're wearing Ministers' robes," I interrupted. My voice sharp, jolting.

His mouth opened and shut wordlessly, his ears reddening. I watched his throat bob, and he turned to address the guard instead of me. "Leave us, please."

"Can't do that," the man said, jutting his chin in a manner of self-import. "Lord Shop said I was to stand by."

"Then you can do so three paces from the door," Theo said firmly. "And allow me some privacy."

The guard seemed to contemplate, but in the end, straightened, replaced his baton at his belt. "Yes, my lord." He walked out of sight.

I held Theo's gaze, thought I saw contrition there. Shame. He seemed inches shorter. "My *lord*," I repeated softly, and then my eyes swept to the window, the city beyond it. "So, you've returned to their side. Just like that?"

He sighed as though hollowing himself. He stepped one pace closer, looked where I looked, out to those enveloping rooftops. I wondered if they'd lost their luster for him as well. What had once appeared to me as beautiful now seemed blandly uniform. Generic.

We might have been contemplating the view in companionable silence if not for all the injury weeping between us.

He said, "I was always on this side, Nina."

"I don't believe you," I said. "You saved them." I closed my eyes and saw the collapsing walls of water putting out Kenton's fires. "You came back when you could have kept going. You came back for Kenton, for all those people."

"I came back," he said, "for *you*."

I swallowed.

"I—God . . . I left a note for Patrick after I spoke to you that day, in the alley. I told him you were looking to uncover the Alchemist."

I turned to stare at him. A shiver of violence ran through me. "You *exposed* me?"

He paled, then nodded. "I wasn't thinking clearly, and I . . . I was trying to hurt him."

I gasped, turning my body from him so that he couldn't see me crumble. Hadn't he known the danger of implicating me? Had he really been so angry with me that he wished me harm?

Was I anything but a possession lobbed back and forth and scrapped over?

"For all you knew, I could have been executed."

"That's why I had to return. In the tunnel I had time to think, to come to my senses, and I realized what I'd done, what Patrick might do—"

I slapped him. My body whirled as I did so, my good arm hitting him with all my might.

He stumbled back, more shocked than injured, eyes welling.

The guard rushed in through the door, but Theo held up a hand to ward him off. "Go," he said, and after a moment of hesitation, the guard disappeared.

Theo had the good sense to look down at his feet. "I'm so sorry, Nina," he said. "Truly. I had to say it, even if you'll never forgive me. I just wanted you to know that I came back for you, and when I saw the flames . . . all those people dying. I kept thinking you might be stuck in the cross fire."

"You saved them because it was *right*," I spat. I saw the way he tried to glaze his mind in excuses. But this wasn't about me or him—there were things of greater significance. "You can try to deny it and say you're still on their side, but what you did for those Crafters was only what was moral and decent, and you know it." My hands shook. I twisted my fingers together and swallowed some emotion. Desperation, perhaps. "You were prepared to die for them. That can't have changed so quickly."

But here he stood in that blue three-piece suit and navy robe, and I felt, though I couldn't explain it, that I was losing yet another critical piece of Theo, the one I knew to be good.

Theo's tongue rolled around his mouth, as though testing the words to explain himself. "My grandfather was a Charmer of fire," he offered. "Did I ever tell you that? And his father before him was a Mason. Quite a renowned one, actually."

I said nothing. My eyes began to film over.

"But my father," he said it with gravity, "is a mere Cutter of emerald."

I looked up. Had I known that? Had I ever asked? It seemed impossible, a mistake. Lord Terrence Shop was one of the most formidable persons I'd ever met. I imagined someone of such persuasion to be of a higher rank. But a Cutter? Cutters were novelties. They sold pretty jewels to wealthy gentlemen and ladies. The made a nice living in useless remits.

"He was expected to do nothing great. The way he tells it, he was practically cast aside by his parents and professors. And yet, he graduated with high order, was ordained a few short years later as a minister for the House, the greatest honor any of our name had ever received, and all of it for a *Cutter*." Theo's shoulders rose and fell as he spoke, as though he were barreling toward something. "And then it was my turn to siphon, and I was terrified. Terrified I'd be nothing, the dead end in a long succession of Artisanal distinction. You cannot imagine my relief when I was named a Charmer, of all things."

"I was there," I said then, seeing again a dark-haired boy in high attire, tipping water from a quivering glass.

Theo continued as though he hadn't heard me speak. "I thought I might stop being scared then, that my Charmer status alone might be enough to satisfy my family name. But my father had been made a Lord of the House *without* the advantage of a high-ranking medium, and if he could do that, then what might I, the Charmer, achieve?" Theo looked at me, and he was colorless. "I was always going to end up here, Nina," he said, as certain as death. "My own wishes were never of any consequence."

Tears fell freely now. Down my cheeks, over my lips. "Perhaps you didn't hold much love for Kenton, or it for you—"

Theo scoffed. It was brittle.

"But for a moment, however brief, you wavered. Somewhere inside of you, you know the truth. This House, it's a farce. Its lords serve themselves before all others and call it religion."

"And the Miners Union kill and thieve and blow up buildings—"

"—to feed their parishes. To take back what's owed to them." I stood, my hands itching to shake him, scratch him, to find the boy I knew beneath. "You once had enough heart to admit that the scale was never even. Not all of us were born in this city. *You* had the advantage of waltzing through your childhood. Most of us crawled through it kicking and screaming."

Theo looked at me with red-rimmed eyes. I wondered what he saw.

The silence extended.

"My father is expecting me," he said. He looked to the door, then fervently at me. "I've come to convince you—no, to *beg you*—to denounce the Miners Union. Pledge yourself to Tanner." His lip trembled at this last, his fists balled behind his back as though to stop them from reaching for me. He looked out the window, Belavere spiraling out beneath us. "Please," he said, a tear shaking free of his lashes. "Please, Nina. There isn't another choice."

My hand lifted of its own accord. It brushed the droplet from his cheek.

"Even if you must . . . if you must pretend." It became a mere whisper. "Pretend to be repentant. Tanner *needs* you. He'll forgive quickly. The terranium stores are near empty. He won't have you killed, but that doesn't mean you won't *suffer*, Nina. I'm pleading with you. Do what must now be done." He took my wrist, leaned into the cradle of my hand, and closed his eyes. "I'm sorry," he murmured. "More sorry than you could know." And he pressed his lips to the soft flesh of my palm.

Beneath the cuff of his robe I could see the white bandages, so similar to my own. The skin around his eye had turned a sickly yellow from its battering. Was he only pretending?

"Who sent you?" I asked him. I did not deliver it harshly, but took back my hand and stepped out of his reach. "Was it Tanner himself?" I asked. "Or another minister?"

He sagged slightly, shoulders rounding.

"Was there a deal made?" I pressed. "Will Tanner pardon your lapse if you set me straight?"

"I don't need a pardon. My father is the second in command. He invented some excuse for my . . . lapse." I watched cords pulsate from jaw to collar as he turned away. "You think so little of me now," he said, and it was quiet, sad. "I can barely stand it."

I couldn't deny it. Couldn't suddenly strip myself of the damage wrought.

He turned back then, eyes downcast, and from his pocket he took a piece of parchment, folded imprecisely. He tucked it into my hand and held on an extra second, squeezing my knuckles. "From your mother" was all he said. And then he quickly made for the door.

"Theo," I called before he could close me in again. "Please. Who sent you?"

He grimaced. "No one," he said. "I came because I wanted to." He glanced down at his wrist, where his brand still hid beneath the dressings. "You have to take care of yourself now, Nina. Remember that."

And then he was gone. The locks snatched closed in his wake.

I looked down at the parchment and saw that it was torn on one side. I unfolded it slowly.

The ink bled outward from every letter like the legs of an insect. Not a scribble, but a handwrought message in trembling cursive:

Hide, hide the witches,
The Stewards, they hid three

CHAPTER FIVE

PATRICK

His father hovered over him when he woke.

"Patrick?" John mouthed. Sound followed retrospectively, the cogs of Patrick's mind whirring into place.

"Patty?" his father said to him, then shook his shoulders and smiled so widely his bottom lip cracked. He laughed as Patrick remembered him laughing, a desiccated bark, tempered by coal and tobacco. "It's good to see you, son." John Colson pulled his son up by fistfuls of his clothes, wrapped his arms around Patrick's back, and pounded his shoulders.

"Dad," Patrick said, blinking wildly. He gripped his father's shoulders, closed his eyes, tried to believe that this was real and not just the sorry consolation of dreams. "You're alive."

His father laughed again. Always laughing. "Course I am," he said, though Patrick could smell the old blood matting his hair, staining his earlobes.

He wrenched Patrick back to look at him, pushed the hair out of his eyes. "My boy," he said, eyes swimming. "How's your ma? Your brothers?"

"Alive," Patrick said. "S'far as I know." Though Gunner had been wounded badly, Donny was no good in a fight where the sound came from all sides, and his mother . . . "But Kenton. It's—"

"I know, son. I know."

"I held it as best I could."

"It ain't your fault."

But the squeezing of his ribs told Patrick it wasn't all true. He'd let them in, the swanks. Polly, Theo . . . Nina.

"I'll get us out," Patrick said now, though for the first time in his life, he didn't have a plan.

John Colson, the man of endless inventions spun from the loom of his mind and into his hands, the man who'd reimagined Kenton Hill from the ground up, did not nod his head. He did not take Patrick's shoulders and laugh and say, *Of course! We'll think up somethin'.*

Instead, he grew furtive. His eyes flickered to the door and away. His tongue skimmed his top teeth, and Patrick was suddenly fourteen again, his father waking him after midnight with glowing eyes and a finger to his lips. *We've business tonight*, he'd say. *Don't wake your mother.*

"Patty," he started, and he sat back on the tiles, brought one knee up. "There's somethin' else in the works. An opportunity, perhaps, if you keep an open mind."

They'd once had a conversation that started much the same. One in which John proposed capturing Domelius Becker and blowing the man's brains out.

Unease trickled through Patrick.

"I've thought of every which way to get out of this fuckin' place," John continued, eyes skirting the rafters above. "There ain't none. Filled to the brim with soldiers and swanks at every hour. And they charm the locks here, did you know that? No keys, just a whole bunch of Smiths nailing us in. I'd admire it if I weren't on the wrong side of the door." John shook his head. "Still, they've kept me alive, son. And there're some who may be willin' to do a lot of things for us—a lot of things for the family, if we were to make a deal."

A deal. His father had made a hundred deals in his lifetime already, a thousand. Patrick used to wonder how he kept them all straight until he himself became the dealer.

"Now, Tanner?" John said urgently. "He's a lost cause. The man wouldn't cut a bargain if it came with a free horse. And I've tried, Patty. Two long years, I've said everythin' just right. Leveraged what I could to keep my neck out of a noose. He's stubborn as a mule." He licked his upper lip and leaned forward. "But Tanner ain't gonna be sittin' where he is forever, son. He's old, nearin' seventy. The one that'll take the helm thereafter ain't so mulish."

"Who's that?" Patrick asked, though he felt he already knew.

"Terrence Shop," John said. "Second in line to preside over the House. And he's got more vision than Tanner, Patty. More ambition. He's taken an interest in me. This is all secret, mind you." John scooted across the tiles, took Patrick by the shoulder.

Patrick saw his father's collarbone jutting out from beneath his shirt collar. His cheeks seemed more sunken beneath the scruff than he'd first noticed. The red in the corners of his eyes pulsated. There was an air of desperation to him Patrick hadn't seen before.

"If Shop comes into power, we can work him over, Patty. He's a puffed-up bastard, but he ain't so rigid. He knows agreements need to be made. We could take Kenton Hill back. Have the family looked after, bluff sent out to every parish. Ink enough for every Colson."

A deal too good to be true. "What of the rest?" Patrick asked. "The ceremonies."

"We bargain slow at first," John said. "We ain't in a position to do more than that yet. We keep our priorities straight. The rest will surely come in time."

Time, Patrick found, never rendered much more than trouble. With time, deals eroded, alliances drifted, the rabbit slipped the trap. "And you're willin' to wait?"

John scoffed. "There ain't a choice in it, son. We're no good to the Union otherwise. The swanks have us by the balls."

Patrick rubbed his temples, his eyes cinched shut. "You told me once; the animals scratch and claw and chew through their legs to free themselves, but business men bide their time, walk away unharmed if they got their wits about them."

"Aye."

"Which one walks away first, that's the question," Patrick muttered. "What did you leverage?"

John seemed taken aback. "What?"

"You said you leveraged what you could," Patrick reminded him. "What did you give up?"

John shrugged. "Crumbs, son. Whatever kept the rats out of Kenton."

"The Dorser docks, I presume," Patrick wasn't talking to his father anymore. Not really. His mind had raced ahead. "The shipments."

"Like I said, crumbs," his father's teeth gritted.

Patrick nodded, but he could see that Dorser woman in the tunnel, her apron bloody. And he'd promised her he'd return the very next day. He'd promised her bluff.

He pinched the bridge of his nose. "I assume Lord Shop intends to speed along his succession?" he asked.

John nodded. There was a certain mania about him—that, Patrick was familiar with. The cusp of plans about to unfurl. "He assures me it's all well in hand."

Patrick pulled in a breath that lanced his throat. He felt every particle of his body shout a reproof, but ignored it. "Tell Lord Shop I'll speak to him."

John squeezed the flesh on Patrick's shoulder, and it sent spikes of pain into his chest. "We'll get back on our feet, Patty. One way or another. We've just gotta be patient."

Patrick lay back on the tiles, stomach rolling, thinking that if nothing else, at least his father was here. And hadn't that been what he'd wanted? To hand back the reins?

Instead, he found his fists clenching.

He wasn't alone. Surely there was something to that.

CHAPTER SIX

LORD TANNER

Beyond the clock tower, on the bridge between silk tailors and the dispensary, Geoffry Tanner had once asked a woman to marry him.

She'd been lovely, quite a bit older than him, and a Craftswoman.

The restaurant she'd worked in, plucking chickens and scrubbing pans, had just hours before sacked her. She met him on the bridge with raw eyes, her apron still fastened. Seeing her like that had made him want to cry.

Instead, he had proposed. He had promised her a safe life, in a town house somewhere just outside the city, where a marriage between Artisan and Crafter was sneered at far less. He'd been just a lad, only twenty or so. She had been fair-skinned, dark-haired, beautiful, her cheeks perpetually scorched by kitchen steam. This is all he remembered of her.

The engagement did not last, of course. Geoffry's father was a Lord of the House, and a lord's son did not marry just anyone. Certainly not a dish maid he'd lost his virginity to beside a chicken coop.

The dish maid was now dead. He heard she'd been involved in a factory accident just south of the city, not months after he'd rescinded his offer of marriage. By then, he'd married a Masonry woman instead—Olivette.

Unfortunately, Olivette took much longer to die.

Geoffry Tanner had loved his wife in the perfunctory ways of men at the peak of society. He helped her out of carriages, kissed her cold fingers, offered a laugh when she tried out a joke. He fucked her with lessening enthusiasm as they aged.

Thankfully, while a Lord's son did not *marry* Craftswomen, bedding them was no matter so long as one was discreet. The House's servants were normally quite willing. It rarely took much persuasion—a promise of bluff, a little spare coin. "Perhaps," he would tell them. "I can put in a good word with the board of enrollments for the Artisan school?" In this way, he endured a dull but respectful marriage. Until, that is, his wife became wise to it and threatened the shameful prospect of divorce. Such a scandal would have crippled his ambitions.

Olivette seemed to abhor him after that. Even his ascension in the House of Lords could not impress her. She complained incessantly about the long hours he worked, the company of the other lords. The continent's idium quotas shortened and shortened, and even this crisis did not free him of her carping. She called him obsessive and single-minded. She did not understand that the entire legacy of Artisans rested on his shoulders alone. He grew to resent her, to pray for her early demise. She bore him no children, and so her death, when it finally came, had been as plain as their marriage, with only him to mourn her.

Olivette had never quite compared to that Crafter girl on the bridge, despite her impressive Artisanal feats. The thought continued to anger him, even years after both women lay rotting in separate cemeteries.

Women, he'd learned, were the single-minded ones, incapable of grasping what he himself had long ago grasped. Idium was everything. Without it, people were nothing but animals scrambling up the rungs of a food chain.

"I seem to remember your son and the earth Charmer being quite taken with one another," Tanner said to the glass panes of a window. It offered a view of the clock tower. He could imagine the bridge below it. "Young lovers, perhaps. Am I wrong?"

Behind him, Tanner heard shoes whisper over the floor, a music box played a soft opera to an audience of two. Lord Terrence Shop sipped his tea. "They were indeed."

"So then, have the boy fuck her back to sense. It shouldn't be so difficult."

"You want me to prostitute my son?" Shop said on a laugh. "Come now, Geoffry."

"Then what do you propose?" Tanner said, turning on his heel so abruptly it squeaked. His nostrils flared. For weeks, months, he had slowly morphed from man to bull. Now he rampaged, directionless.

Lord Shop replaced his teacup on his saucer and stood. His full height was quite astonishing, his chin among the rafters. Though his limbs seemed reedy, he held them in a way that implied strength. He was bespectacled in round gold-framed glasses, and his hair was a mix of black and silver. Terrence Shop was a man so angular it was unsettling. Everywhere he went, he brought with him an emerald-capped cane, though his gait did not show a need for it. Tanner assumed it was a flaunt of some kind—a Cutter turned ordained lord, despite the odds.

"Nina Clarke won't be persuaded," Shop began, in a voice calmer than Tanner's. "Not with gentler measures."

Tanner paced to the ancient, unimpressive book that lay on the desk, its binding barely tethered, the cover badly preserved. It had been written, Tanner believed, in a time before Artisans, when men here were hardly more than those in far-off continents. It was titled retrospectively, as though someone thought, hundreds of years after it were made, that it ought to have a title. Embossed on the cover were the words *The Stewards' Testament.*

Tanner remembered the first time he'd seen it on his desk. He'd thought it irrelevant, at first. A strange relic. Those tales of the Stewards—witnesses of Idia's time on Earth—were a Crafter's myth. The Book of Belavere mentioned no such people. The true disciples were those who had followed Idia into war and watched her sacrifices firsthand.

The Stewards were the ramblings of heretics. Accounts of them had dwindled in history. There were nearly no believers now, yet here was this book.

Frustratingly, it was written in a language no one could read. *Verian Script,* he was told. An infantile Crafter code supposedly used by the Stewards, but more likely used in wartime to communicate on the battlefield. Some impressions of Verian Script had been found and studied in Belavere's great history, but there had been little reason to pay attention to these so-called Stewards until now. Inked into the margins of the first page with an unsteady hand was a faded annotation:

THE SEAM OF IDIA.

It had been Shop who'd alerted him to it. To suggest that, if by some miracle, the myth of the Stewards was real, then the Seam was, too. It could be the answer. The end to this crisis.

But months had passed, and they had yet to find a single living Scribbler who could read Verian Script.

The book now sat on his tea table. They balanced saucers upon it.

How long had he stared at its porous pages, the ghost strokes of ink? How many times had he tried to find a lick of something recognizable in those strange glyphs.

But if any bloody *seam* existed, it was hidden in the nonsensical scratching of some archaic Crafter, and if Idia watched somewhere above, she laughed at Tanner now.

There must be some scholar, some Scribbler somewhere on this godforsaken continent that could draw meaning from it. He would find them.

And once he found the Seam, he would need the means to unearth it. There was only one Artisan with the means.

"It was *you* who insisted I employ gentler measures with Nina Clarke," Tanner said through clenched teeth. "You made a case for courting her to our side in her years as a student."

"Yes, but I fear that route is now foiled. Perhaps if you hadn't taken her mother as your hostage—"

"Do not *lecture* me. She deserted her station. Refused her duty!"

"And spent seven years no better than a beggar. You might've employed a willing agent, had you offered her rewards instead of threats. You've made her into a revolutionary."

Tanner chewed his tongue, simmering. He was inclined to take the teapot and throw its contents in Lord Shop's face. "Careful," he said. "We are schoolboys no longer."

"No, my lord," Shop nodded, no less grave. "I only think it prudent we speak plainly. Time is of the essence, as you know."

Tanner bloody well knew. His last dose of idium waited in a safe beneath his bed. After it was spent, he'd be as base as the man who'd written that damned fairy tale.

"It is imperative that the girl do as we bid her, and if my son cannot persuade her, then we should revert back to the course you originally set."

Tanner raised his eyebrow. "The mother?"

Shop seemed to consider it for a long moment before sighing. "I'm afraid so," he said. There was no small amount of reluctance in it.

Artisans were not creatures of cruelty. They were merely pragmatists. Every representative of their House knew that the cost of success, while substantial, was carefully weighed. They were the gatekeepers of Idia's enduring life source, after all. That duty did not come without its share of the unsavory.

"The hand must be heavier this time," Shop continued, his mouth a grim line.

"A demonstration, then," Tanner said, and though he tried to put on an expression of regret, there was no help for the thrill that cycled up his spine.

CHAPTER SEVEN

PATRICK

Theodore came in first, his father after him.

The two were both alike and not. Theo's father was taller, more severe, his face cast in shadows. Beside him, Theo looked hopelessly young. A boy. They shared the same grave expression, the same posture, but years in Kenton saw Theo with broader shoulders, calloused hands, bronzed skin. It made him strange in his navy robes.

They found Patrick alone where he'd been left in the dusty room of shelves. John had been collected and led away long ago. The only thing left of him was a clot of drying blood by the door.

The terranium on the table remained untouched.

Theo brought food. Potatoes, judging by the smell. Green beans. Bread. Gravy. Patrick's stomach volleyed painfully.

Terrence Shop introduced himself in his affected way.

"What do you want?" grunted Patrick.

But the lord shook his head. "A meal, first, Mr. Colson," he said. "Then we shall speak like humans."

Patrick needed no further persuasion; he went to the counter as though a separate force compelled him, wolfed down the food with his fingers as utensils. He drained a jug of water, thought seriously about throwing up.

To his credit, the lord's nose did not wrinkle in response. He simply waited patiently, his hands clasped behind his back. A soldier by the door looked in with his baton extended.

Theo watched Patrick solemnly, his expression bleak, as though he'd come to impart terrible news.

Patrick froze at the thought. "Is . . . is she—"

"She's fine," Theo said quietly. Then he looked away.

So did Patrick, neither man able to separate feeling from business.

Terrence Shop cleared his throat as Patrick wiped his mouth on the back of his sleeve.

"Mr. Colson, I'd much rather have this discussion in private, but the guard behind me will fret on the other side of this door, unable to see if you decide to pummel me with that terranium. You should know that he is a fire Charmer and a little quick on the trigger. It'd be best if you didn't give me cause to shout for his assistance."

Patrick gave the guard a cursory glance. "A fire Charmer, you say?"

Lord Shop nodded once.

"Bullshit."

Shop's eyebrows lifted slightly. "I assure you—"

"Ain't ever seen a fire Charmer with burn marks on their hands," Patrick said. He looked back at the guard, who only scowled. The hand around the baton clenched, knuckled white where the scars stretched over bone. "Either you're the poorest Charmer in the Trench, or you're an iron worker, and the lord here is lyin' to me."

Terrence Shop did not react.

So then, he was a careful man.

"To have an iron worker pose for you must mean your own medium is somethin' piss-poor. Are you a Scribbler, maybe? A Cutter?"

The lord's jaw flexed, just slightly.

"A *Cutter*," Patrick whistled. "Well, hope you don't bury me in fuckin' jewels."

"I didn't come to threaten you, Mr. Colson. But if it must be said, my son *is* a Charmer—"

"You didn't promise to drown me though, did you?" Patrick continued. He looked at Theo. "And I know him capable of it. He drowned a whole lot of men recently. Did he tell you? Fire Charmers and all."

The lord was quiet again. Contemplative. "Nevertheless, if you choose to be foolish, Mr. Colson, it will end quite badly for you. I came to speak, that is all."

"Pat," Theo said, voice like gravel. "Just listen. Please."

Patrick looked at him. In Theodore he saw two separate men. He couldn't trust even half of him. "Ain't got a damn thing else to do, Teddy. I'm all ears."

Lord Shop nodded to the guard, who backed out of the room willingly enough, closing the door behind him.

Patrick took stock of the lord and found him difficult to read. But not impossible.

"Mr. Colson, the matter on which we speak is delicate."

Patrick laughed again. "The matter of treason? Yeah, I'd say it's pretty fuckin' delicate."

The lord's face darkened. He seemed to evaluate Patrick where he stood, his eyes skirting over every part of him. Eventually he said, "I asked my son to relay to me his time in your employ. He told me you shot men who defied you, or else beat them. He described you as a man who uses brutality to get what he wants. It was all rather unimpressive to me."

Lord Shop took a step toward the sack of terranium and eyed it curiously. "I've known a hundred men who have governed the way *you* govern, Mr. Colson. With fear and might. I find it base. Uninspired. Wolves scrapping for kill."

"And what're you?" Patrick asked. "The fox in the trees?"

Lord Shop smiled. "I am taking the den while the animals fight."

Theo shifted uncomfortably. His father grasped his shoulder as he passed, a warning.

"Lord Tanner is a wolf," Shop continued. "He's grown preoccupied by the blood. It has distracted him from more important business."

"Findin' ink," Patrick murmured, a headache brewing.

"Indeed. Even with the earth Charmer finally in his grasp, he thought it prudent to send her out into the brink, rather than use her where she is most needed: unearthing new terranium."

"Swanks think of people as nothin' but tools," Patrick said.

"She was a tool for you, too," Theo parried.

As he was for her. "So, you'll use Nina to dig, and me to siphon the ink, and in return you'll offer us what? Nice accommodations?"

Lord Shop turned grave. "A truce," he said, and it seemed a difficult word to utter. It was reluctant to escape his lips. "The terms of which can be negotiated by your father and you."

Theo looked at his feet.

Patrick marked it.

"I would agree to a new order of Belavere Trench," Shop continued. "Where a quota of children from each parish would siphon idium and be trained into the fellowship of their mediums. More Artisan schools could be built outside of Belavere City, a larger workforce of Smiths and Masons and Charmers in the next generation available to aid the brink towns. Bluff would be controlled. No premiums. It would mean less hawkers, less bad bluff on the streets—"

"Utopia," Patrick said darkly.

"As close to it as we can manage."

"You must've started shittin' terranium ore, or he has," Patrick nodded to Theo.

Lord Shop was undeterred. "This continent is rich in terranium yet."

Patrick shook his head. The continent was barren, it seemed. The mines empty. "And you plan on workin' Nina to the bone to find it, is that right? Will you have her move every mountain in the Trench till she keels over?"

"You think like a wolf, Mr. Colson," Shop seemed suddenly impatient, as though waiting for a realization to dawn on Patrick. "Not everything needs to be gained by force."

Patrick's head tilted. It seemed the lord was on the cusp of something, some gloat he would not say aloud and undignify himself. A man like this did not prance about with ideas of treason if there were not a clear path to success, if the terranium he spoke of were not already guaranteed.

"You've found a seam," Patrick guessed. He thought the lord's eyes flashed. He appeared to Patrick suddenly ravenous.

"Not yet," he said. "But I have found the surety that one exists."

Patrick pinched the bridge of his nose. "Where?"

"Those answers will come in time Mr. Col—"

"Then you don't know," Patrick pushed away from the counter, paced into the center of the room and gave the lord his back. "You're makin' hollow promises."

"I assure you, a seam exists."

"*One* seam, when what you need is a dozen."

"Not if that one seam is greater than any the continent has unearthed before," Lord Shop made his voice low.

And Patrick turned on his heel. In Lord Shop's face, he saw no deception. Only fire. "Idia's Seam," Patrick uttered. It felt strange to say it. A fable. A forgotten myth. "Bullshit."

Shop presented his hands, a magician indicating no trickery was at play. "What else would I risk my life for, I ask you? Nothing less, Mr. Colson. Nothing less than magic for the next five generations."

Nothing less than idium, which meant everything. "It's a kids' tale."

The lord tsked. "Yes. No matter how hard history tries to bury the truth, it tends to find its way into stories."

"And if the story is accurate, Idia's Seam is damn near the earth's fuckin' mantle."

Theodore shifted nervously again.

"Then it is lucky we have Nina, if indeed she can be persuaded to help us."

Patrick swallowed. Inside him was a hound, lifting its muzzle to a scent. He could not pretend that his fingers did not itch, that his spine did not quiver. "I need proof," he said. "If you believe Idia's Seam to be real, then you must've found somethin'."

"A detailed account of its existence, in fact," Lord Shop nodded. "It will be shown to you in time."

"I'll agree to nothin' until then."

Lord Shop stepped forward, spoke so lowly Patrick had to watch his lips to decode him. "There's an order to everything," he said, then patted Patrick once on the shoulder. "First, the wolves fight, then I'll give you what you need."

"And in the meantime?" Patrick asked, an insistent warning knocking at his skull.

"In the meantime, I'll need a favor from you," he said. "If indeed I am to remove our Head of House, I'll need the means to do so, and it must be subtle."

So, then, he was to be Lord Shop's wolf. He'd happily rip Tanner limb from limb.

"I'll do it," Patrick said, fists curling.

"No," Lord Shop said sharply. "No need. Though you can grant someone else the ability."

Gooseflesh trailed Patrick's neck. "Who?"

"Someone who won't let the opportunity pass them by."

"My father?" Patrick grimaced. "I'd have it be me instead."

Lord Shop's eyebrows rose. "Why?"

"Because it would scratch an itch," Patrick said. "And because I'm guessin' you'd moniker my father an assassin and have him hung for it."

Shop was silent. He let loose a sigh. "I need allies, Mr. Colson. Particularly in the brink towns. I have no intention of severing my alliance with your father. He has been . . . most instrumental."

"Then I'll do it myself, and he needn't be implicated at all."

"No, he needn't. And he won't. Nor will anyone. From the outside, it will appear Tanner suffered a failed heart, or some other episode." Lord Shop grasped his son lightly on the shoulder. "My son is quite the accomplished Charmer. He can bend water at the molecular level—even water in the blood, in a person's very pores. He can draw it back into a person's lungs, if he so chooses."

Theo met Patrick's eyes and thought he saw a hint of panic there.

"My son has much to make up for," Lord Shop said, and though he squeezed Theo's shoulder gently, the boy still flinched. "Produce the idium. Just a single dose. Theodore will do the rest."

Patrick spent long minutes considering. He'd made enough deals with bad men to know Lord Shop was the worst kind.

He thought it likely the lord would renege his offer of truce or underhand the negotiations. But Patrick was the last Alchemist, and there was power in that, at least.

There was little choice.

Patrick wished he could speak to Theo alone. He wanted, badly, to ensure that he could see this plan through. Not all men could kill in cold blood.

"When will it happen?"

Shop shook his head. "In good time."

"I want to see it myself," Patrick said. Hunger in him reared up, teeth gnashing.

Lord Shop, discerning as he was, saw that, too. "You shall."

With that, Partick siphoned a single dose of idium into one of the many vials. It dribbled like oil into the glass base, and he thought only of sweet crimson blood and stained navy. Two sightless gray eyes staring straight to the depths of hell. He pressed it into Theo's palm and watched him stow it safely in his robe.

"Remember what he did to her," Patrick said to Theodore. "And what he did to you."

He nodded.

Lord Shop departed, but Theo lingered. His mouth opened and shut like he was drowning. He followed his father out the door without saying another word, chasing his robes.

Patrick did not sleep that night.

He closed his eyes, and for the first time since he was a boy, he prayed.

He prayed that his father, always surer than he was right, wasn't one of Shop's wolves.

He prayed that he wasn't walking from one cage into another.

He prayed that Nina, whose face circled his mind every minute, would cease this relentless haunting.

CHAPTER EIGHT

NINA

Tanner entered my room after dark, stepped right over the brink towns on the rug, and stopped somewhere near Gilmore. The Gyser River ran between his shoes.

His nose wrinkled at the ceiling. "My word, are those starlings?"

The birds in the rafters above tittered nervously. They had become accustomed to me, but they fretted now in Tanner's presence. "I suppose you endured worse confines in Kenton Hill."

I said nothing, though I wanted to spit at him.

"I've come to tell you that at this moment, Patrick Colson is agreeing to ally with the House. He will be our Alchemist."

I damn near laughed. These were desperate words. I said, "When hellfire swallows the continent, perhaps."

"The only barrier that remains," Tanner continued doggedly, ignoring my jab, "is you." He moved forward suddenly, and I found myself shifting back on the mattress, seeking distance. A girl once more, cowering in a drawing room.

"Your impudence puts me in a very difficult position," Tanner continued. Mania swarmed his eyes, turned them brilliant. "Do you understand that, girl? Do you comprehend what is at *stake*?" He shook with unfettered rage. It bloodied his cheeks, brought his forehead to a high shine. I watched his hands carefully, my insides winding tighter and tighter.

"I could have thrown you back into the swill before you ever stepped foot in our halls, and instead I let you remain, I offered you a *place* among us!" And now it seemed he spoke to himself, pacing frenetically over Trent, over Scurry. "I allowed you a *chance*, opportunities of which your peers could never hope to see! And you discarded it." He seethed, sucking air between his teeth. He stopped his pacing to look at me, and I wondered if he imagined pulverizing me to mince. "You've forced my hand, Clarke. I've come to give you your very last opportunity. You belong to the House now. You will do as you are bid for your nation. If you refuse, Rose Harrow will die for your futile rebellion."

I wanted badly to be the kind of woman who bared her teeth in the face of threats. Instead, I was shrinking, attempting to become nothing.

That was what I really wanted—to be saved by obscurity. I wanted to mean nothing, to have nothing the men of this world could try to possess.

Tanner had caught the scent of my fear, and he bore down. "And I'll have you watch that execution, Nina, if that is what you choose."

I closed my eyes. I pictured my mother as I'd last seen her. Skeletal, tormented. My voice shook. "If she dies," I said, "I'll give you nothing."

You have something the House needs. It gives you power.

I wouldn't yield. Couldn't.

Tanner's eyes bulged. He raised his hand as though he might strike me. I flinched and felt ashamed for it.

But his hand never landed. He lowered it slowly, inch by inch with whatever willpower he retained. "We'll put your words to the test, then," he snarled. He stalked to the door and opened it.

On the other side, in the grasp of a guard, was my mother.

A waif. So insubstantial her clothes overwhelmed her. As with before, her eyes swiveled from place to place, and she seemed unable to set them on any particular thing.

In her hands, clutched against her chest like a baby, was a small embroidery hoop.

"See this as your last meeting," Tanner said to me. "Unless, of course, you choose to save her life." He reached out and clasped my mother's upper arm, pulling her into the room.

Then he strode out and slammed the door behind him.

I breathed once, twice. "Ma?"

She'd once been so big to me that she'd filled every corner of every room, filled my sleep, her body wrapped around mine, my hand in hers, her apron cleaning my face, her fingers twining through the knots in my hair, pulling me down the lanes, all the way through the first years of my life. Then there was a blanket of empty years where she hadn't been there at all.

She wasn't here, either, not really. She'd retreated inside herself.

My throat strained painfully. I'd hated her longer than I'd loved her. Before I'd known what she'd done—what she'd felt forced to do for my betterment.

How long had she worked for the Artisans, I wondered? Cleaning their plates and sweeping their floors, before the secret came to haunt us both?

All that sacrifice, all that suffering. It had brought us only more of the same.

"*Ma*," I said more insistently, my voice waterlogged.

Finally, her eyes turned to me.

Slipping from her shaking lips, in quiet repose, came the stumbling chorus of a song I barely remembered. "*Sweet girl, Caranina*," she whispered. "*Sing sweetly for me . . .*" The rest faded off into a rasp of breath, continuing without voice.

"Yes," I said. "It's me." I wanted to wrap my arms around her, add another layer to her, but I was sure she'd shrink away. Just looking at me seemed to take tremendous effort.

Slowly, she held out the hoop of fabric toward me and pointed to a flower she'd stitched, the petals a deep burgundy. It grew everywhere in Scurry, choking the ground. A weed so resilient, even the soot couldn't kill it.

"Widow's lace?" I said softly. Again, she flinched.

In Scurry, she'd sewn clothes for an extra few farthings, I remembered. We'd wash scraps of discarded fabrics and rags, and she'd patch them together, turn them artful and new. She'd embroider embellishments on them and sell them to the neighbors.

When she continued to point at the cloth, I thought perhaps she meant it for me. I approached carefully and took it from her, ran my fingers over the thread. "Thank you."

She only backed away and hummed softly, as though soothing herself. It was so pitiful I wanted to kill the ones who had brought her here.

Instead, I rubbed away the tears clouding my eyes and said something gentle. Her life had been anything but gentle.

"In the spring, we'll go down to the river and get the very first flowers," I said, the way she used to promise me in Scurry. She'd make that promise all the way through the winter. "We can weave the stems into little boats."

More muttering, louder now.

"And we'll pretend we're aboard." I swallowed, sinking beneath the sorrow of it all. "We'll pretend we're sailing away."

"To a big place," Rose said, only this time her eyes finally saw my face, taking on awareness.

"That's right," I breathed, forcing a smile. "And any door we knock on will open."

She smiled thinly. "An' we'll go dancin'."

I nodded.

There was an all-encompassing silence, and I thought perhaps she'd returned to the surface. Her eyes fell to the embroidery in my hand, then back to my face.

Hesitantly, she stepped close enough that I could touch her, close enough that she could reach for me. Her fingers lifted, as though she meant to touch my hair, tug on the blond coils of it again.

They stopped short. "I . . ." she began, floundering. "I'd do it all differently." She shut her eyes tight, perhaps so she wouldn't break once more.

I took her hand in my own and found it cold. She squeezed my fingers. A sob broke free.

The door burst open then, and a guard strode two paces over to my mother and took her forearms in his hands.

She didn't fight, didn't struggle. She let me go and went away.

The door closed behind her. Daylight slunk back from the corners of the room, and all was quiet except for my labored breaths.

My fingers still cold, I took out my mother's note and read it twenty times. Thirty times, eyes pinched in the dim. It was just an old children's song. One of a hundred she'd sung to me.

I buried my face in my hands and screamed until my throat tore.

She wouldn't die. They wouldn't kill her. Tanner was desperate, but not foolish. I still had something the House needed.

These thoughts cycled, turning to a sort of madness. Twice, I almost called for the guard. Twice, I came close to surrender.

But I'd surrendered once already, hadn't I? Now Kenton was torched and crumbling.

So, I sat and let my insides feast on themselves. Let my throat tear itself to strips.

At some clockless hour, the door unlocked yet again. A tray was pushed in, bearing a dish of fish and vegetables. A cup of water. No cutlery.

The door slammed shut. I was too sickened to eat. The tray could stay there until morning, when someone would come to reclaim it.

But then something beneath the plate's edge caught my eye. Something small, wrapped in parchment and tucked out of sight.

I ignored the food and pulled the parcel free, the parchment immediately uncoiling in my palm.

A stoppered vial—the contents almost black.

My battered heart reanimated.

On the parchment was a tidy hand—one I recognized, though I hadn't seen it since I was an apprentice.

From Patrick, it said, though the writing could only be Theo's.

And I stared at the ink, puzzling for hours, picturing this vial passing from Patrick's hand to Theo's, to mine, and I felt relief.

There's a plan, I thought. *Patrick has a plan.*

I stared at the embroidered widow's lace, then gulped down the idium all at once.

CHAPTER NINE

LORD TANNER

Lord Tanner did not return to his residence that evening. He was too filled with a need to act—to do *something*. He was the bloody Head of House, for God's sake. He could not sit on his hands and allow a fucking chit from Scurry to bend him over.

When he returned to his office, he knocked a glass sculpture of Saint Merlo off his desk, drank a generous pour of port, and ripped his robes from his arms, feeling as though they had suddenly become snakes, constricting him. He was soon drunk, muttering at the walls. Who was he but an Artisan who had only ever sought to protect this continent, its heritage?

He stood over the old book, Idia's Seam hidden somewhere in its fibers, and considered, briefly, throwing it into the hearth.

Lord Shop appeared before him sometime after that. The clock chimed low—a midnight dirge.

"I'm afraid there's no avoiding it," Shop said to him, and he couldn't make heads nor tails of the words. How long had the man been talking?

Shop shook his head when Tanner offered him the bottle of port. "You were never one for fun," Tanner said bitterly, then upended the bottle into his own glass. A fair amount splattered onto the floor.

"My lord." The bottle was removed from his hands. Shop laid heavy palms on his shoulders, shook them slightly. His eyes swam into existence. "Time is of the essence. Can the earth Charmer be convinced?"

"No," Tanner said. The mention of her brought venom to his mouth. "Scum *bitch*," he muttered.

"Then what are your orders?"

Tanner was the Head of House. A Mason of high order. An Artisan.

Nina Clarke was a fraud. A rebel. A traitor to this continent.

"Have the gallows prepared," he said. "We'll see how her loyalty fares then. Bring the Alchemist, too, and the Union chairman. Bring everyone." Let them be reminded of who he was. "At dawn, we'll have a willing earth Charmer."

At dawn, Tanner was sober. Washed. He had replaced his robes and covered the port stain on his shirt with a gold pin. His hand brushed over the Artisan brand on his wrist once, then straightened the cuff. The courtyard beyond the window awaited him. He had listened to the Crafters preparing the platform through the night. The wood Masons were not woken for the task; none had idium enough to snap a stick.

Now, the courtyard was filling in the gray of morning. He could hear the voices rising, feel their presence. They awaited him, their leader.

He was suddenly bone-weary. He wondered what his life might have been like in the outskirts of the city, a dish maid in his bed.

Infantrymen flanked him down the stairs into the atrium. The doors opened onto those imperial steps as they did on siphoning day, only now the sky was bleak, the courtyard attended only by solemn-faced guards, rebels, ministers, and one prisoner, standing at the end of a rope.

Rose Harrow had become a sickening thing to look at. It was difficult to imagine her as she'd once been—a servant of the House, neatly kept, willing to come to his bed on occasion, with the suggestion of idium for her family if she was discreet. Of course, then Olivette had put a stop to it all, and really, he'd never truly promised Rose Harrow or the others a damn thing, had he?

When he'd traced the twelve-year-old Nina Clarke back to the source, he'd assumed this woman had taken matters into her own hands, that she'd stolen idium on behalf of her daughter. He'd thrown her back into the brink for it. How odd, to learn much later that it hadn't been Rose Harrow's doing at all.

She stood in the dawn atop the platform in too-large clothes, in skin that sagged from her skeleton. When Tanner had first brought her out of exile, she'd been more robust, if mad. Months later, she was unpleasantly frail. Blond hair matted, streaked in gray. Soft features turned painfully sharp. Tanner had instructed the infantrymen to make her time in the cellars uncomfortable. He now wondered what exactly that had entailed.

The Miners Union chairman stood to the side of the gallows. His hands and feet were bound, and he appeared distinctly unclean. Even so, he stood with unaccountable dignity. It was infuriating. Whatever had so succeeded in thwarting the spirit of Rose Harrow had done little to John Colson.

At his side was a man who presented a great conundrum to Tanner. A Craftsman who was now the most powerful man in the courtyard, in a way. He, too, seemed oddly prideful. Still strong in body and will. His jaw was set, his shoulders straight. He looked Tanner dead in the eye. That was the problem with Crafters. It was difficult to teach barbarians to be afraid.

The lords stood in their tones of deepest blue before the gallows. Lord Shop and his son headed the pack. Terrence had his hand pressed into young Theodore's shoulder, as though to keep him there.

Tanner descended the steps and stamped over the dust. The ministers bowed their heads respectfully, the prisoners glared, and clouds rumbled overhead, threatening a downpour. The first flecks fell, darkening the dirt.

Uniformed soldiers stood at every interval. Three of them had mounted the platform where Nina's mother stood. The woman had closed her eyes and begun to pray.

Tanner smiled. Even *he* could not find it within himself to put this pitiful woman to death. But Nina Clarke needn't know. The gallows would be convincing enough. She would fold, and quickly.

The guards brought the girl out last, as instructed. Let Nina Clarke see the mess she had made, the lengths she had brought them to.

Her hands and feet were not bound, yet she stumbled, almost toppled in a great heap down the steps to the foot of the gallows.

Her eyes settled over the ropes, the trapdoor, and her mother atop it, shaking like a leaf in the wind.

"Ma," she whispered, mouth agape.

Then she looked over her shoulder at an angle that must have been painful, the soldiers trying not to let her look away.

But there was no avoidance. There was only murderous rage. It was Tanner she searched for.

"LET HER GO!" she bellowed. Loud enough that those beyond the walls would hear. Loud enough to send the pigeons in the gutters swarming into the sky. Her eyes were stark, uninhibited in the frame of her wild blond hair. She fought the soldiers who held her arms, throwing herself toward the platform.

And Tanner, for the first time in many months, felt serene.

Powerful.

CHAPTER TEN

PATRICK

It was a spectacle.

The woman Patrick took to be Nina's mother trembled violently. Fat drops of rain darkened her clothes. The noose swung before her.

First light, and they'd gathered them all there just to witness Tanner's desperate attempt to force Nina's hand. Artisans were showy pricks.

Several feet away, Theodore stood beside his father with glassy eyes. Briefly, his gaze touched Patrick's.

Patrick wondered if this was the moment Theo would take Lord Tanner's life. He imagined the idium now flowing in Theo's veins and thought of what his father had said. *He can bend water at the molecular level—even water in the blood, in a person's very pores. He can draw it back into a person's lungs, if he so chooses.*

Patrick hoped to see it. Right here, before Tanner's lords and constituents. He hoped he got to see the life sputter from him.

They brought Nina out of those doors last. How different the circumstances were from when last they'd stood in this courtyard together.

He wanted to shield her from the sight of the rope and her mother. To take her face in his hands and let her see only him, hear only his reassurance. This was all for show, all of it. She and Patrick held all the cards, not Tanner. *Don't fall for it.*

The trick in squeezing for compliance, Patrick knew, was illusion. You can wrap the rope around the neck, you can take the lever in hand, but you never open the trapdoor. If you do, the squeeze is over, your leverage gone. Tanner wasn't fool enough to hang his leverage. Nina only needed to hold out a little longer—just a little longer.

The blood left Nina's cheeks as she came through the doors, her golden hair tangled, lips parted, eyes blind with panic, exactly as Patrick had feared, exactly as Tanner hoped.

Patrick almost called out to her. He stepped in her direction only to be cut off by a soldier.

"Stay put, lad," John said from his side. "Ain't a thing you can do."

So Patrick stood stock-still, his teeth clenched, and he watched Nina fracture as the illusion took hold. The noose and platform and the woman atop it.

"LET HER GO!" Nina bellowed and stumbled forward. The rain fell in earnest now, turned the navy robes in the courtyard black. It slickened Nina's face as she ran for the gallows.

And Tanner smiled. A cat with a mouse.

Soldiers caught her arms to haul her back, and Patrick lurched forward reflexively, Theodore too. Both were halted by the hands of their fathers and told to be still.

It's only a play, Nina, Patrick thought fiercely. *Come on. Keep your wits about you.*

"Miss Clarke, I bid you be quiet while I execute this woman, since she can no longer be of any use to this House, as you have made so clear."

Tanner turned then in her mother's direction, giving Nina his back. "Rose Harrow, charges of conspiring with national enemies have been brought against you—"

"STOP!" Nina bellowed. There was a howl as she drove her elbow into the groin of a soldier. "MA!"

"I sentence you to hang until you are dead."

The noose was positioned around her delicate neck, and the woman's lips shook. The rain seemed to soften in sympathy. She looked at Nina and smiled wistfully, in the way mothers smile at their children.

"Stop!" Nina howled. Still fighting, clawing. The guards struggled to keep hold of her slick skin.

Tanner's face grew lighter, his voice louder. He read Idia's Last Rite. "And in Her last breaths on Earth, she decreed that all who bled as she bled, and suffered as she suffered, and toiled this land righteously and with the grace of God, should come before her father at the end of their charity, and He would grant them eternal peace."

The noose tightened. Rose gasped as the rope pinched her neck.

"Do you ask Idia, the daughter, and our Holy Father, to grant you mercy?"

Rose's neck craned, the artery red and horribly naked. She could no longer see her daughter. To the sky, Rose spoke in a voice that seemed to have succumbed already. "I don't pray for mercy. He only wants my sufferin'."

"MA!"

The infantryman moved to the lever. The lords in their finery twitched in discomfort. Tanner lifted his hand for the drop.

And Nina surrendered. "I'll give you what you want!" she yelled fervently. "I'll do as you wish. Just let her go! She's done nothing!"

The game was over.

Patrick was shaking. Not for warmth, or for Rose, who was never truly to hang for those weightless charges, but for Nina.

He ignored the soldiers, his father, and he went to her, his feet eating up the ground and hands trying to grip his forearms and pull him back. He barreled through the first two, then a third. The fourth hooked his biceps around Patrick's neck and stopped any further progress. "*Nina,*" Patrick said. "Stand up!"

For she was on her knees now, like a beggar. He wanted to tell her that it didn't matter. A coup was at play. It was only a matter of moments.

He wanted to shout at Theodore to kill Tanner now, to fill his lungs with water and have him silently drown. "Nina! Get up!"

But Theodore only watched Patrick with wide, fearful eyes, and Nina did not lift her head to read Patrick's face.

And before them, with a smile as crooked as the devil, Tanner lowered his hand, his conquest won. "Very well," he said to Nina. He sighed as though she were a child in the last throes of hysterics. He turned to the man at the lever. "Let her down," he said, good-natured now, waving his hand flippantly.

But the lever was pulled.

The trapdoor opened.

And Rose Harrow fell, the snap of her neck rallying over the courtyard.

CHAPTER ELEVEN

NINA

I saw a glimmer of relief touch my mother's face.

"Let her down," Tanner said, and there it came, lifting her eyelids from their closed reprieve, slackening her jaw. Together we let loose a gust of breath. My chest expanded. *Yes*, I thought. *Let her down.*

She fell.

The moment the trapdoor swung away, the relief in Rose's eyes fled. There was only confusion as she sank through, then a pop, her spine disengaging at the neck. The wooden beams creaking as she swung.

And my throat seemed to collapse on itself.

And then Patrick was there, somehow freed of the soldiers who'd restrained him. He dove under the platform, his hands still bound, and looped his arms under my mother's shoes and lifted her torso. The soldiers were slow to follow. Patrick had her neck freed of the rope before they reached him. She toppled into the dirt below, Patrick feeling along her blue-veined neck for a pulse, yelling something to her.

Even from a distance, I knew it was too late. Her body was limp, as though the noose had stripped free her soul. Her final confusion, though, remained. It lingered in death, her eyes forever half fearful, half deceived.

Tanner looked stunned, as though his own words hadn't ordered her death. As though he had not, seconds before, read to her the words of his god.

My mother was dead.

My eyes swam until Tanner's face dissolved. I pushed the heels of my hands into my eye sockets and shouted, hollowing my chest until it protested.

Was it a crime worthy of death, to have been my mother?

And there was Tanner, who had called me a weapon, a knife, a piece of scum. I saw his face on the walls of Scurry pubs peppered with darts and gobs of spit. I saw his name in textbooks and on scribbles meant to frighten me. I saw him standing over me in a long line of men who had stood over me, bending my will until I broke.

Patrick gave up on the corpse and came not to me, but to Theo, his teeth bared. "Do it!" he shouted to Theo. "DO IT!"

I barely heard him.

I stood. My hands lifted of their own accord.

I watched Tanner's face turn ashen, then afraid.

And I'd never hated anyone as much as I hated him.

If I'd had fire at hand, I'd have scorched him alive. With wood, he'd be staked. But I was a Charmer of earth, and so I'd bury him. Let the worms and beetles consume him down to the bone.

Patrick saw my intent first. His bright eyes turned fraught. His lips formed the shape of my name. He began to rush toward me.

It was Lord Shop who stood in his way, and at the exact same moment, the ground shuddered as though in warning.

But there was no earthquake. Only specks of earth lifting from underfoot, from every corner of the courtyard. Tiny particles I could feel with my mind. A rising dust storm.

The rain ebbed, as though it, too, watched on in awe. A billion flecks of dirt, freestanding in midair, awaiting my command.

The lords looked all around, mouths open.

Tanner stumbled back. "Wait—"

"Enough," I said, blood in my mouth. And then I sent the earth hurtling toward him like a plague of locusts.

It blinded him first, invading the crevices between his closed lids, wheedling into the ducts and sockets. The rest funneled through his nose, passed his lips, and he was gagging, choking, scratching at his eyes and throat. Lords and soldiers who rushed to his side quickly found themselves similarly inflicted and stumbled away. They left their Head of House on the ground, ears weeping, mouth spewing earth and root and weed. My mind could feel the way it distended his stomach, his lungs, filling him up, but I wanted it in his blood, in his heart.

My hands shook, and my fingers curled inward.

The ground gave way beneath Tanner. It bowed as though it were a breathing creature, its hands rising to draw Tanner in. Slowly, I bid it devour him, and he sank and sank, heeding its grasp.

And the lords could do nothing but watch. They were weak and fearful and ordinary. They knew nothing of the earth and how it longed to devour them, too. I could make it so, if I wished.

I turned to all the navy blue swimming before my eyes. Rage made my hands into claws.

"Nina!" Theo said. He took my hands, then my face, but he was navy, too.

"DON'T TOUCH ME!" I shouted, shoving him hard. And the ground shook again. A fracture split through the floor of the courtyard.

There were suddenly many hands on me. Guards gripping my arms, my neck. Only now appearing, far later than they should have.

The ground shuddered violently.

And then there was a flash of steel, and for the second time, my arm was slashed and brilliant blood cascaded.

My breath caught at the pain. My heart stuttered, and the earth stilled.

Somewhere beyond, I heard Patrick shout. I saw him buck and kick and free himself from his own wave of guards, throw his fists into their jaws.

I felt the power trickle from me, slowly at first, and then all at once. My vision swam.

A puce-faced lord rose from the ground. "Shackle her!" he roared, pointing a demented finger at me. "Summon the jailer!"

There was an uproar of accession as the other lords recovered, realizing the danger had passed. They rose from the ground with gritty eyes and slack mouths. They looked at the fresh mound of earth where Tanner had been moments ago. Then they looked at me with outright horror. With revulsion.

"She should hang!"

"No, she shall rot in a cell!"

"No," called Lord Shop, stepping into their midst, his eyes hungry. "No sentence will yet pass down to the earth Charmer."

The lords brayed. Some wept. The puce-faced lord stepped forward, his chest heaving. "And who are you to decide?" he spat, eyes pulsating. "Who are you to determine the fate of an *assassin*?"

"I am Lord Tanner's successor," Lord Shop said, and it rang out too loud, too final, the other lords becoming quiet. Realization doused fury. The brays and barks tumbled to a halt.

"I am the Head of House Belavere," Shop said, louder still. "And the earth Charmer will not be touched by a single Artisan or Crafter without my say so."

CHAPTER TWELVE

PATRICK

The guards brought Patrick along to what was once Tanner's quarters—a mistake.

The second he entered and laid eyes on Lord Shop, he sought to wrap his bound hands around the new Right Honorable Lord's thin neck and squeeze the life from it. As it was, the soldiers were prepared, and Patrick scuffled fruitlessly.

"He's rabid, my lord!" one guard panted, wrapping his arm around Patrick's throat. "We ought to put 'im behind a locked door."

"No," Lord Shop said, standing behind the ornately carved oak desk as though it had been his all along. He fingered the whorls on the wood grain with one finger, but his eyes were on the clock. "He'll tire himself soon."

"You fuckin' son of a bitch!" Patrick roared, rearing back. His head connected with a guard's. More howling. "I'll kill you!"

"But then you'd have no authority with which to negotiate, would you, Mr. Colson?" Lord Shop said. "Calm yourself."

But Patrick was seething. *"Where is she?"*

"Having her arm tended to by our staff, receiving blood, resting."

A voice rose from the corner, from a figure Patrick hadn't noticed until that moment.

"This conversation can wait until tomorrow," Theodore said. "Nina should be here for it." He leaned against a wall as though he wished to melt into it. His arms were crossed, his expression hollow.

"You little shit," Patrick hissed at him. "What the *fuck* did you do?" He tried once more to shake free his guards. He'd kill both Theo and his father; he'd never salivated for a revolver more. He imagined it in his grip, his palm collapsing around the cool metal, trigger on the pad of his finger.

Theodore only looked at him though the husk of himself.

"For efficiency, we'll wait for the rest of our party to arrive before discussions begin, Mr. Colson. This conversation is long overdue." He straightened his lapels, smoothed his oily hair, took a teacup from the desk and sipped at its rim. "Kilmartin? More tea, I think. Perhaps some sandwiches."

The guard to Patrick's left hesitated. "Sir?" He glanced questioningly at Patrick.

"Oh, do not mind Mr. Colson. He is not a stupid man." Lord Shop sat on the high-backed chair behind the desk and lifted a small pistol from the inside of his robes. He turned the barrel to Patrick. "I'm sure he'll comport himself like a man of business."

Kilmartin nodded, releasing his grip on Patrick warily.

"Ridgeback, stand outside the door, if you please."

The arm wrapped around Patrick's neck fell away. Footsteps retreated.

And Patrick took a step in Lord Shop's direction.

The pistol hammer clicked. "Ah, ah, now," Lord Shop tsked. "Be wise, boy. I was promised you were the astute sort."

Patrick eyed the small pistol as though it were more an irritant than a threat. He nodded at it. "I shot rats in alleys with a gun bigger than that when I was a boy. You ever shot anythin' before, swank?"

The lord didn't answer. He only leaned back in his chair and sighed.

At that moment, the door opened once more. In filed John, his eyes finding the lord's pistol immediately. He was followed by a maid, a silver platter of sandwiches balanced in her hands.

John looked warily to Patrick. "Go easy, son," he said redundantly. "Haste never wrought no reward."

Patrick heard the warning. The man had perfected a language of sorts with his sons. His words turned to a kind of poetry when there was something delicate to convey among close ears.

But Patrick paid it little mind. He saw red. "What was promised to the Craftsman who pulled the lever?" he spat at Lord Shop. For it was clear that Rose Harrow was never meant to live.

To his credit, the lord did not smirk. Patrick doubted there was a mite of humor in him. He was cold all the way through.

Well, so was Patrick.

"Idium," the lord said blankly. "Which I'll require you to siphon, of course."

Patrick gritted his teeth. "Why Nina?" he asked, pulling at his own hair. "I was *willin'*."

"A couple of reasons," Lord Shop said. "The first is that Miss Clarke—"

"Harrow."

"Miss Harrow, then, was exceedingly prejudiced against the House. I had hoped that taking Tanner's life might sate her bitterness and leave her more sympathetic toward . . . new management." The lord placed the gun down before him, steepling his hands atop the desk, and to hell if the bastard didn't look like he belonged there, in a politician's seat.

Patrick growled, "You had her kin *killed*."

"Nina has had almost no contact with her mother in the past two decades," Shop said prosaically. "In fact, I was concerned her mother's death might not be motivation enough. I'm glad to be wrong."

"You used her," Patrick said, and it was so dark, so thick with violence, that Lord Shop picked up his little gun once more.

"She is an Artisan. Our value is measured by how useful we can be. And Miss Harrow is a most useful individual indeed. You, of all people, should agree. Did you not use the girl long before I?"

And Patrick saw Nina once more, coming toward him through that tunnel with a sack over her face with Scottie and Otto. Shame washed in over his anger.

She used me, too.

Lord Shop sighed as though the debate bored him. Patrick wondered how long he had plotted to take what was Tanner's.

"Miss Harrow was simply the best candidate. I cannot have the other ministers catch wind of my involvement. Honestly, I was surprised you believed I would allow my own son to undertake something as base as killing." His nose wrinkled slightly. "Nevertheless, I do apologize for the deception. I realize that lying to you does not foster a promising partnership, but it was made clear to me that you hold a certain . . . *affection* for the earth Charmer." He waved a hand dismissively, as though affection were a symptom of the weak. "I could not afford for you to intervene. You are, as most are in the brink, unpredictable. If I had allowed another Artisan to be Tanner's killer, they'd be hung. There would be no believable reason for me to stop their execution. But Nina? She is the earth Charmer. No lord or lady in this house will deny the necessity of her survival in these trying times. It will come as no shock when I grant her pardon."

Patrick glared at Theo, who now looked sickly. Good. "You agreed to this plan?" he demanded, hate sliding into the words. Patrick should have shot him the first time they'd met.

Theo didn't answer, but he at least summoned the courage to look Patrick in the eye. What Patrick saw there was pitiful.

"Theo understands that pragmatics must come before emotion," Lord Shop interjected. "The girl will live. Her wounds will heal, and Tanner is dead. This is what matters."

Patrick imagined a bullet boring into the lord's skull, pitting a hole between his eyes. It quelled the clench in his knuckles. "It should have been me," he said, the muscles in his chest aching. "I'm their Alchemist. They can't have me killed, either."

"Ah, but how would it look then, if I proceeded to cut bargains and show sympathies to you and your family, to the towns in the brink? What successor to a murdered Head of House would grant the killer favors?"

"A crooked one," John interjected gruffly, taking a sandwich from the tea table.

"Precisely," Lord Shop agreed. "And I do plan to uphold our deal, Mr. Colson. Your father has told me many things about your mother. Your brothers, too. I can ensure they are protected. Provided for."

"We'd live like bloody royalty, Patty," John said, crumbs tumbling from his lips.

Patrick looked now to his father: his flushed cheeks, the spark in his eye. He had the look of a man on the cusp of something big.

"You knew," Patrick accused, then scrubbed a hand over his face. "You knew they'd do this."

"Aye," John muttered, unapologetic. "That woman on the noose weren't long for this world anyway, Pat."

Patrick felt sick with rage.

"My offer, Mr. Colson, is to make your father governing lord of the brink towns. You as well, if you wish it. You will ensure that thoughts of rebellion are diluted, proclaim that the House of Lords has agreed to a fair solution. You will call a ceasefire, as will I, and if it is successful, then the spoils of Idia's Seam will be distributed throughout Belavere Trench."

"I want it quantified," John said around a mouth full of bread. "How much for the brink?"

"Fifty percent of the bluff, thirty of the idium," Shop said.

John shook his head. "Ninety percent of the population live in the brink. We ain't gonna settle for half the bluff."

"Sixty percent of the bluff," Shop amended.

"Sixty-five. And half the ink."

"Sixty-five of the bluff, and forty percent of the idium. And your family heading the bluff distribution to each parish. You will also select yourselves those children who will attend the siphoning ceremony, so long as their family has no previous criminal activity."

John scoffed. "That's a shallow pool. Might as well give up our share."

"Petty crimes excluded," Shop allowed, bowing his head slightly. "As well as crimes related to this war."

"Deal," John grunted. He spat in his palm and stomped over to the desk, lifting his hand for the lord to shake.

Lord Shop stared at it for several moments, then pulled a piece of parchment from his robe. He passed it to John and gestured to the quill and ink pot waiting atop the desk. "I took the liberty of having an agreement scribbled."

Patrick frowned. "Before knowing the terms?"

The first hint of mirth touched the corner of Shop's mouth. "I also took the liberty of estimating. I'm rarely wrong."

He enjoys this, thought Patrick.

The lord stood and pulled his robes closed. "I will need your signature as well, Mr. Colson."

Patrick shook his head, feeling as though he were hurtling over the edge of a cliff. "No." He paced across the room, trying furiously to think. "I told you I would make no agreements until you gave me proof of the seam. And I need proof that Nina . . . that she's come to no permanent injury."

Shop considered Patrick's conditions for several careful moments. In the corner, Theo turned away, shoulders still slumped.

"Very well," the lord intoned. Then he pulled open a thin drawer at the desk and drew from it a disintegrating leatherbound book no bigger than the span of his hand. The cover's embossing read *The Stewards' Testament.* "This was recently recovered."

"From who?" His eyes stuck to the word *Stewards,* seeing a glimmer of promise in it. It had been some time since he'd heard mention of them. Not many believed.

"A direct descendant," Shop said slowly, clearly sensing Patrick's growing curiosity. "Recently passed, Idia claim his soul. This book was found among his possessions and kindly gifted to the archives."

"What archives?"

Lord Shop did not deign to answer. He merely pressed his lips together and proffered the book with his thin hand. "This is the only conclusive lead we have that Idia's Seam exists, Mr. Colson. I bid you treat it like the relic it is."

Patrick snatched it from his grasp and relished the fury that flashed in the lord's eyes. It was quickly suppressed.

So then, he wasn't unfeeling. Just a man who concealed himself. He could burn. He could hurt.

Patrick opened the cover none too carefully and saw the faded, bleeding lines of symbols he didn't recognize. A language he'd never seen. But in the crevice near the spine's binding was a different hand, this one less faded, as though it had been written retrospectively.

The Seam of Idia, it said, clear enough.

And then there was nothing more to discern. Just page after stained page of symbols vanishing into the parchment after a flash, just as Idia's life source had concealed itself in the marrow of the world.

This was his proof?

Patrick slammed his fist into the tea table, and the glass top splintered. Then he stomped to the hearth, held the book over the flames, and watched as every man in the room lunged toward him, wild-eyed.

Color climbed up Lord Shop's neck.

"Patty!" John cursed, then smoothed his beard—an anxious habit. "Easy, son. That there's an important bit o'—"

"It's a rag," Patrick said. His eyes were on Shop. "You've lied to me twice now."

"There was no deception," Shop said. No snark now. Patrick watched the lord's face change, becoming desperate. "I promised you proof—"

"This book is as useless as a cock on a priest."

"It's a *lead*, boy. Where one piece of the puzzle resides, another will follow."

"Glyphs? On parchment leached nearly clean, thanks to your useless fuckin' archive keepers," Patrick said darkly.

The flames licked higher, touching the very corner, the fibers singed.

A hiss escaped from between Lord Shop's teeth. Patrick suppressed his own satisfaction.

The words came flying from the lord's mouth. "*Damn it.* The whereabouts of the Seam was *protected* by Verian Script, boy! Everything we need to know can be uncovered by someone who can translate it!"

"If there was a way to translate it, you would already have done so." Patrick knew the men could smell the first tendrils of burnt parchment. The edges were blackening.

"I *hid* the knowledge from Tanner," Lord Shop admitted in haste. "I have someone ready to reveal the translation."

"Which someone?"

"The descendant had a child who was taught Verian Script."

"I don't believe you."

"What else would I risk *everything* for? They're employed in the Morland archives—a Scribbler. But even their expertise will be useless if you burn that book!"

Patrick smirked, just slightly, and Lord Shop saw it. He became very still, his eyes closing in defeat. Patrick pulled the book away from the hearth with a flourish, blowing out the embers. "Artisan bullshit," he said to his father. "It's always some Artisan bullshit."

"Aye," John Colson said, a glint of pride in his eyes.

Patrick offered Lord Shop the book and watched the man's fingers unclench as he took it. "I'll need to see Nina," Patrick said. "I'll agree to your deal once I've seen that she's well."

Lord Shop replaced the little book in its drawer, locking it in with a key. He seemed well traversed at the desk of a man not an hour dead. Shop stood to his full height once more, reclaiming his propriety. "Theo? Have Kilmartin bring the lady in."

Theo walked to the door the way men walked to their death. There was a sickness about him, a green tinge to his pallor. Patrick was sure there remained something he didn't know.

"Why does your boy look like he swallowed someone's newborn?"

Lord Shop sighed. "He has a sensitive nature—likely today's violence has disturbed him some."

Patrick patted his pockets absentmindedly for nonexistent cigarettes. "Your swank son has spent the last two years in the soot with me. I doubt there's much sense left in him."

Shop's brow furrowed. "You know of his affections for the earth Charmer."

"She has that effect," Patrick said darkly.

"He only worries for her condition, as you do."

"Which leads me to think there's reason to be worried," Patrick said. "And you're about to tell me why, or I'll not sign a fuckin' thing."

Lord Shop looked at Patrick as though he were a thorn now, boring deeper into his flesh. He lifted his chin, assessing him anew. "You are perceptive, Mr. Colson."

"Taught by the best I'm afraid," John grunted. "Boy was hagglin' with shop vendors before he was walkin'—"

"What're you planning to do to her?" Patrick said, his voice ringing into the vaulted ceiling.

The lord looked down his nose at him, likely calculating whether he should bother lying. It took long moments, and in Patrick's frustration, he advanced toward the man, his chest heaving, and the lord dropped his cane, scrambling for the pistol—

But before Patrick could grab the lord's throat, before the lord's finger could cradle the trigger, a voice rose from the door.

"He'll have her beaten," it said, thick with venom. "Then imprisoned."

Theo stood just inside the door, his fists clenched, the green in his cheeks now blotted with red. His eyes lay heavily on his father.

A shiver of violence coursed up Patrick's spine. He found Lord Shop once more with a gun between the two of them, as though it would be enough to save him. "No deal," Patrick said. He hoped the lord heard the promise in it.

The lord spared his son a bitter glance before addressing Patrick. "Calm yourself, Mr. Colson. Think about this. The girl just murdered the Head of House. My ministry will want retribution. The *nation* will want retribution—"

"The Crafters will be dancing in the streets tomorrow, all throughout the brink," Patrick spat.

"And the Artisans will *mourn*," Lord Shop countered. "And they will not trust a new Head of House that does *nothing* in response to Tanner's assassination. There must be some punishment."

"Lie to them."

"My ministers are not *fools*, Mr. Colson," Lord Shop huffed. "This is not a child's game. In order for many to prosper, we must make sacrifices—"

"It will be public," Theo cut in, his cheeks still aflame. "She'll be whipped in the middle of the city, so that we may appease the ministry. Isn't that right, father?"

The lord looked for a moment as though he wished to shout. Instead, he took several steadying breaths. He laid a black stare on his son and said, "I've tried in earnest to mentor you, and still you act like a boy." To the room, he said, "She will be whipped, yes, but she will heal. She will not be killed. After that, she will look, for all intents, like a prisoner of the House, working to meet our ends. It is a *performance*. This is politics, gentlemen. We walk a treacherous tightrope. But, if no one oversteps, we will achieve what we set out to do."

So, this was the price for truce. Nina would be forced to her knees to take the whip from the very people who needed her.

"To use a woman as your scapegoat," Patrick uttered, still shaking, "you must be the worst sort of man."

Shop hardly seemed moved by the comment. "Your soldiers have killed countless women and children in your rash explosions and bombings. Nina will *live*. She will help us bring peace to the continent."

And she'd be a slave to the House again, digging up their terranium for as long as she drew breath.

"This is the way of it, Patty," his father said, coming to clap a hand over his shoulder. "The road to glory's a bloody battlefield."

If there was a hidden message in that, Patrick couldn't glean it.

He eyed the contract atop the desk, the barrel of the gun in Shop's hand.

"We have the same goal, Mr. Colson," the lord said. "As regrettable as the means may be."

Patrick closed his eyes for a moment, trying just to *think*. To find a solution.

The doors opened again. Ridgeback and Kilmartin came through awkwardly, each of their arms looped under the slack form of Nina.

Her head lolled. Her eyes blinked, unseeing, and then closed. Both arms were tightly wrapped in white gauze.

"You can leave her on the settee," Lord Shop said, but Patrick had strode forward and taken Nina in his hands. He shouldered Ridgeback and Kilmartin away, and they relinquished her with relief.

She seemed to weigh nothing. Her face was younger, her eyelids purple. He was momentarily startled by the memory of a girl with a lopsided ribbon. He walked her to the settee, all of her bones and organs in his hands. He was suddenly terrified that he would break her.

Nina barely twitched when he lowered her down onto the cushion. Her blond hair was matted in places, her lips bloodless. There was gore on her neck, and he wiped it away with his thumb.

"She's right powerful, ain't she?" came John's voice over Patrick's shoulder. "Shook the whole bloody ground. Thought we were all goin' to hell for a bit there."

Patrick had the alarming thought that if Nina died she would look like this, and he placed the palm of his hand tentatively against her chest. Her heart beat reassuringly against it.

She stirred, eyes slitting open. Hazel and green-flecked, they caught onto Patrick's immediately. They were so painfully close.

Patrick swallowed. "You're all right," he told her, though it couldn't be further from the truth. He only knew that he couldn't stomach the crumpling of her face. Perhaps unconsciousness was better. Soon, the visions would wallop back. The noose and the lever and the snap of the neck. He could see it happening now. Her eyes misted. He felt the compulsion to strip her of the memory and hated that he couldn't.

She shut her eyes again as if shutting out reality, and after several long moments, slipped back into unconsciousness. Patrick cursed beneath his breath.

He stood and turned to face the newest in a long line of enemies, crooked thieves, and thugs. They were all the same, whether branded or from the brink. They were all men clawing a lofty existence out of a world that owed them no more than their breath.

Lord Shop stared back at him expectantly, as though he had already choreographed Patrick's every move.

Patrick thought him a man at least as cunning as he. Maybe more so.

Poison coated Patrick's tongue. He'd bet the bastard's jaw would shatter with a single punch. His ribs would snap like twigs. There was nothing to him—he was as reedy as the cane he held. The man had surely never seen another man bleed to death, never gouged out a man's eyes, never smelled the burning flesh of a town on fire. He'd die badly, screaming and pissing himself.

Patrick's bloodlust couldn't be satisfied, though, not yet. Lord Shop was a man of games.

If Patrick was to win, he'd need to play.

"When will it happen?" he said.

"Noon tomorrow," replied the lord. He held the quill aloft. "I'll ensure it is quick."

THE TRENCH TRIBUNE

HEAD OF HOUSE SLAIN BY EARTH CHARMER

By official scribble from the National House, The Trench Tribune *was informed this evening that our Head of House, the Right Honorable Lord Tanner, is dead.*

The scribble stated, in no uncertain terms, that Lord Geoffry Tanner was assassinated by the infamous earth Charmer, Nina Clarke, during a routine courtyard inspection, where he was left vulnerable to Clarke's arsenal.

The 23rd Head of House, an accomplished stone Mason, will be remembered for his legacy in architecture, including the Gyser bridge and monoliths in the city's south. He is surely reunited with his late wife, Olivette Tanner, in the arms of Idia herself.

Succeeding Tanner, Lord Terrence Shop has already ascended to the highest seat of lords by rightful default. He was contested by none of his fellow ministers.

Lord Shop stated to this journalist that the murder of his predecessor was "tragic" and "heinous," but stressed that his mind was turned wholly to the needs of the nation, and in particular, to Artisans and innocent Craftsmen:

The actions of the earth Charmer are the result of radicalization by the Miners Union, who have washed her brain in their wicked propaganda these past months. But she will be a weapon of the Union no longer. She has already exhibited remorse for her actions and promised to atone and assist in the prosperity of our great Belavere.

Nevertheless, her actions cannot be undone, and our great Lord Tanner lays dead by her hands. For this, I order Miss Clarke a prisoner, and to be punished in ways deserving of an assassin.

Nina Clarke will receive a public lashing beneath the clock tower at midday, and the workers of Belavere City will be ordered to cease operation, so that all who are able may attend.

Long live Belavere.

CHAPTER THIRTEEN

DONNY

If he fossicked his memory, Donny could dredge up the pictures of Kenton Hill before his sight left him.

It was dull there, in that rendering of Kenton. Shades of brown and gray. Dry grass and soot and tea-colored canals. The cobbles caked over in horse shit. This was what his sight had left him with before it evaporated completely.

As a child, Donny had been most afraid of that moment, when the black edges of the world finally closed in on itself and he was pitched into permanent darkness. What he didn't know was that blindness wasn't dark. It was color.

Kenton Hill wasn't brown and gray. It was gold. It was yellow and bronze and copper. It was the sharp tang of steel and reflecting onyx. It was constantly morphing, prisms of light bursting into kaleidoscopes. Eventually, he'd come to see his memories as dull interpretations.

Donny walked down Main Street and thought Kenton was now pockmarked in gray once more. The smell of burning houses wouldn't leave the air even now, long after the fires had been smothered. He imagined the cobbles, beneath the salt and ice, still tacky with blood.

Beside him, Otto exhaled smoke into the air, chewing, as he always did, on the end of his cigarette. He was restless, the mechanics of his body giving him away. His hands couldn't seem to settle in his pockets or at his sides or even clasped around a lighter and smoke. Donny gripped his sleeve at his elbow and felt him thrum beneath his clothing, like a swarm of hornets.

"What kind of man am I?" he'd asked Donny the night before, holed up in a sorry corner of the pub. "What kind of man falls for a woman like that?"

But they'd all fallen for it. Every one of them. They were each as red-handed and stupid as the next.

And now Kenton had lost its color.

They were on their way to the infirmary, the only place left in Kenton that still bustled. The streets were eerily silent, the bodies cleared away. The remaining clutch of Colsons and their employees left to burn them, or if they wore navy blue, throw back down the hole in Margarite's in a mash of limbs and buried.

Scottie and Briggs were, at that moment, in Dorser, giving the all-clear to the Kenton refugees to come home. They'd return with food supplies, too. Kenton would rebuild, and its color would return.

Donny clapped Otto on the shoulder. "Don't pout, old boy," he said. "You and I are gonna eat like lords tonight. I've told Briggs to sneak us some Dorser brandy."

"Scottie'll drink the whole lot before it comes topside," Otto muttered.

"Aye, well that's why I asked Briggs, didn't I?"

"Don't feel much like celebratin', Donny." He took his cap off his head to pull at the hair beneath. "Just leave me to my misery, would you? Stop tryin' to cheer me up."

But Donny had his own miseries. He could think of nothing worse than yielding to them.

Underfoot, the cobbles turned to brick pavers. The lip of a threshold reared up, and the wails of the infirmary curled in his ear.

The smell of too many bodies in too close a space came over Donny like a wave. The sting of antiseptic, of hot flesh carved open. Donny saw it in shades of vicious red.

The only remaining Kenton doctor was listing off an inventory of medicines. "Laudanum, meadowsweet, opium," he was saying. He heard the scratch of a pencil, the shallow breaths of the orderlies and their clipped steps. They'd filled the clinic with as many beds as could be pilfered from nearby houses, and Donny imagined them lined up as though the wounded men were laid out on a conveyer belt, moaning or snoring or spitting curses through their teeth.

But none were so loud as the man braying from the back corner. "*—swear to almighty God I'll have the lot of you lynched!*" he said, and Donny imagined the spittle flying from his lips.

"A fuckin' break is all I ask for," Otto muttered at Donny's side.

"Ain't none on the horizon," Donny said, throat stricken. "Come on."

Otto led Donny right to the epicenter. A cart crashed, and its items scattered over the floor. An orderly named Delta swore. "Lord, give me patience," she grunted, setting about picking up the items. "I ain't got the fortitude, Donny! Speak some sense into him, would you?"

Donny clicked his tongue, felt something angular beneath his boot, and bent to retrieve it. A pair of scissors. He held it out to her.

"It's your lucky day, darlin'. I've come to relieve you of him."

"*Don!*" called Gunner, a hand reaching forward and fisting his shirt, bending him nearly in two. "Don, they won't give me nothin' for the pain. I'm dyin'!"

He could hear the titanic breaths of Gunner's lungs, smell the sweat coating him. The wound in his side had been stitched and bandaged. The pain he spoke of was more in his mind than outside it.

Their mother called it withdrawal.

"Ain't nothin' left, brother," Donny told him, prying Gunner's fingers free. "The swank's dogs took it all."

"I'm dyin'," Gunner whimpered, pulling at the clothes on his own body as though they were strangling him. "I'll be dead by mornin'."

"Well," Otto said thoughtfully. "It'd save us draggin' your sorry arse back."

"Doctor says you're fit as a fiddle," Donny told Gunner, already reefing the big man off his back. "Come on, brother," he grunted, swinging one of Gunner's arms over his shoulder. "And you'd better sharpen up 'fore Ma sees you."

"Ma," Gunner said, as though just now remembering her. "Fuck it, Donny. We need Pat."

"Well," Donny said. "We ain't got him. There's you and there's me." *And we hardly make up a whole man between us.*

"But there ain't any bluff," Gunner whined, allowing Otto to take his weight on his other side. "What'll we do?"

"Business as usual," Donny said with far more confidence than he felt. "Just business as usual, brother. I need you back on your feet."

They half carried him from the infirmary. He howled and bucked and shivered. He threatened Donny, then apologized in quick course. "If I ever see that fuckin' Charmer again," he said, as though his hands were already throttled around her throat, "or that Scribbler, *I'll rip their fuckin' heads off!*"

Donny was of much the same sentiment. All of Kenton's light stolen.

But they'd get it back. He'd make sure of it.

And Patty would return . . . He had to. Containing him would be like lassoing a storm.

Right. Patty would return at any moment, and all Kenton's problems would feel lighter.

They dumped Gunner unceremoniously in his childhood bed on the second floor of the house behind Colson & Sons. He groaned soundly, then sobbed. A man the size of a giant reduced to the whimpers of a boy.

Their mother was pacing about the kitchen. Donny could hear her prayers from where he stood on the landing. When he passed her again, she snatched his fingers up and squeezed them, not saying a word.

"He'll be all right, Ma," Donny told her, kissing the crown of her head. Every year she seemed shorter. "Let him clean himself up."

She said nothing, her breath hitching as though she might cry. She patted his cheek.

Donny and Otto left to the sound of Gunner's shouted pleas.

They walked to Kenton's edge in silence. They let the panic and anguish rise and fall between them but did not speak of it. Tomorrow would be better, Donny thought.

It was nightfall when at long last, Scottie and Briggs returned down the eastern tunnel. He and Otto were waiting on a wooden horse fence, just outside of town, the fillies behind them nuzzling their pockets for food.

Otto climbed down to his feet when the lantern lights finally came over the hill, Kenton's residents returning. "Looks like stars," he told Donny in a voice that cracked: a dam punched with leaks, emotion toppling through. "Like a hundred stars running over the ground."

Donny felt their feet pound over the earth like a drum, an ensemble welcoming them home.

He laughed. Rockets of light detonated behind his eyes.

They convened in the pub—Donny, Otto, Scottie, Briggs, and Tess—where Gunner's wails couldn't reach them. A sorry collection of crates meant for the kitchen sat instead atop the bar: vegetables, kerosene, machine oil, flour, and salt. Tess picked through each, her voice shot through with exhaustion. "It ain't half the agreed amount," she said. "Not a quarter of it."

Scottie grunted. "Dunnitch bluff stores are low. They're demandin' more before they trade anythin' else."

Donny sighed. "Well now, you can waltz back down the line and tell 'em we got none."

"*No*," Tess said abruptly. "No. In fact, none of you breathe a word of it." She paced the length of the pub. Isaiah whined from the corner. He'd done so endlessly in Patrick's absence.

Tess's tongue clicked. "You'll tell 'em the bluff is needed here for our wounded, and in Dorser after their raid. Tell 'em it's a matter of duty between us now. We're Union. Remind them of the fuckin' creed, if you have to. It's a favor we're askin'," Tess said. "And doin' the leader of the Miners Union a favor ought to be motivation enough."

Scottie sighed. "They know Patty's been taken, Mrs. Colson. It's in the newspaper. They named Kenton Hill."

The news sounded to Donny like a siren. A warning.

"It's more delicate now," Scottie continued. "They know where we are, that we're vulnerable."

"If we don't promise 'em somethin', Ma, they'll soon come lookin' for it themselves."

"Fuckin' *Dunnitch*," Tess muttered darkly. "Always with one fuckin' hand out."

"Dorser is another story," Briggs added. "It seems Patrick promised them a whole lot o' bluff after their raid. Told 'em if he didn't show up with it, then he was dead."

There was a strangled kind of silence. No one voiced the possibility that Patrick might indeed be dead.

"We told 'em it was business as usual, but I'm not sure we left 'em with much confidence," Briggs said. "And their toll was much greater than ours."

Donny felt a tiredness come over him. He imagined Dorser and Dunnitch on the fringes, closing in. Gunner in his bunk, crying for bluff, the infirmary stacked with wounded fighters, the kitchen behind the bar with not a single vial of bluff.

At that moment, Tess's coughs racked the air.

Donny stood. "Remind the Dunnitch members of the time Patrick ran their coppers out of town," he said. "And if they still have their hand out, cut it off." He took his coat up, wrapped it around his shoulders.

"There's the cows and the chickens that can be brought to market," he continued. "It'll hold us over until Patty gets back. Until then, its business as usual, boys," he said. "Plenty that needs doin'. Otherwise, he'll have our heads."

CHAPTER FOURTEEN

THEO

In the dead hours after midnight, Theodore remained in the National House rather than return to his father's estate. Some Crafter curled over the driver's bench atop a coach parked on the drive, waiting for him to emerge.

He wouldn't. He stayed instead by Nina's side while she slept, her wrists shackled to the iron bed frame. An overly decorative quilt covered her to the throat, and Theo pulled it higher still. She looked softer this way.

It wasn't chivalry that kept him here, but quite the opposite. His father's manor had a dozen empty rooms all with portraits of his ancestors looming on the walls, and they watched his every move. The walls listened. They saw each failing and triumph, and at one point in his life, he'd cared about little else. Eventually, though, it had all started to feel backward. The triumphs felt more like a cost. How long had he ignored that pit in his stomach?

Surely it meant something, that sickness. It shouldn't feel so foul to win.

The door opened, and a steel-jawed maid stepped around the guard to offer him tea.

Theo frowned. "No, thank you," he said. "I didn't call for tea."

Her eyes shifted to the tray she held. "I ought to leave this here . . . in case," she said, setting it on the bedside table and muscling a cup and saucer into his hands.

He took it reflexively and saw that a piece of paper was caught between them.

"I'll leave you be," said the maid. She couldn't seem to close the door behind her quickly enough.

Theo set the cup down and pulled the paper free, reading the message scrawled on it.

The Alchemist has asked to speak with you.

Theo frowned once more. He wondered what could be said between them at this late hour.

Nina slept on in her deadened way, and Theo sighed. He knew he oughtn't lock himself in a room with a man who wanted to flay him.

But then, perhaps he deserved to be flayed.

The man guarding Patrick's door didn't question Theo's arrival. He wore the robes of a minister, after all. The Crafters who worked in the House moved about as if he weren't there, though their eyes occasionally glanced off his chest buttons, never venturing upward. On younger, drunker evenings in the years after Nina, he'd led women from the grand ballroom to this hallway and hitched their skirts up. The maids and guards had continued on then, too, completely dialed to task. Theo had found it was easier to think of them that way—as machinery. It grew confusing when you remembered they weren't.

Theo went back into the little laboratory. It was webbed over and caked in dust. This entire floor was filled with rooms just the same—there had once been an Alchemist per office, but they were now vacant except for Patrick.

The man was standing in anticipation of his arrival. The shadow of a beard was forming over his jaw. Moonlight washed over the acreage of his chest. His hair stuck up in the places he'd clearly pulled at it.

"How did you convince the maid to bring me a note?" Theo asked. Even to him, his voice sounded hollow.

"Bluff," Patrick said dismissively, and Theo saw then the empty sack that had held terranium ore. Patrick sighed, looking more tired than he'd ever been. "It's always bluff they want."

Theo waited, but Patrick seemed thousands of miles away. "And what do *you* want?"

Patrick looked straight at Theo, and he hated the way his insides shuddered a little. The breath in his lungs clung to the sides.

"The same as you," Patrick said in resignation. "I want to get her out of here."

Theo's tongue lodged in the hollow of his cheek. He tried to keep his voice plain. "Thought she was a stranger to you now," he said. "A traitor—"

"They'll strip her from the waist up," Partick interjected, his voice black as pitch. "They'll kneel her down in the dirt, and take her blouse, and then her bra, and some copper will crack a whip over her back until she's cut from neck to waist." He was breathing hard now.

But so was Theo. His eyes had shut tight, but the image came anyway.

"And everyone in the city will watch," Patrick continued. "Every man and woman will see her like that. And once that picture's in their minds, nothing'll scrub it out. They'll *gorge* themselves on it. There'll be caricatures in the newsprint, ain't nothin' you or I can do—"

"Don't," Theo said, his fists balling, something hot cutting at the back of his throat.

"You'll have to watch, too."

The thought was unbearable.

"And you'll know you helped put her there. You stood by while the pieces were put in place. Waited for 'em to fall."

"There isn't another *way*!" Theo shouted. He turned his back to Patrick and covered his mouth with his hand. "The pieces were set long before I arrived."

"That doesn't absolve you."

"I don't wish to be absolved."

"Don't you?" Patrick pushed, stepping closer. "Not even by *her*?"

Theo swallowed. Was that what he wanted? In truth, there was a part of him that prayed she'd stay sleeping. In sleep, she couldn't hate him. Couldn't know what he'd done—or hadn't.

"She's strong," Theo said. "Far stronger than most." Lord, he was a sounding of his father. A direct imitation.

Patrick laughed mirthlessly. He leaned over the desk, bracing himself, his fingers to the oak. "You ever get a beltin', Teddy?"

Theo balked. His mouth opened and shut. "No," he said eventually.

"No," Patrick repeated. "Well, I have. *She* has. Every fuckin' kid in the brink, besides. She'll look at you like you're the devil after tomorrow. Do you understand?" His stare bore into Theo. "Ain't no forgiveness after that. She won't work for you and your father."

"She'll see that there's no choice," Theo persisted. But even he didn't believe it.

"That's just it," Patrick said. "You'll have taken all the choice out of it. And the worst thing you could do to a woman like Nina Harrow is take away her choices."

Theo's hands rose slightly from his sides, then fell, hapless. "Choice is an illusion," he said numbly. "There's none of it left on either side."

"You can stop it, Theo," Patrick said now.

But Theo was already shaking his head. "Do you think I didn't try?" he asked. "That I didn't beg my father to find another way? Whatever you think of me, Colson, surely you've learned that I can't rid myself of her!" He said this last in a sudden onslaught, the words crashing over themselves. It took him several moments to catch his breath. He knew he was unraveling. He ran his tongue over his bottom lip and tasted sweat. "If there was a way . . ." The sentence lingered.

Patrick looked at him as though he found him unfathomable. But he didn't know Theo's father. He didn't understand that the man lived up in his mind, and nothing breached his heart. But he was a *fair* man. He was logical to the point of pain. He understood that the continent could not continue on as it had. "Despite any of our feelings, this is the only way forward. This is the cost of armistice, Colson. Of truce."

"There won't be a truce," Patrick said now, looking dead into Theo's eyes.

Theo frowned. "What?"

"Your father won't hold up his end of the bargain, Teddy. Con men like him never do."

Theo waited several moments. But Patrick didn't expound, and his eyes continued digging into Theo's. "He's a man of his word."

"Ask him," Patrick said. "Ask him tonight, in person. Look in his eyes when he answers." Theo never thought he'd see the man plead.

But surely he pleaded to Theo now.

"Look for the lie," Patrick said. "If I'm right, then Nina goes under the whip tomorrow for nothing. You can *stop* this."

Theo was shaking. His hands betrayed him. "And if you're wrong?"

"I'm not."

Theo sighed, felt nausea swarm him. He turned to leave, but just before he reached the door, he turned back to Patrick Colson. "It's not her forgiveness I want," he said, his voice choking something back. "She was happy here once, in this city. Like she was born for it. I still want that for her."

Patrick only looked on in pity, but perhaps also understanding. "Might've been true once, Teddy. I wouldn't know." He looked back to the stained glass, pulled that infernal coin from his pocket and weaved it through his fingers. "But I know this; she won't kneel. Not now."

"She knelt to Lord Tanner," Theo said weakly.

"She knelt when her mother's life hung in the balance," Patrick said distantly. "Now you've no leverage, and she won't be forced."

Theodore's chest concussed. "It's not my wish, nor my father's, to force her."

"Ask him," Patrick insisted. He tossed the coin, and it levitated before his eyes, spinning rapidly in the air. "Ask him how he intends to control a hostile earth Charmer. And you can be sure she'll be hostile, Teddy." Patrick looked over at him. The coin continued its pirouette. "Neither of us know her as well as we'd like to think, but I think we know enough between us to agree on that. There's no forgiveness for this."

Theo knew that already. Had known it the moment the lever was pulled.

"What about you?" he asked Patrick. "Can *you* forgive her?"

The coin froze.

Theo left him like that, staring into nothing.

Eleven hours remained. The clock tower chimed low over the city. Midday would find Nina beneath it.

Theo walked through those hallways of the National House and past the soulless Crafters and portraits of dead lords. He found his feet on the stairs, and instead of descending to the cellar again, he climbed. He found himself floating to the quarters belonging to the Head of House as though detached from his own body. When he knocked on the doors, the sound was muted.

"Come in."

His father hovered near the hearth, looking into the flames some Charmer had summoned. Purposeless, really. Why did they need Charmers to light their hearths and lamps when a match could do the same?

"Theodore," his father greeted on exhale, irritation apparent.

Theodore inclined his head mechanically. His neck fought the act.

"The hour is late."

"There's something I want to ask you."

"I'd urge you not to want for anything," he replied. "And not for a good while. You still have much to atone for."

Theo collided with his body again, smacked with ire. It was always this when it came to his father. Always what he'd done wrong.

But he'd agreed to that fabricated scandal and gone to Kenton Hill for two years. Two years in the hole with Crafters who'd loathed him. Two years of scurrying around the parish like a rat, looking for the Alchemist. Only one slip of loyalty, in the end. And hadn't he returned and taken his penalties with good grace?

Hadn't he tucked his tail and heeled, the way a son of a lord should?

Hadn't he forsaken the one thing, the only *real* thing he cared about?

"Nevertheless, I must ask," Theo began, though the words were difficult to pass, "once Nina . . . recovers, where will she go?"

Again, his father sighed. "She will remain here, of course."

"She ought to be offered something more comfortable."

Lord Shop pulled his spectacles down the bridge of his nose and pressed his fingers to the pockets of his closed eyes. “These are trivial details, Theodore. They can wait.”

Theo felt his neck heat, but he bit his tongue. “She ought to be moved.”

“There are plenty of available rooms in this building.”

“Which offer no privacy,” Theo argued. “The conditions are hardly appropriate for a lady of her station.”

“A lady of her station,” his father repeated, as though feeling the words on his tongue. “And what station do you imagine for her?”

Theodore frowned. He watched, as Patrick had told him to. “She’s a Charmer. She graduated with a high-order fellowship—”

“And now, she is an assassin,” Lord Shop interrupted, finally turning from the fire to face his son. “Perhaps the most infamous in all of our country’s history.” He had his hands clasped behind his back. His face was expressionless. “Where should such a lady be accommodated, Theodore, if not the cellar?”

Theo’s molars ground together. What he said next was quiet, tampered by embarrassment. “I could offer her my living quarters temporarily. Or—or they could be shared.” He heard how pathetic it sounded. Had he really imagined carrying her over that threshold? Nursing her back to health?

He had. He must have been mad.

His father was laughing now. The sound was cold. “You still believe yourself in love with her, boy?”

His skin burned hot; sweat collected along his collar.

“Love is the strangest illusion, don’t you agree? I think it was the great poet Lady Pennyrook who once said *Love is the reflection of the agony beneath*.” Lord Shop picked up his cane and tapped it on the floor. He exhaled once more. “At the very least, it would serve us, if she could be convinced to love you in return.” He glanced up as though dissecting the thought. “Though I don’t hold much hope.”

Theo felt the blade of a guillotine overhead, balanced precariously.

“For now, Theodore, Nina will need to play the part of prisoner to appease the ministry, and every other Artisan besides.”

"For how long?"

"Until she has won enough favors," Lord Shop quipped, having grown tired of the conversation.

"By finding terranium."

"Of course."

"And if she is unwilling?" Theodore asked now, the guillotine blade slipping free of its hold.

"If she ever wants to escape this House, she will have to," Lord Shop answered. His knuckles cracked as they flexed around his cane. "Or perhaps you can atone by persuading her to our side."

Theodore closed his eyes. "She'd be persuaded, I think, if she knew it were for a worthy cause. If she saw the bluff and idium distributed to the brink."

There was no answer from his father, who had pulled *The Stewards' Testament* from his pocket and flicked idly through its unreadable pages.

"You *do* intend to distribute to the brink, do you not?" he pressed, his heart beating a requiem.

Terrence Shop closed the book with a slap, then walked unhurriedly to that overlarge desk, shutting the old tome away in its drawer. "I intend to show them whatever illusion is necessary," he said. Then he collected his coat and shrugged it over his robes. "If that illusion eases your conscience, Theodore, then by all means, do not look beneath."

CHAPTER FIFTEEN

PATRICK

Patrick paced interminably.

He willed himself to conceive any viable plan. He heard boots on the floorboards beyond his door and wondered if it was Theo returning. Was there any hope in the man at all? Or was he tucked in bed, sleeping off the guilt?

Patrick had siphoned idium from the remaining terranium and stored the vials in his pockets, downing one for himself. He beat at his own forehead, breathed too rapidly. *Think*, he berated himself. *Think.*

But the hours disintegrated, and soon there was light dawning beyond the window, illuminating the stained glass God in all His bare glory. Patrick threw the remnants of the terranium ore at His face. The window didn't even scratch.

Nina would be beaten today, and there was nothing he could do to stop it. There were no more deals to be made, no strategies at play. He was locked inside this room with nothing but terranium and God.

He was useless. Horribly mortal and weak, to have let this unfold beyond his control. And whatever Nina's transgressions, he wondered if he had failed her in more ways than she had failed him.

She had traded his name and his town to free her mother, and he'd traded her freedom for his own means. She'd been his captive before she'd been his partner.

She'd pleaded once, and he hadn't listened.

He'd used her for her medium, just as Theo said.

And now she would pay for a truce that had been bargained over her unconscious body.

Patrick knelt, and the contents of his stomach climbed his throat and spilled out. He heaved until his stomach was empty.

This is what needs to happen, son, his father had told him. *She'd want it for us, if she's truly on our side.*

"Fuck," Patrick cursed. He wanted a blade. A gun. He felt the desperate urge to fire in any direction. And he thought he understood then, how she'd been able to betray him to save her mother. How could he fault her, when he'd kill through ranks of beating hearts to get to her?

He spent those final hours feeling the way he had as a boy, his mother lying prone in her bed, fading with gray fever. He'd been as useless then.

In a last spasm of desperation, Patrick threw his fists into the stained glass window, his knuckles breaking. But the glass remained intact, another reminder that Patrick was an ant of this world.

In this mania, Patrick lost his sense of time. He spent long moments with his head in his hands, heart thundering. He looked to see how high the sun had climbed. Was it already over, or was Nina on her way now to that city square, the population of Artisanal Belavere gathering to watch?

Then, when the sun seemed at its highest, a crumb of mercy.

The bolts of the door slid back. The hinges creaked.

Theodore slunk in with mottled cheeks, oscillating eyes, and closed the door carefully behind him. There was a wildness about him, a determination.

Patrick leapt to his feet.

"I—*God almighty,*" Theo said, seeming to steel himself. From the inside of his robe, he pulled a bundle of navy and threw it to Patrick. "Put this on. We're leaving."

Patrick hesitated for only a second, but Theo, who yesterday was gaunt and shamed to silence, was now feverishly awake. Patrick's blood sprinted. He unraveled the Artisan robe and donned it. "Is there still time?"

"Time enough," Theo muttered, and he held out his hand. "There's a guard outside the door. I've got about ten seconds before he comes in to check on me. I need idium."

Patrick rummaged in his pocket and came up with a trembling vial. He was out of schemes. He could only follow.

Theo pulled the cork and swallowed the ink in one gulp, shivering as it went down. It only took seconds for idium to meld with one's bloodstream.

"Come on," Theo hissed, already backing toward the door. "And be quiet."

Patrick rushed forward.

Theo took a singular breath, wrapped his hand around the handle, and opened the door to a baffled guard, who looked between the two men with dawning realization. In his hand was an uncorked bottle of finest brandy, which he'd evidently been drinking from.

He raised his baton with wide eyes.

But Theo raised one of his hands, and whatever shout the guard meant to emit stuck in his throat.

Instead, a bubble of brandy spluttered from the man's lips, dribbling down his chin. The guard coughed, the baton fell to the carpeted floor, and his hand gripped at his own throat before he stumbled back into the wall and fell, unconscious.

Theo released a shaky breath. "We have to hurry," he said. "Follow me."

Theo led Patrick to the end of the corridor, where a servants' passage waited beyond a nondescript white door. A hideously narrow staircase spiraled endlessly into the dark, and they raced down the spine of it, Patrick's heart thundering against his rib cage. "Where is she?"

"In a coach, headed for the city center," Theo panted. "I had to wait for her and my father to be clear of the building. He took half the guards with him." He finally pushed through another door, barreling into a basement kitchen currently occupied by only one Craftsman, stirring the contents of a large steel pot. He looked up from beneath hooded eyes as they raced around the benches and boilers, apparently unsurprised to see them. Theo slipped a handful of coins into the cook's waiting palm as they passed, then led Patrick to an exit.

They pushed their way into the cellar stairwell, daylight ahead, and scurried headlong up them and onto a drive—the very same passage Patrick had once pulled Nina into, daring her to sneak into the National Artisan House.

Only now, there were overhanging sycamore trees above, and one lone horseless wagon before it, the driver's seat occupied by none other than John Colson.

Theodore's face paled at the sight. "I told you to steal a horse from the stable!" he hissed.

But Patrick's father, dressed in the same navy blue as Patrick, only donned a driver's bowler and pulled it low over his eyes. "Don't need one," he said.

Patrick smiled. He felt the first shivers of hope returning.

"Hand it over, son," John said, grinning.

And Patrick jumped into the back of the wagon, pulled a vial of ink forth, and gripped his father's waiting hand with it.

Theodore's forehead creased. "You're a wood Mason?"

"The very best, kid," John grunted. "Get in the fuckin' wagon."

Theodore clambered in. John downed the idium, tilting his face to the sun as though seeing it for the first time. Then, groaning in satisfaction, he looked over his shoulder to Patrick.

"Let's go get your lady." He winked.

He threw a blanket of burlap over Theodore and Patrick both, and as the wagon began trundling precariously down the drive, the two men lay curled, just barely out of sight, their breaths swarming in the close space.

CHAPTER SIXTEEN

NINA

I awoke in increments.

I saw first a parade of hovering faces, then intervals of nothing. I blinked back stubborn clouds of film again and again but felt mired in them. I woke briefly when they changed my clothes and had the wherewithal to cover my breasts with my hands. I woke again to a nurse tipping something noxious down my throat. I was terrified of my uninhibited body lying just beyond the fog, where I was unable to defend it. I imagined hands roaming over my stomach, ink slithering into my nostrils and pooling in the corners of my eyes.

Moments or hours or years later, I was being shuffled downstairs on leaden legs, strong hands encasing my arms. Then there were the cobbles rising up to meet me, tripling my nausea. I blinked up at spires and vine-entangled gutters to see the sun, somehow still there, and had the wherewithal to ask, "Where're you takin' me?"

I sounded like a child.

"In you get" came the answer, and light dimmed, sound condensed. The bench seat beneath me felt solid and anchoring.

The voice that met me through the fog did not.

A figure sitting across from me. We were closer together than I wanted, our knees touching, walls either side, and a ceiling too low. A coach, I realized. And sharing it with me was a man I knew.

"Miss Clarke," Lord Terrence Shop greeted, his neck taut, face pinched. "Forgive the interruption to your sleep."

I blinked. Gripped the wall. "Wh—where?"

"Where are we going?" the lord finished on my behalf. He moved his cane to the side, looked pensively out a window. "Tending to some business," he said. "My first as Head of House, in fact."

A dull throb pulsed at my arm, and I looked down to see both wrists bandaged, both shackled.

And the rest came rushing back.

The noose and the rain and the lever. The snap and my mother's white lips, her frozen terror. The stampeding sorrow. A bone-breaking anguish.

Earth rising, rising, and then devouring.

Bloodlust.

It coated my mouth again, and I was freshly ravenous. "Did you do this?" I whispered, voice sapped. I was a husk now, I realized.

They'd bled me dry. All of them.

The lord took stock of me over his spectacles with an air of distaste. "*You* did this," he said simply. "No one wrapped your finger around that trigger, Miss Clarke, did they?"

"Harrow." My voice was a tremor, rippling out into the space between us. Did he hear my wrath knocking at his chest? "Where are you taking me?"

"You are to help me repair some of the fractured tensions between *our* people," he answered.

I couldn't make sense of it. Couldn't see where I had been led, like a tethered dog. I only knew that I felt the rope at my neck, always pulling.

A sob climbed my ribs.

Here I was, shackled by the newest Head of House—the last one already forgotten, easily replaced—speaking to me of my duty to help him.

And I was so tired.

His voice droned on, just like Tanner's. "It is the very least you can do. Do you understand? You can humble yourself before your countrymen, pray to Idia for forgiveness."

But if Idia existed, she had frayed every last thread of me, and God was a villain.

"I advise you be gracious from here onward, Nina," Terrence Shop said, my newest puppeteer. "Be thankful I didn't order your throat sliced along with your wrist."

I laughed, a new kind of hysteria in it. I could have hurled myself from the coach or simply closed my eyes and slept forever, right there on the carriage floor. "Kill me, then," I said, then I leaned as far forward as I could, offering him my neck.

But long moments passed, and he did nothing. By the time I rolled my face back to his, he seemed sallow, strained, as though just now smelling the madness in me. "You and your fuckin' ministry," I said slowly, so that he could hear every rasp. "You wouldn't kill me even if I begged you."

And he seemed caught off guard to hear my voice was no longer that of a child's, and that the world hadn't stripped away my spine.

He righted himself. Crossed his legs. "The theatrics are not necessary, Miss Harrow," he said. "But, where your life is concerned, you happen to be correct. I've brokered a compromise with the other lords to spare your life. If not for me, you'd be hanged this day."

More deals. More bargains. My eyes rolled skyward. A school of fish had been painted on the carriage ceiling. "Do you fear death, my lord?"

He was quiet. Contemplative.

The fish swam in a mindless circle. "I find those who fear death have something to live for."

Lord Shop shifted uncomfortably. "I'd hoped you'd see this as an opportunity to renew yourself. Fulfill your purpose. There is much we can achieve together."

For the millionth time, I reimagined the siphoning ceremony, wherein I never made myself the world's only earth Charmer. "Then you might as well take me to the gallows, my lord. I don't care for my purpose, and I no longer fear death."

After all, what remained that I should live for?

The lord chewed on his own tongue for a long moment. A sinister satisfaction seemed to come over him. "As I feared," he said quietly, turning his gaze away. "You'll take the whip on the citadel steps for assassinating the governing leader of this country."

A dull dread rippled up my sternum.

"It will be . . . quite severe. We need to send a clear message that murder is not tolerated—"

"If it is an *Artisan* who is murdered, it is not tolerated."

"—and that the punishment for sedition is grave."

The coach swayed from side to side. The horses out front whinnied and shook their great heads in protest. Somewhere beyond, the city grew limescale and lost its glimmer by degrees. The Artisans scratched at their useless brands and paced their drawing rooms, purposeless, just like me.

For what was left for me here? Certainly no friends or family. All were dead or believed me a traitor. Patrick screamed to mind, and I shut my eyes to stem the onslaught of him. There was no me and Patrick. No Kenton Hill. Nothing to fight for but remnants of my dignity, to be promptly lost on those citadel steps.

Clanging in the hollows of my mind, the shell of my mother said, *God only wants my sufferin'*. Tears ran past my self-restraint.

The coach jostled violently then, alarmingly so. The horses wrenched sideways. Lord Shop gripped his cane and turned to look through the window. "What in God's name—"

But the sound of his voice was cut off by a sudden buckling of wood, an almighty crunch, and we were both thrown sideways as the coach toppled, as though an axle had been snapped in two.

My head hit the wall of the coach, and I groaned, the world now on its side. Lord Shop's body had half collapsed over mine, and he roared indignantly, cursing as he tried to right himself.

Voices beyond the coach called out. The driver barked orders to the runaway horses. The sky spilled in as the door was finally wrenched open from above, and the driver's blotched face appeared, distress making his eyes wide. "Everyone all right, my lord?"

Lord Shop seethed. "Get us *out*!"

"Bloody wheel snapped in two," the Craftsman said, reaching one arm down to pull the lord free. "Like someone took an axe to it."

I watched then as a knife appeared at the driver's throat and pressed against his airway.

Another face blocked out light. This one was bearded, sported a bowler, and gave a long, low whistle. "Scuse the interruption, my lord." His voice was thick, heavily accented. He smiled, stained teeth glinting. "They don't make these swank carriages the way they used to."

Lord Shop's eyes blackened. His lip peeled back in fury, and he tried to find his footing. "Colson. You Godforsaken *fool*—"

"Uh, uh, now," the man I took to be John Colson said, and suddenly, a piece of splintered wood levitated, carved itself with rapid precision into a stake, and then hovered out of reach above Terrence Shop's head, its tip pointed at his cranium.

Patrick's father seemed euphoric. There was a fervor in his eyes that I was sure I'd seen before. "'Fraid I'll have to renege on our deal, Shop," he said, and then to me, "Up you get, darlin'."

He was shoved aside then, his face and that of the driver's replaced by one that, after everything, seemed heavenly.

Patrick held one arm out to me, something pained crossing his expression. "Come on," he said, urgency marring every line of his face. "Hurry."

I lifted my injured arms, and he grasped them. If the wounds split, or fresh pain tore free, I didn't feel it. I only felt his sure fingers, circling around my wrists, hauling me free of the wreckage, out into open air.

"*You scum!*" Shop spat from below, the stake still hovering threateningly above him. "Half the city's policemen are moments behind!"

"Them coppers ran into a spill some ways back" came John Colson's elated voice once more. He still had the Craftsman by the throat, still grinned as though this were sport. "Fuckload of barrels toppled onto the road and blocked 'em in. Horrible luck."

"Patrick," Shop now appealed, turning his attention away from John

Colson. "If you run now, you remove the last hope of amnesty for your people. I will burn every town, every Craftsman in the brink to ash."

Patrick looked down at the lord as though he were a plague. "Pray to God we don't meet again, Terrence," Patrick said, voice murderous. "Next time you see me, I'll be the one puttin' a bullet in that empty chest."

We left Terrence Shop in the buckling carriage on an empty street, the windows of buildings above overcrowded with onlookers pressing their noses to the glass. Patrick jumped from the remaining rear wheel and turned to reach for my waist, and I went to him as one turns to the sun.

He caught me as though I weighed nothing, and then my feet were on the ground, and he was turning me around, urging me onward. "Run," he insisted, gripping my hand beneath the shackles. "As fast as you can manage."

And he led me back down the lane, the faces above tracking our path, until the shadows of an alley bore down on us and the cobbles turned to dirt.

We sprinted through stagnant black puddles, through the grimy underbelly of the city, through a skinny maze of steaming drains and houseless Crafters, who barely lifted their chins to watch us pass. I stumbled often and Patrick caught me twice, his voice insistent. "A little farther," he said. "Come on, just a little farther."

At the end of an alley so narrow we could barely squeeze through, Patrick came to a sudden standstill. Heavy footfalls approached from behind, and I turned, panicked, only to find the man who was surely John Colson thundering in our direction, a radiant smile of triumph splitting his face in two.

He winked at me and put his index finger to his lips.

Ahead was a wide dock, filled with waiting passengers dressed for long travel. Narrow boats stuttered to their pylons and waited for passengers to alight and board. Gray-faced Crafters smoked and manned the steering wheels in long coats and wool caps.

A policeman bellowed names of destinations from the dock, funneling the harried crowd into their prospective queues, his mustache quivering with every shout.

"Shit," Patrick hissed, and reached back with his arm toward me, as though he could push me out of sight.

"Coppers fuckin' everywhere, Patty boy," John said, pulling his bowler low over his eyes. "Look there." He nodded to the left, where three more policemen huddled over a lighter, smoking their pipes apathetically and leaning against the brick.

"He said he'd be here," Patrick said through his teeth, his forehead glistening with exertion. "Where the fuck is he?"

"Who?" I asked.

"We gotta move, Pat," John said over my shoulder. "Won't be long before the cavalry comes chargin' in."

"I know," Patrick said.

"We've got minutes, Pat. Now or never."

"I *know*!" Patrick cinched his eyes closed and muttered to himself, as though a private consultation were occurring, then turned to look at his father and me both. He took the bowler from his father's head and pulled it low over my own, then pulled the navy cloak from his shoulders and threw it around me, pulling the collar up high over my hair. "They'll recognize Nina before they recognize us," he said to his father. "Distract them, if it comes to it."

John Colson nodded. "At all costs, my boy. No more time to lose."

"Stick as close to me as you can get," Patrick said. "And keep your hands hidden."

We walked out of the alley and into the chaos of the dock with John in front, and me tucked so tightly into Patrick's side I could feel every breath, every heartbeat. He slung an arm around my shoulder, and it served to hide half my face. He looked about in a casual way—just another weary traveler awaiting their fare.

"Baymouth on four!" shouted the copper. "Morland on three!"

"Morland," Patrick repeated, and his father nodded once.

But pylon three was crowded with those coppers smoking their pipes and watching the crowd. "Patrick. The police—"

"Morland," he said again. "It has to be Morland."

I swallowed dryly and buried my head farther into the recess of him. I didn't pray. I simply held my breath.

We shuffled into line, the coppers not a foot from my back, so close their conversation was easy to overhear. The tobacco in their pipes wafted over my hat.

". . . begged him to trade shifts with me. What I wouldn't give for a little entertainment," one said. Then came the sound of his spit hitting the dock.

"Not me, I'm squeamish," said another. "If I'm to see a woman's back I'd rather it not be whipped to tatters."

I stiffened. My tongue seemed to swell in my mouth.

"Still," said the remaining, this voice younger. "As good a reason as any for a little sport, wouldn't you say?"

The first grunted a laugh. "What's your bet?"

"Fifty shillin's she can stay on her knees for the first ten lashes."

"Naw. It'll be lights out before the second. Swank skin's as thin as they come."

Patrick seemed to seize beside me. His feet cemented to the dock.

"Heard she ain't well bred, though," the coppers continued, voices damningly loud. "From Sommerland or some such. Might've given her a bit of grit at least."

There was a low whistle. "If a Sommerland girl is good for somethin', it's bein' on her knees."

Harsh laughter carried on the cold air, and Patrick, oblivious to my nudging, turned.

"*Don't*," I whispered to him.

There was now a notable space in the queue before us, waiting to be filled, but Patrick seemed incapacitated, his fists balling, eyes sparking, and I watched in horror as one of the police looked up to meet his eye, jutting his chin toward him. "Oy!" the man called, pipe slipping from his lips. "Move along there!"

"*Patrick*," I intoned, desperate now, but Patrick seemed possessed, as though the violence of the past week had only now caught up to him, and his blood couldn't cool. His chest filled.

"I said, get movin'!" the copper emphasized, stepping past his chums and shooing Patrick as though he were a man who could be shooed. "Or get out of the fuckin' way."

But Patrick stepped toward the man with intent, dropping his hold on me, and it only served to raise alarm in the others, who widened their eyes.

And before Patrick's punch landed, I watched recognition dawn across their faces.

First of me, dressed strangely in a bowler and a minister's cloak, hands shackled and frantically grasping for Patrick's winding arm. Then for Patrick himself, who by now must have been pictured in bulletins throughout the city.

His fist came down on the copper's face like a hammer, blood erupting from a split in the man's eyebrow, his knees buckling, and Patrick caught his collar and wound his arm back again, then again. Before his colleagues could react, the man was bludgeoned and limp, and Patrick was rearing for a fourth blow.

They wielded their batons, catching Patrick's back and shoulder, and he barely seemed to register their attempts.

The crowd dispersed around them, men and women backing away from the chaos with shrieks and clutched throats. More police were funneling onto the dock—whether summoned by the racket or sent by Lord Shop, it couldn't be known, but in they came, shoving would-be passengers out of the way, black helmets bouncing above the sea of people, closer and closer.

Suddenly John was there, pushing Nina back behind him, wielding his blade and pulling a copper off Patrick by his collar, and I watched him jam the knife into the man's shoulder, and retract it just as fast.

Gunshots next, from no particular direction, and I dropped to all fours with the rest of the crowd. Shrieks rent the air. I heard my named called, the false one. "Get Clarke!" they bellowed. "Hold your fire! That's the Alchemist!"

And then hands were at my shoulders, around my waist. Men lifting me off my feet as I fought to free myself, wrenching my body in every direction.

"PATRICK!" I shouted over and over.

Another sound was growing. Beyond the shrieks and the ring of shots fired, above the wet thwack of Patrick's fists and John's grunts, a roar emerged.

The canal was groaning, rising impossibly high onto the docks, harrying feet, then ankles. Passengers tumbled backward and fled. The dock, thick with spores of rot, turned slick, and the men who tried to carry me away slipped and fell.

All breath was pushed from my lungs, but I had the wherewithal to scramble through the rising water, to flee.

"NINA!" came a shout.

Waiting in the canal was a narrow boat arriving around the bend, the water churning beneath it. The moored boats had crashed into the pylons, capsized onto the dock, or else were paddling away as quickly as the driver could muster.

Standing at the wheel of this newest boat was Theo.

"RUN!" he shouted again, eyes wild, hands outstretched, the water rising by his will.

He pushed funnels of it at officers who rushed toward me, pushing them back, but there were too many, and a larger wave would endanger the many innocents still slipping and wading on the dock, trying to escape, some laden with children.

And here again was John, his arm reaching toward me, Patrick close behind him, both of them bloody.

I reached toward John's hand as though it were a life raft, and as it lifted me from the wash I felt relief, even as that rough hand slid around my throat. Even as it spun me so that my back crushed to his front, and the cool metal of the blade pressed under my jaw.

Fear delayed, then stampeded in.

John held me with a viselike grip. "Stay calm," he murmured into my ear. Then he lifted his chin. "GET BACK!" he bellowed out to the dock, and the policemen froze, dripping wet, confused.

"That's it. Back away now, boys! Or we'll have the earth Charmer's throat all over the docks." There was a sharp jostle. Patrick's voice saying, *"No! Not her."*

Then John's, growling in return. "Just get in the fuckin' boat. Don't be stupid."

"Don't move!" one of the policemen shouted, eyes bulging. "Lower your weapons!"

Slowly, through knee-high water and under the straining eyes of a bevy, John shuffled me backward. The blade never left my throat.

I tried to find purchase on his forearm, but it was as immovable as stone. And I was as afraid of him as I was of the Belavere uniforms.

"Nice and easy," John said. "They won't shoot, hen. Don't you worry."

The water receded back into the canals, taking a few officers with it as they lost their footing. And I heard the boat behind me jostle against the dock. Soon I was lifted over the side, and then the dock slipped away, eyes following us uselessly, Theo cursing, John shielded by my own body, and Patrick somewhere on the deck, a stream of hisses emitting from him.

The narrow boat moved faster as Theo pushed the current, and soon we turned a corner out of sight. We were barricaded by high brick walls on either side.

Only then did the blade leave my throat.

I took my first full breath in hours, days perhaps. My knees buckled, and I gripped the boat's side, heaving.

Heavy feet stomped across the deck in my direction, and I threw my arm over my face. But when I opened my eyes, it was only Patrick.

Patrick taking his father by the collar of his coat and dragging him back. Patrick throwing his fist with full force into his father's nose.

"Fuck!" John shouted, clutching his face with both hands and toppling. The boat tipped. John shook his head and groaned. "God almighty. Right jab's improved, eh?"

Patrick's chest heaved with such ferocity I thought he might attack again. Instead, he scrubbed his own face, pointed a calloused finger in John's, and said, "Touch her again, and I'll forgo myself a father."

John raised his hands, abandoning the flow of blood from his nose. "Lord. Easy, son. I weren't gonna hurt her, and you know it."

Patrick advanced again, only this time, he did not box him, he simply leaned to push his face as close to his father's as he could come. "*Not another hand on her,*" he said clearly, deep enough that it reverberated in my own chest. He thrust a finger at me and turned to address Theo and his father both. "Not a single fuckin' hand on her, or I'll cut it off."

He breathed like a steam engine, and he crouched there on the deck, a hand dragging over his face, every muscle in his body rolling beneath the surface.

I silently begged him to look at me. To say something.

But he only growled a curse, stood, and retreated down into the cabin of the boat.

The door slammed against its frame.

"Lord," John said once more, only this time with a sort of foreboding. His eyes moved from the door to me, as though I held a grenade or a loaded revolver. He sighed. "Tore his heart out, I take it?"

My throat closed over.

He grunted in understanding. "The pretty ones always do."

CHAPTER SEVENTEEN

NINA

Traveling out of Belavere City via stolen narrow boat was treacherous.

First was the regularity with which we passed other boats, their hulls gliding within inches of ours, the passengers aboard staring out the windows or from the stern. It forced Patrick, Theo, and me to stay below, where we drew the curtains and hoped John (who had quickly decrypted the coal engine's mechanisms and taken the helm) could guide us in the right direction.

In the city, water Charmers turned the currents of the canals and left Crafters to steer the tillers without steam chests coughing soot into the air, but outside the city's network, the drivers were left to paddle or shovel coal, sputtering to their destinations unaided by magic.

John Colson sat out there in broad daylight, wearing his bowler hat and whistling, hardly the man I'd envisioned him being. I'd imagined a man much like Patrick. Contemplative, watchful, meticulous. But John seemed closer to Gunner in demeanor. There was gravel in his voice, and he carried himself with violence. Like Donny, he spoke unchecked. He was, in every part of his appearance, Crafter-hewn. Tall and broad shouldered, like Patrick. His face heavily lined and bearded. He did not look out of place as he moved coal from bin to chest, picking dry blood from his whiskers.

The cabin of the narrow boat was filled with soft bench seats lining the walls from one end to the other, a tiny aisle down the middle. The cushions, while finely embroidered, smelled damp, and with the windows closed, I soon felt mildew in my hair, spores colonising my nostrils.

I peered out of a hole in the threadbare curtains as yet another narrow boat passed by, and for a moment, a child stared out of his own porthole and met my eye, his forehead wrinkling against the glass.

And then the boat was gone. My view was replaced with the brown water of the black-bricked canal, grass and ravenous shrubbery barricading the entire length of it.

"We should be skirting around Gilmore soon," Theo murmured, his voice unsure, as though it might offend.

And it did. The three of us hadn't uttered a single word to one another since leaving the deck and hiding below like mice. Patrick's knuckles were bleeding. Theo could make eye contact with no one.

I felt shell-shocked, like my bones hadn't yet settled back in place. My eyes begged to close. My ears rang in a soothing way, my nervous system seeking to numb itself.

Across from me, his knees careful not to glance mine, sat Patrick, his head in his hands. He, too, did not look my way.

All that calamity. Now nothing except damp, uncomfortable silence.

Theo cleared his throat. "Does—do you think your father knows the way?" His eyes swept the window at the rear, where John's legs could be seen before the tiller. Patrick's father sang in low tones that floated down into the cabin.

"The way to what?" I asked, my voice odd and hollow.

Theo only seemed relieved that I'd spoken at all. "Morland," he said. "There aren't any canal maps aboard. I checked the storage holds, but—"

"Southeast past Gilmore," Patrick muttered, though he continued to cradle his forehead in one hand. His eyes were now pinched closed. "Due east, seven clicks after Fuller's Pass. Then straight on."

Theo looked at Patrick with a creased brow. "You've been there before?"

"Been everywhere," Patrick said, seemingly with momentous effort.

"And you memorized the geography?"

"I did," he said bluntly. When I finally saw his face, it seemed stricken.

He leaned his head back on the bench seat, a bruise burgeoning slowly over his right cheekbone.

Questions poured in, a river of them, but instead of asking a single one, I slept.

When I woke, it was dark beyond the curtains. Theo's light snores sounded nearby. Water lapped gently against the hull, and moonlight broke over Patrick's face.

He was awake, his fingers steepled in front of his lips. And finally, as though the dim made it easier to do so, he was looking at me. Watching.

His eyes were silver, swirling in unshed misery.

I was curled onto my side and found no energy to rise. My lip trembled. "Will you tell me everything?" I asked, terrified that he would turn away. Terrified of what he might say if he didn't.

If he denied owing me a damn thing, that would be just as well. What would he have to say to Lord Tanner's agent, harbinger of Kenton's downfall? Would he spit and yell this time? Or worse, those same deadened eyes I'd seen after our capture? That slow breaking.

Did he hate me?

His expression faltered, then collapsed altogether. One beat, two, and he left his seat.

Not to leave, but to kneel before me.

He didn't touch me. Didn't reach out to take my hand.

Instead, he said with a depth I could not fathom, "I'm sorry, Scurry girl."

He told me everything. Every wretched detail. From the moment Lord Terrence Shop had stepped into his room and spoken of wolves, made outlandish promises of a truce and idium for the brink, to the moment my mother hung.

"I didn't trust him," Patrick said, "but he wanted Tanner dead, and it seemed we could agree on that."

With every word, I felt fire lash beneath my skin. "And you all decided that I should be the one?"

His eyes flashed. "No."

"Then who?" I asked, just now picturing it, Patrick and John and Theo and Lord Shop, foreheads bent as they concocted a plan I wasn't party to.

"Me" came a cracked voice, and Theo's body rose in the dark. I couldn't see his face, but the register of his voice was soft and pained. "We told Patrick that it would be me."

It would have been more dignified, had I lifted my head from the bench seat, untucked my limbs from the curl of my torso. I did neither. What use was dignity now?

"Why?" I asked. A child questioning the turn of the earth.

Theo sighed like it might be his last. "Because my father decided that it would benefit him most to have *you* assassinate Tanner, and I told him Patrick would never allow it. I told him he'd refuse to siphon a drop of idium if that was the case."

"So you tricked the ink out of him and passed it on to me?"

Theo nodded gravely. I was glad I couldn't see the contours of his face.

"Was my mother to be hanged in the hopes it would *inspire* me to . . . to kill?" The words left my lips on a tremble, the realization that I was now a murderer finally dawning.

For seven years I'd escaped without blood on my hands, and it had caught up to me anyway.

Perhaps it was visible in my expression—the fabric of my being disintegrating—because Patrick's hand came over my wrist and his face hovered before mine, imploring me.

"Shh," he whispered. "It's all right."

Another lie.

"Was it Lord Shop who ensured the lever was pulled?" I asked. I needed this one last truth. I saw my mother's face, terror consuming her, following her into death as she swung.

"Yes," Theo said, hesitant now.

"But you knew?" There were no tears, no cracks in my voice. Just an emptiness I couldn't put a name to. "Did you know my mother would die for this plan?"

They answered one after the other.

A shake of the head from Patrick.

Silence from Theo.

Answer enough.

I rose then, finally gathering my feet beneath me, Patrick rearing back with his hands proffered, as though waiting for me to fall. I faced Theo, compelled by whatever dregs remained of myself. "Did you walk into that courtyard, knowing my mother would die for your father's benefit? Be man enough to answer me."

Moonlight crept through and turned him bone-colored. His jaw shook. "Yes."

And I thought, *we were kids together. We grew up together. Did you forget?*

A painful breath rattled out. "And . . . did you know he'd have me whipped afterward?"

Theo swallowed. His eyes went skyward and then to his shoes, his shaking hands into his pockets. Still, he wore that Artisan blue. "Yes."

Patrick allowed me two hits. The first was open handed and landed across Theo's cheek, a shock of crimson left behind. The second was a closed fist skidding across his jaw, the impact lackluster, my knuckles seizing immediately. Theo's eyes were wild as he raised his arms to fend me off, but there was no need.

Patrick's arms came around my torso like thick iron bands, pinning my arms down, and I settled instead for shrieking at Theo.

And I dug up every foul name Scurry had taught me and hurled it at him, then through him to his father, to Lord Tanner in the ground somewhere. To every minister in the House and all those that came before.

"You *fucking swank*!" I shouted, bucking against Patrick's hold, useless as it was. *"Fucking godless bastard!"*

And it wasn't until Theo's face was awash with tears that I caught my breath, which gave Patrick opportunity to whisper, "He saved us, Nina. I ain't sayin' it makes up for the rest, but you should know he got us all out."

"His *conscience* arrived too late!"

Patrick swore as I bucked again. "You're right. Oy! Listen to me, you're *right*! But his conscience saved you from the whip, and I can't let you kill him, whatever satisfaction it might bring me."

"My mother is *dead*!" I said. And my limbs weakened, my knees buckled. "Did she deserve it, Theo? Did *I*?"

Theo said nothing. From his place on the bench seat, I heard the soft sounds of his regret, and it meant little. It made up for nothing.

"Let go of me," I said, and Patrick did by degrees.

I pulled myself away from his hands, and made my wooden limbs carry me away, back to the steps and out to the deck, ducking my head under the cabin roof and slamming the door behind me.

There was John, a wrinkled, calloused assortment of his three sons, whistling into the icy night, one hand on the tiller.

"Evenin', miss," he nodded to me, spitting over the side of the hull. "Should get some sleep while you can. We'll be in Morland by sunup."

I contemplated him a second longer, then walked toward him with my fist already clenched. What was one more strike? One more split knuckle?

But I was too obvious or too weak, and John stood easily with a slowness that warranted embarrassment and caught my fist in his wide hand.

A short laugh barked from him. "You've got some spirit left, at least," he said, then pitched my hand off to the side as one shoos a fly. "We'll have to teach you to box properly."

I descended to the deck then. Melted to it. Buried my face in the darkness of my hands.

After a moment or two, I felt John join me, his hand patting my shoulder. "For what it's worth, hen. I'm sorry for your poor ma. There ain't any justice in it."

Tears plinked off the wood. I wished he would stop speaking.

"And I apologize for the knife," he added. "Didn't mean nothin' by it."

And that was perhaps the only truth. There was no meaning to any of it. War was a gentlemen's game. Women were just the currency.

CHAPTER EIGHTEEN

NINA

In the first dregs of daylight, we drifted into Morland canals.

Our narrow boat was not followed or intercepted by any other vessel along the way, but I did not voice this strangeness. The canal network was an ever-expanding web of junctions. Perhaps the authorities thought it a waste of time to try and track us down.

I was growing sicker with every sway of the boat, and I suspected fever would take hold soon. The flesh above my bandage was rosy and swollen—the bandage itself still damp with canal water.

I was on the deck as we passed the first Morland buildings. They competed for the skyline, towering above on rickety foundations. Floors and floors of iron rail steps and thin windows. Morland was an ancient province, densely populated, and much like Belavere City, beloved for its fine architecture.

Still, the Artisans preferred to only visit, rather than reside in Morland. The surrounding canals carried a smell up to even the highest of floors, the lanes were too tight, the cobbles buried under layers of dirt, and the churches upstaged by less pious enterprise.

Gambling dens monopolized much of the city's commerce. It was a place where the rich came to play, while the Crafters served and picked at the stray pennies.

I had traveled to Morland twice before. Once with my Artisan class, to visit the relics, and once under a different name, when I'd laundered clothes in the basement of a shiny hotel. Even the latter felt like lifetimes ago.

I'd spent the remainder of the night on deck, watching the quiet water and listening to John hum his songs in a state of disconnect. Several times I cried, and he didn't seem to mind.

"My Patty seems quite taken with you," he commented near dawn, when I'd finally wrung myself dry.

I swallowed. "Not any longer." It stung to say it.

John grunted a laugh, shook his head. "You know, he nearly lost his own ma when he was a boy."

I looked over at him, curiosity finding a way through the anguish.

"Terrible times. I was away on business. Came home to find me sons hoverin' at my wife's bedside. Gray fever. Damn near took her, too. Have you yet met my wife?"

I nodded, Tess's tired face floating to mind.

"She's a force to be reckoned with," John said, shaking his head. "Bet she gave you the hard word once she saw those stars in Pat's eyes."

"She threatened to shoot me."

John chuckled. "Don't mind her. She's threatened to shoot me more times than I can count. Never does it."

"She thinks you're dead," I told him. It was blunt, but I didn't have the wherewithal to care. "She was sure of it."

"Ah, well. Take more than a House of swanks to finish me."

"I suppose she'll be relieved to know she was wrong."

John spat into the canal. "You know, miss. I don't know that relief is the word for it. She was always unhappy to see me go, but she was just as mad when I came home again. I imagine she'll slug me on sight." He smiled fondly. "Deservedly, mind you."

Whether or not he looked forward to this was unclear. Like Patrick, John was difficult to read, and like Donny, everything was buried in humor.

"Why don't you go wake the others," John said as we drifted closer to the silhouette of Morland. He pulled on the air with relish, unencumbered by a night spent awake and upright.

"Why Morland?" I asked him. "You must be desperate for home."

But if John Colson was desperate, it seemed to be for those towering oblong buildings rising up around us, and not for Kenton.

"Business first," he said, pulling on the till.

"What business?"

"The Union's." He seemed to savor the word. "What other?"

Soon enough, the narrow boat was bumping gently against the pylons, and Theo and Patrick came up—Patrick stiff-jawed, and Theo gaunt—all of us surveying the docks for signs of danger.

But that was the thing about Morland: Every square foot was too full, too busy. No man glanced toward another, and everyone minded their own—an unwritten code.

Babies cried and chickens flapped indignantly within cages, and the sheer volume of bodies alighting and boarding boats was unfathomable. No one seemed to question the appearance of our mostly empty vessel. As soon as the narrow boat docked, people waiting on the jetty clambered onto the deck, not much caring whether I was bumped into the water in my negligence to move out of the way.

A hand took mine as though by instinct, and I saw Patrick beside me. He found a gap in the throng and pulled me into it, pushing against shoulders until we spilled out the other side. John and Theo followed quickly behind us.

The whole of Morland wailed and throbbed and perspired ahead. It seemed to invade a person, stopping up the ears and throat. My skin already felt covered in an inexplicable residue.

I'd forgotten how much I hated Morland.

John winked at me, and I recoiled. "Come on, then," he shouted above the din.

Patrick and I held hands only as long as it seemed necessary. As soon as we entered the thoroughfare his fingers left mine, and I tucked my hands away in the pockets of my stolen robe.

The lanes of Morland were despairingly narrow, weaving uphill. Stall upon stall lined the street, their vendors screaming the names of wares to the oblivious traffic. John led the way up the steep incline, and I managed to slip behind Patrick. That way, I didn't have to think about his fingers glancing mine or what it meant.

"Where are we going?" I asked, for it seemed we were certainly heading *somewhere*.

"Perhaps we ought to find a hotel?" Theo suggested from over my shoulder.

"Or perhaps we ought to part ways here, Teddy," Patrick said without looking back. "I've got no desire to be within spittin' distance of you."

"Ah, let him tag along, son," John said. "He'll be swallowed up like a stray in this place."

At that moment, a Crafter woman heavily adorned in glass jewels struck Theo on the shoulder with a tattered book. "IDIA WILL REDEEM YOU!" she shrieked, then blew a handful of white powder in his face. "PRAYER WILL CLEANSE YOU!"

Theo coughed and staggered backward. "Ah! *Fuck*," he uttered, then quickened his step.

"Ain't up to me whether he stays," Patrick said, cutting a path through a queue of people. He nodded to me. "It's up to her."

I skipped a step, stumbling.

In truth, I had imagined we were all to part ways from here. I'd felt a sense of it creeping up with every passing minute. Patrick pulled ahead of me, and I was sure that at any moment, he would disappear into the throng, turn a corner and vanish. He'd broken me out of Belavere City, but surely his charity wouldn't extend beyond that. He wouldn't want me or Theo anywhere near Kenton. Morland, I'd figured, was where we would divide.

But we walked on, and he didn't bid me away, didn't melt into the crowd. In fact, he turned to catch sight of me every so often, ensuring I hadn't fallen too far behind. Not meeting my eye but not letting me out of his sight for long.

I did not give my clumsy heart permission to hope. I could not afford to hope for *him*.

I'd ruined us, hadn't I? And men like Patrick Colson didn't forgive.

Perhaps it would be better if I once more slipped into the cracks of the Trench and disappeared, and I could have done it, right there on that winding incline. I could step back into the crowd and erase myself.

The only thing stopping me walked just slightly ahead.

We reached the summit of the hill and turned down interminable corners until I felt dizzy, but Patrick and his father continued to lead us with intention, some invisible beacon guiding them, and I did not have the energy to question it.

We finally halted outside a skinny building with a blood red door. The sign swinging from the awning read THE MISTRESS in flaking gold paint. It was otherwise nondescript, made from the same clay as the buildings at either side, eaves kissing.

The inside was another world entirely.

A narrow entrance hall stretched before us, thickly papered in deepest red and impeded with frame after frame of themeless art: a banana tree, the citadel in Belavere City, a fisherman, two naked men intertwined, a parrot. The floor was thickly carpeted and stifling.

Nailed to the ceiling, oddly, was a selection of different-sized mirrors.

Two doors waited ahead, one labeled MANAGEMENT, and before I could ask what kind of hotel this was, an elaborately dressed man came sweeping out of it, arms out in welcome.

He wore a black satin cloak with a crudely cut hem. The tails were frayed. His suit underneath was a contrast of patterns—a purple waistcoat embellished in roses, pinstriped pants, a satin shirt that was perhaps once white, but was now yellow. Three long exotic feathers hung from the hoop at his earlobe, and these, too, appeared tired and crumpled.

But his shoes were polished, his black goatee was shaped precisely, and he stood with the air of a man who could sell snake oil to the most stubborn of skeptics, his smile wide and glinting.

It fell abruptly, however, at the sight of John and Patrick in his hallway.

"Meester Colson?" he said with strange inflection. It was impossible to know which Colson he meant. His eyes slipped back and forth between the two. He pulled his glossy cloak around his torso, as though for privacy. "A-hem, excuse me, gentlemen. I was not expecting you."

"We need rooms, Tamir," Patrick said without preamble. "Four of 'em."

The man named Tamir hesitated, his many-ringed fingers steepling together clumsily. "I—erm, I may not have the vacancy—"

"Best you start evictin' folks, then," John quipped, peering closely at the painting of the naked men.

"I . . ." Tamir stumbled. "Might I suggest you inquire at The Ferryman Inn? They have an exceptional view—"

"Last I checked, Tamir, we don't *own* The Ferryman Inn," Patrick said. His exhaustion seemed to give way to menace. "Own every bed in this place, though. Includin' the one you're sleepin' in."

Tamir flushed.

Minutes later, we were led up a claustrophobic stairwell of velvet carpet. The walls either side boasted further art that grew more provocative with each flight. First, it was merely the suggestion of nakedness and sex—couplings shielded by swaths of curtains, heads thrown back in ecstasy—but soon, every frame depicted limbs flung at impossible angles, and my cheeks grew hot.

Theo remained silent behind me. John whistled or snorted with increasing regularity, and Patrick, by the third flight, cursed incredulously. "You've taken some creative liberties, Tamir."

Tamir held his cloak away from his feet and continued to ascend. "Yes, well, the lease says I can decorate how I see fit."

"We imagined it with less tits, is all," John said. "Not that I'm complainin'."

I rolled my eyes.

Tamir led us to the third floor and indicated two opposing doors. One door was labeled THE MENAGERIE and the other, BELLA'S TRENCH.

"This floor is yours, as well as the one above," Tamir said, nervously looking anywhere but at Patrick. From a higher floor, there came a rhythmic thumping, a shout, a woman's laughter.

Patrick tracked the sound as though he could see its source through the ceiling. "For fuck's sake," he said, closing his eyes, and then to Tamir, "I pulled you out of a gamblin' den and handed you this place on a silver platter."

"And I've made a good business of it!" Tamir exclaimed, every word a performance. He grasped his chest in affront. "Never once have I been late in my rent."

"Our company name is in the deed, Tamir. You were instructed to keep a low profile, run a quiet hotel."

"It *is* a hotel!"

"Yeah? And what do you call that?" Patrick asked, nodding to the ceiling, where the thumping had resumed.

Tamir bit his lip. "It's . . . a creative liberty."

"It's a fuckin' brothel."

"Oh. Well, yes."

Patrick looked away from the paintings, ears reddening. John only hiked up his trousers, a chuckle breaking free of his lips. "Not exactly subtle, is it, Tammy?"

"I keep a discreet clientele," Tamir assured them. "I am also known as Richard now."

"*Richard?*" Patrick repeated, his patience clearly waning.

"Yes. It makes me sound genteel, no?" Tamir pulled proudly at his waistcoat. "All the rich men, they invite me to their swank parties. I am the ball's belle, as they say."

"No one says that."

"I assure you, Meester Colson, they have a fondness for me."

"I can't imagine why," John scoffed. "Couldn't be all the whores, could it?"

Tamir waved away the suggestion. "It is my charm, I think. But I've paid off every debt, Meester Colson. Do not worry."

Patrick remained unamused. "Just unlock the damn door."

After a moment of stern contemplation, Tamir produced a key for The Menagerie.

The door opened onto a wardrobe of a room with badly clumped emerald carpet, exotic birds papered onto the walls, and a lumpy canopy bed complete with fake hanging vines.

"Fuck me," Patrick hissed, then proceeded to push Tamir inside.

John put his hand at my back to guide me over the threshold, and I balked.

"Just need to convene before we part, darlin'," he said gruffly, holding his hands up for show. "In you get."

Theo followed warily, closing the door softly behind him, and we were all assaulted by sudden darkness and thick incense. Tamir rushed to open a curtain, and light sprayed across the dust motes.

"Before we rest," Patrick said, his voice somehow deeper, gruffer. "We should know where we all stand."

I eyed what appeared to be a loincloth hanging over the arm of a chair. "In here?"

Patrick's jaw ticked. "This is the only Union-owned enterprise in Morland. It's here or it's the tunnels, and last I heard, they were filled with mud."

I pictured that tunnel, lurking somewhere beneath. "And why are we in Morland?"

"And, er . . . how long will you be staying?" Tamir added. "Not that you aren't most welcome—"

"As long as we need, Tamir," Patrick said. "And you'll not be breathin' a word of it to anyone. Not even Union members."

"No," Tamir agreed sagely. "But I must say, this is quite a dangerous place for an Alchemist to be. These streets are filled with these important government types, you know? They love the drink and the topless ladies—"

"How do you know he's an Alchemist?" Theodore interrupted, his arms crossed tightly across his chest.

"Oh, everyone knows this," Tamir said, gesturing flippantly. "It is all about the gossip in town! Even the newsprint! This is why I am most surprised to find you *here*, Meester Colson. The papers say you are finding a truce with the House?"

"Tomorrow, I think you'll find 'em sayin' somethin' different," John muttered darkly.

Tamir gulped. "This city is not a good place for hiding," he implored. "So much navy blue, Meester Colson. Better that you head for your tunnels, I think. I can provide some provisions—"

"We need guns and clothes," Patrick said bluntly. Indeed, Theodore and

I were still adorned in Artisan blue—ministry garb, no less. "But we'll be goin' nowhere yet."

Tamir seemed to deflate. "Of course."

"What word is there of Kenton Hill?" Patrick asked now.

Tamir bowed his head. "My condolences on your loss, my friend. I heard the infantry broke through like a battering lamb."

"A battering ram."

"Yes, that. The Union have been tittering since you were captured, Meester Colson. It was quite a shock. The members are in disarray. But the whispers assure me that Kenton Hill is resuming its business. It seems its people were quite eager to return once the navy dogs retreated to the kennel." He eyed Theo warily as he said this, sensing that one of *their* kind stood among us.

Then he looked at me. "And you must be the infamous Nina." His eyes swept over my face and all the way down to my feet. "The posters did not do you justice, my dear." His smile was not unkind. "You are a very brave woman indeed."

I gave an awkward nod in thanks.

Tamir tilted his head as though I confounded him.

"I'll ensure you're repaid," Patrick told Tamir, regaining his attention. "As soon as possible."

"Ah, it is not necessary, Meester Colson. When last you saw me, I was in the hands of those book men—"

"Bookies."

"—and they were threatening to cut off my testicles, do you remember?"

"I could hardly forget."

"But thanks to him"—and he addressed Theo and me as he slapped Patrick on the shoulder—"I am now a fashionable businessman!"

Patrick eyed the bird feathers at the man's ear dubiously. "Just get the guns, Tamir. And the clothes."

"I'll bring supper, also," Tamir said, bowing his head. He offered Patrick four keys. "And if you please, no urinating in the stairwells." Then, in a flourish of satin, he left.

My lips twitched upward despite myself, and the smile felt foreign.

"Well," barked John into the silence, slapping his hands together. "Let's get to business, shall we?"

"Yes," I said, which served to turn all attention to me. "The three of you can begin by telling me why we've come to Morland, of all places."

I eyed Theodore, then John, but could not bring myself to sweep my eyes to Patrick again, lest I lose the momentum building in my chest. "Since I seem to be the only one who doesn't know."

There was a pregnant silence, John and Theo shirking an answer and waiting for Patrick to speak.

But Patrick only went to the window and turned to lean against the ledge. A cigarette appeared from nowhere, and he put it between his lips. A matchbox slid from his sleeve to his palm.

John whistled. "You pull that from Tamir?"

"The dockmaster," Patrick corrected, lighting his smoke.

"Got another?"

"Haven't yet decided," he said darkly, giving his father a pointed glare.

There was still blood caked in the man's nostrils. "You holdin' grudges, son?" his father asked.

"At least a little longer." Patrick drew deeply on the cigarette, his tired eyes closing as he exhaled. "You remember the deal I told you Lord Shop offered us, Nina? The truce?"

He did not look at me, but I thought it was a good sign, at least, that he said my name. That he hadn't bid me away yet. "Yes," I said.

"The deal was made on the promise of terranium. Enough of it to last the next few generations, maybe more."

My brow creased. "The mines are near empty," I said. My tone was vacant, uncomprehending. "The deal was a con."

"It certainly was," Patrick said. "Though not all of it. A discovery was recently made."

"What discovery?" I asked, turning to Theo and searching his face for answers.

Theo sighed heavily, more drawn than I'd ever seen him, and said, "A book that may reveal the whereabouts of Idia's Seam, if such a thing exists."

The name clattered somewhere in the stores of my memory, a Scurry schoolyard where children clawed the mud with their bare hands. *I'm diggin' all the way to Idia's Seam.*

My gaze flickered between Patrick and Theo both. "Idia's Seam?" I parroted. "The *fable*?"

"Not a fable," Theo said, his face in shadow. "Just a well-covered secret."

And I believed him. The House was built on lies—if they believed this real, then they would have kept it close.

"The book was found in the Morland archives," Patrick added, and the rest of the tale was not needed, for I could feel the sudden fervor in the room emanating from John.

But not Theo, who appeared merely trapped.

"And what now, Patrick?" I asked him, for surely there was some grand plan turning in the cogs of his mind. I could see that he was trying—and failing—to hide his own zeal.

"You're here to thieve yourself a copy of the book from the Morland archives? Is that it?"

"Don't need one," John grunted. And he pulled from his coat a much-abused book. "Young Theodore thieved the original, didn't you?"

Theo looked darkly at the object. "And as I told you back in the National House, I'd feel better if I could carry it *myself*—"

"Don't give a rat's arse how you feel, boy. You just be grateful you've been allowed along."

I stared at the book, my breaths shortening. Embossed on the cover were the words *The Stewards' Testament.*

Hide, hide the witches,

The Stewards they hid three . . .

My mother's face swam in and out of my vision.

I looked back at Theo. "It's real?"

He sighed. Nodded.

"It's written in Verian Script," Patrick added, and my gaze swerved to his. He was watching me carefully now, blue eyes sparking. "That's why we're here. There's some Scribbler who works in the archives who can translate. A descendant of the Stewards, or so says Shop."

I closed my eyes briefly, the first tremors of a headache beating about my skull. "You're going to look for the Seam."

Of course they were.

"If we don't," Patrick said slowly, "then *they* will, Nina. Only they don't have a way to find it. They don't have the book."

"It'd mean the end of the war," John inserted, spinning the little book in his palm like the needle of a compass. "With a Charmer to dig up the terranium and an Alchemist to siphon it?" he whistled. "The swanks might as well kneel now."

So this was why Patrick had yet to turn me away.

"Is that what you want?" I asked Patrick, ignoring his father. "The entire nation on its knees? Do you want to lead all of Belavere Trench?"

Patrick's eyes iced over. It sent a shiver down my spine. "I want to drag the ministers from their nice beds, their nice houses, and have them watch as I burn it all to the ground."

I saw then what he saw: Lord Shop and his fucking cane, the ministers lining the courtyard to watch my mother swing from the noose. The tidy streets of Belavere City, every brick mined by Crafters. Kenton Hill ablaze, Gunner bleeding. Tanner in a drawing room, proclaiming me his weapon, his knife.

A deep cold slithered through me. "Is this why you saved me?" I asked him. "Because you needed someone to dig up your seam?"

I already knew it was. I hated the way my voice shook.

Patrick didn't answer. I looked away.

"It's just business between us now, then?"

He sighed, flicked ash onto Tamir's carpet. "Yes."

I nodded, trying desperately to hold on to whatever pieces in my chest remained intact. It was no more than I'd expected, but twice as painful.

"You don't have to say yes to this," Patrick said slowly, as though it were only us two now. He stepped away from the window toward me but halted in his tracks. Lord, his face was handsome—salt in the wound. "You've got choices. If you don't want a part in it, you can leave."

"Leave?" John stood abruptly from the bed. "Wait a minute, miss. 'Fraid we can't let you do tha—"

"She'll go where she pleases," Patrick said with a threatening finality. "And you'll not be doin' a fuckin' thing to stop her."

Something passed between the two men. "Tell me, Patty," John said, his voice turning low, dangerous. "Who's the chairman of the Union now? Did you usurp me in my absence, son?"

Patrick's expression flattened, and I thought of all the times he'd refused the title of chairman, as though he'd been forced to the summit of his father's venture and found he disliked the height.

He'd been willing to do many things, hadn't he? To get his father back.

"You've been gone too long, Dad," Patrick said. "Too fuckin' long. And now things have changed."

I swallowed.

John inhaled and jutted his jaw as Gunner had. "We need her, son."

"Only if she wants to help," Patrick repeated. "But, she's free to leave. I'll insist upon it."

"Will you now?" John said, chuckling mirthlessly. "Lord, boy. How deep are you?"

Patrick didn't answer. His expression was unreadable, John's veneered in dark amusement.

Patrick returned his attention to me. "What is it you want, then?"

What *did* I want?

I wanted to turn back the hand of the clock. To be a simple person with simple troubles, who had taken only bluff and left the National House with Patrick that day when we were twelve. I wanted to see Kenton Hill restored and revive the dead. I wanted to rip the ache from within me. Tanner, Shop, the House, their soldiers with their bayonets—they'd taken everything.

This itch for idium was never quiet, never satisfied. In truth, though, it wasn't idium that I cared for. How often had my medium become a gun to my head? Perhaps I should want to run. I felt the coil in my muscles now, willing me to seek safety in solitude. Loving someone was dangerous, and it would hurt to stay, to see Patrick every day and know he'd loved me once. I could escape back into the folds of Belavere and learn to live with an empty chest.

But I didn't want that.

I didn't want to take on a new name and new lies and let the idium ebb until I was none of the things I'd ever been.

I wanted someone to hurt.

I felt it burgeoning in me: a yearning for blood. Shop's perhaps, or the man who'd pulled the lever on my mother, or the coppers at the docks. I wanted to feel as I had when the earth clogged Tanner's ears and mouth and jammed his airways—like no one could touch me.

And here was Patrick, offering me a way. Generations of idium, he'd said. A fair fight. If I *was* a knife, then I could rip and slash and gouge until the aching ebbed. It wasn't idium I wanted. It was revenge.

"If we succeed," I said, "I want to bury those lords myself."

A shadow rippled across Patrick's face. He nodded and stepped away.

"Then we'll find ourselves that Scribbler," he said. "We begin tomorrow."

CHAPTER NINETEEN

NINA

I welcomed sleep, yet the first evening spent in The Mistress was restless. The stairwell was irregularly filled with frantic footsteps, drunken murmurs, and once, howling laughter. The walls of the building seemed to hold the echoes of bedsprings and headboards, and I heard the knocking well into the night.

Theo and John had taken the floor above, while I remained in The Menagerie and Patrick in the room next door. The two were conjoined, I realized after the fact, by a door near the wardrobe. I wondered, in the absence of sleep, if Patrick had yet seen it there, if he had locked his side of the door.

I had eaten, washed, painstakingly combed the snarls of my hair until the curls did not resemble a nest, and now I lay atop the blankets in a pale-blue lace-trimmed slip. I didn't dare ask Tamir where it had come from.

Fever had set in, and I felt alternatingly hot and cold to my marrow. I'd discarded the dirty bandages. My arms lay on the mattress, ghastly and swollen, and though I wanted nothing more than to sleep for an eternity, I rose instead and went like a ghost to the adjoining door.

Before I could reach it, a sharp knocking came from the other side of it. I faltered, squinting at the door, wondering if I'd succumbed to delirium.

But when I pulled it open, Patrick stood there, dressed in clean clothing, smelling of soap, his brow so furrowed he appeared decades older.

I frowned, confused. "How long have you been standing there?"

"Far longer than I'll tell you," he said. Immediately, he noticed the sheen of sweat on my skin. "What is it?" he asked, eyes widening.

I blinked slowly. "I'm . . . unwell. Infection, I think." I held up my sliced arms. "I've cleaned them, but they were already starting to swell."

Patrick's jaw rolled at the sight of them. He nodded to the bed over his shoulder. "Sit," he said.

I hesitated. "I—I don't want to impose—"

"Lord, just sit down on the fuckin' bed, Nina."

I went in tentatively and sat on the edge, noticing how high the hem of the slip rose up my thigh. Wishing I'd thought to don a robe, I blinked again and the room doubled.

Patrick was pulling something from his wardrobe. My eyes roamed over the expanse of his back, watching the muscles flex beneath his shirt.

He returned with a vial, half-filled with black swill. "Take it," he said.

He loomed above, doused in lamplight. I found myself disconcerted again. Not by fever this time, but simply by him.

Patrick sighed. He leaned down over me until I could see nothing else. "Drink it," he said. "Or it'll be done for you."

A shiver assailed me. I downed the contents, feeling the immediate flux of my mind, stretching and reshaping. The bluff would spread through my blood within a few minutes, curbing the fever.

Patrick backed away and crouched, hands coming together between his knees. Watching me carefully.

"I'm not about to keel over," I told him. I pulled at the hem of the slip.

"Leave it alone," he said.

I looked down at my hand, confused. "Why?"

"'Cause it's hard enough keepin' my eyes where they ought to be."

I flushed.

His eyes skipped to my arms now, both mottled in injury. He looked at the Artisan brand I had melted from my body, undeterred by the scar.

"What did you use," he asked slowly, "to get rid of it?"

"An iron press," I said, distracted. Relief was finding me. I closed my eyes and sighed. "Broke into a washhouse here in Morland and held it on the plate for as long as I could. A Crafter woman found me passed out cold the next morning. She gave me a job." It was easier to speak to him, there in the dim. In the quiet. Time felt illusory in the earliest hours.

He hid his expression from me. "What happened to her? The Crafter?"

"Shot, I think," I murmured. "She was harboring women fleeing Gilmore, and the police came."

Patrick grimaced. By now, there were a hundred stories the same. A thousand. "But you escaped," he said.

"I hid. We *all* hid, actually, in a cellar beneath the steam ovens. Everyone except her. She covered the door behind us, and we sat like cowards and listened to the police officers scream at her and beat her and carry her away."

Patrick listened intently, lost as I was, in the strangeness of the night. "Tell me the rest of it," he said, not a command, but a plea, and I did.

I told him about my time in Trent, bartering art for a train ticket, then the china shop in Hesson, where the foreman had his hired guards search our pockets after every shift. I told him about Dorser, where I'd come the closest I ever had to starving, and was saved by two elderly gentlemen who took me into their kitchen and fed me poached quail.

Then I came to the day in Delfield, where I'd lived above a pub in a waterlogged flat for all of three days before the infantry marched in. I told Patrick of how the landlord's eyes had always lingered on my face, of how he'd sold the whereabouts of the earth Charmer to save his own family, and how I couldn't possibly, even now, blame him for it.

I spoke of how I'd woken in the National House, Tanner hovering over me.

"He paraded my mother in," I said, my voice thinning. "And I didn't recognize her straightaway. That's strange, don't you think? For a daughter not to recognize her own mother."

Patrick shook his head, entranced it seemed. "You hadn't known her in many years."

"It was more than that," I muttered. "She was . . . changed. Not herself. She hummed a song she used to sing for me when I couldn't sleep, or when my dad was shouting and she wanted to hide the noise from me, but she wouldn't look at me. Wouldn't speak. She'd already lost her mind, I think."

There must have been tears on my face. I could feel them dripping off my jaw. "Tanner told me . . . he told me that she'd left Scurry *for me*. Somehow, she'd learned the secret, and she'd learned that servants of the House were rewarded for keeping it. Their children made Artisans. That's why she left me. She was trying to barter a better life for me."

Patrick was sitting at his careful distance, one arm around his knee, the other hand weaving a coin through his fingers. The ropes of his tendons were rigid.

He didn't move from this position. He only listened, an unnameable expression on his face.

"They told me to go to Kenton and find the Alchemist, and there was no other choice in it. I couldn't let them kill her." My voice wavered. I wondered if he could see all the guilt I was made of. "I was weak," I whispered. "I'm sorry."

Patrick didn't nod, or rise, or shout. Didn't lift his eyes from mine. The coin ceased its turning. Several long moments of silence stretched. "You could've told me everything," he said.

I sniffed and nodded.

"But you didn't."

To that, I said nothing.

"And I can only presume it was because of your friends, Theo and Polly, and what might happen to them, should they be implicated."

I nodded once.

"Or perhaps you were worried for yourself," Patrick said. It felt like an accusation. "Perhaps you thought I'd throw you into a canal if I knew the truth."

I bit my tongue. I could still see the barrel of his gun pointed at me.

"Ah," he said, reading my expression. "So it was fear, then. You were scared of me."

I stiffened. "I was scared to lose you."

"Yet I was devoted to keepin' you," he said now. "I vowed it, told you I was in love. You didn't believe me."

No, perhaps I hadn't. "Some loves die when tested," I said, voice fading.

He nodded. "That they do."

We sat in silence for a while, the night passing by, and I couldn't bring myself to leave the room, couldn't bear to stay.

"Did you give 'em my name, Nina?" he asked. "You can tell me the truth now. Reckon I've earned it."

I was mere whisps of myself. I felt he could pass right through me. "Of course not," I said. "I'd changed sides. I'd told you that I loved you."

"No, you didn't," he said. "Not really."

"I told *no one* about you," I said, more forcefully now. "Not even Polly."

He ran the tip of his finger over his lips, then nodded, as though to himself.

"I was going to tell you everything, Patrick," I said, fresh tears falling. "I waited all night for you to come back. I waited . . ." I could say no more. I was suddenly bone-tired. When I closed my eyes, images pervaded.

I heard him sigh heavily from his place on the floor. Then he stood. He went to get a fresh bowl of water and a damp washcloth and came to where I sat. He knelt before me and took one of my forearms into his hands to clean it. The cold water stung.

"I believe you," he said, his voice low and close. He moved from one arm to the other. "But I told you once that there should be trust between us."

"And you don't trust me," I finished for him.

"*You* didn't trust *me*," he corrected. "I told you I'd protect you. Keep you safe—"

"Patrick—"

"—and it's clear to me now that you could betray me in the worst ways, and I'd forget every code I have to defend you." He finished his ministrations, wrung the washcloth dry. "A bigger weakness, I can't forsee. So there are lines I can't cross with you again, do you understand?"

My eyes cinched closed, if only so I didn't have to see his perfect face when I asked, "Can you never forgive me?"

I felt him breathe once, twice. "You're already forgiven, Scurry girl, but it don't fix much."

I opened my eyes, and his face was far too close to mine. And I wondered how he could suffer the remaining distance. How he could ignore the compulsion to close it.

"Patrick, do you ever regret going into that cellar?"

After a moment, he said, "Despite it all, I still can't say I do."

CHAPTER TWENTY

NINA

By the following day, my head felt lighter, the infection cleared.

We converged in Tamir's living quarters soon after waking, and John pulled *The Stewards' Testament* from his coat pocket. When I laid my eyes on it again, something more than grief and guilt ignited within me. I felt hunger.

I imagined bursting seams of black ore beneath the earth's crust and Lord Shop digging his way toward it.

We needed to find it first.

The little book lay open on Tamir's unvarnished kitchen table. A scrawl of indecipherable faded symbols stared back at us.

Tamir remained two steps away, his hands twisting together in the sleeves of a teal housecoat. His small flat unfolded behind him in a collection of upholstered furniture and antiques. Compared to the rest of his establishment, these two rooms were quietly elegant, refined. The walls were adorned in mournful abstract landscapes instead of women's vulvas. A cat slunk around the curve of an armchair.

Tamir came to peer around John's frame at the first page, unable to help himself.

"But what does it say?" he asked.

"Fuck if I know," John responded. "But it'll lead us to a treasure trove."

I frowned at the pages, some eaten through by moths. "How can we be sure it says anything about the Seam?"

"I don't know yet," Patrick answered. "Expect that Shop seemed to think it of great importance."

"And there's supposed to be a Scribbler somewhere in this city who can translate it?" I asked. "How are we to find them?"

"It ain't that big of a city," John said, crossing his arms. "We'll find 'em."

"You have a name?" I asked.

"Better. I've got a place," he said. "Some swank club not far from here."

"The problem isn't just in finding someone who can translate it," Theo interrupted. "It's in convincing the Scribbler to break their oath to the House to help us."

"What oath?" John asked.

Theo shrugged as though it were obvious. "Scribblers are entrusted with highly sensitive information. If captured or tortured, they would accept death before revealing national secrets."

"Then capture won't do," Patrick said. "We'll have to swindle 'em."

I stared at the book, plain as it was. A blur of symbols. "If they swear an oath to protect Belavere's secrets, then they've likely been trained to spot such a scheme."

"Well," John said, closing the book with a loud slap, "they're yet to be swindled by a Colson."

Rickers was the name of the club—a restaurant the Artisans in the city frequented, according to Tamir, where they ate five courses and danced to a brass band. The women wore their most scandalous dresses, the kind polite society wouldn't dare accept in Belavere City, where the citadel bore down from every angle.

The Scribblers of the Morland archives favored it, said Tamir. It seemed the only place to start.

"I can secure us a reservation," Tamir said with the wave of a hand. "I am often asked for at these parties, you know."

“In that case,” Patrick said, and looked to his father, “we’ll need supplies.”

“Supplies?” Theo asked.

“A few tinctures.”

Theo narrowed his eyes. “Which *tinctures*, exactly?”

Patrick looked at Theo’s jaw as though deciding whether to lay his fist into it.

Theo leaned away.

“If the Scribblers are inclined to drink, then we’ll give them a little somethin’ to loosen ’em up,” Patrick said. “They’ll be more easily swindled if they’re seein’ double.”

“You’re planning to drug them?” Theo looked to me as though expecting I might join him in his reproach.

But whatever doctrine had sewn together the threads of my morality had been snipped free. I did not blanch.

Perhaps deep down there was a murmur—a tired belief that Artisans were people, not all bad. Not all evil or hateful. But it was damningly quiet. Easy to ignore. Right now, every one of them was Lord Tanner or Lord Shop.

“How will we know which ones are Scribblers?” I asked.

Tamir grinned shrewdly. “They’re proud, the swanks. It never takes much conversation to learn their medium.”

“And which of us is to simply parade through a room of Artisans, looking for a Scribbler to drug?” Theo asked.

“Ain’t that the question,” John chortled, looking at Theodore expectantly.

Patrick clicked his tongue. “There’s a use to you yet, Teddy.”

Theo looked from one to the other. “Not me, surely.”

But it was obvious. Patrick’s hands were pressed to the desk, the knuckles compacted with callouses, arms thickly corded in muscle, his entire stance that of a miner, even if the blood beneath was shot through with ink. John with his thick beard and grating tenor. Neither moved nor spoke in the language of the genteel. But Theo did.

And I did.

"You can't be serious," Theo said bluntly, his mouth a thin line. "You want *me* to drug a Scribbler?"

"That'd be grand, Teddy, if you could," John said, slapping Theo on the back.

Patrick and Theo seemed engaged in a silent scuffle, eyes locked, chins jutting.

Then Theo pinched his eyes closed. When he opened them again, he was looking at me.

"Nina, listen to me—"

"I can't think of a person I would be less inclined to listen to." The words had teeth.

He winced. "The terranium hasn't even been found yet, and already people will be hurt in its pursuit. More will follow. *After* it's uncovered, every man and his dog will come scrapping for a piece. The entire continent will devour itself."

Good, I thought.

"There's another option," Theodore said, his gaze skirting to Patrick and away. "A stalemate."

"There ain't a stalemate to be found," Patrick said immediately. "Either we find the terranium before the House does, or we lose the fight."

"They have no Alchemist, Colson," Theo said. "Without one, the terranium is useless to them."

"And so you'll have them continue razin' brink towns while they hunt me down," Patrick said. "Or perhaps you imagine I'd give myself over to 'em, eh?"

"If it's my loyalty you're questioning, I'll remind you that *I'm* the reason you're standing here and not in a locked room," Theo reminded him. "And no. I don't propose we do nothing."

"Then what, Theo?" I asked. "And to be clear, I *do* question your loyalty."

He seemed to find difficulty in keeping himself impassive. "Burn the book," he said simply.

There was silence for a moment, the ringing kind.

I felt that void inside me shudder.

John seemed amused. "Burn it?" he said. "Son, that there is a map to more magic than we've ever known."

"And it'll do no good in the hands of my father. I know that now," Theodore said, straightening his shoulders. "But your hands are no cleaner."

Patrick's head rolled back on his shoulders, and he laughed tiredly, the blue of his eyes icing over. "Ah, Teddy. You've no need to tell a miner of his dirty hands." His blue eyes swept to Theodore's neatly trimmed fingernails. "A less honorable man I've never seen."

"Far more people will die if you do this," Theo pressed on, imploring me, not Patrick. He turned his back to block the Colsons from my view, stepping closer. "Let the idium die out. Let *no one* have it, Nina. Force a stalemate. My father will have no choice but to negotiate with the Union and find a truce."

But I knew otherwise. I knew men like his father were born ravenous. The currency shifted: if not idium, then coal, timber, until another path to power was found.

Once, I'd have sided with Theo. I'd thought Belavere a slave to idium, and that we were each better off without it running through our blood.

Now, I didn't care for what was right. I cared for that hole carved out in my middle.

"A truce?" I looked at Theo squarely, remembered all those times his father had invited me to dinner, his disgust for me swimming beneath the surface. "I don't want a truce with your father. I want them all in the ground."

I watched Theo war with it; his loyalty to me, to his father, to the Artisans.

"I don't believe that," he said, searching my face, I thought, for remnants he recognized. "I don't believe you want to see people suffer."

A rumble grew then, beneath our feet, beneath the foundations of the hotel, deeper still: a buried titan deep in the earth, clawing for the surface. The pendant light overhead shook. Dust fell. Tamir shrieked and stumbled against a credenza.

"God almighty," John intoned, gripping hold of a chair.

The quaking ceased. Theo and I held each other's gazes. "Do you doubt I could do it?"

He hadn't moved. Hadn't blinked. The only change came from two splotches of deep red, high on his cheekbones. "You don't scare me, Nina." But his jaw was tight. "I know who you are."

Fury reared up. "Not anymore."

But still, Theo stood there, breaths carefully measured.

"Go," I told him. "Crawl home to your father. Pray he doesn't hang you next."

My voice cracked on this last, and Theo's guard crumpled in response, his dark eyes hazing. He shook his head. "I want to stay. I've picked a side."

"Then don't stand in my way."

He nodded stiffly, relenting, but I thought I saw something solidify in his resolve. He lifted his chin and turned to Patrick. "I'll help to find the Scribbler," he said. "But I won't drug them."

Patrick had his arms crossed. He was watching Theodore with barely veiled hatred. "That's where you draw the line, is it?"

"It is."

The look he gave Theo was withering. "Not with the decimation of Kenton Hill, then? Or with the death of Nina's kin? Druggin' one of your fellows is what turns your stomach?"

Theo bristled.

"I'll do it," I said, empty of feeling. "I'll drug the Scribbler. I can talk circles around them as good as Theo."

"You're too recognizable," Patrick said warily, like he could sense I was close to combustion. "They'll know your face."

"I don't see another option," I argued, crossing my arms over my chest.

"A-hem," Tamir coughed. "Pardon. But I have many decorative garments, and quite a few wigs. We can make the lady quite undetectable, I swear to you." He covered his heart with his hand and bowed his head. "It would be my honor."

"I'll bet," John offered, eyeing Tamir's robe dubiously. "Don't think dressin' her like a whore is gonna help the girl blend in, Tammy."

Tamir frowned. "My outfits are of the finest quality, sir. She would not look out of place."

I could feel Patrick's stare. "Nina—"

"You won't be alone," Theo said. "I'll accompany you."

There was little else to be said. Patrick looked on the precipice of arguing, but instead, he lanced me with cold eyes and said nothing.

John clapped his hands together and said, "Ain't nothin' else for it." Theo stood straighter than he had since we'd left Kenton Hill.

"Then it's settled," I said, something violent climbing my throat. "I'll drug the Scribbler."

The following evening, I was dressed in the kind of garb any Artisan in Belavere City would balk at, but not here in Morland, where the constraints of society were loosened after dusk.

Tamir had encased me in an emerald dress with ruffled off-shoulder sleeves, a corset that constricted my rib cage, and skirt that pleated elegantly at my hip bone, then fell to the floor. The bust line was more daring than anything I'd ever worn, and when I glanced in the mirror, I blushed. My hips and backside were too accentuated. My cleavage was, quite frankly, indecent. I tried to stuff it back into the garment.

But Tamir slapped at my hands. "You are a woman!" he told me. "You cannot be faulted for being exquisite."

"It's distracting. I don't want to be *ogled,* I want to go unnoticed."

"You ask for the moon," he tsked, standing back to admire his work. "You cannot hide loveliness. Better to use it." He winked. "Fools are blinded by jewels, you know, and you will be a diamond!"

I wore an unassuming chestnut wig that stopped at my shoulders, heavily shadowed eyelids, ruby-red lips, a powder that concealed my freckles, and a precisely drawn beauty spot on my cheek.

I felt like a trussed-up doll.

"You will devour them," Tamir delighted, then sent me into the stairwell.

Patrick exited his own room at the same time, dressed in simple wear, and was struck dumb at the sight of me.

His eyes stuck first to my face, painted in what I considered to be a grotesque amount of rouge and haloed by hair not my own, and I thought he was taken by the strangeness of it.

But then his eyes traveled over the rest of me. Down the valley of my breasts, to the hills of my hips, and he said nothing. His hand seemed melded to the doorknob, as though it kept him upright.

I could hardly stand the heat of it. Blood rushed up and pulsed beneath my skin.

I cleared my throat. "Tamir said they all dress like this in the night quarter. The Artisan women, that is. I'll blend in."

"You won't," he said. He swallowed, something animalistic in it. "You never did. Ain't any hope for it now."

We were to congregate in the foyer, and Patrick and I walked the stairwell in torturous silence, limbs taut, a scent of wildness emanating from each of us—those desires not yet dispersing in the aftermath.

On the last landing, he gestured I go ahead of him. This was a mistake.

My body came too close to his as I passed. I felt his inhale, felt the planes of his chest expand. I paused there.

I thought of him and I in a different stairwell, the steps flexing beneath our feet as his fingers pressed into my hips, anchoring themselves there, his mouth skirting over the pulse at my neck, drinking in the rush of blood beneath my flesh.

Everything had changed. Nothing had changed.

I lifted my head slowly to look up at him, meeting the hunger in his eyes with my own.

"Don't," he said, but it came out as a groan. He stared down at me, that hunger intensifying. His eyelids lowered. "Just keep on walkin'."

But I didn't move—couldn't, perhaps. Not when his mouth was inches from mine, close enough that I could rise on the tips of my toes and meet it.

Perhaps it was base to still feel this sort of spiraling desire with such wreckage in our wake and a gulf of trouble ahead.

But longing reigned, and it was nice to feel . . . something. Something good.

"You'd let me, wouldn't you?" he said as his eyes roamed over me, and though his hands remained in his pockets, I felt his touch everywhere. "You wouldn't slap my hands away if I pulled this skirt up," he murmured, his gaze moving down to my hips, "and fucked you right here."

I stopped breathing altogether, heat coalescing in my middle, spreading to my inner thighs, climbing my chest.

"Is that what you intended when you put it on?" he asked darkly, and he seemed impossibly close now. "To torture me?"

I shook my head slowly, barely aware of my surroundings, of anything but his scent.

He watched the shake of my head and lifted an eyebrow. "To torture every man in the room tonight, then."

Lord, I wished he'd touch me. I'd have any excuse to touch him back.

"That's what'll happen when you cross that threshold," he told me. "You'll turn 'em all into sweatin', pantin' oafs." His hands clenched in his pockets. I rose on my toes despite myself, but he didn't grant me his lips. "Ah, but they don't know how you taste, do they? They don't know the sounds you make when you come."

His voice slid over me like smoke. My hands reached for the lapels of his coat, but still, he held himself away.

He was the one torturing *me* now.

"That'll be my consolation, I think, knowin' that you'll never give them what you gave me. They'll only ever imagine it, and even a fuckin' swank don't got imagination enough for that."

"Patrick."

"Off your toes, Scurry girl. Keep walkin'."

Slowly, as though falling out of a trance, I dropped back onto my heels, though his face continued to swim around mine. I would have done anything he asked.

"You don't belong to anyone, Nina," he said. "Not a single fuckin' one of 'em."

I blinked, and he frowned. "Say it."

"I don't belong to them," I repeated, heart stuttering.

His gaze held me captive. "*They* belong to *you*." His fingers withdrew from his pocket and pressed something cool into mine.

There was a shot of darkest blue amid the cerulean of his eyes, and I was lost to them, with no mind to the minutes passing. Awareness only flickered in when Patrick moved away, descending the last flight and disappearing into the foyer below, leaving me to my own burning. I looked down at my hands, which felt detached from the rest of me. In one of them was a vial.

Patrick's voice remained in my middle ear, hammering against the bone until it etched, letter by letter.

You don't belong to them.

The plan was this: Theo and I would claim different names and mediums and be ushered into a swank dining establishment in the night quarter, the owner of which frequented The Mistress and knew Tamir by name.

After that, it would take luck, flirtation. If the Scribbler was present this evening, I prayed they enjoyed a drink.

John had left The Mistress earlier that day and returned victorious, having procured what turned out to be mere tulleyroot.

"*Tulleyroot* is the tincture?" I had asked, incredulous. The miners wrapped their abrasions with the leaves to stave infection, but it was otherwise a noxious weed that strangled the moors in the east.

"Ever eaten it?" John had said, shaking the green vial between his fingers. "You'll be numb-faced with just a swig."

I hadn't, but I'd seen enough numb-faced men, which was always credited to bluff. "If that's true, then why haven't the miners started uprooting every last hill?"

"Because tulleyroot rots your tongue," Patrick answered blankly. "Right after you've finished waggin' it."

"And how will the Scribbler translate without a tongue?"

"Don't need his tongue to scribble, does he?" he countered.

He had paused then, as though wondering if that might be enough to turn my stomach, to make me reassume my former principles.

It wasn't.

While I dosed the unfortunate Scribbler, Patrick and John would be waiting in the alley with a wagon and the Testament.

I assumed, though I did not summon the integrity to ask, that the Scribbler would be left outside some hospital, tongue fermenting, their mind made into swill, after, of course, they'd been forced to transcribe the Stewards' book.

Tamir had redressed in a three-piece suit that was so inoffensive, he was almost unrecognizable. His goatee was neatly oiled, his top hat meant for the theater.

He led us to the lamp-lined street and hustled us into a lopsided coach with two wooden wheels and two steel. "I'm quite a good driver," he reassured all four of us, and shut us in.

We spent the carriage ride hitting our heads on the ceiling, or else slamming into the walls, our arses bouncing inelegantly the entire way. I was seated opposite Patrick, who watched with slow-moving wrath as I slid at each turn into Theo's side, my thigh pressing into his.

If Theo were a smarter man, he might have committed his mind to the passing viaducts and vendors and street performers and plumes of smoke cloying the purple sky. To anything but the dress I wore and the parts of me it clung to.

I drew my shawl higher and higher until I was strangled with it.

"Did you leave your genteel manners in Belavere City, Teddy?" Patrick growled beneath the clatter of horses' hooves on the cobbles and the bray of Tamir egging the poor creatures onward.

Theo, distracted until that point, tore his gaze away and turned a delicate pink. "I'm more gentleman than you'll ever hope to be."

"Yeah? Best you don't forget it," Patrick said darkly, hatred settling over his face.

John gave a low whistle, apparently entertained. He covered his smirk by way of smoothing his beard. "Lord. We ain't got time to duke it out in here, boys," he grunted. "Settle it away from the lady."

I was food. A hide on a meat shank.

The image of a banquet came to mind, with all the men seated and the women carved up and dressed before them on platters. I pulled my shawl closer still.

Tamir called "whoa," and the coach came to a bruising halt. Light beamed in.

The establishment was a solid concrete wall made of a thousand orange-lit windows and iron-grate balconies, pillars stamped with carved cherubs, slain mares, faces missing eye sockets. The doors were a glass-plated bloody maroon that betrayed the chandelier beyond, as well as the pearly tiling and polished ebony banisters.

Already, the noise from within the building drifted down to us, wave after wave of heavy chatter. Theo and I knew the scene from heart. Crystal glasses and crisp white shirts speckled with wine or meat blood. Hands clasping hands, lips on knuckles, pompous laughter.

Already, I felt sick.

Theo exited the coach first and proffered a hand—a routine from another lifetime we'd shared.

But Patrick caught the very tips of my fingers at the last possible moment, still sitting back in the shadows of the coach, and his expression swallowed me. I watched a thousand words pass over his lips, felt the tingling warmth that passed from his skin to mine.

"They belong to you," he said, voice grave. "Make sure they know it."

And I looked away, lest I be captured again.

CHAPTER TWENTY-ONE

THEO

Theo and Nina entered the dining room of Rickers hand in hand, Tamir ahead of them, and Theo's chest brimming with dread.

On his last visit here, he'd been thirteen. His father had taken him to the smoking room, said "This is your chance to prove you're a man of some worth," then tendered him round a circle of aristocrats, mistresses hanging off their elbows. Theo had spoken well, he thought, laughing diplomatically when it seemed right. He'd smoked his first cigar, encased vomit in his cheek, and swallowed on his next inhale. His father had been proud of that, Theo thought—that his son hadn't gagged in front of his fellows.

There had been a man named Gumble: a fire Charmer, semiretired from his military career. He was pigeon-chested, generically handsome in the way of most heroes. He wore pins awarded to him by the Head of House and spoke about them at length. In the late hours, he drew young Theo aside, sloshed neat scotch onto his own chest, and said, "See any you like?" He was gesturing to the women strewn about the room—all of them Crafters—feigning interest against bookshelves, staring blankly out windows, or else nursing Artisan men in their deteriorating states.

Theo knew this game. Gentlemen did not blush or concede. He had looked Gumble in the eye, fashioned a smirk, and said "*That* one."

In truth, he hadn't an eye for any of them. He was still just thirteen, and these women were all old. The woman he'd nodded to at random was rake-thin and wore too many necklaces for comfort. There was so much rouge on her cheeks, you could hardly see the shadows beneath. She was only pretty if you could see past the desperation.

"Then I'll be having that one," Gumble had said, finishing the remnants in his glass. "You've got to be careful with the Crafter girls, son. Mostly they're diseased. You have to check them over very thoroughly first." His eyes took on a manic glint then, like some bolt in his mind had suddenly snatched free. "*You* can check her for me." He declared it as though a favor had been traded, passed generously from his hand and into Theo's.

That was how Theo had found himself inside a coat closet with a much older Crafter woman, and she'd looked, momentarily, as though she might cry.

And Theo had thought, *Does a gentleman bring a woman, any woman, to tears?*

He hadn't checked her for disease, whatever that meant. He hadn't done a single thing other than look into the dank diminutive light of the closet and wish to be swallowed by it.

After a moment of stillness, of silence, he'd simply exited the closet and left her there, winking to Gumble, who'd watched on with a moronic smile. He'd dedicated himself to a corner for the remainder of the evening.

Later, after he'd been bid good night and sent back upstairs to the suite owned by the Shop family, he'd passed that same Crafter woman again, this time in an upstairs parlor, the doors wide open. And with her was not just Gumble, but two of his compatriots, all in states of hasty undress, bull-eyed and gleaming.

And the Crafter woman looked not at Theo, but through him, as though neither of them were truly there at all.

It only occurred to Theo now, that those women might have had children at home. Maybe partners, as well. Perhaps leasing the warmth of their flesh was better than the mines, better than the mills and factories.

Theo shuddered. He'd spent enough time in the mines now to know that he never wanted to be belowground again, that he'd do a good number of ungentlemanly things to avoid it.

Tamir was greeted by a man in a red suit jacket and white gloves, who resembled a ringmaster but was more likely a maître d'.

"Meester Peters!" Tamir exclaimed, and reached out to clasp the man's small hand in both of his.

"Tamir," Peters said tightly and in a way that inferred reluctance. His eyes swept quickly to Theo and Nina. "These are your guests?"

"And what fine guests they will be," Tamir offered, bowing low enough that he might press his lips to Peters' knuckles. Peters retracted his hand abruptly.

The man cleared his throat. "They are not to eat from the serving trays," he said. "Or enter any of the sitting rooms—or the kitchens, or the stables—"

"But you misunderstand!" Tamir interjected, waving his hands in a frenzy. "These are guests from *Belavere City*!"

Peters blanched. "You mean, they aren't . . . ?"

"They are not under my employ," Tamir laughed. "No, no, Meester Peters. You have put your foot in your arse, you see?"

"In his mouth, Tamir," Nina corrected.

"Yes, right in his mouth. These are *Lord* and *Lady* Pontino, and they are my very best acquaintances come to visit me! Did I not tell you I have many good friends in Belavere City?"

Peters looked as though he'd heard of Tamir's "many good friends," and hadn't believed a single tale. He turned to Nina and Theo repentantly. "Please, forgive me, my lord. Tamir . . . well, he often visits with an array of guests."

"Yes," Tamir nodded. "But these ones will not be found coupling in your stables. Now, we should be shown through, yes?"

Peters, now the color of puce, nodded and led them through the foyer and then left into a grand crescent dining room, complete with three tiers of seating, brass banisters, all the occupants looking down from their round tables at the band in the bottom most tier, the dancers pulsating around their stage.

This party was not one to be found in Belavere City, where the woman wore dresses with hoops and necklines to the throat, where the most scandalizing thing to occur would be a spilled drink or a muttered curse.

This was Rickers.

There was more flesh here than Theo had ever seen. Granted, he'd never been permitted beyond the smoking room as a boy. He tried to imagine his father in a room like this, with men wrapping their hands around women's backsides, feeling for the edge of their hems. The laughter was louder, somehow savage. It stunk of abandon. Of sex.

The lights were low enough to disguise debauchery, tinged red to incite sin. The band was made of trumpets, fiddles, a piano, a man in reflective blue tails belting notes into a microphone, and the Artisans fumbled about in their delirium, drunk on the rebellion of it.

This was why Morland still stood, Theo thought, why the Crafters in the street were not yet starving. They offered the Artisans something important. Freedom. Temptation. Discretion.

"Welcome!" Tamir said, taking Nina's hand and leading her to the edge of the first balcony. The men at a nearby table put down their drinks in succession, followed her with widening eyes, wet their lips.

And Theo abruptly blocked their view, staring daggers at them.

"Have you ever seen anything quite like it?" Tamir asked Nina, patting her hand, drinking in her expressions.

She was slack-mouthed. Her eyes stuck to two Artisan men dancing, connected stomach to stomach.

"No," she said, incredulity making her quiet. It was her habit to become silent and thoughtful when she was overwhelmed. There was not so much of her that had changed, Theo knew, even if she insisted she was different. Her eyes would oscillate of their own accord, reams of thought shifting over them and never settling. Theo still thought he could read some of them.

He took her unoccupied hand. "Don't be concerned," he told her. "They might be drunk, but they're still Artisans."

Her torrent of thoughts seemed to halt abruptly, and her gaze flashed to him. "They aren't Artisans," she said, snatching her fingers free of his. "They're animals."

She lifted her chin, and the light turned her chest alabaster, then red, then gold. Theo reminded himself to look away. He placed his hands behind his back. "Still, they won't cross any lines with a fellow."

"I'm *not* their fellow," Nina said bluntly in a voice Theo didn't recognize. "And I don't want your assistance." Somewhere in his chest, where Nina had left his heart hacked and bleeding, another cut was etched.

He swallowed. For years she had clung to him, had welcomed him leading her, shielding her. He'd done so willingly, been proud to do it. He'd helped her, hadn't he? Made school easier for her?

Now, he stepped back several inches, swallowing his shredded ego. "Of course," he said, inclining his head.

Cold. She was always so outwardly cold toward him now.

And he'd earned it.

If only she could see inside him where guilt churned, slowly ruining him, enough that it had eroded the calcification of his former loyalties, his beliefs. Enough that none of it—honor, duty, tradition—seemed to matter now.

There was hurt in her hazel eyes when she looked at him, fissures of hatred. Blame. He deserved that, too. And if she bid him away again, he would go.

Though he thought it might break him to do it.

He'd tried to once, hadn't he? He'd admitted defeat and left Kenton Hill. He'd only lasted a day before the draw of her thinned the anger, made it impossible to continue on.

It had taken him seven years to find her again. Seven tortuous, wretched years. He'd be damned if he lost her a second time of his own accord.

So he followed Nina and Tamir around the tables, around the standing parties, and to a group of men whose gaze traveled down the length of her before ever meeting her eye, and he didn't say a thing. He'd stay for as long as she'd let him. He'd hope that one day those fissures would close, and he would show her that she wasn't made for destruction.

She didn't want this, not really.

And she hadn't bid him away yet.

CHAPTER TWENTY-TWO

NINA

Tamir introduced us first to an elderly man with arthritic knuckles. He took great gulps of liquor and spat when he talked, his lips luridly wet. His frame was bent almost double, yet he attempted, with great effort, to straighten as I approached.

"Richard!" he brayed first, toasting him, and Tamir lifted an eyebrow at me. *See?* he seemed to say.

"And who is this ravishing lady? One of yours?" the man asked now, threatening the shirt buttons protruding from his chest. At the mention of a lady, the other men in the grouping turned from their conversation and perused me.

Tamir introduced me as Miranda, a Cutter, and Theo as James, a Smith, and there was not a flicker of suspicion among them. They were too impeded by drink, too struck by the prospect of new flesh. The clawing commenced.

"A pleasure to meet you, my lady. I'm Mr. Langley."

"Mr. Tunney, Miss. Might I tempt you to dance?"

"You may have heard of me already. Frederick Dunce? Purveyor of special artifacts at the archives?"

I was the diamond, sharp and glinting. And though my stomach twisted, and the rage gnashed, I lowered my eyelids a fraction and tilted my head to the side.

"The archives?" I repeated with just the right amount of breath intertwined that I seemed like an idiot.

Oh, how men *loved* an idiot.

"Yes," Frederick said, a smile laced in it. He lowered his head as though the gravity of his duties were a burden. "In the relics tower. It is quite a heavily guarded department. In truth, I'm not supposed to speak of it."

"But then"—and I pressed my hand to my bosom—"you must be a Scribbler of high order?"

The other men guffawed into their drinks, and Frederick glowered at them.

"High order?" Mr. Langley laughed. "Quite impossible. Frederick has never turned in a single article on time."

Frederick downed the rest of his whiskey in one punishing swallow.

"So then, which of you is?" asked Theo, and the laughter ceased.

Each of their eyes flickered to his, as though just realizing him. The music belted in.

Mr. Tunney seemed to sober immediately, his eyes narrowing. "Where is it you said you were from?"

Theo stared back coldly.

"Fenway," I offered, brightening my smile to a sickening voltage. "He supervises the timber mill."

The men rolled their eyes, grunted laughter into their drinks, dragged on their cigars as though they could not imagine a lesser fate.

"And what of you?" said Frederick. "What brings you to our fair Morland?" He seemed the youngest of the group and was the only one without a wedding ring. He had damningly thin auburn hair and a weak chin. But he watched me with the most intent, tottered the most often. Already he'd commandeered another drink from a passing server.

I tried to look small, willing. "I'm most curious to know its people."

It was difficult to tell if Frederick was, firstly, still in possession of his magic, and secondly, a Scribbler accomplished in translation, but he was, at the very least, enthusiastic. He took me first to the bar and collected a glass of champagne for me. He didn't seem to notice when I refrained from drinking it. He spoke at length about the archive towers, their rich history (which I already knew), the view from his office window (which I needn't know), and more about Morland. When I prompted, he assured me that he was still receiving biannual doses of idium despite the shortage crisis. When I pushed gently on his chest, rolling my eyes and calling him a liar, he caught my hand in his. "Shall I prove it?" he slurred, leaning in.

I then felt a scratch on my thigh, the skin just above my knee itching momentarily.

I let the split in my skirt fall aside, revealing the wet ink he'd left there. The name of a building. A room number. A question mark.

I smiled coyly, looked deep into his eyes, felt bile pocket in my throat. "What other marks might you leave on me?" I whispered.

Always, Theo remained just over my shoulder. I felt him burning in my periphery. He was approached by countless women, all of them dressed impeccably, and he gently declined them all.

I ignored him entirely.

It didn't take all that much to turn the conversation back on itself, in the end. Frederick was practically sideways with drink. I was beginning to suspect the tulleyroot wouldn't be needed. "I once corresponded on behalf of Lord Tanner!" he was saying now. "Did you know he had a mistress? A *Crafter*?"

I feigned shock, leaned in close enough that he blinked, licked his lips. "Lord Tanner himself?" I said. "But then, you must be quite accomplished, to be trusted by the Head of House."

And Frederick grinned foolishly, his eyes on my lips. "Oh, I am, my dear," he said. "Accomplished in many things, in fact."

"An important man," I said, my fingers pinching his collar. I let my nails trail along the skin of his throat, watched his eyes glaze in satisfaction. "I suppose you translate, as well?"

He scoffed indelicately, slipped sideways from his stool, and caught himself. "In many languages, since you asked!"

"Really? How about Verian Script?"

Here, Frederick faltered. He gaped like a fish. "What?"

"Verian Script," I said slowly. "Do you know it?"

He frowned, "Well . . . no one does, my dear. It's not much needed, you see. Quite archaic."

I kept myself from visibly deflating, hoping he was wrong.

Perhaps Frederick sensed my disappointment, felt me slipping from his fingers.

"I do know *one* person," he said. "Though I shouldn't speak of it—"

"A friend of yours?" I asked, my interest reigniting.

"No—I mean, yes. That is, my friend is no longer a colleague. Quite an interesting scandal, in fact. But I'm not sure I should be talking about—"

"You are a well-connected man, then." My hand settled gently on his knee, and he looked down at it, as though unsure of when it had arrived there. "What I wouldn't give for an introduction. I'm so curious about you Scribblers and your work."

Frederick seemed entranced. He stood and stuck out a wavering hand. "Then you're in luck. Let me fulfill your dreams." He led me then into the red-tinged gloom.

I knew Theo followed. I could feel him trailing close behind, teeth on edge, most likely.

Frederick wove me around the high-top tables, down the red carpeted steps, and around the banisters. He became waylaid by a change of song and asked me to dance. I declined.

"Your friend?" I reminded him gently, smiling. "The one you mentioned, the translator."

He tapped my thigh with one finger, a reminder of payment. "And then to our other plans?"

I hid my revulsion with another smile and a nod.

By an exit, where white-clad servers trafficked silver platters back and forth, clustered several round card tables. Each seat was occupied by a player, spectators hovering by their shoulders. The dealers were Crafters, performing deft tricks for spare shillings in between hands.

Frederick pulled me between tables, his eyebrows lifting in an attempt of seduction. "I'd wager you've never seen anything like this."

I had, actually. But there were fewer brass buttons in the brink, more lager, less money per wager.

At the farthest table in a dark corner, the patrons clustered in a state of rapture, the dealer slinging cards to five faceless players, their heads bent.

"There," Frederick nodded. "At the end."

He could've been referring to any of those five players—the gray mustached man, flipping farthings clumsily in his palm, the two top-hatted gentlemen with pinched mouths, the man who seemed, the longer I looked, to be asleep, his chin resting on his chest, or the woman who splayed her cards in her hand and looked about the group with a sobriety none of them could match.

But I knew which one Frederick would take me to immediately, and so did Theo.

He was there at my shoulder, his eyes pinned where mine were and narrowing by the second.

"Introduce me," I said to Frederick, and it was an effort to keep from spitting it.

But Frederick suddenly turned pink, contrite. Panic dawned. "Er . . . well, there was a scandal, you see? I shouldn't be seen—"

"You *are* friends, aren't you?" I said through my teeth. "Am I not allowed to meet a friend of yours?"

"Well, we're not exactly friends in the *traditional* sense—"

I moved around him, tired of the charade, shaking now. I stepped on the feet of the onlookers, pushed through gaps until I was right over her shoulder. Close enough to see her cards, the five of hearts morphing into an ace. Close enough to see her pupils dilate in fear when she looked up at me.

"Good evening, Polly," I said.

CHAPTER TWENTY-THREE

NINA

Polly Prescott was unchanged.

Unless you considered the gown she wore, her red-painted lips, and the deep circles beneath her eyes.

She didn't wear a wig like I did. Didn't hide from her name.

The music thundered on, the dealer called for the first player, the spectators drank and fumbled for parts of one another and took no notice of the slow collapse between me and her.

Could she feel it? The depth of her knife in my back.

Her eyes told me she could, that the guilt of it had whittled her down to nearly nothing. She looked furtively over my shoulder to Theo, terror turning her ashen. "Nina," she said simply, on a breath. "Please."

The hole inside me expanded, swallowing me. I shook my head, displaced tears on the brim. Here she was, in all this finery, while Kenton Hill swept its ashes into piles.

I turned to take the pistol from Theo's jacket pocket. The bodies pressed in; someone laughed raucously and dropped their champagne glass. The dealer flaunted his shuffle to a rapt audience. No one saw the glint of steel as I pressed it to Polly's side. "Get. Up," I said, voice shaking. "And walk."

Polly's eyes closed, and when she opened them, I saw surrender. She stood.

"Nina," Theo warned, his hand at my elbow, his mouth at my ear. "Nina, put the gun away. *Now.*"

But my hand was cinched so tightly I thought I might fuse myself with it. It shook uncontrollably in my hand. Everything shook.

The chandeliers overhead rattled and swayed, the band stopped mid-song as the celloist toppled sideways from his stool. Dancers and cardplayers shouted and grabbed hold of banisters, of one another. The sound of breaking glass rebounded. "Union attack!" they shrieked.

"Stop, Nina!" Theo panted in my ear, his hand around mine, trying to pry my fingers from the pistol. I was barely aware of anything but the tremor in my core, finding pathways into my blood, into the earth. The balcony teetered. Polly lost her balance.

"*Nina!*" Theodore pleaded.

CHAPTER TWENTY-FOUR

PATRICK

The coach and its nags perched by a coal bin in a muddy alley.

Patrick leaned against the coach's exterior with his father, accepted a cigarette when he offered it.

"Got us a few provisions earlier," John said, lighting his own with a match, then Patrick's. He took a deep draw, as though he wished to suck the marrow from it. "Lord almighty," he said, curls of smoke unfurling from his lips. "Even better than I remembered."

Patrick might as well have been ten years old following his father out onto Main Street after supper. John pointing up to the night sky and saying "See, son, even the moon has its eye on me."

Patrick looked skyward now, drew on his cigarette, tried to imagine Kenton Hill, his brothers, his mother, Nina in a pale blue dress bursting through the pub door. He exhaled, feeling a heavy bout of homesickness pervade him. He'd never been away from Kenton so long.

"There'll be snow on the ground back home," John said then, as though he could read Patrick's mind, see the quarry and the hills and their snail-shell town curled up in the middle. "The water'll start freezin' in the tanks."

"The Coal Works held," Patrick grunted. Theodore sprang to mind, sending torrents of water over its rooftop. "Gunner'll turn on the boilers to heat the tanks."

Gunner, with a knife in his gut, blood seeping through his fingers.

Partick's stomach twisted.

His father clapped him on the shoulder. "No tougher pelt ever seen than the one on Gunner Colson. I'm sure he's healed already."

But Patrick couldn't see how, not if the infantry had raided their bluff stores and taken it all.

John sighed. "You were always the solemn one." He threw his stub to the ground, crushing it with his boot. "So bloody serious. Take after your ma."

But he'd been a boy once. Back before the tunnels. Back before his father had taken him to the police house to watch it burn. Back before John had tugged on his collar and told him that one day, he was going to be the world's only Alchemist.

Patrick inhaled. "Once we have the translations, we need to go home."

One of the horses nickered and stomped, and John barked a curse at it. "No can do, son. I ain't lettin' those Charmers within a mile of the place again."

Patrick turned a glare on his father.

"Relax, boy," John said, lighting another smoke. "Can hardly cut the girl loose, can I? Once we know where the Seam is, we travel without delay. No point returnin' to Kenton unless we got somethin' to show for it."

He spoke of Nina the way he spoke of bad trades, of shady arms dealers, and shipyard thugs. Unsavory folk with whom business must be tendered. Sooner or later, those people ended up injured or dead. He'd seen his father pull a blade enough times when the deals went south. He imagined John now, turning a knife on its edge, its point between a pair of hazel eyes.

"She ain't yours to cut loose," Patrick said slowly and very clearly. "She'll go where she pleases."

John seemed to expect this. He rolled his eyes to the heavens and scoffed. "You've turned soft on me, lad," he said, with a voice hewn a hundred fathoms below. He turned his eyes to Patrick and looked him over. "You've grown a fondness where you shouldn't have. I warned you and your brothers to keep your eyes and your hands on the work, didn't I? The women'll come and go, but the work ain't goin' nowhere. This is the important business, Patty. This is what we've been fightin' for. It ain't the time to go fallin' in love."

Patrick looked away from his father, lest he see the truth. That it was too late. That love had already invaded him, and try as he might, he couldn't banish it. "She's on our side, now."

"She's a swank, son. You forgot that once, and it's cost me half the fuckin' parish."

Defensiveness punched through, sent Patrick's blood boiling.

But composed men fared better than the bulls. He closed his eyes and blew smoke up at the moon. "There was a mudslide," he said. "At the eastern pit. The whole fuckin' tunnel collapsed."

John's face became immediately drawn, feeling, as all miners did, a shiver of terror. "How many dead?" he asked soberly.

Partick flicked ash to the mud. "Four."

John hesitated, his brow furrowed. "Just four?"

Patrick remembered how he'd crushed his mouth to Nina's by the shaft, made her promise to come out alive. "Just four."

John stared, wide-eyed for a moment, calculating.

"Nina stopped it," Patrick told him. "You should have seen the way the hill fell. Great fuckin' wall, headed straight for the school. All those kids would've been buried, and the street beyond it, too. And she held it all up." Patrick paused for a moment, remembering the way she'd looked at the bottom of that hill, how impossible the task had been. "Never seen anythin' so godlike. Then she went into the shaft herself, brought out every man waiting to die in that pit. Nearly killed herself doin' it, too." He threw his cigarette to the ground, thinking that Nina hated the smell of it. How it reminded her of Scurry. "You say she cost you half the parish?" Patrick looked his father in the eye, noticed how much older he seemed. "I say if she hadn't been there, half of it would have gone under."

John watched him for a long time, his expression never changing. That was the power of John Colson—he was far more perceptive than anyone would believe, all of it hidden beneath a beard and a miner's grit.

He opened his mouth to speak, but it was cut off by a sudden tremor. The ground shuddered, panicking the horses and rattling the coal bin. Above them, the orange windows of Rickers splintered.

"Fuck," John swore around his smoke, gripping onto the coach for support. "Earthquake?" he asked above the growing roar.

But Patrick was looking up at those windows, imagining Nina within, picturing a hill sliding toward him. "No," he said, turning immediately for the street. "Just a girl from Scurry."

CHAPTER TWENTY-FIVE

NINA

The balcony jolted, and shouts rebounded in my ear.

"Please, don't kill me," Polly prayed, her eyes shut tight.

But she had left us all to die, left all of Kenton to burn, hadn't she? The vendetta rotting out my insides—some of it was saved for her. I understood then, with abrupt clarity, how those soldiers on the battlefield could lift their bayonets again and again without hesitation, adding to an already littered graveyard. An eye for an eye.

I could shoot Polly Prescott right then and add her to the heap. Step over her to the next.

"Nina! Stop!" Theo said, his fingers pressed harshly to the wound on my arm, and the bite of pain sliced through my consciousness, brought a halt to the rush of my mind.

The tremors ceased.

Polly shook like a child. Like a whipped dog.

Reality came sputtering back.

The card tables had slid sideways into the banister, the Artisans hiding beneath stark-faced and looking in every direction. "A bomb?" one of them asked. "An attack?"

But the first to point the finger was the Scribbler named Frederick.

Where the liquor had made him simple, the shatter of a fallen chandelier sobered him. The cracks in the banister and the falling plaster seemed to clear his head, enough that he looked up from where he cowered on the floor. Enough that he saw the pistol I was holding. "Union!" he shouted, scuttling backward on his arse. *"Union!"*

"Shit," Theo breathed, my elbow still in his hand. "*Run*," he said.

But the voices were growing, a carousel of contorting faces crying "*Union!*" "*They're Union!*" And before Theodore could shove me farther than a heap of fallen stools and glass, three men came scrabbling through the mess toward us, cornering us, their party attire making them plain but their guns making them coppers, silver barrels lifted.

"Stop where you are!" one said. "Drop the gun!"

There was no way past them, only the drop over the banister to the stage, and one pistol against three.

It couldn't be over yet.

It rang through me like a struck gong. Desperation, conviction. *I'd rather die*, I thought, idium screaming in my veins. *I'd rather die than go back.*

"Nina, it's over!" Theo said. "Please, they'll shoot."

Better than capture. Better than the House and the whip.

"She's the earth Charmer!" came Polly's voice, rising from somewhere over my shoulder. "She's Nina Clarke! Don't shoot."

The barrels wavered, confusion marring the coppers' scowls, the quake of the building taking on new meaning for them. One reached beneath his suit jacket, and the glint of shackles peaked out.

No, I thought, and I lifted the gun. Pointed it straight at him. I'd open a mouth wide enough to swallow a building. Let us see who survived in the rubble.

For the second time, I felt my mind expand, let it sink into the earth beneath the building. Deeper still, to the fault lines. The tremors reawakened. The coppers toppled.

And I spared no thought to any Artisan in this building who might die. I spared no thought at all but for the sheer power coursing through me, the sharp, vicious satisfaction of it.

Shots rang out in quick succession. Orange blasts in the dark. From left to right, the coppers fell, their craniums bursting, legs collapsing.

The quaking ceased, and people shouted, ducked, crawled for exits while they could.

And from the scrummage came an advancing Patrick, his own gun smoking, legs sturdy and sure. He didn't slow as he reloaded the barrel, stepped over the bodies. He didn't take his eyes off me.

I saw him as I did in dreams.

More blasts. This time from John, who pointed his gun at the ceiling and shouted, "Party's over, swanks! Out you get!"

A siren was wailing. I could not discern from where it came. All I saw was Patrick. The apparition of him.

"Nina." His hands firm on my cheeks, my shoulders. "Nina. Focus. Look at me."

But he was faded at the edges, tilting sideways. Was that him shaking me? Or was the earth shifting again?

"Come on, darlin'. Don't collapse on me now, the night ain't over."

"We have to run, Colson" came Theo's voice.

"Nina, eyes on me." He gripped my chin, and I blinked. Nodded.

Gunshots rang out. John called to the last of the Artisans as though he were rounding up cattle.

"Found the Scribbler," I tried to say. It was difficult to tell if the words passed my lips.

Partick scowled. "It don't matter," he said. "Listen to me. We need to run."

But I was turning on my heel. And somehow, for reasons I couldn't fathom, Polly was still there, between the fallen card tables and buckled chairs. She was kneeling, hands raised.

Patrick laid eyes on Polly.

"Don't shoot," she said to him, not quite meeting his eye. Tears shook off her lower lip.

The building groaned. Plaster molding fell. But Patrick had stilled. A tick made its way into his neck, and then his jaw.

Without saying a word, he leveled his gun at her and advanced.

It was Theodore who put himself in Patrick's path. He lifted his hands. "Pat, *wait*!"

Patrick halted, the back of his neck burning red. "Move out of the way."

"No," Theo said, and the sirens howled on. They seemed closer now. "Don't shoot her. You *need* her."

"Time to go, Patty!" John called. "Before the whole fuckin' thing collapses!"

"She's the Scribbler," Theodore insisted, Patrick's gun now aligned with Theo's own chest, Polly whimpering behind him. "The one you're looking for."

"We gotta *go*, Pat!" John shouted. *"Now!"*

Patrick inhaled once, twice. Then pushed Theodore aside easily. He took Polly by her upper arm and hoisted her to standing. She kept her chin to her chest and closed her eyes.

"Whether you live or die," he said, ushering her forward. "Will depend on what you do next."

We left Rickers through servant halls and stairwells, Patrick holding Polly at gunpoint, me following in a haze. We were already in a back alley when I realized Theodore had his arm around my waist and was holding me upright.

John picked me up the way one would a child and deposited me inside the coach.

Beneath dim lamplight, we escaped to the street. Police coaches careened toward the club's entrance, the road behind us flooding with shaken Artisans, their evening wear now garish, their night turned abruptly sober and discordant.

On the air, following us down the steep decline, was the repeated murmur of my name as it was passed from person to person.

Nina Clarke was here.

The earth Charmer.

The lord's assassin.

CHAPTER TWENTY-SIX

PATRICK

On Patrick and Polly Prescott's first meeting, she'd been face down on a pier, her nose bent and bleeding against the sodden wood.

She'd been grateful to see him that time, and doubly grateful for the bullets in her two assailants.

As he recalled, she was conscious as he rolled their sorry bodies off the docks and into the wash. They would catch in the nets, or else curl bloated against the pylons, he told her. She didn't need to worry.

He saw her brand then, the whorls of Idia's hair fanning out beneath the hem of her sleeve, and he helped her to her feet.

She'd been just as rattled then as she was now: eyes wide as a deer's, her breaths escaping in tiny gasps. Patrick had guessed she was moments from collapse. "What's your name?"

"Polly," she'd murmured. "Prescott."

He'd pitied her. How could he not? Artisan or no, there was a certain place in hell for a pig who used his body against an innocent. "And what breed of swank are you, Polly Prescott?"

It was there in the paper cuts lacing her fingertips, in the mere fact that she was in Dorser, too far east of the river for any lady with a brand on her arm.

And he couldn't simply leave her there on the docks or dump her in some Dorser hovel, could he? Patrick was hardly a gentleman, but he was no devil, either.

Besides, he thought Kenton could use a Scribbler.

And she *had* been useful. Far more so than even he'd bargained for. Before Polly, messages were sent via Otto and Scottie, through the tunnels. It could take days to send a warning, a week to settle a deal. With Polly, the raided towns received necessary bluff sooner. Betrayals were caught in the wind and silenced quickly. The coppers in Kenton sent their missives by Scribbler to the National House, and no one came to see what had become of their quiet parish in a continent booming in bullets and smoke.

That is, until Polly had sold them to the slaughterhouse in a single scribble.

Until she'd undone an entire rebellion.

Now here she was, dressed in high fashion, gambling in Morland—the prize for setting Kenton Hill alight and bringing the House a living, breathing Alchemist.

Patrick breathed deeply. In their line of business, the last man standing was the one with all his cards still pressed to his chest. When rage found him, he'd learned to temper it.

Right now, he was the dark void of a serpent's mouth. He was filled with venom, lined with teeth.

Polly sat tied to a chair in The Mistress. Tamir's apartment was lit by candle, turning his trinkets orange and morbid. He was pacing in the periphery, his hands together in prayer, mumbling apologies, curses, a growl of profanities in a foreign language. Every so often, his eyes strayed to the window, as though he expected a barrage of coppers to break through it at any moment.

Tamir would have to run, too. Patrick would need to find a new Union member to take over the establishment, to keep ears and eyes on Morland.

As though Patrick had said it aloud, Tamir yanked a large bag from beneath the bed and began filling it at random.

"He's flighty, ain't he?" John said from where he lounged in a kitchen chair, a cigarette dangling from his lips. "Calm down, Tammy. Coppers don't work that quick. They won't be round for a while yet."

"And I suppose you'll just shoot them when they arrive?" Theodore asked.

John winked. "You're a quick fuckin' learner, kid."

Theo had his back pressed to a wall. "They were lowering their guns," he said bitterly. He had a soldier's look about him, the light all burned out. "We could have walked out of there."

"Aye, well, that all went to shit when the lady here decided to start a fuckin' earthquake."

Patrick thought Nina on the brink of starting another any moment. Like him, she was wire-taut, set to trip.

They were, each one of them, the head of a pointed spear, glancing off the other. How long before the hostility pierced through? And who would lunge first?

There was only one thing tying them together, and it was the book clenched in Patrick's hand.

Polly looked at them all in turn, her eyes shaking in their sockets. Patrick tried not to see the flames of Kenton reflected there.

There was no tulleyroot. Theo had dumped it all on the way back. If not for him, Polly's tongue would be decaying before his eyes.

"Do you read Verian Script?" he bit out. Sometimes he made his voice quiet to incite fear. Tonight, he couldn't find the wherewithal.

Polly blinked at him in surprise. "I—s—some," she allowed.

"Are you a descendant of Stewards?" he asked next. He saw no benefit in dancing around the point.

She paused, frowned in earnest. "My grandfather believed we were," she said eventually, twisting her hands together. "He's the one who taught me the language. But . . . my father didn't like it, and my mother was an Artisan. Mention the Stewards around any Artisan, and they'll react as if you've told a joke in poor taste."

"But your grandfather is a Craftsman," Patrick said, leading her. "And he believes."

Again, Polly paused before answering. "He *was* a Craftsman," she said, her brow lined in confusion. "But yes, he believed."

"He passed?"

"A few years ago," she said, looking from one set of eyes to another. "What is this about?"

Patrick took the book out and placed it on the table. He slid it across the surface to her.

"This," he said blankly, "was supposedly written by the Stewards."

She stared at it, then exhaled all at once, as though he'd punched a hole through her chest.

Patrick watched carefully. "You recognize it."

Her mouth opened uncertainly. "I—yes. It was his, I think. My grandfather's."

"And he taught you how to read it?"

Polly hesitated. "In a manner of speaking."

"You'll translate it."

She stared at the book, still trying to puzzle through something. "How did you find this?"

"It was in my father's possession," Theo answered.

Polly looked at Theo. "You stole it from him?" she asked, only it wasn't accusatory. It was almost . . . impressed. Like she couldn't imagine anyone crossing Terrence Shop, choosing to place such a target on their back. "Why?"

Theo shifted uncomfortably, clasped his hands at his back. "My father . . . There is little he wouldn't do to get what he wants." His eyes trailed to Nina. "I couldn't just stand by."

He didn't mention his hand in getting his father what he wanted. Didn't tell Polly that he was only here, it seemed, because Nina was here.

Polly shook her head, turned her attention back to Patrick. "Pat, I—I want to—"

Patrick slammed his fist on the table, and all the trinkets on the shelves, the clocks and windchimes and dishes, they all quaked in response.

Polly's face crumpled. She drew herself inward, away from danger.

"You'll translate it," Patrick repeated, waves of wrath swelling from the cords of his neck, the tendons of his arms. "Or you'll die here. I'll do it myself."

She swallowed. Her eyes flickered to Theo, sensing her one alliance among them. The only one who might still hold some sympathy.

And she might have found it there. If it weren't for his infatuation with Nina, he'd be as much a traitor to the Union as Polly.

It was hard to say which of them Patrick despised more.

"I had to do it," she said then, her voice breaking in desperation. "You know I had to. Tanner—"

Patrick stood. He took the chair beneath him and lifted it by its leg, hurled it at the wall behind him. The parts splintered and scattered across the room, and though Patrick wasn't nearly sated, the sound was enough to make an impression on Polly, enough for her to hear her own bones in the snap of the wood.

Patrick leaned against the arms of Polly's chair, his face inches from her own.

"You don't get to explain yourself. You understand?" He thought she did. "I don't want to hear how you didn't have a choice, or how sorry you are about all those dead people and their burnin' houses. Their deaths are on *your* hands, Polly. *You* killed them, just as surely as if you'd set them alight yourself."

She sobbed, disintegrating by pieces.

"Otto survived the attack. Did you know that?" Patrick asked now, and he watched the information sink into her like a knife. "Did you care, Pol, if he lived or died? Or were you only ever dreamin' of the day you'd sit at a card table in Morland, in your fancy fuckin' dress?"

She closed her eyes, as though shutting out the world. "They were *coming*," she said brokenly, her voice a rasp. "The infantry were coming anyway, and I couldn't stay. I didn't want to die."

"You led them safely to the very middle," Patrick said. "You know, Pol, beneath hell, there's a place that's worse. They save it for traitors."

Tears shone in her eyes. "They were already *coming*—"

"THEN YOU SHOULD HAVE LET THEM COME!" Patrick seethed. "Let them be blown apart on the fuckin' hills!"

"And then live as a fugitive?" she asked. "Hope the soldiers didn't eventually make it past all those landmines? Try my hand in the brink again, alone? That didn't work out so well the first time."

Patrick saw the faces of those men, bearing down upon her on the pier.

"I traded Margarite's tunnel for a chance at safety," she said, eyes cinched shut, tears washing her face. "And if it brings you any comfort, Pat, you should know I didn't find any. I wasn't brought back to the city. Tanner ignored my scribbles, and now he's dead." The shadows beneath her eyes seemed to extend. "I was ousted, shunned as a deserter. The archives here won't have me—I've already tried. I'm sitting in swank gambling dens now, using the last scraps of the idium left in me to ink cards into aces for money." She looked as hollow as any factory worker. "I promise you, Pat," she said in a voice not more than a whisper, "you could never hate me as much as I hate myself."

There was more he could say, more wounds to carve, but that would do nothing for him. So he stood straight again, counted the passing seconds while Polly composed herself.

"You'll help us," he said. "And save your fuckin' apologies for someone who believes 'em."

She sighed, caught tears on the cuff of her sleeve. "And once I do help you," she said, resigned, "you'll throw me into the canals." She'd spent enough time in Kenton Hill to know what befell traitors. And none had betrayed Patrick quite like her.

"As I said," he lied, "whether you live or die will be up to you."

Polly's jaw twitched. She knew, just as Patrick did, that he couldn't let her live after this.

"Any moment, the police will come," Tamir murmured, fretful. "Any moment!"

"If you don't start sayin' somethin' useful in your next breath, it'll be your last," said John to Polly, lifting a knife he'd procured from Tamir's kitchen drawer. He buried the tip into the woodgrain, balanced it with the pad of his finger. "Rats are meant for canals, ain't they? Just like you said. Translate the fuckin' book, or I'll take you swimmin' myself."

To her credit, Polly didn't beg for release. It seemed to Patrick as though she was fighting herself, weighing outcomes. He understood then that she was a creature bent on survival above all else. Above the Artisans. Above the Craftsmen.

Such a person was, at the very least, predictable. They always chose the path of least resistance.

She folded now, not bothering to look at the book again. "I can read it," she said. "But there's something I want in return."

And John stood, pulled the knife from the timber. In a blur of movement he was behind Polly, his forearm banded around her neck, the knife at her throat.

"If you kill me, there's not a single other who can translate it!" Polly said, the warning slipping quickly from her lips, her voice pitching. "And there is nothing to stop me from sending a scribble right this second to the head of Morland police, or directly to the House."

"You got a death wish, miss?" John said, his arm tightening.

"Then kill me," Polly whispered. It didn't sound brave. It sounded like defeat. "Lord knows there's nothing left for me in the Trench."

Realization struck Patrick then. "You want a way off the continent."

She looked at him. Then, slowly, she nodded. "There's nowhere else I can go," she said miserably. "I've been turned out by the House, by my own family. I've betrayed the Union. Betrayed every friend I have." Her eyes met Nina's briefly. "I want something more than gambling dens in the brink. The ship in Hoaklin," she said. "I'll trade the translation for passage on that ship."

Patrick didn't intend to give her a damned thing. "Translate the book, and I'll get you on that ship," he told her. "It's due to anchor by the end of the month. I'll give you the location and instructions. We'll part ways tomorrow, and I'll rest easy knowin' I'll never see your face again."

Polly swallowed, eyes pricking with tears. "I want you to take me there yourself. Ensure they allow me aboard. It will give me time to translate the entire text," she said.

"We're on the clock actually," John said. "You'll read it tonight. Skim for the important bits."

"Verian Script is more complex than you can imagine!" Polly insisted. "Each symbol encases multiple meanings. Sometimes entire phrases. It takes time to pull them apart properly."

"What do you mean 'pull them apart'?" Nina asked. "Explain."

Polly shook, the knife edge still balanced at her throat.

"Leave her be, Dad," Patrick said to John.

Polly exhaled in a gust as John's blade disappeared back into his shirtsleeve. Her forehead was coated in perspiration. "Was there a cypher text with the book? A sort of . . . glossary?" This question, she directed to Theo.

Theo frowned. "No, none that I know of."

Polly frowned. "My grandfather had a book of glyph cyphers. I—I can try and translate it from memory, but it's been years. I haven't practiced."

Patrick rubbed frustration from his eyes. "Dig deep, then, Pol, or that steamer is sailin' off without you."

She sighed, chin wobbling slightly. "I'll need paper," she said.

Tamir procured some parchment from his Scribbler's cranny, and Polly opened the book to its first porous page. The first symbol was strange. A snakelike curve cross-sectioned in several places, encased in a house, or a pyramid maybe. The lines tessellated.

Polly traced the pattern with one finger as though memorizing the shapes, and as she did so, ink appeared on Tamir's blank page. A perfect imitation.

Polly paused and looked up at us. "Each symbol has layers, do you see? If one can find the layers, they can decipher the code."

"We ain't in class," John said. "Get on with it."

Polly swallowed. Then she considered that symbol on the page, the strange lines that both connected and diverged.

At first, nothing happened, and Patrick began to wonder if it were all a ploy. Perhaps Polly was only delaying them, betting on the police arriving sooner rather than later.

But suddenly, the ink on the page warped. Disentangled.

Slowly, ink melted and reappeared. Certain lines evaporating, as though Polly were merely testing it, like moving a game piece around a board to check its merit.

No one spoke, except Polly, whose lips moved while she worked, whispering to herself. Her forehead creased in concentration.

But soon, the ink seemed to separate in a permanent manner. Polly's eyes widened with fervor.

The single symbol became three. One oblong, one serpentine, one cutting.

"Joan," Polly read, her finger beneath the first symbol. "Dione," she said for the second. "Idia."

Patrick's hand went to his jaw, grazing the stubble there. He'd not heard the names in many years. "The three daughters," he said quietly.

It seemed he wasn't the only one rattled by the names. John had paced away, his hand dragging through his overgrown hair. Nina stared at the book, lost in her own thoughts, though her face had softened. The wrath in her diverted for now.

"What does it mean?" Nina asked no one in particular. "What do the three daughters have to do with Idia's Seam?"

Polly balked. "Idia's Seam?" She turned then to Patrick, to Theo and John. "That's what you're searching for?"

"Lest I didn't make it clear enough, Miss, you ain't in a position to ask questions," John muttered, but his eyes were on Patrick, his tongue running over his bottom lip.

Nina's eyes were distant. "The three daughters. But it's only a Crafter's myth."

"So is Idia's Seam," Patrick countered.

Theo scoffed. "They're not the same. The three daughters was a story concocted by heretics. God had only *one* daughter, and she sacrificed herself in the Battle of Belavere. There are no records, no evidence at all that another two fought alongside Idia."

"Learn that in school, did you?" Patrick asked. He imagined Theo dressed like a swank schoolboy, still wet behind the ears, some soft-faced nursery maid tightening his belt and wiping his nose each morning.

What a smug little bastard he must have been.

Theo's mouth tightened. "I did."

"Pardon me," said Tamir, inserting his head into the circle. "But who are these 'three daughters'?"

Of course, it was Theo who answered first. "A group of apostates—the self-proclaimed Stewards—once claimed that there were three daughters of God, and that they lived as simple farmers. Some of the less . . . educated folk still propagate it as fact—"

"Crafters," Patrick uttered darkly. "Have the bullocks to say what you mean, Teddy."

Theo bristled.

"And these Stewards." Tamir pressed, steering them away from a fight. "What do they say about the other two daughters?"

"That their blood was just as magical. Just as powerful," Nina said. "That they could grant wishes."

"*Wishes?*" Theo asked incredulously. Patrick imagined that Artisan children never heard *that* part of the tale. Never snapped a chicken bone at midnight. Never blew a strand of hair into the water the way Crafters did at the beginning of spring. "That sounds like a nursery story. But there are actual *written* accounts of witnesses who were there the day Idia threw herself onto enemy battlements. There was a bright white light, an explosion, and the other side was slain immediately. Her blood seeped into the ground that day."

Patrick didn't like the tone of his voice. His foolish certainty.

"It is quite far-fetching, this war story," murmured Tamir.

"Not as far-fetched as the idea that God had *three* daughters, two of which have never been accounted for," Theo countered.

Patrick spared him no more of his attention. He instead focused on Nina, who looked as though she were reaching into the trenches of her mind to bring forth something forgotten.

And did Patrick imagine it, or were the corners of her mouth extending? Her cheeks, too, grew rosy and full by the light of the candles. She touched the Stewards' book with the tips of her fingers, mesmerized.

Theo sighed heavily and shook his head. He was a swank, born to the stories of the Artisans. But Nina and Patrick? They were born in the brink, where the legends wound so deeply into marrow, they were reborn in the chests of children. Towns with no archives, no written records, just skeletons full of stories.

Lord, how he'd love to bend Theo's neck and make him see the tethers he and Nina were made of. *See?* he'd say. *She and I, we're just the same.*

"How long will it take to translate the rest?" Patrick asked.

Polly was passing the pages of the book over the pad of her thumb, the weight of this remit already descending upon her. She looked up warily. "A while," she said. "Several weeks, most likely."

Patrick and his father shared a look. It was far longer than they'd bargained for—enough time for something to go wrong.

"When I'm standing on a pier in Hoaklin with a ticket in my hand, you'll have your translations," Polly said. "Not before."

Patrick felt a familiar exhaustion wrap around his spine. He stood. "You ever hear of a miner's shiver, Pol?" he asked her darkly.

She hesitated. Shook her head slowly.

"It's a bad omen. An instinct, if you like. Some miners get it right before a tunnel collapse. It starts in the middle of your back, works its way to your skull. We learn to trust that shiver. Sometimes it's the only warnin' we get that it's all about to fold in." Patrick put his hands on the table and leaned in, until Polly had no choice but to meet his eye. "You'll have your ticket out of the Trench," he told her. "But if I feel that shiver, Pol, you won't see me comin'. There's a bullet in my pocket with your name etched on its side."

He watched a familiar fear gloss her eyes, her lip tremble, but she nodded.

Patrick stood upright. "Get your things," he said to the rest. "We leave before dawn."

"Leave for where?" Theo asked.

"Home."

But John grunted his reproach. "Might as well make our way to Hoaklin," he said. "We'll need to make arrangements there if the Scribbler is to set sail."

"We need to return *home*," Patrick repeated. With each passing hour, he felt his skeleton rearing forward, as though it would wrench itself outside his body and retreat to Kenton without him. He turned to his father. "Especially you."

Time for John Colson to take back his seat at the table. For the rungs of Patrick's life to fall back in order.

John leveled him with a glare. "Ain't nothin' I want more," he said. "But I'll be in hell before I let the likes of these swanks waltz back into my parish."

In a former life, Patrick would have shrugged, sighed, and heeded his father's wishes. But not anymore. There were problems awaiting them both, no matter who was chairman.

"We're going home," he argued. "There're damages and broken trade arrangements—"

"And no bluff to trade with," John reminded him. "Unless we find the means to make it."

Patrick gritted his teeth.

"We'll have the Scribbler write home to Kenton," John said now. "Tell 'em we're still standin'. Tell 'em we're on business so they don't worry."

But Patrick worried. It was like a bolt slowly threading into his skull.

Despite it, he nodded. He would bide his time.

To Polly, he said, "Best you use a different hand for that scribble, so they don't know it's you sendin' it."

Polly nodded once, her eyes empty.

"Tamir," Patrick said, "we can send word to Kenton Hill that you're comin'. They'll give you a place to sleep."

Tamir nodded dolefully, touching the wallpaper of his brothel as though he were saying goodbye to an old friend.

"Teddy," Patrick said next. "Do the honorable thing and be on your way."

Theodore glared back at him. At least he was man enough to do that. "I'm afraid my *honor* compels me to stay, in case I need to fish Polly from a canal."

Polly gave him a weak nod of gratitude.

Nina simply stared down at the Stewards' book.

Patrick wished that she'd say the words and send Theo on his way, save both men from the contest that would soon come.

But she didn't.

And Theo stayed.

CHAPTER TWENTY-SEVEN

PATRICK

They were to leave that very evening.

The police would be out in numbers tonight, hoping to corner the earth Charmer.

Patrick checked the barrel of his pistol and counted the bullets. Three missing.

They'd parted to their rooms to redress, Tamir providing them with clothing fit for travel. Before dawn, they'd be gone.

In the hour before, Patrick paced his room, vowing not to go to Nina's.

He saw her again as she'd been in Rickers, face white, eyes fixed on something far off, the tendons of her neck and hands so taut they threatened rupture. The whole world shaking on its axis.

She was breaking a little more each day, with each new blow. There was no preventing it.

Patrick was accustomed to fixing things. He was a man of solutions, a man who obtained what he wanted.

Lord, if his body didn't still want hers.

He'd crossed a line with her earlier, so soon after vowing he wouldn't. He had no trouble admitting he was weak where Nina was concerned. One look from her, and his mind was sprinting ahead to dim lighting, flushed skin, her skirt above her hips, her hips above him, trust be damned. He could feel her weight still. What harm would it do? To have that just once more?

Some things, though, were too broken to be rebuilt. He'd resist the urge to taper his hands to all the cracks and fissures of her in a desperate ploy to salvage what they'd had. Or at least, what he'd imagined they'd had.

I was going to marry her, he thought. God, how deep had she entrenched herself in him? How far would he have to cut to get her out? He'd been stupid with love. Blind with it, just as his mother had said. Hadn't he felt that miner's shiver? How quick he'd been to ignore it.

But surely, he hadn't imagined all of it. He wasn't so creative that he could have invented feelings where there were none. He'd seen love requited when she'd looked at him. No one, not even Nina Harrow, was that good an actress.

But therein lay the truth of the matter. He would long for her, even as she lied to him. And she would scheme against him, even as she fell for him. Round and round it would go, the web tightening, constricting.

It had to be left alone. Patrick had turned away from the adjoining door, jaw fastened, head shaking a reproach. "Get your wits about you," he muttered to himself, pulling his shirt over his head and letting it fall to the bed.

He was running a wet cloth over his skin, avoiding the healing flesh on his shoulder, when he heard the door open, Nina's distinct steps walking through.

Patrick grimaced, made a poor attempt to gather himself, then looked over at her.

And immediately away.

She was still in that fucking dress.

Already he felt blood rushing south.

He groaned, his head dropping forward. "Do me a favor, Nina," he said. "And don't come any closer."

"Why?" she asked, taking an unmistakable step in his direction.

"Because I'm a man like any other, and not a very good one."

He heard her bare feet move closer, and he was sure she stood directly behind him, and her forehead touched his spine, and a pent-up breath escaped her, permeating his skin.

He shivered.

"I don't want a good man," she said. "I want the one in front of me."

Patrick closed his eyes, at war again. Always at bloody war.

He abandoned the washcloth. "We'll be leavin' any minute," he said.

She nodded against his back, and he felt her retreat. He breathed in relief, in sufferance.

When he turned, he found she had stumbled back, looking so unlike herself that it scared him. She pulsed with something, her hands interlacing before her, then clutching her rib cage as though holding it together.

Here it was, the breaking. Right before his eyes. Nothing to do but let her. She would crumble and rebuild.

"Breathe," he said.

And she did. "I think I would have sent the entire building into a crater," she said, her voice quieter than he'd anticipated. "I would have killed every person trapped inside. What does that make me?"

"Heartbroken," he said immediately, watching her face. "Only that. You don't need to look any further."

He watched her eyes oscillate from collapse to rage with astonishing speed. "They'd deserve it," she said, words shaking. "Wouldn't they? They'd deserve it. They stand by and do *nothing*—"

"Yeah, Scurry girl," he said. "They'd deserve it. But that hole inside you? You won't stitch it up that way."

She turned from the window to look at him, eyes burning. "Then how?" she asked.

He was tempted to lie to her, to tell her something beautiful waited beyond all this, that her struggle would all find its end.

He shook his head. "When I figure it out," he said, "I'll let you know."

Tears filmed her eyes. From between gritted teeth, she said, "It hurts."

"I know it does, darlin'."

She closed her eyes, struggling to give voice to the thing gnashing at her insides. "I'm furious," she said. "I feel I'm going mad with it."

He knew the feeling well. Knew that people in the brink sated it with bluff or fists. What other way to curb generations of anger?

God, but he wished he could take that from her, even now. But all he could do was win a war. Make it so she'd never feel powerless again.

"Better to let the madness come and go as it pleases," he said. "No point tryin' to stop it."

"Is that what you do?"

"Definitely not," he said, smirking slightly. "I bottle it all up, then unleash it on hawkers at the market."

She laughed once, but it was borrowed. She stumbled back a step, falling into a chair by the wall. The split in her dress fell to one side, revealing her thigh, far more of it than was fair.

Even from a distance, Patrick could see the ink smudged there. Could see some other hand's scrawl.

"What is that?" he asked, eyes flicking up to her face.

He imagined she saw something dark cross his visage. Because she sat straighter, pulled the skirt of her dress down, made the markings of some other man disappear.

Patrick tilted his head, felt something horribly improper invade him. Heat coated his tongue, simmered behind his eyes.

"Patrick—"

"I asked you a question," he said slowly.

She swallowed. "There was a Scribbler in the club. He was . . . easily distracted."

"I can imagine," Patrick rumbled. That was precisely the problem, he was imagining it with piercing clarity. Some Scribbler leaning in, talking into her ear, scratching his fucking ink onto her thigh. "Who?"

"Does it matter?" she asked. She seemed to sicken as she spoke. She pulled her skirt down farther. "It worked." She buried her face in her hands, as though she couldn't bear to look at him. He hated that even more—that she was ashamed.

He watched her, seething, for several moments. Then he turned.

From the basin, he took the washcloth. He swallowed fire as he crossed the room toward her, and, for the second time in as many days, knelt before her like a damned acolyte. He ignored the alarm on her face as he took either side of her skirt in his hands and tugged it apart, ripping it to the hip.

She looked down at him with open desire, her legs parting for him already.

And it was torture not to take that invitation, not to rip that godforsaken dress to the bust. She was all too willing. Always so fucking eager. And there was still so much they hadn't had time for.

There was a room number inked into her. A meeting time. A question mark. As though there were ever a possibility, a hope in hell, that a Scribbler who wrote on women's thighs could be indulged by someone like Nina. Patrick rubbed the pad of his thumb over it, and the ink smeared.

Nina inhaled.

"Think about this," Patrick said. Letting the water from the washcloth drip onto her thigh, the droplets racing over the curve. She shivered. "We're going to find the Seam, and I'm going to make you more powerful than anyone's ever been." Patrick wiped the cloth over the Scribbler's ink. Her eyes lowered to his lips. Her breaths lengthened.

"And you'll watch 'em all cower at your feet. Every lord, every minister. You'll go where you like, do what you like, and there won't be a single person who takes it from you. No one will ever touch you again. And if they *try*, Nina . . ." He gripped her thigh with one hand, washed the ink away with the other. "I'll pull them apart myself, piece by piece."

CHAPTER TWENTY-EIGHT

NINA

We left Morland by tunnel, of course, the mouth of which was hidden in a brick culvert in the city outskirts. We slithered to it single file, Patrick leading, the night always on the verge of dawn.

Tamir was desolate, cradling a heavy trunk to his chest. He slipped into the culvert last, shivering. "I ought to return to the dockyards, Meester Colson. Perhaps find passage to my homeland."

"You'll be looked after in Kenton Hill," Patrick assured him. "They're expectin' you. You'll be welcomed."

"Will it be safe there?" I asked Patrick. Kenton Hill was no longer shrouded in anonymity, after all.

"By now, Gunner and Donny will have ensured Margarite was caved in. The hills are still wired and protected. Kenton is as safe as it can be, even if it's no longer a secret." Patrick opened a drain cover, revealing a ladder.

"We'll point you down the right path, Tamir. It will take you to Dorser. A man named Otto will meet you there and escort you into Kenton," John told him.

At the mention of Otto, Polly blanched.

"Send him the scribble, Polly," Patrick said now, lowering himself onto the ladder. "Be sure to change the handwriting."

Polly's jaw twitched, but she stayed silent and obeyed without protest.

The tunnel was, as Patrick had promised, a stinking, waterlogged mess.

The roof sagged threateningly, roots bursting between struts. The mud came up to our knees; a chorus of water leaks fell.

I was struck by a memory of me and Theodore in a Gilmore field, Professor Dumley watching as we slipped through the mire and tried to charm the soil into something fertile. I remembered falling, sinking into the bog, Theo laughing and taking my hand over and over, his cheeks smeared with the grime.

He offered me a wary smile. "If only Dumley could see us now."

I didn't yield even a twitch of my lips.

We worked in tandem, as we'd done in that field, him pushing the water back into the walls and me compacting the earth, stabilizing the ceiling, the timber frames groaning in relief. We moved quickly at the spearhead, the presence of those behind us nearly forgotten. Escaping into one's medium was all-consuming. I wrapped my expanding mind in the weight and texture of the earth, and it was a relief. I did not batter Theo with questions about his attempts at redemption. I didn't think of Polly, who had betrayed us, betrayed Kenton, or even of Patrick, who, after everything, carried my heart around in his hands. I didn't think about his fingers on my thigh, his voice in my head.

I thought of nothing but earth.

Hours passed before we parted with Tamir at an indiscriminate fork, and I wondered how Patrick knew the way to go, how many times he'd traveled under the Trench. The tunnel opened and dried underfoot, and Patrick led the way to Hoaklin, holding a lantern. John whistled a miner's tune happily from behind them in place of a canary. I got the sense he was at home here, where ribbons of dark distended and took shapeless forms. He spoke ahead to Patrick as though he were stretching his tongue, sinking into a language he'd longed for.

"Thirty fathoms or more here, Patty."

"Thereabouts."

"You need intersectin' struts every three feet, son. These are every four."

"They're bearin' just fine."

"Get Welsh down here. Tell him to reinforce every other cross section."

"Welsh is dead," Patrick said tiredly. "Got buried on the south line."

"Bullerman, then."

"He's in the Coal Works now," Patrick said. "And I'll be gettin' no one down here anytime soon. There's more to do at home." There was finality in it, a trace of ire.

John clicked his tongue loudly, mockingly. "Well, now. Got it all figured, have you?"

"I do."

John chuckled. It weaved darkly into their midst, a monster rising. "Careful, son," he said. "Don't overstep." And for the first time, I heard in his voice the ghost of Patrick's—smoky, smooth, unsettling.

I shivered.

Ahead, Patrick showed no outward reaction, though I thought I saw the expanse of his shoulders go taut, tasted a tang of violence in the air.

Or perhaps the aggression was my own. Perhaps only I felt the sting of the barb. "*Overstep?*" It had escaped some cage in my chest. I'd stopped on the path, turned to buck at John. "Patrick has run Kenton Hill for the past two years." And he'd hated it. Hated every second of it. "*You* were nowhere to be seen."

The entire party stuttered on the path.

I could hear John's tongue rolling about in his mouth, hear it flick out and slide over his lip as though readying it. "And in that time, he found himself a bunch of swanks and let 'em run the whole fuckin' thing into the ground."

He was amorphous in the dark, a grunting, spitting outline, dissolving into men whose faces were indistinct, men from Scurry, my own father. He might have been any one of them.

I bypassed Polly and collided with Theo's arm, barring me from passing. "*Nina*, don't—"

"And what were *you* doing?" I asked, my voice tripling down the fathoms. "Two years a prisoner, and there's not a mark on you to show for it!

You look like you've eaten three square meals a day. Less can be said for your Union members in the brink."

"The other Union prisoners were hanged," added Theo, now frowning in thought. "It is a wonder that you were kept alive."

"Information," said Polly, breaking her self-imposed silence. "The House only trades in information."

There was the sound of a pistol hammer drawing back, the flash of steel in the lamplight, the hollow middle of a barrel pointing between us in no particular direction. "You know," mused John, "there's a lot I've endured in the last two years, caged like a *dog* in that fuckin' swank city." His tone turned gravelly, as though he were spitting the words through gaps in his teeth. He came into the nimbus of the lamp. "One by one, the other prisoners swung from the gallows, but a smarter man knows how to give 'em a proper runaround. How to get inside their heads. And I won—I managed to keep myself alive. So now, I won't be lettin' a trio of *fuckin' swanks* imply that I've been on holiday."

The pistol oscillated between us, but John's gaze was for me.

The moment hovered dangerously, stretching to its limit, the recoil sure to be punishing.

Instead, the sound of Patrick's voice filled the tunnel. It was calm. Calculating.

"There's not a single bullet in the barrel, Dad," he said. "Put it away."

The gun wavered, John's face turned terrible, then abruptly expressionless. "Just makin' sure they were listenin'."

"Darin' of you," Patrick said, "to threaten an earth Charmer all the way down here." It might have been lighthearted, except for the glare Patrick leveled at his father.

"It's a matter of family honor, Patty," John replied, pulling bullets from his pocket and rolling them around on his palm. "It's Colson law to put holes in bastards that test our loyalties," John's eyes flashed with menace at us. "That way, we ain't got to worry about people comin' between us." John's eyes flicked upward to where Patrick watched him as closely as one could here in the crust of the earth. "Remember that man who picked Donny's pockets, Patty? How you took off his finger with a paring knife?"

"I do," Patrick said slowly. "He was takin' advantage of a blind boy."

"He was."

"Just imagine what I'd do to the man who took advantage of me." His voice was full of dark promise, and perhaps he meant it for Theo, or even Polly.

But he was looking at John.

"Tell me again, Dad," Patrick said. "Who was it that gave my medium to the House?"

John gave no response. The two stood lock-eyed, a gun and three traitors between them.

And I volleyed my gaze between the two.

A distinct crack of timber suddenly echoed down the tunnel. The sound ricocheted back to them and they all ducked on instinct, as though bullets were flying. We froze.

Silence for a moment. Then a subsonic groan. A dawning awareness on Patrick's face as he stared down the tunnel, and then he shouted, "*Run!*"

He picked Theo up by the scruff of his neck and shoved him back. Another crack rang out, the sound of falling earth, the yawn of a monster at their backs.

"Get up!" John shouted at Polly, lobbing her forward. "Go!"

The lantern light swung over Patrick's eyes. In them, I saw pulsating fear.

I scrambled to my feet and bolted back the way we'd come.

We threw ourselves back down the tunnel, the snap of timber chasing us, each strut giving way as the earth above us bore down, sought to devour us, jaws closing. I poured my mind to it, felt the idium thrum beneath my skin, already lethargic. I couldn't slow my feet enough to concentrate, couldn't hold it all up after expending myself earlier. The ceiling above us held only long enough for us to pass beneath it, my mind releasing it again soon after and letting it buckle. Patrick kept one hand in the middle of my back, and I kept one hand to the ceiling.

I felt the earth hounding us. Eventually it would catch our heels and we'd be sucked under.

A fork ahead. John moving for it like a snake moves through grass. He disappeared sideways, pulling Polly after him, then Theo.

Patrick hooked his arm around my waist, and with a tremendous push, hurled me around the bend.

I toppled on top of Theo, my knees hitting metal.

And we were plummeted into deepest black.

CHAPTER TWENTY-NINE

DONNY

In the first dregs of morning, Donny roused Gunner.

They had slept once more in their bunks, like kids. Gunner above and Donny below, beams of dawn breaking in through the small window. Patrick's childhood bed lay empty. There was a silent agreement that neither of the men use it.

Of course, Donny had never left. Gunner had married and taken a house on Penance Street, and Patrick, when he did sleep, preferred sleeping in the hotel. But Donny knew these stairs and each individual floorboard. He knew every surrounding inch of the house. He thought he could draw it, if he were artistically inclined, to near perfection. He stayed for the persisting comfort of it.

Gunner groaned and rolled over heavily. "Lord, kill me now," he rasped, as though his lungs had emptied themselves overnight.

"Time to return to work, brother," Donny said, pulling on Gunner's earlobe, then the hairs on his bare chest.

"Ow! *Fuck.*"

"Get up," Donny said. "No more shirkin'. There's men in the western tunnel."

"There's always men in the western tunnel," Gunner growled, pushed Donny's face away.

"Well, these men ain't from Kenton."

Donny felt the mattress shift as Gunner sat upright. "Who?"

"Dunnitch lads, it seems," Donny said, patting him twice on the shoulder. "Get your wits about you, Gun. On your feet."

They carried a sack each over their backs down the western tunnel. Gunner held the lantern, and Donny the canary. He heard the dirge of the underground rising up beneath them, heard the minute shifts of earth, mites chewing at the mineral-rich bacteria, black beetles burrowing tiny crevasses, water tables, somewhere beneath them, cutting silver pathways.

Gunner walked with a limp, his gait heavy-footed on the right. Intermittently, Donny heard him gasp and clutch his side where the knife had shanked inward.

Donny remembered the wet sound of it, the easy split of the tissue, the reels of red streaming into his mind.

Gunner didn't shout for bluff anymore. He only wasted away. For three days or more he'd slept. Ate and spoke and moved about like a ghost. In the night, when he thought Donny asleep, he prayed. Mostly, he prayed that Patrick would return.

It reminded Donny of when their father had first been captured. How they'd counted the passing days and hoped against fading odds that they'd awaken to John strolling back down Main Street, announcing his next grand plan. Patrick had prayed harder than any of them. He'd never faltered. He went about running Kenton Hill as though John would waltz in at any moment and light into them all for letting his town fall to ruin.

Donny wondered where his brother was now. He wondered what Patrick would do if he found Dunnitch men wandering uninvited down the western line.

An hour into the tunnels, Gunner called out, a weakened rendition of his usual menace, but menace enough. "Oh ho!" he yelled, as though he were calling across a vast cavern and not a six-foot-tall tunnel. His voice rebounded off the walls and rang in Donny's ears.

“Mornin’,” came Scottie’s voice. “Found us a couple of visitors.”

Six pairs of feet shifting the mud—his own, Gunner’s, Scottie’s, Otto’s, and two others. Two unwanted guests.

“Hello, boys,” said Gunner. “Just what in bleedin’ hell can we do for you?”

A scuffle, one of them likely detained in Scottie’s fists. “Tell this fuckin’ oaf to get his hands off me.” The voice was tremulous, rough.

“He only does that to people he fancies,” Gunner said casually. “What’re your names?”

“Dirk,” said that first voice. From farther down the tunnel, a smaller one said, “Warner.”

“Found guns in the backs of their trousers,” said Otto.

Donny could feel the silver in them from here, now protruding from the pockets of Otto’s overalls. Two small pistols. His mind reached for them.

“Now just what were you plannin’ on doin’ with those, eh?” Donny asked the men. “Was it to be a two-man raze?”

“We only wanted to *talk*,” Warner said, and Donny thought he might be younger, on the cusp of manhood. “Your men didn’t come at collection time.”

Donny shrugged. “They didn’t come to collect, ’cause there’s nothin’ we’re needin’.”

“Or they didn’t come ’cause you ain’t got a single ounce of bluff to trade,” said Dirk. There was a strangled sound, as though Scottie had gripped his throat a little tighter.

“Let him down, Scottie,” Gunner said. “For fuck’s sake, he’ll pop.”

A thwack of limbs in the mud. A groan.

Donny clicked his tongue. He pulled a damp cigarette from his pocket. “Now, didn’t we make it clear to your members that the bluff is bein’ allocated elsewhere?”

“Aye,” said Dirk. “And it ain’t what we agreed to. We need the bluff as much as anyone else.”

“Once the infirmaries clear up, we’ll send some down the line.”

"It ain't just us," Dirk continued. "The Union members in Hoaklin want to know when to expect the next trade. Same with Dorser and Trent." Dirk panted as he stood upright. "Trades ain't ever failed before."

"Times are hard," Gunner responded. "From each what they can give. To each what they need—"

"And we need it," Dirk spat. "We've fought just as hard, sacrificed just as much! If there's still bluff in Kenton Hill, then you're favorin' your own parish."

Gunner stepped forward then, his feet sloshing through the muck. Tension bloodied the air and turned it red. "A smart man," he said. "Would not utter the name again."

Warner cleared his throat, seemed to work his tongue around his fear. "We came to deliver a message. That's all."

"I love mail," Donny said. "A poem, I'll bet."

"The Northeastern contingent—Hesson, Dunnitch, Dorser, Hoaklin—have agreed to halt our trades with Ken—with the *Miners Union*," he faltered with Gunner bearing down on him, "until we see some evidence that any bluff remains in the brink."

With that came the flourish of paper. Thin, wispy. Newsprint, not parchment. It was snatched up and read aloud by Otto. "*National House of Belavere Trench celebrates as new Alchemist, and former leader of the Miners Union, Patrick Colson, forms alliance with new administration.*"

Quiet descended, damningly thick.

"The papers lie every day," Scottie said with a laugh. "You ought to know better than to believe swank gossip."

"You ain't got your Alchemist," said Dirk. "He's makin' idium for the House now. And you're leadin' us all along like fuckin' sheep, takin' from us what you can't repay!" He spat a gob into the mud. "There's a debt not settled. The Northerners won't trade until we know the facts. We want proof the Union is still operational."

Donny sighed inwardly, replacing his unlit cigarette back into his pocket. *It's come to this*, he thought. And then, *Forgive me, Patty.*

"Message received," Donny said with a smile. "And if you wouldn't mind sendin' my regards . . ." Here, he let his mind reach once more for those silver pistols in Otto's pockets. He felt the way they lifted in the air as though held by his own two hands. He felt the barrels and the muzzles and the smooth curve of the triggers. He pulled back the hammers on both in tandem and pointed them in the direction of Dirk and Warner.

The silver went in the direction his mind bid it, even if he couldn't see where. He imagined the hearts of Warner and Dirk, and knew that if he were to fire, the bullets would puncture them both.

Swank magic, he'd learned, was in the mind, not the eye.

"Tell your members in Dunnitch, and the ones in Hesson and Hoaklin and wherever else, that if it's proof they want, we'll gladly come show 'em."

He heard Warner stumble backward.

"God almighty," Dirk cursed.

"Don't shoot, *please*," Warner said, the words warbling off the walls.

"Shoot?" Donny said. "Now, why would I shoot a fellow Union member, eh? What kind of comrade would I be then?"

Donny pulled the sack from his shoulder and let it fall into the mud. The rifle muzzles within clacked together. Gunner followed suit.

"A gift," Donny said, kicking the sack in their direction. "Consider it an act of good faith."

Warner's feet hesitated. Dirk finally hauled up his awkward body and stood. Calculations ran taut in the quiet.

"You boys need any further demonstrations?" Gunner asked.

More silence. Donny heard the mechanics of their bodies, the air dragging through their teeth, the reproach of the canary. "We ain't short of ink," Donny finally said. "The Union is as operational as it ever was. But just so we understand each other, we don't take kindly to guests waltzin' down our tunnels." He let the two pistols drop to the floor with a wet slap.

"Thanks for comin', boys," Gunner said. "Take your partin' gifts with you."

"How will we know?" Dirk asked. "When the next trade is. We ain't received a single scribble."

Even from a distance, Donny thought he heard Otto's chest caving in on itself.

"No scribbles," Donny responded. "We'll send a telegraph the old way."

They left the Dunnitch men with Scottie and Otto, with a sense that the walls were closer. In his mind, Donny imagined the cold-rimmed edge of Patrick's old pocket watch, its cogs pushing the needle round a wheel, the seconds and minutes and hours ticking down to an eventual end. "What did he mean, Gun?" Donny asked. "What did he mean about a debt not settled?" Patrick never left a debt unpaid.

Gunner lagged. Eventually it wasn't him leading Donny, but the other way around. By the time they exited the pit, Donny was carrying half his weight.

"It's this fuckin' wound," Gunner was hissing between his teeth. "Keeps reopenin'."

Donny had the sudden, terrifying notion that without their father, and without Patrick, it was he who stood at the helm. Hot fear flooded his veins. He saw Kenton Hill then, colored in steel-gray, like iron bars. An apocalyptic city. He stumbled under Gunner's weight.

They practically tumbled down the hill and into town. Halfway to Main Street, they were intercepted by Sam and Isaiah. The dog licked at Donny's fingers. Sam had been looking after him in Patrick's absence, the two of them like orphans left to roam directionless without him.

"I can take him," Sam said, and Donny felt Gunner's weight leave his shoulders.

"Mrs. McCallister wants to know why she can't open her shop. She's requested a meetin' with you and Mrs. Colson. And Briggs said to tell you the trolley's righted. He can have it runnin' again by tomorrow, but there was a gas leak reported on the east side, near the brewery. He said the street ought to be evacuated while he takes a look."

Donny heard it as a barrage. But he nodded, swallowed. "Right. Yeah."

"Stop blatherin' and get me inside my pub," Gunner groaned. "I need a fuckin' drink."

Tess was waiting for them when they returned. Donny heard her pacing behind the bar, the crinkle of parchment. Sam deposited Gunner into a chair and departed with a feeble "Mornin', Mrs. Colson."

"Go do somethin' useful, lad," she said in response.

Donny bent his head to his chest for a moment before sitting. Patrick had done that a lot, conceded to the weight of his head for a moment before proceeding, as though needing a second of surrender.

"Well, they took the guns," Gunner started. "Not that they had much choice—"

"There's been a scribble," Tess interrupted.

Donny lifted his feet to a chair and stretched. "Ah, from one of my many lovers abroad, no doubt."

"No. No, it's . . ." This was a tone Donny had rarely heard her use. Tess Colson's voice was a deep river water, forcing over stones and overpowering the flight of fish, a great relentless push. But here, it had reduced itself. The words seemed to bank on her tongue.

Donny sat upright. "Who?"

In answer, Tess read aloud. "*Escaped and fled into the brink. John is alive. There's a lead on rock keeping us from home. Know that I'm finding a way back. Everythin' has its fix.*"

A cavern seemed to open up inside him, swelling the jacket of his rib cage. "Patty," he said, then stood and laughed aloud, his hand searching for Gunner's shoulder. "What'd I tell you!"

"It ain't signed," Tess said carefully, never daring to hope. "And I don't recognize the Scribbler's handwritin'."

"It's him, Ma!" Donny insisted. Between them, they'd referred to terranium as *rock* near untrusted ears. A code word. And he'd said, *Everythin' has its fix*. How many times had they all heard that in their household? Their father always singing it out when the problems shuffled in. He'd say it while patting Donny's shoulder, pushing yet another pair of makeshift spectacles over his deteriorating eyes. He'd said it until the problem of his sight was no longer a problem, but a conclusion.

"Dad," Gunner said, the same way he'd said it as a boy. "He's with him?"

Tess's teeth sucked at the edge of her lip. "I don't know," she said. "I don't know."

"That's what it says, Ma!"

"That don't mean it's *true*." She sounded close to the edge of her control. "We can't pin our hopes on it."

Bubbling up inside Donny, however, was a geyser of relief. "He's goin' after terranium," he said on an expelled breath. He slumped back in his chair and dashed his hands over his face, felt his eyes wheel in their sockets. "Thank fuckin' Idia."

"Goddamn Patty," Gunner was saying in wonderment. He coughed out a laugh. "That slippery little fucker."

Donny wondered, in a detached way, which Gunner longed for more, their brother or the bluff he'd surely bring with him. "And Dad," Donny said. "Holy god, Patty was right after all!"

"If that ain't cause for a drink, I don't know what else is!" Gunner brayed, slapping the table.

Tess slapped back in response, the reverberations of her hand sending quakes through their limbs. She heaved breaths like a thoroughbred, like a steam train. "We have the surroundin' parishes breathin' down our necks!" she said, a river churning up the bed once more. "We've got not nearly enough food in the market, houses to repair. It's not yet the middle of winter, and the Coal Works ain't got its foreman." Here, Donny felt Gunner shift, felt the air thin. "Everyone knows where we are now. *Everyone.* If you think those Dunnitch men will be the last headin' down the tunnel, you've got gas in your heads. We can't let 'em know we've run dry, or we're cut off. And for as long as we can convince 'em we've got bluff on the way, they'll come knockin' for it."

The parchment of the scribble crackled in her fist. "This ain't the fuckin' time to *celebrate*," she said slowly and clearly, as if they were both simple. "None o' that until Pat returns. *If* he returns. Until then, we're weak. Soon, everyone'll believe we're weak enough that they can kick in the door, take what they want—"

"Just let 'em fuckin' try," said Gunner.

"—and if we lift our boots off their necks now, more of 'em will come."

Her words hung in the air, and Donny swallowed them. That cavern of hope in his chest caved inward. But as always, he lifted his chin and fashioned himself a cocky smile. "He's comin' home, Ma. He's too stubborn not to," he said. "Dad, too."

But Tess was righting herself, pulling the parchment into the pocket of her apron. "Patty will do whatever's necessary," she said. "But if your father lives, Donny, I doubt we'll see him anytime soon." He heard her turn on her heel, heading for the kitchen. "He'll know better than to show his sorry face round these parts, unless he wants me breakin' it."

CHAPTER THIRTY

NINA

My elbow wedged into my own sternum, the bones there grinding against one another. Dirt seeped inward, clung to the inside of my nose and stifled the air.

Earth had a tendency to behave like water belowground. It threaded into every space, found impossible pathways, drowned its venturers.

I coughed, tried to find a remaining bit of power to push the dirt back, push it out of my lungs.

Bodies on every side of me, angular and unnatural. The blade of an arm, or a shin, or a foot at my back and sides. They were just more things pushing the oxygen from me, making it impossible to snatch it back in. In the back of my mind, a thought rose, that if this is what it was to be buried alive, then it was too slow.

But there was grunting, too. Grunting and breathing and shifting. A weight lifted from beneath me and on top of me. I inhaled like my head had breached water.

"Fuck!" came a voice. John Colson's.

Then another, Patrick's. "The pulley," he said. "Someone find it."

Slowly, I became aware that the angular bones at my back were rungs. Someone shifted and grunted in exertion. The sound of screeching metal accompanied it, followed by collision.

A lighter flickered—Patrick's, illuminating his own face, then the rest of us.

We were encased in a shaft lift, its metal cage closed, barring out clods of dirt and rock. Patrick bore down on me, held the light so close to my face I could feel its feeble warmth. "You're all right," he said, putting his hand against my sternum, reassuring me, or himself, perhaps, that my heart still beat. We were alive.

"Fuckin' damn it," John expelled, maneuvering himself hurriedly, his hands searching the walls. "Didn't I say it, Pat? The struts were too far apart. *Fuck.*"

Polly was gasping noisily for air. Theo was struck, it seemed, by the same thing I had been just moments ago, the sensation that we weren't dying by degrees, but somehow, miraculously, still alive.

Patrick stood upright. "Just breathe slow as you can," he said. "Try not to talk. We only got so much oxygen."

Immediately, Polly stopped breathing altogether.

The light petered out, and a moment later, I heard the slap of metal against metal, the chink of chains, the expelled exertion of John and Patrick as they heaved at something. They worked mechanically, as though operating on some sort of default, lifting us upward. *Any moment,* I thought. *Any moment, the chains will break. They'll lose their grip.*

But we jolted upward in increments, the smell of sweat permeating the air. In the dark, I felt we could have been moving sideways, or farther down, delivering ourselves to the heart of the earth.

They worked, alternating. Pull, pull, pull, for an impossible amount of time, until long after I measured a human capable. The air grew thin. I couldn't seem to fish enough oxygen out of it.

An almighty heave, a final shout of exertion from Patrick, from some supernatural reservoir of strength, and the lift collided—or bottomed out, it was difficult to distinguish. I felt, with a narrowing awareness, that I was only halfway there.

"All o' you," John panted. "Get up," he said. "All hands."

There were the sounds of our scrambling, the feel of a hand around my wrist, pulling it toward something, flattening my fingers against a cool metal ridge. "Dig your fingers in," Patrick said. "Pull it apart." And even his voice had begun to err toward a void, reduced to gasps.

"Give it all you got," said John.

Shoulders clashed against mine, all five of us jammed together, and we worked to pry apart the doors. A memory surfaced: Patrick and I in a collapsing mine. *The gate jams in a collapse*, he'd said.

We're stuck, I thought. *We'll all die here in a shared tomb.*

I felt rendered useless, my body no match for the weight of the door.

But then, a whisper of something on my throat. Air, trickles of it. Then light.

Another jolt, another growl of exertion, and the doors shuddered back an inch. My hands fed all the way through and gripped the sides.

We were washed in oxygen and light, made delirious by it. I threw every ounce of weight against the door and heard the others do the same.

Like the jaws of a beast relinquishing, the doors shuddered apart, and one at a time we spilled out onto our fronts, breaths rattling, wailing through our chests.

Polly shook beside me, her ribs against my forearm. She might have been weeping or exalting.

"Till the light comes, Patty," I thought I heard John pant out. His face marred in sweat, in mud. He slapped his son on the back twice, the two of them staring at each other, then somehow, laughing. Falling into great, chest-rattling fits.

"Can't imagine . . . anything . . . less funny," panted Theodore on all fours, trying and failing to stand.

"Try this one then, Teddy," John said in response. "What d'you call a swank in a hole?"

Theodore frowned.

"A good fuckin' start."

Theodore stood, then leaned to touch his fingertips over my knuckles. "Cl—Nina?" he said breathlessly. "Can you stand?"

I blinked grit from my eyes, nodded, then let him pull me up. He did the same for Polly.

"Where are we?" Theo asked now, blinking out into the gray light. The pit exit loomed a short way ahead, the climb abruptly ending with that circle of merciful sun.

"Trent," Patrick said, his eyes homing in on Theo's hand, still wrapped around mine. "We're in Trent."

When last I'd ventured into Trent, it was bustling with industry, heavy convoys of wagons and steam carts packed with tree logs. The roads in and out of town clogged with farming Crafters, the landscape heavily wooded and dotted with livestock, but peppered by police.

When I pointed this out to Patrick, he said, "Nowhere to go but out."

We came aboveground in the outskirts to find it unrecognizable. The woods were stripped of foliage and blackened, the trunks crumpled, half their size—some fire Charmer's doing. Snow piled the forest floor. The cold rushed in from the distant mountains, and without the windbreakers of pine and spruce and birch, it stole my breath. Sheep stood unperturbed, the thick wool of their coats overgrown, but there were no fences to contain them now. No Crafters to herd them.

We journeyed a road into Trent by foot, passing a boundless grave of tree stalks, the necks craning. We never passed a single soul. I reasoned that the weather was too cold, though I suspected something far more horrible.

"Razed to holy hell," John said unnecessarily, passing a broken wagon, its bed heaped in snow. "When did the army march in?"

"Couldn't say," Patrick frowned, concern marring every inch of his face as he took in the surroundings. "Must be recent. I never received word before we left Kenton."

"Aye. Well, let's see who's left."

The town proper was made of wide lanes, big enough for tree logging carts. The roads were made of tar and stuck underfoot in the summer, easily ploughed in the winter, yet Trent was mired in fresh snow. Not a single set of footprints in sight.

Signs of conflict seemed stark against the white canvas of it. The brick exterior of Trent's largest timber mill crumbled into the street. A coal bin had overturned and spilled. Most windows had buckled outward from fire.

"You think any made it to the tunnel?" John asked Patrick, kicking over a stray boot, half buried. "Maybe they're all holed up in the next parish."

Patrick looked doubtful. "I hope so."

I shared his doubt. I suspected that beneath all the snow, blood stained the tar.

In the distance, toward the center of the town, a single chimney coughed into the gray sky, the only sign of life.

"There," I said, pointing to the smoke. "You see it?"

And Patrick let out sigh of relief, nodded. "Let's go introduce ourselves, shall we?"

"You'll be doing no such thing," came a voice from behind us, and I whirled to the sight of Theodore looking stricken, an arm pressed tightly around his throat, his feet slipping from beneath him.

And a woman at his back, the filleting knife in her hand poised near Theo's ribs, resignation written all over her. "You'll stay right where you are and go no further."

There were voids beneath her eyes, a cracked tooth in her mouth. A bruise on her chin had yellowed her brown skin. She couldn't have been older than thirty, though she spoke with authority. She handled the knife like she knew how to use it.

Patrick raised his hands cautiously, placatingly, but it was John who said, "Afternoon, miss." His voice was carefully modulated, the way one would coax a spooked horse. "Before you kill us, at least let me introduce—"

"I know who you are," she said, throat bobbing. "Your face is all over the bulletins. All over the papers. You're the new Alchemist from Kenton Hill," she said to Patrick, then her eyes skirted to mine. "And she's the earth Charmer. You're said to be workin' for the House now."

“We’re Union,” Patrick said immediately. “And we escaped.”

“Then you’ll surely bring the infantry after you,” the woman said, voice wobbling. She looked over one shoulder, as though she might find them marching up from between the skeletons of trees.

“Looks like they’ve been and gone,” John said. It wasn’t unkind.

The woman’s eyes glossed over. A tear fell. “They can’t be beaten,” she said hopelessly. “There’s too many of ’em, and their fire Charmers—” Her lips pressed together, suppressing a sob. She sobered and pulled Theo in tighter. “We need bluff,” she said, eyes leveling Patrick’s. It struck me how courageous she must be, to look in the eye of a man and make demands, while holding a knife to another. Completely alone.

Patrick shook his head. “There’s none to be found in the brink. The infantry took the Union’s stores.”

“Liar,” she spat. “Word is, Kenton’s keepin’ it for themselves. Fuckin’ *speck* of a town.” She shook her head. A lie. “The Union is done,” she said. “It’s every parish for themselves now.”

Patrick’s eyes touched the woman’s collarbone, where a cut had barely scabbed over, to the bruising, the tears in her eyes, the point of the knife. There was calculation on his face, but there was sorrow, too. There was guilt. “I can’t give you bluff. But I can send for coal and rations. Perhaps some medical supplies.”

“We called for it already, sent countless messages down the tunnels.” She laughed mirthlessly, blinking furiously against the tears. “There ain’t anyone on the other end answerin’.”

“But you need it, don’t you?” Patrick said patiently. “Whoever you’ve got holed up here still, I imagine they’re too wounded to have escaped with the rest.” He looked to the woods and pastures, blackened to ash. “Soon there’ll be nothin’ to eat. No heatin’. Even your strongest will grow weak. It’s just a matter of time. It’ll mean a dead winter for you all.”

At the mention of a dead winter, the woman’s expression became sallow.

Patrick grimaced. “But I’m guessin’ there’s already a heap of dead somewhere, still waitin’ to be buried.” Patrick’s eyes fell to the woman’s hands, which were cracked and blistered, grubby with dirt. "Bet the ground was difficult to break. It's near frozen. Bet you resorted to incineratin' 'em, religion be damned."

The woman shuddered delicately.

Patrick turned to the smoke spiraling out of the single chimney. "You'll run out of bodies to burn eventually. And it will feel like a relief, at first. And then the temperature will keep droppin', and you'll wish you had a few of 'em back. It'll feel like a curse."

The woman sobbed. She wobbled on the sleet, and Theo winced as the blade glanced skin.

I imagined this woman trying in vain to break the earth to bury her dead. How long she must have persevered to ruin her hands that way. "I can help you," I told her, my own eyes pricking. "I can give them proper graves."

The woman winced, her eyes searching my face.

"This is the leader of the Miners Union," Patrick said, gesturing to his father. "And this woman is a Scribbler. Whatever you need, we can have it sent quickly. And in several weeks, I'll come callin' again, only it'll be bluff I'm deliverin'. More than you'll need. Enough to bring everyone back to health."

She laughed again in that deadened way. "You say there's no bluff, then promise it anyway? Which is it?"

"We have a lead on some terranium," Patrick said. "And when we find it, the House and its infantry won't stand a fuckin' chance."

The woman seemed distrustful, but she didn't immediately reject the offer, either. Beneath her ferocity was desperation.

"We ain't dead yet," Patrick added, stepping closer. "I promise you that."

Her chin wobbled. The knife fell away by degrees. "There ain't any bluff left?" she asked, voice still guarded.

"No. But there will be." Patrick sounded so sure, so convincing. It was difficult not to believe. "In abundance. And in the meantime, you'll have coal to burn from Kenton. I can have food transported from Hoaklin and Dunnitch. We only ask for a day or two here."

She was hesitating now, the need outweighing her caution. Her arm slackened on Theo's neck, then slowly fell away.

The woman tipped her head to the sky and worked to control her breaths. "Idia help us," she said.

Theo stumbled to the ground, cursing.

"What's your name?" Patrick asked.

"Edith," she said, her cheeks wet now, mottled by the frigid air.

"Edith," Patrick repeated. "How many are left?"

"A hundred n' forty livin'." Her whole body was shaking, like the blasts still tolled through her. Trent had been a population of more than three thousand. "The rest ran to Sommerland, or they're dead."

"I'm sorry," Patrick said, but not in the way of condolences. This was self-blame. Failure. I watched it anchor itself to him.

"Take us to 'em, miss," John said now. "I'd like to shake the hands of the stubborn bastards who outlasted the Lords' fuckin' Army."

Edith laughed wetly at that, her breaths clouding before her.

"Put that knife away now," John told her softly. "The fight's come and gone."

Edith took us to a factory, a sign above its great doors reading BLEAKER'S TEXTILES. The space inside was dense with giant iron machinery, all of it unmanned, unnaturally still, but untouched by fire. Starlings swarmed the rafters high above, escaping the cold. Settled on the floor, between the threading machines and the washers, were a series of pallets.

Men and women lay atop them, gray-faced, their injuries many. One man's face was so bloodied it was difficult to tell if there was anything to salvage beneath.

Moving among the injured with broth, blankets, bandages, and water was an army of women. Some sported injuries of their own, like Edith, but all worked on the wounded like a living engine.

"Where are the men?" Polly asked quietly, her mouth agape.

Edith eyed her with contempt. "Gone," she said, her gaze trailing to the man with the butchered face. "Or half gone." She led us on. There was hardly a single person who lifted their face to look at us. Their hands were too full to care.

Edith walked with slow, weighted steps to the rear of the factory, then out a small creaking door to a ravine. Beyond it was a fast-moving river threading through the trees, eroding the snow on its banks, churning the mill wheels to no avail.

Lined on the ravine's edge was an endless row of bodies, a hundred or more. Only their blackened feet showed. Each one was covered with a fibrous blanket, snowfall piling in the creases of their torsos and necks, care taken to offer them some dignity.

Not even the crisp winter air could completely hide the smell of death.

"We can't bring 'em inside," Edith said, her eyes glazed and focused on nothing, as though shutting out the sight. "They foul too quickly."

Polly doubled over and vomited, coughing violently onto the ground.

"Lord almighty," John uttered, and swiped the hat off his head.

Patrick simply stared, his eyes hardening, jaw ticking. Eventually he wiped a hand over his face and shifted his stare to the river, the trees beyond. "All Union members?"

Edith tracked a small swallow leaving its nest, born too late. It swooped dangerously close to the river before alighting. "We all were," she said. "And a fat load of good it did us." Her eyes closed and didn't open. I wondered how long it had been since she'd rested.

Patrick stared and stared, something wretched in his expression.

"What provoked this?" Theo asked. He stood just over my shoulder. From this close, I could hear the way his voice shook, the stop-start of his breaths.

"I did," Patrick said bluntly, his eyes trailing over the boots, the ashy toes. "We encouraged strike action in the Southeastern parishes through winter, to cut off the city."

"And we listened," Edith mumbled bitterly, her voice fracturing. "Like fools."

Patrick's hands went to his hips, as though he could hardly bear his own weight, then he rubbed his eyes once, twice, thinking.

"Polly, scribble to Donny. Tell him Trent has been attacked and ask for supplies. Food, coal, medical aid. Whatever can be spared should be spared. Call on support from Dunnitch. Make sure he knows it's me."

But John stepped forward, just as Polly nodded and closed her eyes. "Now just a minute, son. They've got enough of their own to tend to back home. Kenton took its own losses."

Patrick barely spared him a glance. "They've got enough in reserve."

"Patty—"

"Polly," Patrick said, taking a step toward the ravine. "Send the message. Tell Donny the Morland tunnel is caved in, they'll need to use the Sommerland line. And for the love of God, don't leave a trace of yourself on the page."

Polly winced but nodded.

"It will take another three days for it to come through the tunnels," Patrick told Edith. "Someone should be waiting on the other side when it arrives. Preferably not with a carvin' knife."

Edith nodded. "What about the bluff?"

"You'll have it," Patrick said, with a confidence plucked from the sky. "I'll ensure it comes. And in the meantime, I assume there are at least a few coppers here who remained."

Edith wiped her hands down her front, fingers shaking. "They evacuated before the army got here. A few came sauntering back in once the fires died out." She looked once more to those bodies lined neatly on the slope of the ravine, and her eyes turned hard, bitter. "They're holed up in the trading post with a few cases of port, last I saw."

John and Patrick traded glances.

"We'll pay 'em a short visit," John assured her. "In return, we need to hunker down a night or two."

Edith nodded her assent. "I need to go and help the rest," she muttered, wiping her nose on her sleeve. She turned and used whatever vestiges of strength remained to drag herself inside.

At first, we five remained, but the snow had begun to fall, and the air bit at our skin, and the wall of corpses became impossible to look at.

"We've earned a bit of rest," John said decidedly, somberly. "We'll recoup for a bit." He pulled a flask from his pocket and took a thorough swig. He held it out to Theo as he passed. "Here, kid. That'll pump the blood."

Theo accepted it and turned his eyes away gratefully, and Polly followed. They needed no other prompt to flee from the dead.

"No rest for you, swank," John said to Polly, slapping the Stewards' book against her sternum. "While we're here, you've got some readin' to do."

Polly pressed a retort between her lips and followed the men inside.

Then it was only Patrick and me, too disturbed to look away from the line of shrouds.

"Nina," Patrick said, and he said it as though it were a lifeline. His throat bobbed. He didn't dare look at me.

I watched the valleys of his expression, the reds in his eyes straining. What was once startingly blue now appeared a bleak gray. "I don't want to ask—"

"You're not asking, Patrick. I'm just doing it."

His gaze was torturous.

I made to move around him toward that first sheet. Something stopped me.

Patrick's hand taking mine. Not pulling, but simply holding it for a moment, his rough fingers encasing my own.

I looked back to find his eyes had closed. He breathed through his mouth in great puffs, gripped onto me like he was clinging to a ledge.

I waited there, unmoving, watching parts of him crack, then knit themselves back together.

A lark cried. His eyelids snapped open. Our hands retracted.

He watched there in the cold while I worked, his hair dusted in snow as I buried the bodies, the earth giving way beneath each and swallowing them whole.

CHAPTER THIRTY-ONE

PATRICK

In the first cold squalls of night, Patrick and his father left Bleaker's Textiles.

They adjusted their coats, their hats, eyes pinched against the cold, and stepped out onto the vacant road, boots sinking as they went. Farther into town, a lone chimney sent curling smoke skyward. Without speaking, they walked in its direction.

Three coppers, Edith had told them. Sent, no doubt, to ensure the post, the police house, and the swank residences weren't looted. After all, those buildings were Artisan-owned.

"What will you do?" Nina had asked him, watching him pull on warmer attire, no doubt from some dead lad's wardrobe.

He'd watched the flecks in her eyes distend. "Better I don't put words to it."

"You'll kill them?"

"Yes."

"I want to come," she said to John and Patrick both.

Patrick sighed. He could see the hunger pulsing behind her eyes, that yawning gulf in her heart again. The way she clamored to fill it. He had a heart to match.

Riddled through, the both of them.

"Not this time," he said. He wanted to explain how these coppers would cry and plead and piss themselves. How they'd reduce to the feeblest creatures. How the look on their faces as they died would dig themselves into the trenches of her brain, drudged up in dreams a year from now, ten years from now. "It ain't your beast to slay," he said instead.

"But it's yours?"

"It is," he said. He was a Colson. The Miners Union was his business.

"I need you to stay with Polly," he'd said then. Polly had found a desk in the back offices. She was bent over *The Stewards' Testament* and a stack of blank parchment.

Edith had given the rest of them blankets and assigned them a corner to keep to. They were handed bowls of stew by a young woman who carried a baby in a sling. She doled out the food with a blank expression, as though they were just more mouths to feed.

Patrick had given his meal to Nina. "Eat mine," he said, then hesitated, his fingers brushed up against hers, and he felt the charge running over her skin. "Every lord, and every minister," he reminded her. "They'll all be beneath the heel of your boot soon."

Then he left, feeling as though he was shedding one skin and taking on another. Transforming from man to wolf beneath the moon.

The fire Charmers had left the town center untouched, as was their habit. Still, ash stuck to the brick, the sills, the gables. The shingles and gutters were black with it. Through the window of the squat trading post, candlelight flickered.

Patrick and his father came to a standstill before it, puffs of breath beating out, their hands winding into their coats and taking an inventory. Revolver, rope, kerosene.

John shook out his arms like he was shaking off cobwebs. "Let's see if they bite," he said.

What most didn't understand about the wolf was that it stalked the night in a perfunctory way. It mauled for its territory, no matter the neck. It tore flesh from bone without much relish; hardly any meat was taken for itself.

The door kicked off its latch easily, punched into the wall with the sound of a gunshot.

And already, they wailed.

Three coppers, just as Edith promised. All in their navy uniforms, their Belavere emblems, waistcoats unbuttoned and guts overhanging their belts. They flailed in their chairs. Their limbs, for a moment, taking flight from their bodies. One fell right off his chair, his mouth holed open, teeth wine-tinged.

Another shouted, scattered the playing cards he was holding. The third had the wherewithal to reach for a vacant holster.

But their guns, all three of them, lay strewn on the oak countertop, where the Crafters would normally line up for an hour or more to give over more than half their stock, their harvest, their textiles.

"Not on your life," John said as one of the men made to move toward it. John cocked the hammer of his own gun, lifted it lazily by his waist. "Take your seats, boys."

Slowly, the mush of their brains finding order again, they resumed their seats, bodies turned toward Patrick and John. One of them held his hands up.

"We're Belavere officers," another blithered, the last refrains of a desperate man. "You can't do this! They'll come for you."

"That's the trouble with you coppers," John said, taking rope from his pocket. "Got a short fuckin' memory." He threw his gun to Patrick, who caught it, moved toward the man closest. "You're a swank's guard dog now, but you were born a Crafter. And just when has the House ever lifted its head to the likes of us, eh?" He tied the first man's wrists to his chair. "One more dead Crafter in the brink don't mean nothin' to 'em."

"They'll hang you," another spat, but his great teeth chattered in his head. "They'll hang both you bastards!"

"A quick death," Patrick said in return. "Nothin' like the ones about to happen here tonight."

The copper shriveled. John grabbed his wrist, but the man yanked it back and tried to stand.

A shot rang out, blistered the insides of Patrick's ears, but the bullet sailed where he'd meant it, right into the copper's shin, and the man fell, squealing and flailing.

"Nowhere to run, boys," he said. "This is where it ends for you. May as well speak with your God now and make peace with him."

John pulled the man, crying now, back onto the chair, tied his hands behind his back.

"I always wonder," Patrick said as the last copper was tied to his chair, "what goes through a man's head when he walks through his town, sees it burnin', sees the kids in the street dyin', and doesn't lift a finger."

They all three sat shaking so much that their noses ran, the tendons of their neck seeming to break through the skin.

Patrick went to the copper closest and held a gun between his eyes. "How black is the soul of a man who lets his townspeople burn?"

"*Please,*" he begged. Always, at the end, they begged.

"Unfortunately for you, boys, I've got my own blackened soul." Patrick stepped back. He put his gun in his coat, took the three from the countertop, and stowed those away, too.

John pulled a canister of kerosene from his pocket and poured the contents over their card table and the floorboards beneath their feet. Patrick struck a match. "For Trent," Patrick told them. "By dusk, our work is done."

Patrick did not follow his father back into Bleaker's Textiles. He knew there would be no sleep for him. It was a kind of penance, he thought, that even bone-deep weariness wasn't enough to let him rest on nights like this.

He stayed out in the cold, his back against the outer factory wall. In his mind, he imagined the route from Trent to Sommerland. From Sommerland to Kenton Hill. He calculated the transit, estimated the number of injured who would die in this factory in the coming days. He devised plans to get supplies here faster. He had contacts in Baymouth he could reach out to. He could—

Boots ground into snow, and Patrick looked up to see Nina sneaking out into the night, sliding back the factory door.

Patrick sighed. He couldn't explain the quiver of relief that burned through him in that moment.

Her eyes fell to his hands, currently pilfering his own pockets to no avail. He hadn't been aware of it until that moment. "What are you looking for?" she asked.

Snow was catching in her hair, in her eyelashes. "A cigarette."

She should be sleeping. She'd spent hours in the cold burying corpses. She'd walked miles and miles underground and almost been buried alive. Instead, she was assessing him, rose lips slightly parted, slender eyebrows pinched. She crossed her arms over her chest and dipped her head against the cold. "I should like to take a walk."

Patrick scoffed tiredly. "No, you shouldn't."

But she shrugged, wrapped her borrowed coat tighter around her, and abruptly set off. She looked back over her shoulder at Patrick as she passed him. "Are you coming?"

"Nope."

"Suit yourself," she said, and marched off into the dark, disappearing around the corner.

"Damn it, woman," Patrick hissed between his teeth.

He shouldn't follow. Lord knew he shouldn't follow.

"Fuck me," he muttered, shaking his head.

He found her again in a smoker's hole. Kenton Hill factories didn't bother with such things, but he supposed in a textile factory, the masters wouldn't want their fabric stinking of tobacco and ash. The workers would come to this outer shed in the winter. It kept out the snow and the wind enough to light a cigarette, though not enough to keep out the chill.

Nina sat on a bench within, discarded newsprint at her side. On it, the headline read *Union Trades Alchemist for Earth Charmer's Clemency*. Nina frowned at it.

"I would have, you know," he said, leaning against the doorframe.

She looked up at him. "Would have what?"

"Traded myself if it meant keepin' you from the whip."

Her eyes shone star-bright. "Why?"

He considered his answer carefully. "I've seen you bleed enough," he said, his eyes slipping to her arms. "Don't think I could watch it again."

She looked down at her feet. "Are you pretending you can't stomach the sight of blood?"

"Not yours," he said observationally. He didn't look at her as he said it, only stayed leaning against that frame, affecting an air of indifference he didn't feel. "Some walk," he quipped.

By way of reply, she held up a single white papered cigarette. "Thought the night called for it," she said. "Take it."

Patrick's head tilted. "And just where did you get your hands on that?"

"In the coat Tamir gave me." Her other hand opened to reveal a matchbox.

Patrick shook his head and took it from her, but didn't light it. He sat in the seat beside her, throwing the newsprint to the floor, and their shoulders brushed.

It was dark in the shed, but the smoker's hole had windows and a wide-open door. The night had turned clear, periwinkle, silent in a way Kenton Hill never was. He now craved the endless rumble of home.

At his side, Nina rubbed her arms, nodded to the stars. "That's Neveretti's Cross," she said softly, in a way that drew Patrick's attention to her lips rather than the constellations. "Do you know the story of Neveretti?"

Patrick put the cigarette between his lips. "Somethin' tells me I'm about to."

She rolled her eyes, and for a moment, they were back in that city courtyard, legs crossed, her explaining the world to him like the meaning of it all was obvious. "Neveretti was a man of the sea," she began, "and every day he stood on the shore and prayed that the waves wouldn't flood his village. His people watched the water come right up to the banks, then retreat, and believed Neveretti was a messenger of God. They called him the Keeper of the Sea. Each day, Neveretti would pray for the waves to retreat, and every day they did. He would return home to his wife, his daughter, and his bird."

"His *bird*?"

"Do you want to hear the rest of the story or not?"

Despite himself, Patrick grinned. "Go on, then."

"One day, Neveretti did not go to the shore, and he didn't pray."

"I'll bet his wife was relieved," Patrick said.

Nina smirked but otherwise ignored him. "He'd been too ill to rise from bed, and so the waves breached the banks and swept into the village. They carried his wife, his daughter, and the caged bird out to sea. Neveretti blamed himself and went to save them. He was the strongest swimmer in the village, after all. Who else would save them, if not him? He found his wife first, taking her on his back. Then he swam further and found the bird in its cage.

"Last, he found his daughter, but when he turned around, he was too far from the shore. The weight of all he carried impeded him, and together they drowned.

"When he arrived in hell, Neveretti was confused. He began listing all the good he had done in his life. He told the devil that he had tried to save his wife from the water, and the Devil replied, 'Your wife could swim.' Next, Neveretti claimed he had tried to save his bird. But the Devil replied, 'The bird could fly.' Last, Neveretti fell to his knees and cried out the name of his daughter. 'Your daughter,' said the Devil, 'was already dead, and yet by trying to save her, you drowned them all.'

"In a final bid for salvation, Neveretti said, 'I am the Keeper of the Sea, and I protected my people from the waves for as long as I could.' But the devil shook his head and said, 'The tide ebbs and flows without you, by the will of God, and you are no god.'"

Patrick watched the frost of Nina's breath dissipate with that final sentence and waited. "Horrible bloody story," he muttered, pulling the cigarette from his mouth again. He had yet to light it.

"My mother used to tell me that one," Nina said conversationally. "Among others."

Patrick saw again the noose, the lever, the woman on the platform who looked so much like the woman at his side. The laughter bubbling in his throat turned abruptly to ash. "I'm sorry."

"Don't be."

"Are you about to liken me to Neveretti?"

"Neveretti was an imbecile. I'm sure you know better than to think yourself a god."

Patrick sighed. "There ain't a god. Just a world full of terrible people."

She nodded, and once she might have disparaged Patrick his lack of faith, but he believed the past months had peeled all charity from her bones. Perhaps now, she was fated to be as cynical as he was.

Lord, he hoped not.

"I'd agree with you, but I've found there's still some good in it." It was whisper-soft, and her eyes did not turn to Neveretti's Cross or to the crumbling main street. They turned up to Patrick as though he were the map of stars.

Patrick raised his eyebrows. "A gangster?"

She shook her head, tilted it. "No, he's just a man, I'm afraid."

Patrick turned the cigarette over his fingers once more, then threw it to the ground, stamped it into the snow. He knew she hated the smell. "I'm not half good enough, Nina," he said. "And if there is a hell, one day I'll be takin' my place in it, right beside Neveretti and his fuckin' bird."

Nina reached up and touched his forehead, sinking the pads of her fingers into the creases. "Does blaming yourself for the deaths of all these Crafters help them?" she asked, and the words struck a chord in Patrick's chest, as though she'd reached in and plucked it. "Does it save you from all the bad you think you've done?"

"I'm not lookin' for salvation."

"You didn't kill the people here, Patrick. Nor the people in Kenton Hill, or Dorser, or Hesson—"

"But somethin' could have been done. There's always somethin' to be done."

"Why should it fall on you?"

"Because it *has* to," Patrick answered. "He left it all up to me."

"Who? John?"

"Yes."

She blustered. "Your father isn't exactly a beacon of virtue."

"But he's my father just the same." Patrick said it calmly. He didn't expect her to understand the tangles of the Colson web, and why should she? She'd swallowed that idium and left her own father behind. How to explain to her that you could both love and hate a man, a place, a purpose, in equal amount? "He left the Union in my charge, and look at what I've done with it." His hands balled, though he didn't mean for them to. "I fell for Tanner's scheme. I invited Polly in, and now it's all in pieces. The Lords' Army will keep on burnin' and razin', and there won't be a choice but to break their strikes, give over their goods, return to the mines and factories, because there ain't anythin' else to turn to. Without the Union, there's no tip-offs, no guns, no bluff. No way to protect themselves. That's what I've done."

Nina looked as though she might cry, and Lord, he hated to see it. He lifted a hand to her cheek, swiped his thumb over the freckles there. "I accepted the responsibility," he said. "So I accept the blame, too."

Nina's eyes blurred with tears, and she shook her head. "This is Tanner's fault. Shop's fault."

"Perhaps," Patrick allowed. "But they're only doin' what the powerful do when the lowly rise up. You can't start a revolution without plannin' for the downfall. And I didn't plan for this. I didn't plan for you."

Her nose had turned pink from the cold, her eyelashes wet. Her chill-burned lips opened slightly. A moment of hesitation. "Am I the downfall?" she asked, and it was delicate, like she expected the answer to come out spitting, swinging at her.

He could see how easily she would take the burden from him, how she would foster blame that wasn't hers, and fill up that hole with it. He couldn't let her. He couldn't stand to watch the slow collapse of her lovely face, turning in on itself, hating herself. He wouldn't let that happen.

The blame would remain his own.

So, he scoffed. "A girl from Scurry who can't box?" he tsked. "A pain in the arse at most."

Her lip quirked. "Broke my thumb once," she admitted. "Couldn't have been older than ten."

Patrick wasn't surprised. He'd seen her form. She punched like she was only thinking about it. "And the victim?"

"A boy from school," she grinned. "Arlo. Used to call me Ninny Nina."

Patrick whistled. "Deserved. A no-good villain."

"He put ants in my hair, too," she recalled.

"Ah, probably he was in love."

She scowled at Patrick. "He had a funny way of showing it."

"Most of us do." He considered her for a moment, then stood. "Get up."

She looked up from her frozen position on the bench. "Why?"

Patrick took off his coat and cap. "So you can learn to throw a punch like you mean it."

She frowned. "You want me to punch you?"

He rolled his eyes. "Don't act like it wouldn't bring you a little satisfaction."

"I don't think it would," she mused. "In fact, you might be the only person I *don't* want to punch."

"That's just my charm distractin' you," he said, taking her hand and pulling her upright. "Didn't have no problems throwin' fists at me in Kenton. Put 'em up."

She looked a little incredulous. Her eyes glanced over his shoulders. "You'll freeze."

"That's the first rule in a fight," he said. "Don't freeze."

She let out a sigh and shook off her coat, as he had, shivering. For once, her hair wasn't pinned back. It lay loose around her collar.

She looked painfully beautiful this way: pink-nosed, curls wild, her borrowed blouse too big for her, slipping down slightly over one shoulder. She pushed the sleeve up.

"Widen your stance," Patrick said. "One foot in front, one behind."

She lifted her skirt to see her boots, then planted her feet.

"Dukes up, in front of your chin."

She held limp fists close to her face, elbows tucked tightly into her body.

"Lord almighty," he said, and he took one of her fists in his grasp and pried the fingers back. He pulled her thumb free, touched each delicate knuckle. "Never tuck your thumb, Nina. No wonder you broke it."

"Hurt like hell," she recalled, looking at his fingers too long. Swallowing. Without exception, being this close to her invaded his senses, tripped his self-control. He backed away. "Did you leave a bruise, at least?"

"Not even a shadow."

Patrick groaned. "It's a miracle you made it out alive."

"I can land a fair kick," she grinned. "Kick a boy in the groin and you don't need fists." Her eyes traveled south, below his belt.

He resisted the urge to wince. "Can't argue with that," he said. "Though I'll warn you. Try and sneak one in, and I'll pin you down."

Her eyes flared.

Damn it. Where was that line he'd drawn?

Patrick held his hands up, swallowing the rush of desire that had pooled in his mouth. "Give it all you've got."

She breathed, then reeled back and threw a fist into his waiting palm. It wasn't so terrible. But he was a man of very little discipline, apparently, so he rolled his eyes and said, "A wet fish would slap harder."

She gasped, huffing into the cold air, and lifted her fists again. The next blow was a little heavier. Enough to rattle teeth if it landed on someone's jaw. But she was too easy to rile up. And it was too easy for Patrick to fall back into this temptation. "Would it help to picture Arlo instead of me?" he said.

She punched again, grunting. "Keep talkin', and it'll be inspiration enough."

And there was the slip, back into that tongue she'd had when he'd met her. He hid a grin.

Another punch. This time, he caught her hand and threw it away. "Ah, come on, Scurry girl. I know you got some of that Eastern blood in you somewhere."

This time, she advanced before he put his hand up, and he had to lean away to avoid her fist. She advanced again, this time aiming for his jaw. He had to block it. "Whoa."

Her leg kicked out, her boot aiming for his groin. He hit it away, smiling, and had her wrapped up in the next second, colliding against the inner walls of the smoker's hole, one of her wrists trapped in his hand and pinned beside her head. The other caught between his chest and hers. His arm all the way around her waist.

The tin walls rattled threateningly, and all the breath punched out of her. Her eyes were wide with surprise, then unshrouded humor.

"The last rule is to not tell the man you're fighting that you'll kick him in the groin. Otherwise, he'll know to anticipate it."

He watched the planes of her face, the flakes of snow stuck in her hair, lips turned upward in a smile that couldn't last. After a few moments, it descended again. A sinking raft. Nothing, not even he, could hold her afloat for long.

She let her forehead fall to his chest, giving in to gravity. She gasped in and out, her whole body slackening. She was all around him, and he all around her.

Patrick made himself retract. He dropped her waist, let her hand fall from his grasp. He stepped away from her and cleared his throat.

His mind churned with indecent images of all the things he could do to her here. Now. He turned his back to scrub his face.

His heart hammered, blood washed his veins, and he almost turned back. Almost.

"You were wrong before," she said from behind him.

He stilled.

"You said I didn't trust you. But I did. You were—you *are*—the only person I trust."

She didn't move, and neither did he. Better that he remained facing away, where the sight of her couldn't overthrow him.

"But I didn't plan for you, either."

He sucked in a breath. No, she hadn't planned for it. They were both cogs in a machine neither of them had much control over. Faulty parts trying to change things.

"But I know I wouldn't have fallen for you if not for your heart."

He turned slowly, raised his eyebrows mockingly. "My heart?"

"Yes," she said, obstinate. "It's in there. I saw it."

"Bet it weren't a pretty picture."

She sighed. "You're not nearly as wretched as you think you are."

"You don't know the half of it, Scurry girl," he told her. "You only know what I could stomach tellin' you."

"Then tell me," she said, stepping toward him. Imploring him. "You think I'll flinch? Tell me what you did to those coppers."

"Burned them alive," he relented, his voice now ice.

To her credit, she didn't flinch. Instead, a wildness came over her. He thought she was seeing, once more, those hundreds of corpses waiting in the snow. "I hope it was slow," she said. "I hope they felt every second of it."

The ground beneath their feet gave the softest of tremors. She eyed the newsprint discarded on the ground, and her breath pulsed out in clouds. "They should all burn."

He felt caught up, suddenly, in that same fervency. A longing to descend into the madness of it with her.

Her eyes were closing. She was pacing in a tight circle now, shaking out her arms. He took several steps in her direction but stopped short of her.

"Sometimes I want to tear off my own skin," she said, tipping her head back, snatching cold air into her lungs. "I feel so angry."

"You sound like a miner."

"How do you tolerate it?" She was practically begging for an answer, pulling at her own clothes like they were suffocating her.

"Booze," said Patrick. "Brawling. Sex. Whatever takes the edge off."

She looked up at him, urgency flooding her. Intent.

And goddamn if his cock didn't side with her, but Patrick forced himself to shake his head. "Ah, don't look at me like that, Scurry girl. That's not what I meant."

She bit her lip, and he suffused a groan. She came close enough to touch his chest, to run one torturous hand over his shirt and up to his collar, then the other. Sense had flown her body. "And if I begged you?" she said, her mouth closing in on his. Erringly close. And already his lips were parting. His cock pulsed painfully. He held himself as still as he could and closed his eyes.

But she was all around him.

"Please," she said, her body vibrating. He felt the stiff peaks of her nipples rub against his chest and he imagined teasing them, running her to the edge with just that touch alone.

She looked up at him once more, her hazel eyes enveloping him. Lord, help him. Soft lips pressed against his, her tongue swept gently across the tips of his teeth, and he felt half his resolve melt. She was too sweet to resist. Too much a torment for any one man. A growl left him, and he pushed her back into the wall again. He had a mind to spin her away from him and pin her hands above her head, to make her forget her own name.

She gasped in relief against his mouth, her body undulating already. Her hands slipped down the length of his torso toward his belt.

He caught her wrist before it could descend any farther. Moved his mouth out of reach.

For a moment he simply held still, waiting for the throb of his blood to slow. Waiting for the night to cool them. He pushed his forehead to the wall over her shoulder. "You don't play fair," he groaned. Counting his breaths.

Her voice rasped when it came. "It doesn't have to be about love," she said. "You . . . you can still have me without loving me."

He went cold. His eyes snapped open.

He dropped his hold on her body abruptly and leaned away, pain lancing him. He made sure Nina looked at him when he said, "If it wasn't about love, then you'd be bent double right now, do you understand?"

Her breath stuttered. She nodded.

Patrick shook his head and exhaled, looking out to the night. "With me and you, Nina. It's always gonna be about somethin' other than fucking. It's too late for that." He wished now that he hadn't discarded that cigarette. He closed his eyes. "It's distance you and I need."

"Because you don't trust me?"

"Because I don't trust *myself* when I'm with you," he said. "And you fuckin' hurt me." He was split open, his heart swinging by its tendons, the meat of his chest on display. He went to the bench by her side and collected his coat and cap.

He paused before passing her, leaning down close enough to speak into her ear. Finally, she flinched. "You ever offer yourself to a man like that again, and it'll be the last thing he ever hears. Got me?"

She nodded, eyes misting.

He went back out into the night, the wind corralling him, whistling in his ears. He wished he could go back and strip them down of all the things they had done, the things that made them feel ashamed.

He wished he'd kissed her when they were twelve and led her onto a train home with him, and they'd both forgotten idium ever existed.

THE STEWARDS' TESTAMENT

JOAN

The three daughters, born one year after the next, were blooded divine, but fleshed in the vessels of humans.

They were born to a sheep farmer and his wife to the name Trent in humble surrounds and were christened Idia, Dione, and Joan.

As they grew, they took to unnatural practices. They could carve riverbeds, divert floodwaters, and till soil with no tools. They blessed the village with their magic as it strengthened. When winters came, they summoned fire from the heavens that needed no kindling. When the river ran dry, they called on water from the mountains.

They were called messengers of God, but this was not true.

The three daughters did not converse with any higher authority. When outsiders traveled to them to be healed, the daughters could not cure. When callers wished to speak with the dead, the daughters could not summon this magic.

The travelers took their stories to far corners and spoke of the false prophets who had refused them, who saw them swallowed by disease and grief and would not save them. They called the three daughters wicked, perverse. Witches.

But in their village, the Trent daughters were loved. The townspeople ran off any traveler who sought their blessing. The village prospered for many years.

But words spread like water. Like hellfire. The lust for power bore an enemy. It rose up like a beast. Like a devil.

And as the enemy formed, so, too, formed the first Stewards of these Trenched lands. They were farmers, millers, and loggers. They vowed to transport the three daughters to places of safety. To defend them against the enemy marching across the land, just as the daughters had defended their lands.

The Stewards planned to take the daughters each to a different secret place.

But Joan would not go. She feared for the safety of her town, her people. For surely, the enemy would trample it in search of them.

So the beast came to Joan first.

She wielded fire and water, arrows and blades, but even a daughter of God is limited. She was separated from her sisters, and eventually her power was drained. The Stewards were mere men and women, and they, too, were quickly thwarted.

Joan was captured. She was tied to a post for three days.

On the first day, they bled her, trying to take from her that which God had given.

On the second day, they took her flesh and consumed it, and still no magic was bestowed.

On the third, the beast's patience waned. Mad with envy, they threatened to burn her where she stood if she did not give up her magic. "You will be reborn each day in hell," they swore to her.

The youngest daughter, Joan, let of her blood, devoured, fell first.

Before fire consumed her, she said to all those who watched, "I die in the solace that my rage dies with me. I wish not to live among these men."

By testament of the Stewards, Joan made no sound as she was released of man's cruelty. If any remnant of her magic seeped free of the fire, then it seeped into the earth, while the eye of the enemy was enthralled by the flames.

CHAPTER THIRTY-TWO

NINA

"Trent?" I repeated, the letters on the parchment fading. They were blotted, and many had been crossed out, rewritten. Polly's fingers were stained with it, her hair flattened in the back, her eyes wild with sleeplessness. She nodded emphatically.

She'd woken me but not the others. Not yet. I couldn't be sure why.

"Surely," Polly said, pulsing with some sort of awareness. "It is no coincidence."

I reverted my eyes to the letters so that I would not need to see her face. Sometimes when I looked at her, I forgot what she was. What she'd done. "Nothing about Idia's Seam?"

"No, nothing yet. But Nina—"

"Then, keep translating."

Polly sighed. "There will be some holes. I don't remember all the glyphs, and some are faded. It takes time to pull the ink—"

"Well, time isn't on your side," I said curtly. "Nor ours." I began to turn away.

"Nina, wait." Polly's hand reached for my elbow, but retracted at the last moment. "I—I just wanted to tell you that I'm sorry."

"So, you've said."

"I mean . . . for your mother," she said warily, like I was a dog baring its teeth. "Theo explained what happened. I know you went to Kenton hoping to spare her." Her eyes pinched. "We were all fools in the end. None so much as me." One lip worried over the other, but she had the gumption to look me in the eye when she said, "I don't deserve your forgiveness, but I wanted you to know, if I could undo it all, I would. I wanted to the moment I sent that scribble."

"A moment too late," I retorted. And I left Polly to return to her tiny foreman's office with her flurry of parchment and the Stewards' book, shoulders hunched over.

Orderlies were the only others awake at this early hour. It seemed they never slept. They carried their items to and from pallets. One woman simply went bed to bed, singing soft Crafter songs in a voice that would break hearts.

I wondered if once, three daughters had resided in this town. I wondered if it had looked the same after the enemy had come for Joan.

Two more Trent Crafters had died in the night. When morning bloomed, Patrick and Theodore carried the bodies out to the ravine, and I buried them.

Theo looked bloodless and sick. John took his hat off and bowed his head. It was then that I gave them Polly's translation. I watched their eyes catch on the words *Trent* and *beast* and *witches*.

I watched confusion dawn, as it had in me.

"The beast," Theo read. "It must mean the invaders from other shores. The ones who came in the Battle of Belavere."

Lines deep as rifts appeared in Patrick's furrow. "Perhaps."

"Fuckin' animals, in any case," John uttered.

"Trent," Patrick said, his thumb smearing over the word. "Their name was Trent?"

"Could it—could it mean this place?" I asked. "Perhaps this town was named after them."

"It's as common a name as any, miss," John said, taking the translation from Patrick. "More likely it's a coincidence. This could've happened anywhere in the Trench."

But I couldn't shake the feeling crawling beneath my flesh and skipping the rungs of my spine. I'd felt it the day Patrick and I hid in a cellar, and again the day of the Artisan School attack. I felt it now, catastrophe in my blood, a relentless pounding in my head.

We ate meagerly, guiltily, knowing we took from what little stores Trent had left. Then Edith came to find us.

She nodded to me first. "Thank you," she said on a choked whisper. But she hardened her jaw, refusing to cry. "Those people—they deserved some decency."

I only nodded. What else was there to say?

"You should be on your way," she said next, already turning from us.

"We'd like to stay until tomorrow," I said suddenly, and Patrick's head turned in surprise, then John's and Theo's and Polly's. "We want to help however else we can."

It wasn't the whole truth. I wanted time in Trent, enough to find answers. Some confirmation of the suspicion unfurling in my gut.

"There ain't any coppers left to kill," Edith said. "But we need scouts, and people who can fetch water and launder. There are houses on the west side, closer to the trading post, that were never searched for supplies."

She left us to it.

"I'll search the houses," I said immediately to the rest. "See what there is to salvage."

Patrick came up close, right to my side, and looked where I looked, out over the beds of the wounded, rows and rows of them. "What are you doin'?" he said beneath his breath.

"It's not a coincidence," I insisted. "It can't be."

That was how I found myself walking through the wide lanes of Trent with Theodore, who hurried up behind me.

I turned at the sound of his approach, and a groan escaped me.

"Not the friendliest welcome," he muttered, slowing to match my pace.

"No welcome about it," I said in answer. "Shouldn't you be charming water from the river?"

"I set out to, but John practically shoved me aside. He's building some sort of contraption with Patrick."

I sighed.

"Where are we going?" he asked.

"*We* aren't going anywhere. *I'm* searching for supplies."

He watched me as he walked. "Then I'll accompany you."

"I'd prefer you didn't."

"You'll have to forgive me eventually," he said softly, a whisper of desperation in it. "I insist. I'll not give up until then."

I turned to him, and he stopped with me. There was snow in his dark hair, on the tips of his ears. He looked a decade older than we had been in Kenton Hill.

"This isn't the House," I hissed. "You're no longer a lord. Your insistence means *nothing* here."

He nodded. "You're right. But I do intend to earn your forgiveness, Clarke."

"Harrow."

"Nina," he settled. "And you haven't turned me out yet. A man has to wonder why that is."

I kept walking, past the crumbling remains of Crafter houses and outdoor lavatories and snow-banked horse carts. Theo followed one step behind. "I don't trust you enough to let you leave," I told him sharply. "You'd be back in the House by morning. We both know your father would round you up, and you'd tell him everything."

"You don't think I know how to lie?" Theo said. "That I wouldn't do that to protect you?"

"I think you turn the shade of the seat you take," I said. "Like a reptile."

We came to the far edges of destruction, the houses and buildings in this part of Trent not crumbling or choked in ash. Windows were broken, and most had their doors flung wide. A lone cat walked between houses, searching as we searched.

I approached the first door and hesitated. The number hung loose. A child's doll lay just over the threshold, its face concaved. Snow, in great flurries, had piled over the stoop. Wind howled through.

The air was too still, the snow too bright, the sky encroaching. Birds in far-off trees rabbled, ignorant to the shiver of abandonment. Without thinking, I moved closer to Theo's side, like a child does when shadows start to take shape.

He looked at me, confused. "What is it?"

I grimaced. "It just doesn't feel right, walking in uninvited."

Theo raised his eyebrows at the open hallway. "Well, we can knock, but I don't think anyone is coming to let us in." He stepped over the threshold and looked back to find me hesitating there. He frowned. "Are you coming?"

"Don't you feel that?" I asked him, and again, the wind swept through, sent gooseflesh up my neck.

"Feel what?"

"I don't know," I admitted. "A bad omen. Like we're disturbing something."

"Like a ghost?"

I pressed my lips together. He made it sound preposterous. I thought it seemed all too probable. I would have bet Trent was full of ghosts, overspilling with them. I stepped into the hallway gingerly, my boots crunching against broken glass. "You don't believe in ghosts?" I went past him and led the way up the staircase and into the first open door. The room was wallpapered deepest green and obviously Artisanal. Who else in the brink could afford a gilded credenza, a harp in the corner, shelves of books? I wondered if this house had belonged to a Scribbler, or perhaps a wood Mason. Plenty of wood to mill in this parish, or at least there had been.

"Ghosts?" Theo said. "No."

I began opening the wardrobe doors, taking the clothing from within. "Crafters say that when you die young, your ghost lingers a day for each you missed. That's why we grieve the death of a child so badly. We can feel them nearby."

Theo gave a sad sort of smile. "Sometimes stories are made where logic fails us." He was looking over the books on the shelves, his fingers running over the spines.

"And *The Stewards' Testament* . . . I take it you think it nothing more than a story?"

He turned to face me. "I think this entire thing is a goose chase," he said. "With no happy ending."

"If that's your belief, then you should go," I said, half of me wishing he'd disappear that very moment, the other half terrified he might just do it.

"Is that what you want?" It was a real question. Vulnerable.

"No," I said honestly. "Better the devil I can see than the one I can't."

Theo's frown deepened. "I'm not your enemy, Nina."

"You've acted as my enemy," I countered, rummaging through blankets, towels, sheets. "Not a week ago, you would have seen me lashed. You've lied to me. Manipulated me. My mother is dead because of your father's scheming, and you didn't do a thing to stop it."

"And I'm more sorry for it than you could know," he said tremulously, biting back some emotion. "But you're not the only one who's been used and spat out. You are not the only one who's lost their mother."

I turned to look at him, at the fracturing in his eyes. His mother, who had suffered the slow death of influenza without the bluff needed to revive her.

"We are all someone's enemy," he said now. "Whether you admit to it or not. I regret what I've done every waking minute. But I don't regret coming back for you in Kenton Hill, even when you didn't want me. I don't regret killing all those infantrymen to save a town that never accepted me. And I don't regret saving you from my father or liberating the man who stole the bluff stores that would have saved my mother's life." His chest seemed to buckle. "I can't bring myself to leave, Nina. I spent seven years wondering where you were. So, even if you love him now, and I have to witness the hate in your eyes when you look at me, I choose to stay. It's better to be near you and know you are safe than to be without you at all."

He looked at his feet, frowning, as though he had said too much. He sighed, looking up at me once more, his dark eyes warmer now. "I only want you to consider the danger in this, the improbability of it. And not because I want you for myself, but because I need to know you'll still live and breathe when this plan collapses."

"I don't much care for living and breathing while your father sits on his throne," I said, though I knew it was unfeeling.

He looked saddened. "You deserve more than a life of vendetta."

"I do." Hot tears pricked my eyes. I wiped them away angrily. "But wishing for it won't make it so."

"And will finding that Seam fix it all?" He stepped closer, eyes beseeching. "Will it bring you peace to see everything the Artisans have built, burned to the ground?"

Pain jolted through me. A reflex.

Theo saw it. "This isn't you," he said, softer still, his hand reaching out across the void. "This isn't your war. You're not a killer."

But I was. His father had ensured it, and I'd taken the shape of the animal he'd caged. I straightened my shoulders, felt my eyes dry, my tongue turning to steel. "You think you know me?"

"I do."

"You used to, when I was softer. I had to be soft—malleable. I was trying to fit into your world, and I'm grateful to you for cushioning me." I took a breath, and though I wanted to square my shoulders, they slumped. "But I'll never be that person again. You and I might as well be strangers."

"If it's easier to reconcile with yourself that way, then I won't argue with you," he said. "But that girl you're talking about? I loved her more than I've ever loved anyone. And to me, she fit into my world perfectly."

Of course she did. She'd turned to his every whim, went gladly in any direction he pulled her.

"Do you remember the night in the library?" he asked now.

We had lost track of time, sitting on the floor between the stacks. Not studying, just reading, sharing a book between us. It rested on our touching knees. We used to compete to see who could finish the page first. But then the sconces flickered out all at once, the wooden doors creaked shut as a distant clock tower chimed, and we realized we had been locked in. That the door was charmed and didn't unlock until morning. We had laughed, sprinted down the aisles, pulled soggy sandwiches from Theo's bag and eaten them in the elemental science section.

I had read to him a piece of poetry from a moth-eaten anthology, and in the middle of it, he'd kissed me, perhaps more passionately than he ever had. We'd kept our lips locked as we undressed each other, one article at a time, eyes cinched shut, hearts hurtling, and we'd made love for the very first time. Slowly, awkwardly, but beautifully, under a ceiling painted to replicate heaven.

I shook my head at Theo, shook away the image. I could see the memory suspended in his eyes, forever golden, impossibly sweet, made brighter with time. He'd polished the recollection until it gleamed.

"Did you ever think of me?" he asked. "After you left? Did you miss me at all?"

I shunt out the hurt, the loss I'd long ago reconciled with. "Yes. At first," I whispered, lifting my chin, turning for the door. "Then a little less each day. Then not at all."

I made to leave the room.

"Can you find it within yourself, at least, to not hate me?" came his voice. It floated over my shoulder, a plea. If shame had a shape, it would look an awful lot like him. "I don't think I can bear that."

I sighed, felt my hands tremble just slightly. "I can't hate you, Theo," I said. "As much as I might try."

I escaped to the hallway, my shoes scuffing off the carpet as I hurried away. I reopened the compartment in my chest that I'd saved for Theo and shut him in once more, but resolved that perhaps I didn't need to treat him quite so coldly after today.

After all, Theodore Shop hated himself more than I ever could.

We went from house to house, finding drawers of thick woolen socks, pillows, blankets. We went back and forth from the factory, emptying the supplies and leaving again, until my feet burned with the cold and I'd lost feeling in my fingers. Theo asked twice if I wanted to retire for the day, but I shook my head and ignored his sighs. It felt better to do *something*, anything. It was when I was still and quiet that my thoughts began to diverge into darker circles.

In a schoolroom I found containers of bandages, a sling, ointment. I pilfered the teacher's desk and found a half-empty bottle of brandy. I shoved the items into a child's satchel, still hanging by its hook on the wall. The name above it read BETH.

More evidence of life disrupted: a half-full mug of tea; a word on the chalkboard, three letters short; a small chair overturned, a knitted cardigan still slung on its back.

I felt for a moment as though I was seven years old again in a Scurry schoolroom, paper flowers stuck to the windows in a poor attempt at cheer.

On the far wall was the emblem of Belavere Trench, precisely where it had hung in Scurry. Beneath it were plaques with names, one for every graduating year. And at their center was one that read IN REMEMBRANCE OF THE FOUNDERS OF TRENT.

Here were names I didn't recognize. Sully, Wynnum, Galileo.

And then, near the bottom, Joan.

My fingers traced over the etching of her name. The wood wasn't so old; the grain hadn't discolored, nor had the letter edges dulled.

There it was—that bristle of knowing. Intuition, perhaps. It staked me there.

I took the plaque from the wall and added it to the satchel. I felt the ghosts of the schoolroom shiver in my wake.

I returned near dusk to find John and Patrick hammering nails into a huge mill. John moved the final planks with his mind, sending them careening down the snowy bank and into the water, where they connected lengths of wooden troughs already carved and waiting.

Sweat had broken over Patrick's neck and back, soaking his shirt through. The sleeves were rolled away from his forearms. He bent over and heaved huge pieces of pipe and whole troughs onto his shoulder, carried them into place and dropped them. For a moment, I stayed hidden and watched. I watched the muscles of his back ripple, watched his chest flex as he dropped another piece into the snow. Soon, it seemed the construction was complete.

The river pushed the mill, the water heaped into its troughs and overflowed, fed into the pipework that disappeared over the snow and into the factory.

I left the cover of trees. "Genius," I called out, and Patrick turned before I'd even finished the word, inexplicably attuned to me.

"It'll do," John called from the river, his legs half-submerged in the frigid water. It didn't seem to bother him.

Patrick wiped his brow as he came up the bank, his suspenders hanging by his hips.

"You should be inside," he said by way of greeting. "There's weather comin'."

"*You* aren't inside."

"I ain't a lady," he said, stopping before me, whorls of steam lifting off his skin. He seemed to recognize the intensity in my eyes. "What is it?"

"I need to find Edith," I said. "Would you come with me?"

Edith was to be found in the factory, sorting the goods Theo and I had brought in. Theodore was emptying a sack onto a metal workbench while she picked out the canned goods, the medicines.

Polly came stumbling out of her office, eyes near-deranged. She blinked in rapid succession as though trying to draw shapes from her surroundings. John came into the warmth behind me and Patrick.

"Edith," I said, pulling the plaque out of the satchel, not revealing it yet. "Edith, what do you know about the three daughters?"

She didn't look up from her ministration, but I thought her hands stumbled over the clothes she was sorting. "The three daughters?" she mused, then shrugged. "As much as anyone else I'd guess. My ma used to tell me to make wishes on 'em."

"Mine as well," I said, a weight falling heavily into my stomach. "And what did she tell you about the founders of Trent?"

She stopped then, looked over her shoulder at me, seemed to realize for the first time the people convened around her, listening. She eyed the plaque in my hand furtively. "What've you got there?"

I gave it to her, let her eyes fall to the names. "The three daughters were born of the name Trent?" I asked.

Edith shrugged. "So they say."

"So *who* says?"

"People here got a long memory," she sighed. "The first Stewards—they came from this parish, see? That's what the old folk think. Their grandmas and grandaddies taught them the same, that Trent were Idia's birthplace." She handed the plaque back to Nina. "But the Book of Belavere don't agree. It don't think there's more'n one daughter of God, neither."

"And what do you believe?"

Edith shrugged, her eyes straying over the factory. "Don't matter much either way. Coppers here beat anyone tellin' stories about it. The name Trent came from a woman named Joan, they say, who was one of the first Artisan daughters. But we ain't supposed to think differently. Coppers even tried to cut down the tree, 'cause the kids would sit under it and make wishes."

"What tree?" Patrick asked.

"It's a kids' fancy. But some believe it's where she's buried," Edith said in an undertone, as though policemen might thunder in even now. "The thing is, the coppers can't cut it down. Not even the wood Masons they sent from the city. Nothin' fells it." She said it with pride, a slow grin lifting a corner of her mouth. "Don't know if there's a lick of truth to it. The Stewards might've been a bunch of puffed-up fools, for all I know. But there's somethin' about that tree. We used to sneak into the woods at night, dare each other to get close to it, you know?" She shook her head. "Can't touch it without gettin' the shakes."

Even now, Edith seemed doused in chills. She rolled her shoulders back. "If it's a wish you're wantin', it still stands out there in the woods. The fire didn't touch it none. But don't get your hopes up," she said, the moans of a man rising as he convulsed on his pallet. "Ain't ever granted any fortunes to us lot."

Partway into the woods, an oak tree towered, unmarred by fire, just as Edith had promised.

There was nothing about it that should mark it as a grave. No engravings, no discerning features. But still, it stood before us as a monolith, and in turn, each of us shivered.

Winter had taken its foliage. What was left was the spine, its branches reaching desperately outward, and perhaps that was the quality that made it somber.

The clouds overhead pushed down, turning the snow ashen, dulling sound. There were cold fingers on my neck, tracing the shell of my ear, but when I turned, no one was there.

"Bad omens, Patty," John said, his eyes lost in the network of empty branches. "Bad omens."

Miners were a superstitious lot. A shiver of wind was a bad omen, a crying swallow meant death. I used to laugh at how grown men cowered at the breeze.

But I thought John might be right. There was decay in the air.

And yet, the oak tree stood taller than any I'd ever seen. Wholly alive.

"It's only a tree," Theo said, rubbing his bare hands together. "Doesn't exactly prove the existence of the three daughters."

The clouds parted then, weak beams of light dousing the oak.

It bleached and shadowed in the gnarled wood, turning it monochromatic, as though an artist had used it as a canvas, turned a tree into a woman. A knot in the trunk became a hand clutched to her chest. The lines in the bark were now her head bowed, eyes closed, jaw defiant. Her body cascaded into the earth and the heavens both.

I staggered backward, winded.

"Well," John said. "Will ya look at that."

The light dissipated, and the woman was gone.

There was a beat of silence. Logic failing to find its way to anyone's lips, to offer an explanation. And then Theo sighed in a gust, eddies of snow spinning before him. "Just more myths," he said calmly, his neck craning to see the tops of the branches. "It's freezing. We should go back—"

"You don't feel it?" I asked, my voice sounding distant.

The look he gave me was half pleading, half pitying. He shook his head. "Any decent Mason could've carved something like that into the wood, Nina."

"There's somethin' here," Patrick mumbled, as though to himself. Then he lifted his blue eyes to me. "Do you hear it?"

Of course I did. It was roaring in my blood, sparking my nerve endings. Something thrumming beneath the surface.

It was a sort of muted violence. A wave of it.

I felt it wetting my feet, poisoning my veins. In my mind, I saw men with blood beneath their fingernails, gorging on the body of a woman, burning her at the stake for the crime of having something they could not.

Acid coated my tongue, as though I'd bitten into rotting fruit.

I took in every branch of the ancient tree, every root delving into the earth. The sound of the ground here was different. It was festering, and I thought that if what the Stewards said was true, and Joan's remains had been left to feed the soil, then she'd found no rest here. No peace. She scratched from beneath the surface.

"Nina," Theo called to me, blocking my view. "This is ridiculous. It's near freezing. We need to get inside."

"You don't think it's strange?" I asked him. "That the tunnel should collapse and bring us here of all places?"

"I think the struts were too far apart," Theo answered, taking my shoulders in his hands as though he might shake sense into me. "Just as John said."

Patrick reared up in my periphery, but I'd already knocked Theo's hands away. I was thinking of wishes. Of retribution. Justice. I couldn't feel the cold at all. "Go back without me. I'll follow later."

"You haven't eaten," Theo insisted. "You've hardly slept."

"Careful now," Patrick said slowly, his eyes hardened. "You're oversteppin'."

"She's dead on her feet!" Theo said, his voice rising to the last crows still braving the frost. They went flying. Theo lifted his arms and let them slap against his sides. "This is madness," he exasperated. "We should be moving. Every moment we remain gives the Lords' Army a chance to catch up. And thanks to the Colsons"—Theo waved his hand in Patrick and John's direction—"we've got a trail of dead police officers in our wake."

"If it eases your conscience," John said. "We only cooked 'em. Didn't cut anything off 'em."

Theodore shook his head, bewildered. "This is a fucking pointless treasure hunt," he said, to no one in particular.

"You're welcome to get off at any stop, Teddy," Patrick said, blowing warm breath into his cupped hands. "Lord knows it'd spare us the sound of your whinin'."

Puce-faced, Theo turned on his heel and stomped back through the snow. Polly followed, seeming relieved to escape the cold.

"Well," John said, patting Patrick on the shoulder. "Think I saw a bit of brandy back at the factory, son. If you're of the mind."

Patrick let his father walk on. "You comin'?" he asked me.

"I want to stay here a while," I answered.

He nodded, but he touched my hand as he left. A reminder. A reassurance.

I stalked back and forth in front of Joan's tree, trying to find the curves and valleys of the woman that was now amorphous. The sun remained obstinately behind the clouds. Even the earth beneath my feet had turned quiet, restful. I closed my eyes for a moment, tipped my head back so that I could see the last leaves clinging to the branches. "I don't know what to wish for," I muttered. In truth, I'd never felt more adrift. I thought of Theo, claiming that I'd lost myself, and worried that he was right. That perhaps I was just angry enough, just broken enough, that I didn't care for myself anymore. I imagined Joan upon that pyre, slowly bled and devoured, and I thought if I were her, I'd wish for the men who feasted on me to be poisoned by my flesh.

I wondered why God insisted on leashing women with power only for men to come harvest it. Joan had been wrong to think that her rage would die with her.

It was in Edith wielding a carving knife.

In blunt-faced women nursing the injured.

In Polly, her tongue so bitten down she hardly spoke.

And it was in me.

The wind picked up. The last hem of light seemed to surrender to the blanket of cloud. A howling ensued, first through the spines of black-trunked trees, then through my lungs. I let it carry me back the way I'd come, like a hand between my shoulder blades. I felt the whip of snow catch at the backs of my ears and hurried faster.

A feeling of urgency rose, from the ground, the air, and I felt like an animal scenting the first hint of danger.

I hastened, boots sliding, sinking.

Then, from Trent's belly came the first labors of a dying siren, whirring out once more into a parish devoid of almost everything but its ghosts.

CHAPTER THIRTY-THREE

NINA

The wails grew louder near the river and the graves of Trent's dead. It swallowed the sound of the door crashing against the factory wall as Patrick ran out of it, his face drawn, eyes wild. They grew relieved when they saw me climbing the bank, using my hands for leverage in the slip of snow.

The factory was a chaos of movement. The orderlies loading shotguns with shaking, unpracticed fingers, moving heavy machines together to barricade the doors and windows. John was boarding them with planks of wood that moved at the will of his mind, pounding nails into them with loud grunts at shocking speed.

"The army?" I asked, Patrick shunting me into Polly's office. Theo was already inside, his hands tearing at his own hair. Polly had the Stewards' book clutched tightly to her chest.

"Can't be anyone else," Patrick said, and without warning, he stalked toward Polly until she backed herself into a wooden cabinet, the doors clattering. He took the gun from his pocket.

"I didn't send for them!" Polly exasperated, her lips trembling. "I swear it, Pat!"

"Three to one says you did," he told her, the barrel poised beneath her chin.

Theo started forward. "Let her go, Pat."

"Patrick, please. It wasn't me—"

Patrick gritted his jaw and shook his head. "Odds ain't in your favor, Pol." He cocked the hammer. "Not another Scribbler in sight."

"Perhaps there is," came the voice of Edith. She stood in the doorway, her hand clutched around the knob. "Did you clear that fuckin' tradin' post before you burned it down?"

Patrick's face paled. He didn't take his eyes off Polly.

"They leave a Scribbler in every town, Colson. Surely you thought o' that?"

"You said there were only coppers left," Patrick reiterated. "I asked, and you said three."

"Three coppers," Edith nodded, "and a Scribbler. My bet is the swank was in his bed on the second story, with enough time to send a call for help to the House before he ran off or died in the smoke."

"Fuck," Patrick growled, his gun lowering. He paced madly, pinching the bridge of his nose. He spoke to himself with the air of someone completing immense equations.

"We need to leave," Theodore said. "Now!"

"No," Patrick said, his eyes closed. "They'll burn this place down lookin' for us."

John came up behind Edith, sweat glistening down his neck and sinking into his collar, beyond him, the last survivors of Trent in flux. "They're comin' in from the west," he said. "The hearths've been smothered. But it ain't gonna take 'em long to sniff us out."

As though on cue, the lanterns in the factory were snuffed, the candles extinguished. Darkness descended.

The only remaining light came from a match suddenly lighting in Patrick's fingers.

"I'm sorry" came Edith's voice, her face only just visible. A collection of disconnected features.

There was the glint of a knife in her hand, and she snatched my arm.

Right as Patrick lifted the gun once more.

Right as the first horses respired down the thoroughfare.

I felt a body slide behind mine, the tip of the blade rest between ribs. "I can't let you leave," said Edith, her breath in my ear. "And I won't be lettin' 'em burn us down, neither."

"Whoa, now," John said from behind me. I heard the click of his hammer, another gun leveled Edith's way. "Let's be smart."

"You're the reason they've come back!" Edith said, shaking now, her voice too loud. "So you'll be the reason they turn round and leave. You'll walk yourselves out there and give yourselves up to 'em."

Patrick shook his head, dread forming in his eyes. "They'll kill you all anyway," he growled. "They'll smoke you out for sport."

"Then we're dead either way," Edith said, a strange laugh bubbling up from her throat.

I held my breath in terror, knowing the blade would sink in at any moment. "Patrick," I pleaded, though for what I couldn't say.

His eyes met mine. A beat of silence, then his expression shuttered. "We'll go," he said.

"Pat," John started warily. "She's got two guns pointed at her. She ain't in a position to make any demands."

"If we walk out there, they'll take us captive," Theo said, his voice strained.

"They ain't takin' us captive, Teddy," Patrick said, his eyes pinned to Edith. "We're fightin'."

I felt the knife at my side shift, slide over a rung of bone.

"Let her go," Patrick said to Edith. "And we'll walk out those doors now."

"And do *what*?" Theo blustered. "You plan on shooting every last one of them?"

"Me?" Patrick said. His gun lowered. Outside, the wind battered against the walls. Loading rifles clacked and it was impossible to discern whether it was in my mind or in the street. "No, Teddy," Patrick said. "I plan on havin' you drown 'em."

Edith's blade lifted away. "Go," she said. *"Please."*

Patrick looked at Edith one last time, his thoughts inscrutable, the tangled remnants of duty still warring along his jaw, down his throat. "Thank you for your hospitality," he said, pulling me behind him, leading me out the door. "Make sure I don't see you again, miss. Or that'll be your last moment on this earth."

"And don't call on Kenton," John added. "There'll be no help comin' down the tunnels."

We left Edith standing alone, the knife sliding from her limp fingers, her face buckling.

CHAPTER THIRTY-FOUR

PATRICK

This is mad," Theo said, his voice trembling. But he helped push the barricade away from the door, his breaths coming in large gusts.

Patrick couldn't contest it. Beyond those doors were several ranks of approaching soldiers.

"How many bullets you got left, Patty?" John asked, his face pressed to a gap between the wooden boards on a high window.

"Just the one."

"I've three," John counted, rolling the barrel. "Here they come. Five on horses. Thirty all up, I reckon. Forty at most. They're goin' door to door."

"They don't know it's us," Patrick said in response. "If they did, there'd be more."

"Then why have they come?" Theo asked.

"Because they think a few angry Trent Crafters killed their coppers and a Scribbler, Teddy." How oblivious he was to the ministrations of his own House.

"Holy god. I can't kill them all," Theo said, his head shaking back and forth. "They've been ordered here. Most will have families. It isn't right." He was beginning to shake, to lose his grip.

Patrick grabbed his collar in his hand and pulled him close, felt the button at Theo's throat pop. "Sharpen up, Teddy," he said. There was command in his voice. Theo paled. "They'll aim to shoot at anythin' that moves. They won't stop to ask what family *you've* got waitin' at home. Won't think of the right and wrong in it. They'll open fire, and you'll be dead on the ground before you can wave your white flag. And so will *she*."

Together they glanced at Nina, who was peeking through a window.

Patrick watched how Theo's eyes seemed to stick to her. "Use the river—"

"I don't need your instruction on my medium, Colson."

"Do it as soon as they're in reach," Patrick said in undertones. "Before they have a chance to recognize her. *Please.*"

Finally, Theo's gaze turned away from Nina, surprise coloring his expression to hear Patrick plead with him.

"This is the side you chose. You chose *her*," Patrick said, though he hated to say it. "And you'll watch her die or be captured tonight unless you do this."

"They're here," Nina called, backing away from the window, her eyes wild now. "Patrick?"

He clapped Theo on either shoulder, so hard his teeth rattled. "If there's any worldly way to prove yourself to her," he said in desperation. "It's *this*."

He watched Theo galvanize, his pupils dilating, eclipsing. The stalk of his neck cocked. A deep exhale rattled from his chest. A soldier's last breath before the first spray of bullets.

Lord, Patrick thought. *Let us survive this.*

"Do it now, Theo."

Theo went to the window. Patrick saw the way his eyes shuttered to what was in front of him, all senses honed elsewhere, to the frigid river that slunk behind the factory.

Patrick heard the calls and whistles of the soldiers beyond the door, felt the clutch of tension in the air, heard the first rolls of thunder—not from the sky, but from something closer. Something monstrous. Patrick stepped toward the boarded windows, peered through the slats.

"Be ready to run," he told the rest. "When I say."

Here were the soldiers, weary from their trek through the snow. Trading flasks and cigarettes that sputtered out in the wind. Bayonets slung over their shoulders as they cupped their hands around their mouths to warm them. The horses clopped sleepily, necks bent against the snow belting against them, the generals atop shouting orders. The foot soldiers broke down doors where they were bid. Three men stalked sullenly toward the factory, their eyes tracking over its dark silhouette.

Three feet from the heavy doors, they halted.

Patrick saw it in their eyes when they realized the roaring was not wind. He saw terror distort their faces as the sky seemed to fall atop them.

The freezing water fell in heavy sheets, toppling the soldiers from their horses and crushing them.

"Go!" Patrick pushed through the heavy doors.

John shot three who stirred in the snow, spitting and trying to rise. Patrick shot another as he reached for his bayonet, and their bullets were spent.

Theo held the rest hostage in the stillest water Patrick had ever seen. It blanketed them as if a spring had suddenly appeared in the middle of the main street, its surface already icing over in the cold. The bodies beneath it did not move, either too broken or already dead.

Theo's hands were raised in front of him, his brow furrowed in intensity. The wind lashed in, but he seemed impervious to it. "Run!" he said.

Patrick took Nina's arm, John took Polly's, and they took off without Theo, running through the snow. The only remaining tunnel was to the south, in the farming pasture behind the loggers. It might as well have been on another continent. The terrain made them slow.

They hadn't made it more than a few yards before a door burst open into the street and two soldiers in full regalia appeared, stomping out into the night, halting abruptly when they saw the group pounding toward them.

"Fuck," Patrick muttered, and lifted his pistol, though there were no bullets to fire, only the hope of the con. He pulled Nina behind him as they hastened to lift their bayonets.

"Halt!" they called. "Stay where you are."

John pulled Polly in front of him as a shield.

"Hello, boys," Patrick said carefully, eyes flickering between them. "You can let us pass, or we can trade bullets. Which will it be?"

Behind them, cut logs rose very slowly from a mound of firewood, snow sliding gently away. Patrick didn't look at them as they rose silently into the night, waiting over the soldiers' heads.

But there was the matter of the loaded guns pointed at them, fingers already wrapping the triggers, reflexively pulled on a flinch.

Patrick glanced once at his father.

"Drop your weapons!" shouted one of the men, his voice carrying, probably in hopes it would reach his comrades.

"They can't hear you," Patrick said. "They're dead."

The men looked at one another. "Bullshit."

Theo stumbled up then, sweating and panting. Every breath seemed to pain him. Patrick didn't spare him a glance. "Get 'em all, Teddy?"

"Y—yes," he said shakily. He was likely moments from vomiting.

"Well, there you have it, boys," Patrick said. "Last ones standin'. That's got to be worth a medal, eh? Let us pass, and you might just collect it."

"She's Artisan," one soldier said suddenly, his eyes landing on Polly, whose forearm hosted a red, puckered brand on her dark skin. The soldier regripped his weapon, looking through the scope of his rifle, muzzle trained on John.

"And that one . . ." the other soldier was looking over Patrick's shoulder at Nina, eyes narrowing. Patrick moved in front of her.

"The Alchemist?" Patrick said. "That'd be me."

That served to draw their attention, at least.

"Patrick Colson," he said, empty gun still lifted. "It's a pleasure."

Likely this contingent had come through the cold expecting a fightless raid. Perhaps a few bottles of whiskey on someone's shelf to pilfer. Home by morning.

"How would you two like an even bigger medal, eh?" Patrick felt for Nina behind him and pushed her toward Theo. He stepped forward, let his gun swing loose on his finger. He held his hands up in surrender. "You can take me right up to National House yourselves."

It was their only choice. That, or shoot him, which would get them hanged. They weren't Artisans, after all.

Patrick saw opportunity gleam in their eyes. But still, their guns didn't move. "Can't take us all in yourselves, though," he pointed out. "We'd out-muscle you, wouldn't we? Better odds if there's two on one. Tell my friends to be on their way." Patrick dropped his revolver to the snow and waited for them to deliberate. He prayed they were fools.

Eventually, the one closest to Patrick nodded to himself, readjusted his footing and stood taller. "Yeah," he said, his shoulders rolling back. "Yeah, all right. We'll take just you." He jutted his chin at the others. The log waiting over his head hovered precariously. "The rest of you, get walkin'."

Slowly, they did so, Theo with Nina behind him, John with Polly in front, and Patrick would wait until the bayonets were drawn away from their group and trained only on him. John would let them fall. Patrick would duck the bullets.

"Patrick?" Nina said, edging away from Theo, ignoring his insistent tugs.

Patrick groaned internally. *Keep walkin', Scurry girl.*

"Hang on," grunted the second soldier, recognition dawning. He looked between Patrick and Nina, some uncompromised part of his mind quicker than the rest of him. "Wait. Is that . . . That's the earth Charmer!" he said, jaw swinging open. His bayonet lifted at her torso.

And Patrick was too far away.

The logs fell.

A shot rang out.

The soldiers struck the snow, knees first, then faces. The backs of their skulls caved in.

And next to Patrick lay another body, its stomach blooming red beneath clothing.

CHAPTER THIRTY-FIVE

THEO

When Theo had first arrived in Kenton Hill, a man had aimed a shotgun at his stomach outside the Coal Works. Called him a swank. Told him to go back to the city or be sent back in a box.

Theo had wondered then, with a sort of detached curiosity, what it would feel like to have a bullet sink into his skin. Whether he would feel anything at first, or if the pain would seep in slower, like melting ice.

He'd been wrong on both counts.

Agony splintered through his gut, made worse by the jostle of movement as Patrick and John leveraged him on their shoulders. His feet dragged over snow, then soil, then the metal slats of a mine shaft. He heard the groan of the pulley, the music of chains, the rhythmic plink of dripping blood.

"Theo?" Nina's voice. Ice-cold hands on his cheeks. "Theo! Don't close your eyes."

"It's gone all the way through," Patrick was saying. "A graze, I think."

Fuck off, Colson, he wanted to tell him. But his mind was turning to swill. He couldn't find his eyes to open them. Something heavy pressed into his stomach, and he bucked with a new onslaught of pain.

"Easy," Patrick said to him. "Nina, keep pressure on it."

When Theo opened his eyes he saw nothing. Just encroaching darkness. Fingers insistent at his neck. "Why did you do that?" she asked him.

But he was being swallowed. Into the earth, into some black reprieve, and he couldn't force the words beyond that heavy barrier. In his mind, he saw Nina's face in Dumley's office levitating soil, in the shadows of an Artisan theater, in the rubble of the first attack, and in his dreams every damned night.

Because I love you, he thought. He hadn't found a way, just yet, to make it stop.

In his disorientation, Theo awoke with the surety he was in Kenton Hill, deep underground. He felt the damp earth beneath him, heard that suffocating quiet, and tried to organize the tangle of his thoughts. Where was Scottie, or Briggs? Where was Gunner, shouting at him for daring to rest? Why was he here, seated? Had he fainted again? As he had on his first descent?

But pain lanced him, spiking up his side and into his lungs, stealing his breath. "Fuck," he groaned, and cupped his hand over his waist just above the hip bone, where a coat covered him.

"It's all right" came not Nina's voice, but Polly's. Theo blinked, and her face pieced together. "Don't sit up," she said. "The bleeding will start again."

He realized then that her hand was gently pressing a wadded rag over his wound.

He frowned, his eyes wanting to close again. Fuck, but it stung. "You're not planning to sleep?"

She shook her head. "Truth be told, I'm terrified of the tunnels."

He nodded. He was, too. He looked farther down the tunnel, to where John and Patrick were also awake, their back pressed to the walls and a lit gas lamp between them. Nina was curled onto her side, asleep.

Theo nodded in the direction of their party. "You didn't want to be closer to the light?"

She grimaced. "It's a little crowded down there."

"I'll say."

She smiled at him wanly, then looked into her lap, shame spilling across her expression.

Theo exhaled, then winced. "You don't need to fear them, Polly. They can hardly be rid of you, can they?"

She looked at him dubiously. "And how long does that last?" she murmured. "My usefulness runs out the moment they find Idia's Seam or give up on the endeavor entirely."

He scoffed. "Men like Patrick and John—my father, too—they don't give up on things like this."

Polly's stare was distant. "Do you remember that drunk back in Kenton?"

"You'll have to be a lot more specific."

"The one who cursed at Mrs. Colson and kicked Isaiah?"

A man from Dorser came to mind. He'd been granted amnesty at Colson & Sons, just like Polly and Theo. He'd said he was a businessman, though Theo suspected he was just a criminal to whom they owed a favor. He'd gotten carried away one evening and turned cantankerous, knocking over a table, throwing his brandy onto an unsuspecting woman, screaming at Tess when she came to clear him out, then gave Patrick's dog a firm kick in the ribs as he left.

He'd been a novice to Kenton Hill. He'd yet to understand the codes of the Colson empire, and the rest of those in the pub had watched on in quiet anticipation.

It surprised no one when Patrick downed the rest of his drink and stood, or when Gunner adjusted his belt and opened a switchblade, both of them following the Dorser man calmly out to the road.

The man ended up on his back in the middle of Main Street, his cheek slashed open and his shoulder bleeding from the puncture wound beneath.

"Deal's off," Patrick had said around the length of a cigarette. "Take the long way home. Just watch the hills now, they tick."

An hour or so later, there had been a distant blast to the South. A landmine tripped. And Kenton barely stuttered at the sound.

Theo nodded. "I remember."

"Well, that man kicked their dog," she said. "What do you think they imagine doing to me?"

Theo grimaced. "You were doing what you believed was right."

Polly shook her head sadly. "The word *right* didn't factor much into it."

"You were backed into a corner."

"I was," she said on a whisper. "And so was Nina. So were *you*. But I was the one to give Tanner the tunnel. I kicked the dog." She turned to look at Theo then. "And I don't deserve your compassion. I'm exactly the coward they believe I am."

Theo considered her for a moment. "Do you remember when I arrived in Kenton Hill? The mining boys started in on me straight away. Trying to rile me up, I think. Test my mettle. I'd never met men like them before, throwing their weight around, beating their chests like apes. I thought them moronic. Only Scottie didn't take too well to that observation."

"Well, you called him a witless degenerate, and I don't think he knew what either of those words meant."

"And he and Otto took my chair out from underneath me, and I was lying there on the floor thinking they might beat my head in. Then you rose up like a guardian angel and scolded them both like they were toddlers. Told them to sit down before you knocked their heads together."

She smiled, just slightly. "Scottie's harmless. He only looks like a troll."

"And Otto was butter in your palm from the very beginning."

Her expression splintered at the sound of his name, and she turned away, eyes back on the Stewards' book in her hands. "Are we just reminiscing? Or does this story have a point?"

"You're not a coward, Polly. Not truly. You survived the Artisan school, and then countless towns after it, most of which were far from welcoming. You've seen far more than I would care to see, I'm sure of it. Whatever it is you are, you are not a coward. You simply want to survive. I can't reproach you that."

She turned in on herself, her spine curving. When she next spoke, her voice was reedy. "What kind of person forsakes an entire town just to save their own hide?"

Theo sighed heavily and looked out into the gloom. "Funny how things shook out in the end," he said quietly. "I hated that damned parish, yet I stayed to help salvage it. You liked Kenton, and yet . . ."

"Yet I sent in the bloody infantry." She sounded like she could hardly believe it herself. "Knowing full well that it might kill the man I—"

Theo watched the word stick in her throat, her eyes rimming with tears. "Loved?" he supplied. "Was it love? With Otto?"

The hollowing of her throat told Theo enough.

He did the gentlemanly thing of changing the subject. "What will you do after this? Without scribbling?"

She shrugged lamely. "If I'm being truthful, I don't care, so long as I'm not shot dead somewhere along the way."

"For what's it worth," Theo said. "I won't let the Colsons kill you."

"And if Nina were the one holding the gun?" she asked now, turning her head to watch his reaction. "Would you stop her?"

Theo frowned. "I wouldn't have to. She'd never do that."

"Wouldn't she?"

Theo thought he saw something flash across Polly's irises. Perhaps she was remembering the night they had found her in Rickers, Nina's knuckles blanching around the butt of a pistol. "However angry she might feel, she isn't capable of something like that, Polly. She isn't one of them."

Polly tilted her head as though she pitied him his naivete. "That's exactly who she is, Theo. However much you might wish it otherwise."

He bit his tongue to stave off a retort. She didn't know Nina as he did.

"Do you think we'll ever move on?" Polly asked now, shivering. The cold was closing in.

"I hope not," he said in earnest. "Then it was all for nothing." Theo had been too long with that ache in his throat, grown used to it.

She looked at him sadly, as though she couldn't imagine a worse fate.

"I think I'd be more content to, though, if I knew there was some part of her that was . . . *changed* by me," Theo allowed. "To know that I'd altered her half as much as she altered me."

"She loved you once," Polly said simply. "You carved your way into her heart back then. It stands to reason the marks would still be there."

Theo took a tremulous breath. His stomach seemed to seize. After a moment, his muscles relaxed back against the wall of the tunnel, his head tilted to the ceiling. From the void of his chest, words rose unbidden. "I do worry, you know, that we aren't the ones who find their happy ending."

"No," Polly murmured. "No, I don't think we do."

When the others rose from their rest, Polly helped Theo to stand. They traveled on, Theo clawing dying embers of memory and Polly rubbing her right arm with her left hand, as though warming that one small part of herself.

CHAPTER THIRTY-SIX

PATRICK

Patrick felt a wave of homesickness so acute he had to clamp his eyes shut.

In truth, it might also have been the air in the tunnels.

They were fleeing in the exact opposite direction of Kenton Hill. And the farther south they traveled, the more detached he felt from home, from his brothers and mother. He'd never been gone this long. Worry wheedled in. Voices in his head told him he couldn't be sure they were even alive.

It would have been enough to send him back if it weren't for the fear of it. Fear of seeing it half reduced. Anytime the urge to steal home swarmed him, he would try to imagine the view from the surrounding hills and how different it would look now, and the feeling was swallowed by the urgency to find the fucking Seam.

He would be returning with nothing if he couldn't return with a plan, with a fix. When he did return, he would be filled to the brim with idium, with enough in surplus to give to every man and woman in Kenton. Let the House come then. Let them breathe fire and spray bullets. Let them shake as Kenton returned in kind.

The next time he stepped foot in Kenton Hill, he'd make it the most formidable parish in the world.

He was filthy, covered in mud and Theo's blood. One endless night and day in the tunnels. They walked as far as Theo could be carried before surrendering to the ground, resting, then rising to do the same again. Nina and Polly weren't accustomed to walking the tunnels in the dark, and between John and Patrick, Theo's deadweight had quickly become encumbering. When they set him down for the night, the relief was immense.

Nina slept opposite Patrick, sitting upright. He held his sickness at bay by listening to her breaths. Farther away, Polly curled in on herself. Theo was slumped against his own part of the wall, his side as well bandaged as they could manage with the sleeves of Patrick's shirt.

John rested beside him, though Patrick knew he was awake. He heard the quiet pop of his lips as he spoke to himself, the same way he had when Patrick was a boy. Always scheming, strategizing.

Odd to have him so close again. To be able to ask one of the many questions that had banked up in his mind over the last two years. Now, he found little to say.

Patrick had imagined their reunion would feel like surrender. Like mercy. Instead, he felt heavier now than he ever had.

"You haven't asked Polly to send a scribble to Ma," Patrick murmured, only just loud enough for John to hear it. Not loud enough to stir Nina from her dreams. She slept so seldom it worried him.

He felt John shift, turn to peer at him through the dark. "You say somethin', son?"

"You haven't asked the Scribbler to send a message to Ma," Patrick repeated.

There was a moment's hesitation. "There a question in that?" John uttered eventually. "Ain't much business of yours, Patty. For all you know, I've sent her a bloody sonnet."

"Have you?"

His hands rose and fell, slapping the dirt. "We've been a bit preoccupied, son. I ain't thought much about love notes."

But that wasn't his way, Patrick knew. Always there had been notes. He'd left them under her water glass beside their bed. On the stovetop, in the heel of her boot. *One day, you'll have a castle, love*, they'd say. *Soon, we'll have it all.*

A lifetime ago, his mother had seen those notes and smiled shyly. Later, she'd squeezed her eyes shut, like she was praying for patience, and the note was tucked in her housecoat. By the time Patrick was an adult, she'd walk right by, refusing to read them at all.

"It's been more than two years," Patrick rumbled. "Two years she's gone without a word from you. Now we've got a Scribbler at our disposal. You'd think a man in your shoes would have sent a message."

John shuffled. "Watch your tone, son."

"She's your *wife*," Patrick growled, his volume climbing. His eyes slid in the dark to Nina, but she didn't stir. In whispers, he said, "What man worth a damn neglects to send word to his wife and sons?"

John groaned, scrubbed at his face wearily. "You're young, Pat," he said slowly. There was a warning in it. "You don't know yet how marriage works. But your ma does. She knows there's things more important than love notes and fuckin' poems."

He tipped his head back to the wall again. Crossed his arms over his chest as though the matter were closed. "And you'll mind your mouth when you speak to me of your mother, son. You hear me? 'Fore I knock your teeth out."

The same hollow threats from Patrick's childhood. He'd never followed through on a single one of them. "You haven't asked about them," Patrick continued. "Gunner or Don. Two years, and you ain't got the wherewithal to ask." He looked over at Nina. Not his family, not *his* at all. Still, he heard her slow breaths draw into her chest and said, "If I had a wife waitin' somewhere, there ain't a thing I'd think about more."

To that, John said nothing.

"I took the liberty of havin' Polly write to Ma and the boys," Patrick said now. "I told 'em you were alive and well. It's a mite of what they deserve." Then he turned away, unable to think of his father, of his mother and brothers and Kenton Hill a moment longer.

The tunnel came up into a stinking culvert, as far from Hoaklin and Kenton Hill as one could get without crossing the Gyser River.

Lavnonshire had somehow evaded the grasp of winter. It remained humid, the air thick as soup, gulls still swooping lazy circles over the sea. It was a lean-to town, structures half-rotted unfolding to the cliffs, the streets narrow and uneven. When the wind rolled in off the ocean, it would pick up stray cats, discarded rubbish and blow them down the lanes, but as much as it battered the walls of Lavnonshire, they never folded. The mortar between bricks was mostly eroded. Everything smelled of salt and fish innards. An interminable roar harried the ramparts and the cliffs, drowning out the drawls of fish mongers. Lavnonshire hardly changed. It seemed condemned to churn with the ocean it bordered. Not even a war could halt it.

Theo came out of the tunnel looking ashen. He held his side as though he were holding in his organs, the bandage bled through. Patrick and Nina held most of the man's weight, but with every step, Theo grew more tight-lipped, more drawn.

"Where are we?" Nina asked, blinking into the assault of light.

But it wasn't Patrick or John who answered her. It was Polly.

"Lavnonshire," she said breathlessly.

Patrick recalled, from some cavity of his memory, that she'd professed to have been raised here. It made sense, he supposed. Lavnonshire was a strange collection of Crafters and lower-ranked Artisans. He frowned. "In case you've got ideas of visitin' old friends, I'd remind you there ain't any ships left in Lavnonshire that still leave the dock."

Polly raised an eyebrow. "There are no old friends," she assured him. "Just a mother and father who'd be embarrassed to see me darken their doorstep."

Patrick heaved Theo onward. "Why? Did you send an army after them, too?"

Polly looked off to the distant rooftops. "I'm not exactly a prized Artisan daughter," she said. "I was supposed to return home with accolades, not a dismissal."

Accolades, status, social repute—the things of value to an Artisan. Perhaps the mines weren't the worst fate one could face in the Trench.

"Where to now?" Nina asked, taking up Theo's other side. He groaned as she lifted his arm over her shoulder. The culvert emptied out into a dust yard, weary-eyed Crafters picking out metals and bones left to burn in hearths. It was astonishing what some tried to burn. The poorest Crafters sold the bones to glue factories. The fabric could be washed and reused. The metals melted down and traded in. Dust yards were only good for scraps, for meetings of a dark nature. For hiding.

There were several gaunt Crafters here. They barely paid the group any mind as they passed. One kept their business to themselves in a dust yard.

Ahead of them, though, was the thrum of Lavnonshire, and it would be full of infantry and police watching the docks, ensuring the fishermen strayed no farther than the immediate coastline.

"There's no Union-owned establishments here," Patrick grunted, heaving Theo along.

"What about Leethrow's?" John asked, turning abruptly. Leethrow was a butcher and a neutral. He'd given over the deed without much persuasion back when Patrick was still green. He still remembered his father striding in and holding a meat hook to the man's eye.

"He's in the wind," Patrick responded. "Scarpered two years ago." Right around the time John had been captured.

John cursed. "Slippery little weasel, ain't he?"

Patrick didn't argue. The man had been paid handsomely every month for his indenture, but had also brought two daughters into the shop each day. It was likely he'd valued their safety over money.

"I have an idea," Nina said now. The sun had turned her hair golden, her cheeks distractingly pink. "Though there's no telling if it will be safe." She grimaced and looked directly at Theo, and he at her. A silent message seemed to pass between them.

Patrick felt something primal rise up and bare its teeth.

"Mrs. Trunk?" Theo asked.

It was a name that meant nothing to Patrick, but Nina nodded.

"Who is Mrs. Trunk?" Polly asked.

"When we were apprentices, Professor Dumley used to bring us both here. 'Field work,' he'd call it. Sometimes, we'd stay with . . . an acquaintance of his. An antiques shop proprietor."

Patrick gritted his teeth. "Is she a swank?"

Nina hesitated. "A Mason."

"No," Patrick said immediately. "We'll figure somethin' else out."

"She's harmless, Patrick," Nina said, panting under the weight of Theo. "A society outcast. And she liked us."

Patrick rolled his eyes. He doubted there was nary a person alive who'd met Nina and not fallen for her. "It ain't enough."

But Nina pinched her eyes closed in frustration. There was mud smeared into her hair. A cut on her cheek, sweat glistened over her brow, and he was suddenly suffused with guilt.

"Trust me, Patrick. She couldn't raise the alarm even if she wanted to."

He frowned warily. "And why's that?"

"She's mute," Theodore grunted, looking as though he might pass out at any moment.

"It don't mean she can't flounce down the street wavin' her hands over her head," John grunted. "She'll turn you over the moment she recognizes you."

"I'm not sure she'll think much of it," Nina muttered, her voice turning reluctant. "Mrs. Trunk isn't . . . all there."

Patrick stared at her. "She's a lunatic?"

"Not a *lunatic*," Nina said indignantly. "But she's getting on in years, and she's a recluse. She doesn't care much for society."

"I imagine not," John muttered. "Can't fuckin' speak, can she?"

Nina glared at him. "Have you got a better idea?"

"None," John said, then looked to Patrick. "Gotta stop somewhere, son. The Charmer ain't gonna last the night unless he's seen to."

Even as he said it, Theo's head fell forward, his face collapsing in pain.

Patrick sighed and looked at Theo. It'd be simpler to leave him here to recover, to continue on without stopping, but one glance at Nina told him it wasn't a question. He'd gone and saved her life, after all.

"Lead the way," he said to Nina, taking Theo's full weight from her. "And keep your head down."

The walk was treacherous. Lavnonshire was littered in open market stalls and street vendors selling their haul of cod and crab. Patrick put his cap over Nina's head and pulled it low over her brow. He closed Theo's coat to hide the bloody bandages as they weaved down the streets, closer and closer to the ramparts. A row of shop fronts clustered perilously close to the cliffside, sewn together like a patch quilt.

Theo's weight was starting to hinder him when, thankfully, Nina came to a stop. Her eyes trailed over a grimy door, bulging shopwindows so filled with lime and salt they were impossible to see through. The sign dangling precariously from the roof guttering said TRUNK ANTIQUES AND ODDITIES.

There was a claustrophobia about it, even from the street. It was too narrow, too tall, the competing shops either side pulverizing it.

"Waitin' on an invitation?" John asked Nina.

She turned on him and Patrick, eyes steeled. "No threats," she said. "No guns."

John clicked his tongue. "We ain't in the habit of shootin' old ladies, darlin'."

When they stepped through the shop's door, the sound of the sea was swallowed, replaced by the kind of unbearable hum Patrick only ever experienced when a hundred fathoms beneath ground. Polly let the door shut behind her, and the tinny bell rattled overhead.

Its windows were cluttered top to bottom with art, hat stands, newspapers, books, cat cages, embroidered cushions, lamps, vases, empty wine bottles, candlestick holders, rat traps, and, strangely, a miner's pick.

There were few places to stand, all available room having been taken up by some piece of dusty furniture. Shelves crowded the walls, and even the ceiling was cluttered with hanging pots and cages and cookware. Patrick couldn't think of a place less Artisanal if they were in Kenton Hill.

He grinned.

They each took off their hats, relaxed their shoulders with a groan. Even if the general of the fucking Lords' Army were to look through a window at that moment, they'd see naught but towers of junk.

"Mrs. Trunk?" Nina called out carefully, turning to pass her hips through piles of newspapers and a cello. "Hello?"

From behind a fort of books came someone so short as to appear a child, but was on closer inspection a frightfully old woman with dark skin and thinning hair.

She licked her gums, took her spectacles off, and rubbed them against her blouse. Her chin quivered as she peered at them all. After a moment, Patrick realized that she was speaking to herself in silence. Her lips forming words they couldn't hear.

She came around her piles and stacks in a practiced way, her squat form somehow avoiding any obstacle, until she came before Nina. She looked at her as though she were a collectible to peruse, picking up her hands and turning them over to see their backs, pulling on her curls to test their spring.

Then she smiled, patted Nina's cheek.

"Hello, Mrs. Trunk," Nina said warmly, smiling back.

Patrick felt punched through by that smile. She'd used it on him once or twice. He doubted there were many with hearts and eyes who could refuse it, Mrs. Trunk included.

The old woman's eyes then swept to the rest of them, not stopping until they found Theo, propped between Patrick and John, recognition dawning.

"We're sorry to call on you without an invitation," Nina said to her. "But I'm afraid we had no choice. Theo is . . . injured," Nina said.

Mrs. Trunk patted her cheek again. There was a shake to her hands. She wore a gentleman's dinner jacket and dungarees—hardly swank fashion—and if it wasn't for the piano that started playing of its own accord in a dusty corner, Patrick might have thought her a Craftswoman.

Except that the keys trilled suddenly in a strange and complicated ascension of notes. It made John spin and lift a pistol from his coat, made Polly duck and cover her head.

But it only made Nina smile.

Patrick watched the dark wooden keys settle back into place and frowned at them.

"Mrs. Trunk is a wood Mason," Nina offered.

At that, the piano warbled again. One solitary, piercing tone, as though to affirm.

"She uses the piano to speak."

Mrs. Trunk's lips moved soundlessly. She moved to a chair overturned and took it by its legs. With precarious movements she righted it on the floor and pointed abruptly to Theo. The piano sang again.

"I think she wants to see Theo's injury," Nina offered, and Mrs. Trunk nodded brusquely.

Theo groaned as he sank onto the chair, but he had the wherewithal to nod his head to Mrs. Trunk—the perfect gentleman. "Pleasure to see you again," he said through gritted teeth.

Mrs. Trunk unwrapped the sodden bandage, shook her head in reproach, her lips moving, piano playing in double time, the tone somber, as though she were giving them a tongue lashing.

Without warning, she went shuffling off into the maze of junk.

"Lord," John said in her absence. "Ain't a single marble left, eh? Complete nutter."

"Mind your manners," Nina said, eyes stuck on the weeping sore on Theo's side. His head was hung back over the chair, his eyes closed. He drew deep, deliberate breaths through his nose.

"Well, she ain't a threat, that's for certain," John continued on, going to an old wall clock discarded on the floor and picking it up, turning it over to view its cogs. "We ought to take advantage if we can. Lay low for a few days or more, let the Scribbler work on the translations."

Patrick was already shaking his head. "We haven't got time. The longer we sit still, the more likely it is we're caught." Patrick felt that screw wind itself tighter. "We need to find the Seam. I need to return to Kenton." He felt it like fingers clamped around his windpipe. Every day, his dread compounded.

"Theo can't travel like this," Nina said, her eyes roaming over the man, brow furrowed.

At the sound of her voice, Theo's eyes opened. They caught hers.

Patrick heard bones break, the spray of blood. He swallowed. "Then he ought to stay here." He said it with deliberate slowness. He wanted her to hear the sense in it. To bring this juvenile bond to an end. "He can stay in the care of Mrs. Trunk, and we'll carry on to Hoaklin as planned. Polly can translate on the route. Then we head straight for the Seam."

Nina turned her head to Patrick, and he thought her expression was laced with apology.

His stomach fell.

"We can't leave him here."

"Don't make much sense to drag him along any further," John interceded.

But Nina paid him no mind. She stepped closer to Patrick, her hands balling the way they did when she was scared. Was she afraid of him?

"He followed your orders with those men. He killed them for us, and he took a bullet to save me," she said. It was damningly soft. "I—I can't just abandon him."

Over Nina's shoulder, Theo's eyes became star-bright. His shoulders lifted just a fraction.

Patrick let the air pent up in his tired lungs go and swallowed a stream of vitriol that wasn't intended for her. "Fine," he said. "We'll stay." Lord, but he was loathe to. Loathe to be sitting still while his broken parish stitched itself back together and the Lords' Army circled in on them and somewhere in the Trench, miles of terranium sat waiting for the taking.

"Thank you," Nina said, and back she went. Back to Theo and his shining eyes, his wound—visible proof of his loyalty to her. She watched over Mrs. Trunk, who had returned with a carpet bag clinking with medical supplies and begun to pull out foul-smelling antiseptic and yellowing gauze.

Patrick couldn't stand here another moment watching. He went to the piano with his jaw sticking. He rounded precariously stacked pots and a chest of men's boots with his nails digging into his palms.

The standing piano was made of Sitka spruce, he guessed, its keys unsurfaced. Atop each key was a letter, or sometimes a word. Patrick saw a *Yes*, *No*, and oddly, the word *Bastard*. Each of these was etched into the wood in neat script, no doubt by Mrs. Trunk herself. Patrick ran his fingers across them. They came away dusty.

The keys compressed discordantly, the words spelled out too quickly. Patrick tried to track the letters as they were belted down but was helpless to follow along. He looked back over his shoulder to Mrs. Trunk, who was half bent over, dabbing at Theo's side in a practiced way.

"What did she say?" Nina called, watching him.

He shook his head. "Could you, uh . . . go a little slower?"

Mrs. Trunk's shoulders rose and fell on a sigh, and then the melody played again, lagging now. Partick couldn't describe how, but he felt as if the sound mocked him, like speech slowed down for the irreparably stupid.

The notes rang out, and Patrick read them aloud. "Don't . . . touch." He grinned down at the keys, then turned to say. "Pardon me, Miss."

John came to Patrick's side, his tongue tucked into his cheek in the way he was prone to when deep in thought. For a moment, Patrick was waylaid by memories of him turning over the working parts of some device, his concentration fixed.

"Clever," John said, bending to see beneath. "She had her tongue cut out or somethin'?"

Another singular note, this one a dirge. The key with the word *No* compressed, and John huffed a guttural laugh.

"She's not *deaf*, John," Nina called out.

Another note. *Bastard.*

Patrick grinned again. John chuckled. "Ain't half-stupid, neither."

More notes. This time spelling W-H-O-A-R-E-Y-O-U?

"Mrs. Trunk, my name is Patrick. I apologize for the intrusion."

Mrs. Trunk simply kept on with her ministrations, hovering over Theo, blotting the antiseptic on his wound.

"Please forgive John here. His manners are trapped somewhere between his arse and his mouth." It was a risk, Patrick knew, to speak crassly to an Artisan lady before asking her a favor, but Patrick had learned to read people. No regular swank opened an antiques store on a cliff in Lavnonshire and piled it with Crafter treasure.

Mrs. Trunk's eyes twinkled. Patrick knew caged laughter when he saw it. Nina rolled her eyes at Patrick, and he winked at her.

"We're in dire need of a place to stay, Mrs. Trunk. Just for a few nights," Nina said. "We'll keep out of your hair. And we can pay."

Mrs. Trunk was already nodding absently and waving off the idea of payment as though it were hardly a favor at all. More notes rang out. T-R-O-U-B-L-E-?

Patrick hid his hands in his pockets. "No trouble," he said easily.

A run of notes followed, one key after another, so dizzyingly fast that Patrick hardly made heads or tails of it.

Nina grinned. "You'll have to forgive them, Mrs. Trunk. They're simple Crafters. They don't read quickly."

Patrick smirked.

The melody came again, this time elongated.

"Studying?" Patrick read aloud.

Theodore and Nina shared a look, his eyes popping open and his jaw slackening, lost in some memory.

"Yes," Nina answered heavily. "We're studying."

Patrick wondered if Mrs. Trunk was in fact addled, or if the passing of so many years had simply blended them all together while she collected her wares and curated her piles of junk, oblivious to the turning of the earth.

Mrs. Trunk had pasted the wound and covered it in gauze. She wrapped a clean bandage around Theo's waist, smacked his hands away when he tried to touch it.

She held out a dusty vial then, on it the words BLUFF TINCTURE reflecting light from the window.

Theo hesitated to take it.

"Drink it, Theo," Nina said.

Like a dog greedy for the approval of his master, he did.

Without another word, Mrs. Trunk turned and began her slow progression to a slight stairwell in the back of the shop, between an overladen china cabinet and a silent grandfather clock. She indicated for them to follow.

Patrick saw John take one last glance at the piano, his finger reaching toward the keys. He was beaten to the punch by a single note.

No.

Mrs. Trunk's upstairs apartment was much like her shop: cluttered with odd assortments of things, too cramped by far. There was a minuscule kitchen, a tea table with two chairs, shelves of pottery and candlesticks, a boarded floor covered in a faded red rug, and a settee. Nina helped Theo limp to it and lay down there, where he closed his eyes immediately, the dose of bluff taking effect. He was snoring within moments, and Nina looked down at him with concern etched in her brow, her hands pressing anxiously on her hips.

"He'll recover, won't he?" she asked aloud. To whom, it wasn't clear.

Mrs. Trunk showed the rest of them to two spare bedrooms piled with newspapers and books with peeling covers. There were two iron beds with lumpy mattresses per room, a skinny window that wouldn't open, empty candlestick holders on the sill, wax gumming them to the paint.

Mrs. Trunk shuffled the girls into one room, then Patrick and his father to another, like they were schoolchildren being herded into dorms. When Patrick looked over his shoulder to watch the back of Nina disappear through the door, Mrs. Trunk put a finger to the side of his head and turned his face away, shaking her head, her messaging clear. She gave them bowls of water and towels to clean with, brought them tea and toast. Patrick ate and drank unconsciously. He tried to lie down but found it unbearable. Instead, he settled for trying to open the jammed window, pressing vehemently against the hinges.

His father chuckled behind him. "Like a caged animal," he said fondly. "You always were. You and your brothers."

Patrick glanced over his shoulder. John was shirtless, washing his face over the bowl, his beard dripping rivulets. He looked about the room as though it was of great interest to him, and Patrick couldn't understand how he wasn't jumping out of his own skin.

"It's been weeks now," Patrick said, throwing his shoulder against the window frame. It didn't budge. "Weeks since the attack on Kenton. Since they took all the bluff."

"Your brothers are there, Patty," John said. "They'll hold down the fort just fine till you return."

"Till *we* return," Patrick corrected, pausing in his assault against the window, looking once more to his father.

John was drying his face with a towel. "Yeah," he said. "Till we return."

Patrick shook his head. "Gunner's not right in his head," he said. "He's worse than you'd remember. I couldn't keep him away from the hawkers. And Donny's just a kid."

"He's no more a kid than *you* are," John told him. "And their mother ain't gonna let 'em go astray. She'll kick him in the arse if need be."

"The trades'll be slowin'," Patrick continued, pressing the tips of his fingers into the window crevasses until his fingers turned white and his nails protested. "If they haven't stopped already. There's debts, and not a lick of bluff to trade with."

"There's coal," John said prosaically. "Your brothers'll hold 'em off till the end of winter at least."

"It won't be enough," Patrick argued, an ache forming behind his eyes.

"Then they'll throw their weight around, Patty. They know the business."

"This should concern you," Patrick said, pinching the bridge of his nose and cinching his eyes shut to stave off the pain. "You should be worried for them. For Ma."

"Composure, Patty," John said, as though his son were still thirteen and trying to split lumps of stolen terranium. "Men who don't learn it don't make a single right choice in their lives."

Patrick threw his shoulder into the window again, harder now. There wasn't enough air in the room.

"Guard your temper. You fly off the handle, you might as well fold your hand."

Patrick pushed at the window again, heard something creak.

"This is the business, Patty. It's a hundred problems, each as urgent as the next. The only one that matters is the one in front of you."

Patrick threw his fist into the window in desperation, and the glass splintered. His father's hands were on his shoulders, his chest, holding him back.

"Just breathe, Pat," he was saying. "Come on, lad. *Breathe.* Till the light comes, remember? Till the light comes, we keep at it. Everythin' has a fix."

His lungs were howling as he inhaled, his eyes shut so tightly he thought they might never open again.

"Jus' breathe. That's the way," John's voice swooped in. "Ain't anythin' so big we can't handle, Patty. We find a way. We'll get us all the bluff we'll ever need, son. All the bluff your *mother* could ever need."

Tess's face swam on a carousel. Younger and gray as smoke. Then older, wearier. He braced himself on the windowsill, felt tiny shards of glass embed in his skin. He breathed heavily, sweat trickling into the corners of his eyes.

"Nothin' we can do for 'em if we go back empty-handed, Patty. We find the Seam first. This is the problem in front of us."

Patrick nodded. There was nothing to do but nod.

"I rely on you, son," John was saying now. "I gave you this burden 'cause you were the only one who could bear it. We're so close now—I can't have you fallin' apart."

His father slapped his spine between his shoulder blades, the reverberations reaching his heart. It was a reset, a jolt of strength.

"Till the light comes, son. Say it."

"Till the light comes." He could barely shove the words past his lips.

"That's it." John mussed his hair. "Come on, now. There's gotta be a cigarette somewhere around here."

Patrick opened his eyes to the broken window, the glass now a web. He traced the path of a fissure with his finger, and he thought to himself, if only he could see where it would all end, where they would all fall, he would know if he could live with himself in the aftermath.

He turned to his father pulling a shirt over his head, pulling up his suspenders as though preparing for second shift in the mines. As though he might thunder down the stairs and kiss his mother on the cheek, pat Gunner's shoulder, and pull on Donny's nose.

"Till the light comes," Patrick murmured to himself, searching for composure, shunting fear into his center and locking it away. "Down we go."

CHAPTER THIRTY-SEVEN

DONNY

It'd been several weeks since Donny had slept soundly. Every day, he felt as though he were morphing into a poor substitution for his absent brother.

He wondered if this heaviness he felt in the crane of his neck, in the bedrock of his stomach, had been carried by Patrick before him and his father before that. Had it felt to them as though their boots were sinking farther into the mud by the second? Had Donny truly been so absorbed in himself that he'd never noticed?

For the first time in seven years, the Coal Works was short of coal. Hearths would start emptying around the parish, the pipes would bring naught through its channels. The waters in their tanks and boilers would freeze over.

"A dead winter," Gunner muttered. The gong of his boot kicking a copper drum rung hollow. "A dead fuckin winter, on top of *everythin'*!"

The factory floor of the Coal Works sweltered. In his mind, Donny imagined it bulging, the steam collecting along the walls and curling to the roof until the whole place distended. "God bloody help us," he said.

"Ain't any way round it," said Otto. His voice was weary from a shift already spent in the mines. "Nothin' left to trade with. Gotta keep the Union members happy with somethin' if not bluff."

Therein lay the problem. With no bluff to trade, there was only coal. Triple the amount outgoing than usual, and not half the men to mine it.

There'd been too many good miners lost in the attack. Even working more than they ought to, the miners that remained couldn't replace what they were exporting.

"Fuck," Donny said, pulling his cap from his head and mopping his face. "Someone light me a smoke."

"Can't smoke in here, Donny," said Otto.

"Don't see no signs."

"Won't see my fist flying at your chin, neither," Gunner growled, his temper barely contained. These days, he was like a feral dog backed against a wall. He'd lash out at anything.

Donny fished a bent cigarette from his trousers despite it. He felt his blood thinning, retreating to his heart. His hands shook.

Gunner slapped the cigarette out of his hand. "I'll box you till you're deaf as well, Don!"

"That'll be the fuckin' day," Donny said, fists clenching.

"You need a drink is all," Otto said on a sigh. "We all could use a night off."

"I need a fuck," Donny countered. "Anyone will do."

"Didn't you lay with that lad last night?"

"Aye," said Donny. "And it's been too many fuckin' hours since."

Gunner was prowling, back and forth. Donny couldn't help but count the minutes ticking by while they stood there, useless. *Patrick would've come up with a solution by now*, he thought. *He wouldn't just be standin' here thinkin' about his cock.* But Donny had never been as cunning as Patrick, nor as quick, nor as decisive. Donny could be counted on for the sport of the business, not the strategy.

"Fuck the members!" Gunner was braying now. "Never once thanked us, have they? How many years've we spent breakin' our backs for 'em? I say we keep the fuckin' coal for ourselves."

"Can't feed the parish with coal though, can we?" Donny sneered. "A warm body ain't any good if it's starved, you dolt."

"Call me dolt *again*."

"Why does Gunner's head look like it might burst?" came Scottie's voice. His footsteps approached, muffled by the hiss of the boilers.

"Don't worry none. It's thick as a ram's. Nothin's busting through it," Donny answered. "What news?"

Scottie sighed wearily. "The bad kind."

"Have mercy." Donny wondered if there was a bottom to the well, or if they'd drown reaching for it.

Scottie had been to Dorser for an arranged trade in the night. He was late to return.

"Dorser didn't show," Scottie said, and Donny heard the cracks of his bones as he stretched. "Waited there half the fuckin' night."

An incomprehensible silence ensued. Otto began to pace. There was the sound of a lighter striking.

"Oy!" Donny cried, "Thought you said no smokin'?"

"They're sendin' a message," Otto intoned, voice distant. He exhaled heavily. Smoke infused the air.

"Left a note, too," Scottie said. There was a crinkle of paper, the slap of it as it collided with someone's hand.

Gunner read aloud.

"*Alchemist and Earth Charmer Sworn into Governing Administration as Lord and Lady*," he said gruffly, voice darkening on the final words.

Donny's chest concussed. Beyond the pounding in his ears, he heard the sound of paper tearing, flames thrilling as they were fed.

He turned his back on the others, closed his eyes, and tried to think.

"They think we're colludin' with the swanks," Otto growled. "Donny? Did you hear—"

"Yeah, I fuckin' heard," he muttered.

"Donny . . . they won't trade till we prove we're on the right side of things. That's what they're tryin' to tell us," said Scottie.

"I know."

"Soon they'll be comin' down those tunnels lookin' for bluff."

"We ain't got any!" thundered Gunner.

"But we told 'em we did," Donny said. "And then we flaunted like show ponies for those fuckin' Dunnitch men." He dug the heels of his hands into his eyes, wishing, for the first time in his life, that he could block out the spurts of color and plunder himself into the quiet, fathomless dark.

Patrick wouldn't have made this mistake. He would've been miles ahead of it.

"Rally up some of the lads," Gunner was saying now. "Give them some rifles. We'll pay those ungrateful fuckers a visit ourselves."

"And turn against our own comrades, just as they fear we have?" God bloody damn, but he needed silence. He needed sleep. He needed someone else to take this burden from him. "That's how this whole fuckin' thing unravels, Gun. From within. It starts with lies. And then we grow distrustful of each other, then fearful, instead of rememberin' who we're fightin'. That's what the House is hopin' for when they write those fuckin' headlines."

The other men grew quiet. Donny felt their stares on the back of his head, felt the gooseflesh rise along his neck. "This was our fault, brother," he said heavily. "*Better to lead with something true.* That's what Dad used to say."

"Aye. Well, he ain't fuckin' here."

No, he wasn't. It was just the two of them now to look over the business, the Union, their mother, and they were making a mess of it.

"What do we do with the coal meant for Dorser, Don?" Scottie was asking now.

"Fuck those Dorser *cunts*. We'll have it here, where it's needed," Gunner heaved.

"No," said Donny, and he felt the decision land in his gut, felt the fingers of it strangle his organs. "Leave the coal at the end of the tunnel in Dorser. They'll find it."

"What? Donny—"

"Their population is three times ours," he continued. "And they've suffered their own attack. They're just as much prone to a dead winter as we are. That's what Patrick would say."

“Fuck that! Patrick would tell you to turn your attention to Kenton Hill first. He’d tell you Dorser was someone else’s village!”

“Patrick promised Dorser bluff,” Donny answered. “And until we can make good on it, we’ll act in good faith. Let them see it as a sign that we remain on the right side of this war.”

Scottie cleared his throat. Otto exhaled again, and the smell of sweet tobacco found Donny.

None argued, and Donny wondered if he didn’t want them to. If he wanted them to stomp their feet and tell him no, that he was wrong, that this, too, would prove a mistake.

“What about the market, Don?” said Otto. “We need to fill it with somethin’.”

Donny sighed, pictured Patrick somewhere in the brink, fossicking for the last dregs of terranium this continent had to offer.

They only had to hold out a little longer. Any day now, Patrick would return.

“Call a Union meetin’ in the pub for tonight,” he said. “And be ready for trouble. They ain’t gonna like what we got to say.”

“And what’s that?” Scottie asked.

“That their food sundries now belong to Colson & Sons and will be redistributed evenly, and that all southside residents will be relocated to the north to conserve coal.”

“Fuck,” breathed Otto, and Donny thought he sounded wearier than he ever had.

“Then I’ll get to work divertin’ the gas lines,” Gunner said. “Be easier to persuade ’em to leave when they come home to cold houses.”

“Are you sure you’ve got the words to convince ’em, Donny?” Scottie said carefully, his tone grave. “You better put some balls behind it, or we’ll have mutiny on our hands.”

Donny sighed long and hard. “I’ll find ’em.”

CHAPTER THIRTY-EIGHT

PATRICK

When he woke, the sun beyond the broken window was orange. The shadows in the room had elongated. His father snored obscenely.

Patrick pushed himself upright and stretched out the strain in his neck. He pretended that the lethargy he felt was credited to the lumpy mattress and not to a greater fatigue. For a moment, the room rotated around him like a mirage, and he himself was bodiless. He pressed the heels of his hands into his eye sockets. He couldn't stay in this room with its towers of books another moment.

He stood and half dressed himself. The clothes Mrs. Trunk had left smelled like must and time. Socks, no boots, an unbuttoned shirt, no suspenders. He fought the door against the draft in the hallway.

Polly and Nina's door was cracked open, and inside was Polly sleeping with the Stewards' book on her stomach, parchment spread around her, those strange symbols bled onto the pages, scratched out, rewritten.

Nina was missing.

She wasn't with Theo, either, who lay prone on the settee, the bluff making his jaw sag, his eyelids slack in sleep.

A jolt of panic struck Patrick, one that was becoming familiar to him. He went to the stairs and pounded down each one, mumbling beneath his breath about how the woman couldn't go more than a handful of hours without fraying his nerves.

He found her in the shop, sitting on the piano bench alongside Mrs. Trunk, who spoke to her with music.

Patrick didn't approach immediately. He simply watched, letting his thundering heart settle.

Nina was smiling softly at the older woman, her hair escaping its clasp and framing her face, dimples appearing in either cheek, lashes fanning tired eyes. He knew their color to be beautiful, though he couldn't see them. He knew when they caught the light, a spectrum of green swallowed the hazel, the apples of her cheeks glowed pink and the column of her throat, too. It often unsettled him.

It was becoming difficult to remember why he couldn't love her. Over and over, he replayed the times she'd lied to him. He was trying to convince himself that really, she was a mystery to him, that he'd sprinted ahead to love and ignored everything else. A goner, Tess had called him. He hadn't had the time to understand the half of her.

But it was so easy to feel like he did.

Mrs. Trunk played stories to Nina, who sat with rapt attention, grinning, answering in kind, throwing her head back and laughing earnestly at whatever the elderly woman told her. She treated people with a blanket fairness Patrick couldn't allow, gave pieces of herself over freely and closed off other parts in a vault.

He felt that she'd been born in the wrong world. In another life, she was the sort of woman who got all the things a lady deserved. A house and beautiful dresses. A flowery wedding. A bed in which she'd be worshipped. All the children she wanted, or none if she didn't. Every ounce of bluff or ink she'd ever need so she'd never know a day of pain. Someone who would take on the brunt of the world until it felt soft to her.

He'd imagined himself to be that champion once. It seemed laughable now. Neither of them were meant for that life. Without her, there was no terranium. Without him, there was no alchemy.

And without idium, there was nothing.

Patrick stepped into the shop, and the women looked up, finally noticing him. Patrick tried and failed to grin. "Pardon the interruption."

Mrs. Trunk nodded when she saw him, then touched Nina's cheek and rose. As she passed, she stopped to look up shrewdly into Patrick's face. Whatever she saw there, it saddened her. She crammed into the stairwell, her frame disappearing.

Patrick put his hands in his pockets, stifling the sudden unease he felt. "Do you ever stay where you're supposed to?"

She lifted an eyebrow at him. "Not recently, no."

"Anyone could walk in," he reminded her, nodding toward the door and its open sign. "Recognize you."

"I've been here plenty. Never seen a single customer."

"Woman, you couldn't just humor me and stay safe upstairs?"

"If I say no, will you threaten to carry me up there yourself?"

His blood spiked. "It wouldn't be a threat."

Nina rolled her eyes at him. Lord, when she did that, he wanted to take her jaw in his hand, tilt her head back until she was looking only at him. "What were you two doin'?"

She glanced her fingers over the piano keys. "Just gossiping."

"Through *song*?"

Nina's lip quirked.

"Artisan bullshit," Patrick muttered beneath his breath. It had the desired effect. There was sustenance for him in her scowls. He thought he could live off them until he was an old man. He smiled to himself as she began to prattle.

"You don't seem to have a problem with ingenuity until you learn it's an *Artisan* who's responsible. And you're awfully superior for a man who is, by any reasonable measure, an Artisan himself."

He sighed. "We ought to get you your own piano. I might even enjoy it if you scolded me in song."

She looked at him with that flat expression of hers, one finger rising to the key entitled *bastard*. The sullen note rang out. But a grin broke through. A blush crept up her throat from beneath her collar, and he watched it. She looked away.

That was just as well.

"Why aren't you resting?" he asked. "We've had a long journey."

She shrugged. "I couldn't sleep," she said. "Polly was scratching away at her translations half the night. Your dad's snoring was coming through the wall, and I couldn't be in the living room."

"Ah," Patrick said. "Theodore."

A small hesitation. "Yes."

"Because you can't stand him?" Patrick asked. "Or because you can't stand the thought of him being hurt?"

She bit her lip, looked down into her lap. "Because I can't stand knowing . . . that he would have died for me."

Patrick sat on the bench beside her, his chest heavy. "More agonizin' company I couldn't imagine."

Her eyes were wet with something unspent. "It was easier hating him," she said. "That, I could reconcile with."

Patrick nodded. In truth, he felt the same way. It was all made simpler before he was indebted to Theodore. But he'd saved Nina twice now.

"I know we should leave him here," Nina said tightly. "But I can't, Patrick. I wish I could."

It sounded like she was saying something else. That she wished she didn't care for him.

Patrick tasted metal and blood. He grimaced. "If you could be anywhere else," he asked, needing desperately to change the subject, "even for just a day, where would you choose?"

Her fingers traced the keys. There was a rigidness to her posture now. "I don't have an answer for that."

He wished he could read her thoughts. "Try."

"Won't do much good."

"Why?"

"There's no place that'll have me, Patrick," she said. "Unless you count the House of Lords."

And for all his troubles, he couldn't imagine that cruelty. To have no place of retreat. Nowhere that felt like home. But he wouldn't let his pity show. He knew she would hate it. "What about Kenton Hill?"

She scoffed, the sound unexpectedly sad. "I suspect I outstayed my welcome there." There was a shake to her hands. Enduring shell shock.

Patrick clasped one large hand over hers to still them. He counted to three and then removed it. "I only meant . . . did Kenton Hill mean somethin' to you?"

Nina looked at him and sighed. "I'd rather not say."

"Why?"

"Because I don't think you'll believe the answer," she admitted. "And you have a certain way of looking at me when you don't trust me."

He watched gooseflesh rise along her collarbone, saw the way her legs crossed tighter. "How do I look at you?"

"Like we've never met," she said. "Like you're looking at a stranger."

He pushed his molars together. "We don't know each other in the ways that matter."

"Yes, we do," she said, looking up at him. The same freckles she'd had as a kid. Same hazel eyes, same clenched fists. "Better than most people would. Because I've seen the tarnished side of you, the one that flies into a rage and throws around his muscle. And you've seen the ugliest parts of me."

He knew he should get up and leave this very minute. "It don't mean we're good for each other."

"I'm not saying we are," she said reluctantly. "I'm just saying we know each other. If it eases you to think of me as a stranger, then so be it. It hardly makes it true."

She didn't know the half of his thinking. He shook his head minutely. "In truth, Nina, I've been tryin' to wipe my mind of you altogether."

She winced. "Any success?"

He paused, thinking that his answer should stay locked away. "None at all."

She nodded, looking down at the piano keys, fingers playing a phantom of a song from her memory. She swallowed. "That will become easier when we part ways."

Patrick very much doubted it. "You didn't answer my question."

"Which one?"

"Kenton Hill," he said. "Did it mean somethin' to you?" He'd taken her to the hills and through the village, to the Coal Works and the market beneath the lamps. And he'd thought he'd seen the parish work its magic on her. Had he imagined it?

Nina suddenly filled with something. She expelled it in one heavy breath and said, "I've traveled the Trench over, and I've never loved a place more."

A lump rose in his throat. "And when you thought you might still bury it . . . what did you tell yourself?"

She hesitated before responding, as though knowing the weight of her answer. "Polly told me something back then," Nina said. "She told me that I had to try not to see it—all the good in Kenton. Scottie and Otto and your brothers. The dancing and the music. The community. You." Nina's hands pressed to her stomach like something had punched her. "But I saw it all anyway. In truth, I told myself I had time to find a solution. I made bargains with myself. I was drunk, I think. On the parish. On you." She looked up, smiled sadly.

He tried not to show his understanding, how conflicted she made him feel. "Then we were both drunken fools."

She nodded weakly.

Patrick turned back to the piano. "Can you play?"

"A little," she said. "Though I was my music professor's least favorite student."

"He was a fool, too, then."

Nina smirked. "In my first year, I used to sneak into the conservatory to practice at night. The headmaster caught me once, but he walked right by like he hadn't seen me. After that, I was never chastised again in my music lessons. I think Professor Dumley had something to do with that." She frowned at the wall for a moment, lost in thought.

It was odd to imagine her in the Artisan school alongside the other swank kids. Patrick could only imagine her as she'd been at the siphoning ceremony: lopsided bow, poorly stitched blouse, dirt on her nose, fire in her eyes. "Was it difficult?" he asked. "To try and fit in where you didn't belong?" For it had always been so clear to him where she truly belonged.

"Impossible," she said. "Polly and I were the only brink children in our year. They called me *worm* and her *squid* beneath their breath. I didn't know how to fight back. In Scurry, it would've been fists and slurs. In the Artisan school it was gossip, whispers, jokes. The violence was all silent. I think it turned me into a coward. It didn't get any better until . . ."

Here, she came up short, something lodged in her throat.

"Until what?"

She looked away. "Until Theo," she admitted.

Patrick tensed, the poison rising in him against his will. Like Nina, he was born in the brink, where a person was measured by how well they fought. He wished he could eliminate any other man from her thoughts the only way he knew how.

"Did he defend you?" he asked, trying to hide the flash of jealousy. "Rough up the other boys in front of you and make you swoon?"

Nina scoffed. "Artisan boys don't *rough each other up*."

"Ah, pardon me. Then he picked you flowers and drew you pictures?"

The blood pooling in her cheeks told him he wasn't far off.

"He was a friend to me," she said. "For no good reason other than I needed one."

Patrick clicked his tongue. "Oh, there was a reason, darlin'."

Nina glared at him. "We were *twelve*, Patrick. I don't think romance was a factor."

"I was twelve when I saw you for the first time," Patrick mused, "and romance was *definitely* a factor."

Nina rolled her eyes again, and this time he did take hold of her jaw, turning her face to his. His fingers were neither harsh nor gentle. "Do you want me to tell you what men see when they look at you?" he said, voice deepening. Here was the madness taking over again, flooding him, muting all sensible thought.

He ran his thumb over her bottom lip, and she released a small gasp for him. He felt it resonate low in his abdomen, in his groin. "They see every sinful imaginin' they've ever had, all at once," he murmured. "Every beauty that existed before vanishes from memory, until their whole head is crowded with you. You in their hands, their beds, in every improper way that can be imagined. They see a woman they'd commit terrible crimes for. Just for a chance." He was close enough now that the words were skating over her mouth, down her throat. "They'd kill for it if they had to."

She shivered, her hand rising up to flatten against his chest.

"They might pretend to be gentlemanly for you, Nina," Patrick said, coming close to the edge of his restraint, "but inside every man, Artisan or not, lives a beast. Some only hide it better than others." Fire erupted in her eyes, on his chest where she touched him. "Some of us don't bother to hide it at all."

He released her chin and drew away, removed his gaze from her mouth. Tried to redraw the line.

He felt her gaze on him. "Play me a song," he said.

She sighed and repositioned herself on the seat, shoulders slumping. "What do you want to hear?"

"Only songs I know came from a church or a tunnel," he said. "Play me somethin' I don't know."

After a moment of hesitation, her fingers hovering over the keys and their carvings, she did.

And Patrick was sure, then, that whoever that Artisan professor was, he had gas in his head.

The song expounded in his chest and his blood like idium, expanding his mind tenfold. Made him forget all the wrong she'd done, all the sin in his head.

How could something so beautiful be so wrong?

THE STEWARDS' TESTAMENT

DIONE

The second daughter, Dione, traveled with the Stewards to the southern cliffs along the shore. They sought shelter there, but were met with solemn welcome, for the people had already heard it told of witches in the Trench.

But Dione hosted a magic the likes of which had never been seen. She kept the escarpment from crumbling into the ocean, and with it, many of its houses. She tamed demonic waves before they could sink their boats. She built them a church to prove her faithfulness to God, and for this, the townspeople gave her refuge.

Dione married in the church she herself in weeks prior had erected, to Mister Rackley Duponte, the founder's son. She was, on the day of her marriage, ten and four, and no family passed her hand to her betrothed.

She became round with a child quickly, and when the beast invaded the moors, the infant was born into the night. Her husband was not to be found by her bedside, nor her father by law, for they had fled the land and taken to sea. Only the Stewards remained.

Dione was discovered quickly, for the village was promised its safe return to its custodians if Dione was surrendered. The enemy was led to her birthing bed, and her child taken from her arms. In doing so, it awakened in her a terrible monster.

She held her captors at bay for three days and three nights, drowning the men with giant waves until she tired. She was tied to the sea boulders and bled dry. She wilted there to the audience of her captors, until the ocean, as though sent by God, came mercifully to cradle her remnants down to the depths of the sea.

CHAPTER THIRTY-NINE

NINA

In Mrs. Trunk's living room, my eyes rose from the parchment.

"Well," John said gruffly, glaring at Polly. "Still don't say nothin' about the Seam though, does it?"

We were gathered around Polly's latest translation—all but Mrs. Trunk, who was tending her shop, and Theodore, who was still resting on the settee.

Patrick closed his eyes in frustration. "What else is there, Polly?"

She was weary, drooping further with every hour. She shook her head. "That's all I've managed."

"It ain't enough, Scribbler," John said, clicking his tongue. "Not enough for a fare out of Hoaklin."

"I can't remember it all, no matter how hard I work at it," Polly said. A capillary had burst in her right eye. She stretched her shaking fingers as though they were calcifying. "I told you it would be difficult."

"How long to translate Idia's story?" Patrick asked her. "It must be comin' next."

"I don't know," she said despairingly. "Weeks, maybe." But she looked as though she wouldn't last another day.

John scoffed. "Weeks!" A cruel smile twisted onto his face. "Then you best forgo sleep and pray for a miracle, darlin', because that ship of yours only comes round once a year off our shores, and it'll anchor down in a fortnight."

Polly's head shook, fervor returning to her eyes. She gripped the fringes of her coiled hair between her knuckles. "There are too many symbols I don't know. Too many gaps to make sense of the rest! It's slowing me."

"It's all right, Pol" came Theo's feeble voice. "There isn't a more talented Scribbler anywhere. You'll find a way."

But Polly was biting her thumbnail, pacing around the room. "I need a bloody cypher. I'm just stumbling through without it."

Patrick sighed. "And if you had it, how quickly could you translate?"

She concentrated for a moment. "Hours," she said. "Only a good few hours."

"Well," said John, "your luck ends here, Scribbler. We ain't got a cypher between us."

"But your grandfather had one," Patrick said to Polly. "You said he taught you Verian Script with it."

She nodded.

"And he died here in Lavnonshire?" Patrick asked.

Polly's lips thinned. "He . . . did." She seemed to know where the line of questioning was headed.

"And who would have been charged with his possessions after he died?" Patrick asked. "Who would have donated his books to the archives?"

Her brow twitched. She hesitated before answering. "My parents."

"Locals, I'd bet."

Polly nodded stiffly.

Patrick exhaled in a gust and pulled his coin from his pocket. "Then you'll be payin' old Ma and Dad a visit."

Immediately, Polly shook her head. "That—it isn't possible."

"Sure it is," said John, teeth glinting in the thicket of his beard. His energy seemed restored. "Call on 'em for a spot of tea."

"You don't understand. They've forbidden me to return home," she said. "I'm the very last person they'll help, and not especially with anything that pertains to the Stewards."

There was shame in her now, weighing down her posture.

"Let me be clear," Patrick told her. And he flipped the coin over again, watching the face turn tails to heads. Canary to lord. "If it's not you goin' in to find that cypher, then it's me."

It was threat enough. Polly's eyes drifted shut. "All right," she said. "I'll need different clothing."

Patrick paused in the act of turning away, his eyes skimming over Polly's form with little interest. "Nothin' wrong with what you're wearin'."

"I look like a Craftswoman," she said, her voice extinguishing at its end. "My father . . . won't like that."

Patrick sighed. "Then find yourself somethin' suitable from downstairs," he said, stalking down the hallway to his room. "We're leavin' now."

I stepped forward. "I—"

"Don't bother," Patrick called over his shoulder. "You're stayin' here."

I gritted my teeth.

"I might as well come along," John said, interlocking his fingers and flexing them. "Wouldn't mind stretchin' me legs." He ambled off behind Patrick.

Polly's eyes flitted to me once with something I thought was pleading. But then she gathered her skirt in one hand and went for the stairs.

With the translation in hand, I moved to the window. I listened to Patrick's muted voice coming through thin walls, to John's boots plodding over the floorboards, to Theodore's steady breaths. I looked out over the sun-drenched ocean, ranks of whitewash barreling toward the cliffs, and I reread Dione's story another time, then started again. I wondered if the town that had used and abandoned Dione was now the seaside parish of Lavnonshire. I didn't see any reason why it couldn't be. It was a sign, surely, that we were on the right track. Perhaps after everything, Idia was leading us.

Theodore cleared his throat.

"It's quite something, isn't it?" he said, not without effort. "Quite a different account from the one we were taught." Theo snatched his breath in, gripping his side.

I looked at his bandaged wound, swallowing hard. "You're starting to sound like you believe."

His nose wrinkled. "It's a fascinating story," he said. "But if there's any truth to it, the Artisan historians would have written their own accounts."

"And what if this was just another secret the House took pains to keep buried?"

Theo seemed to consider it seriously, then he shook his head. "What motive would they have? To protect the nations who invaded Belavere?" he scoffed. "Doesn't sound like them."

No, it didn't. If anything, the House promoted hatred of the enemy nations who'd once come to these shores to take their terranium, just as they promoted hatred of the Miners Union now.

I bit my lip, looked back to the cerulean sea. I didn't want to admit that Theo had a point, that maybe this book was a work of fiction, and we were barreling toward a dead end. "I need to believe it's real," I said aloud. "Or what do I have left?"

When I looked at Theo again, he stared down at where the bullet had entered. "In case it wasn't obvious, Clarke, you'll always have me."

I was transported, for a moment, to a time when this sentiment might have moved me. How different I was now.

But I nodded. It seemed the least I could do for someone who'd stood in the way of death for me.

I gripped the parchment between my fingers. "Do you remember what Dumley told us about Lavnonshire? That the waves never breached the cliffs. Never crumbled them. He said it was likely the work of ancient stone Masons and earth Charmers."

Theo nodded. "I remember."

"What if it was Dione all along?" I said. "What if she died here in Lavnonshire, and they didn't even have the decency to remember her name?"

"We can't know that for certain," Theo said simply, shrugging.

But already I was running away with the idea. "She saved their whole fucking town from sinking into the ocean," I fumed. "And they served her up for slaughter anyway." I felt that familiar rage in my core, seeping outward again, ravenous.

Theodore looked at me long and hard. "If there's one thing you can trust in people, it's their tendency to save themselves first."

But that didn't quite encapsulate it. Those townspeople hadn't just forsaken Dione to save themselves. They'd wrung everything from her first.

I closed my eyes. Saw a young girl on the cliffside.

"It's just a story, Nina," Theo said.

But the waves were already rushing overhead, hammering down. And I was tossing in the depths, lungs burning, fingers reaching for the surface, curling into claws.

CHAPTER FORTY

PATRICK

The Artisanal influence of Lavnonshire seemed to worm in, seeping into the black brick rendering of houses as though they were mid-transformation.

The wagons became horseless, the people weak-chinned. The building facades cleared themselves of soot. The briny air, though still tinged in the stench of industry, lightened.

The Artisan houses were made of stone and looked to Patrick like mausoleums. Wrought-iron garden gates rusted with salt and columns at the entrances. Polly walked ten paces ahead with her hands clasped in front of her stomach. She was now dressed, he supposed, in what Artisan women deemed proper. It entailed more skirt layers than he cared to understand. He wondered if the swanks had their Crafter maids peel the clothing away for them every evening.

She dragged her feet like she was walking to the gallows and ducked her head from the people she passed.

Some ways behind her, John and Patrick pulled their caps low over their brows and toted chimney sweeps over their shoulders, lit cigarettes between their lips. Eyes slid right by them. There were plenty of Crafters mixed among the swanks, selling fruit from shoulder bags, playing fiddles, begging on street corners, selling newsprint.

Polly stopped abruptly before a picturesque limescale house, ivy climbing trellises to the gutters, opposite jewelers and a tea parlor. It wasn't the largest of homes, but there were rosebushes by the gate, a neatly edged path, a polished brass knocker on the door. A chimney flue puffed. Someone was home.

Polly took moments to galvanize, straightening her spine rung by rung, then stepped through the gate.

John tsked. "How do you figure the odds here?"

Patrick sighed. "Not a fuckin' hope in hell."

They crossed the lane to the street corner, where a coal bin and streetlamp created a mite of cover. John and Patrick warmed their hands with their breath and languished against the outer walls of the jewelers. The swanks passing with their canes and parasols would only think them lowlifes, shirking their labors in favor of a smoke and some weak sunshine.

The window at Patrick's back showed a collection of shining pocket watches. He eyed their ticking hands. "We'll give her till quarter past the hour," he muttered, settling in.

John stalked toward a nearby Crafter stand selling limp produce, and said, "Johnny!" as brightly as though he'd known him from birth.

The young Crafter frowned some. "Johnny's me Dad," he said warily.

"Bugger me. Goin' blind in me old age," John barked a laugh. "You look right like him."

Patrick leaned against the brick and crossed his arms over his chest, watching his father as he struck up conversation about the weather next, then politics. His hand disappeared into his coat frequently. First with a box of matches, next a packet of rolled smokes, then a handful of plums. He bid the vendor a "fine afternoon," and returned, already lighting a new smoke.

Patrick hesitated when his father offered him his own, but the needle on the watches had already revolved twice. Anticipation cracked open in him like a beast hatching. He took the cigarette and dragged deeply. "Are we regressin' to cheap tricks now?" he asked his father. In Kenton, they'd take a man's finger for theft.

"Still got some sleight left in these old bones," John said, leaning beside him. He whistled as an Artisan woman passed them, her waist so tightly corseted it looked painful. “They do got some talent among these swank ladies, though, I’ll give ’em that.” He tipped back his cap to better see.

Patrick’s sights were oscillating between the windows of that limescale house. He pulled smoke into his lungs as though it gave him sustenance. “Lord, that’s good,” he muttered, his muscles relaxing some.

John was eyeing him. “You sound like a man starved, son,” he said.

Patrick flicked ash to the pavement. “Nina don’t like the smell.”

John shook his head pityingly. “Lord, boy. She’s got her talons in you.”

“No help for what’s done,” Patrick said absentmindedly. Another minute lapsed. No Polly.

“She’s a pretty girl, Pat. I won’t deny it. But you gotta keep your sights in the right place.”

“My sights ain’t your concern,” he said, his irritation mounting. Artisans continued to intersect in the lane. The door to Polly’s family home remained shut.

“She’s a liability, Patty,” his father was saying now. “I taught you this, didn’t I? Everyone we let close to us becomes a weakness. A crack in the hull.”

“She ain’t my weakness anymore.”

“We need her to perform a job,” John continued.

Another minute fell away. His fists clenched. “And she’ll do it. She’s on our side.”

“I don’t doubt it,” John grumbled darkly. “But when the hammer falls, she may revisit her former principles, Patty. Women are funny like that. Their hearts get in the way of their heads. Logic don’t play a part. She might grow nostalgic or tired or bored of the work. She might decide she don’t want to get her hands dirty for the Union—”

“You don’t know her.”

“—and if that time comes, she’ll fall into your lap cryin’. She’ll tell you how she can’t go on. How she’s had a change of heart, and she’ll beg for your understandin’. And you’ll have to rip out the talons then, Patty. You’ll have to ignore the weepin’ and turn her back to the dirt.”

"Stop." His vision was closing, narrowing, the way it did before it turned red.

"It don't matter what she says, Patty, even if she says it with her mouth 'round your cock—"

Patrick took his father's collar then, the same way he would with any other pig. He rammed John's back into the wall hard enough for his head to crack into the brick, hard enough to rattle his teeth.

John laughed. "Ah," he said knowingly. "How deep do the talons go, Patty. Eh?"

"Deep enough," he said, seething. His breath seemed hot as blood, flooding out his nose an inch from his father's. He squeezed his hand tighter around the scruff of his shirt. He was stronger than his father now, he realized. When had the scales tipped? "Mention her mouth again," he said. "And consider yourself short a son."

John's grin melted into something much more sinister. Something he generally reserved for dark business. "So that's the order of it, then?" he asked. "Your Charmer girl first, then the rest of us."

Patrick realized too late that he'd been baited. He'd seen his father do it before, and he should have seen it now. His hand loosened. "She's on our side," he repeated. "My loyalty is to the fuckin' Union. As its always been, and so is *hers*."

"But is she willin' to do what we are, son?" he asked. "Is she willin' to shed herself of the softer parts to get the job done?"

He thought of the way Nina clenched her teeth together now. How she lost herself, at times, to the churning of her thoughts. How anger bloomed across her expression even in the quietest moments. "She's been stomped on enough times," Patrick said. "She'll do what needs to be done."

Patrick let his father go then, noticed the way he sagged on the wall for a moment before straightening, as though he, too, was surprised to learn just how much stronger his son was.

Across the way, two Artisan women had stopped to gape at their confrontation but hurried off when Patrick scowled at them. The jeweler's watches showed a quarter past the hour. On the limescale steps, Polly appeared.

Patrick glanced once more at his father. "If there comes a time when Nina wants no more to do with the Seam, then I'll cut her loose," he said plainly. "And we'll mine it ourselves. And if you try to move against me on it, Dad, I will beat the breath from you."

John shook his head as though there wasn't a river of boiling anger funneling beneath the surface. "I stayed away too long, I know," he said to Patrick. "I left you with a lot of . . . burdens, and it pained me to think of you shoulderin' it all without me. But perhaps you've grown fond of 'em. Perhaps it's a threat to have me back. Is that it, Patty? Is it the *chair* you want?"

Patrick looked at him with as much venom as he was capable. "You know it ain't," he said. "Of all people, you know it ain't."

John made a noise of disbelief. "When did you start turnin' away from me, son?" he asked. "When did you start seein' me as your adversary, eh?"

"The moment you gave my name to Lord fuckin' Tanner." He looked his father straight on and saw him flinch. "Yeah," Patrick muttered darkly. "Tell me, Dad, what father sells out his own son?"

Silence, just whorls of smoke, ash dropping to the toes of John's boot. Polly retreating down the lane.

"It weren't me," he denied, and yet it was quiet, uncomfortable. "Lord, Pat . . ." But he found nothing more to say. His mouth hardened into a grim line.

And Patrick nodded, feeling as though he'd only ever seen his father from afar, that a veil had been lifted. He turned his back on John Colson and walked down the street in the direction Polly had gone, feeling a weight settle itself inside him.

CHAPTER FORTY-ONE

POLLY

A Crafter she didn't recognize answered the door of her family home.

She was dressed in typical maid attire, her bun ribboned, blouse broached at the throat, apron around her skirt, and her eyes averted.

"I'd hoped to call on Mr. and Mrs. Prescott," she said to the woman.

"And who should I say is calling?"

A moment of hesitation, and then, since there was no avoiding it, "Their daughter."

She was let in to the sitting room immediately thereafter, and Polly assumed that the Crafter maid must indeed be newly employed. Their previous maid would have known not to let her over the stoop.

It wasn't the grandest home, and certainly not the most affluent parish for an Artisan family to live in, but her mother's jewelry shop was across the street, and their father would never be accepted in a more prestigious part of the Trench, so Polly's parents remained in this same lane, where Polly had grown up before she'd been made a Scribbler.

The same hearth, the same mantel with its same candelabra. The same portraits and paintings on the walls. The same books and piano and tea cart. She sighed wistfully.

Her father, Reginald Prescott, entered and closed the doors behind him, lips tight. "Polly," he said by way of greeting.

He was a proud man, or perhaps a defensive one. After all, he was a black

Craftsman from the brink. The Artisans whispered that he'd swindled a marriage from a perfectly respectful Cutter woman and sullied her good reputation. He lived each day clamoring to maintain propriety, the appearance of perfection, to bridge this unbridgeable gap.

Having a daughter denounced by the House? No, that would not do.

"Your mother will remain upstairs. She does not wish to see you," he said. He did not take the seat beside her or gesture for Polly to resume hers, and so the two stood awkwardly across from each other, a tea cart between them.

Polly nodded, felt acid in her throat.

You'll need to work harder than the rest of them, he used to tell her over and over. *Twice as hard as any other apprentice, to be accepted.*

But she'd been sent right out into the brink anyway, to the very worst pockets. This had been the first betrayal to her family name, this disappointment, and there had been nothing but treachery since.

"We said it very explicitly, Polly," Reginald said now. He'd once gone by Reggie. "We told you not to return here. Your mother's business is not a stone's throw away. How does it make her look, to have you at our door?"

His face was cleanly shaved, his hair cut neatly. If you looked hard enough, you could still see the scar over his right eyebrow—some scuffle from his scum adolescence. Polly had asked him about that scar once. He'd only smiled and tugged at her hair ribbons. *It's nothing you will ever need to worry about*, he'd said. How wrong he'd been.

"I don't mean to embarrass her," Polly said stiffly.

"Embarrass her?" he said, exasperation getting the better of his temper. "I think we are well past that, Polly. We heard you were boarding in Morland, frequenting the gambling dens." He looked at her like she was a stain on the carpet. "I hope you haven't come here to ask for money."

Polly shook her head, swallowed bile. She was horrified to find that tears were threatening to spill over the rims of her eyes. She blinked them back. Once, she and her father had sat in this room until well after midnight, locked in a never-ending chess game, candles burning down to their stubs before Reginald had finally knocked over his own king, pride beaming from him. *A formidable player*, he'd said, shaking her hand. *Far too formidable for your poor old dad.*

Now they stood apart with tight chests, that same chessboard still by the window.

"No," she said, and she tried to keep her voice free of fury. It would not serve. "I only—I've been offered an opportunity for work."

Polly had thought this would be the best way to approach her father. It was the only thing she could think of that might make him consider helping her. The only thing he would care about now.

His eyebrows drew together. "A Scribbler's remit?"

"Yes," she said. "At the Morland archives. They have a position in the translations department." It was as close to the truth as she would get.

Reginald took several moments to respond, as though calculating. "You were denounced," he said. "The House stripped you of your fellowship."

"They did," she nodded. She had to word it carefully. "But they would reinstate it, I am told, if I was to offer them a skill not easily found elsewhere."

At this, Reginald's expression darkened. He looked away and muttered something beneath his breath.

"They need someone to translate Verian Script," she said. "And I'd hoped that you could provide me with—"

"Please, Polly. Stop this," her father said now, turning away from her. He shook his head, as though there'd never been a worse fate than having a daughter such as her. "You know, we received a heinous scribble the other day. Quite indescribable. From the House of Lords, of all places." He addressed the mantel, unable to look at her.

Polly's stomach fell away.

"They were asking for your whereabouts," he continued, his voice wretched, shoulders drooping. "It implored us to provide any information we could, as a matter of urgency. Somehow, I doubt that has anything to do with them wanting to reinstate your fellowship."

A tear fell free, and Polly wiped it away. "Father—"

"So why don't you tell me, daughter, just what trouble you're in now." He sounded dangerously close to tears.

But she couldn't tell him. "I need grandfather's cypher," she said. "Please."

"For what?" he asked. "What have you promised them, Polly?"

"Verian Script," she said. "That's all."

"No honorable lord of the House would be bothered with it," Reginald countered, spitting the words between his teeth. "Stewards. Utter nonsense."

Polly fought back a sob.

"I should never have let your grandfather fill your head with it," he continued on, pacing, agitated. "If the House is looking for you, and *you* are going around talking about Verian Script, I can only assume you've ruffled one too many feathers. They think you a *heretic*, is that it? Do they think you a sympathizer?"

She struggled to breathe evenly.

"I want you to leave," he said. "For good this time, Polly. Before I do something I cannot undo."

Polly balled her hands. "I can't leave without the cypher. I'm sorry."

"It is not here," he seethed, his lips curling back. "Do you truly think I would want any of that rubbish in my *house*?"

As she'd feared. "Did you burn it then?" she asked, there was an edge of new hurt in it. Her grandfather might have been eccentric, but those texts were his most prized possessions, and he'd been a good man.

Reginald closed his eyes. "Of course not," he said. "Lord, but I should have. Couldn't bring myself to in the end."

Watery hope trickled in. "So you donated it?" she asked. "To the Morland archives?"

He scoffed. "That hovel?" he said cuttingly. "Absolutely not. They didn't get a thing. Everything was given to the library here in Lavnonshire."

Polly frowned. But *The Stewards' Testament* had been filched from Morland. That's what the Colsons and Theo had said; that it had been donated after her grandfather had died.

It didn't matter now. If the cypher was in the Lavnonshire library, then it was free for the taking. It was a better outcome than she'd imagined.

"I don't want to hear of you walking about society," her father was saying now, rubbing his forehead. "Your mother—I don't think she can bear any further disgrace."

Polly nodded. "Tell her for me . . . that I'm sorry—"

"Oh, a sorrier child I cannot imagine," Reginald agreed. His eyes swept over her moth-eaten clothing, at least four decades out of trend. "You had it all before you," he said, and Polly wasn't sure if he were speaking to her or to himself. "Everything that I never did. And you squandered it."

The last time Polly had sat here, her father had used the same words, only then, she'd been cowed and shaking. Now, she stood tall. She still felt the shame, but she didn't let it curl her spine. If she was to disgrace her parents anyway, then best to not disgrace herself, too. She would do what she thought was right.

"I went where the House told me to go," she said. Her voice was soft, but sure. "Without question. I gave them the information they sought, at great personal cost." And at the cost of others. So many others. "And all I asked for was safety. A modest remit in a place that wouldn't be razed by the Lords' Army," Polly's lungs swelled. "They took that information, and in return they stripped me of my fellowship." Tears sprang up in her eyes. "I was *loyal* to the House."

"You were a Union *sympathizer*!" he volleyed, and then he went to the bookshelf and opened a drawer there. He pulled out sheets of parchment in his fists and slammed them down on the tea cart, bouncing the cups on their saucers, the milk overturning. "Three letters in the first *week*!" he spat, rage overspilling. "*Hand-scribed*, if you can believe it! All of them sent personally to our door."

Polly saw the crude quill work. The too-big letters. The first word on each was her name. The last was Otto's.

I still can't bring myself to believe it . . . Tell me it's not true, Pol . . . I only want to know that you are safe, and I'll write no more . . .

Reginald measured each of his breaths, reuniting with some severed part of his early days, his fists balling as though he might swing on someone. "Some *Crafter* kid," he said. A voice he'd shed long ago came up his windpipe, foaming and seething. "Some piece of brink scum, sending notes by fuckin' hand to *my* daughter. To *my* house!"

You ought to know I loved you, though I was too much a coward to say it . . . I love you still, even though I shouldn't . . .

Tears fell free, coursing down Polly's cheeks. Damn it, but she was shaking after all.

"Do not stand there and preach about your *loyalties*!" her father said. "What of your loyalty to *me*? To your *mother*? Do you have any idea the deals that were made to instate you as an Artisan in the first place?" He sent the letters and sugar cubes and milk flying. He stormed across the room, trying to leash that part of him that was born in the brink, that he'd buried long ago.

And did he hate that part so much that he couldn't bear his own daughter loving a Craftsman?

Polly picked up each letter, one by one, crumpled now and soiled with milk. She did not give her father the courtesy of a goodbye. She did not apologize to him like she had the last time, bawling and begging as her father shoved her over the threshold.

This time, she walked out with her chin lifted against the weight of three millstones. She pulled along behind her every terrible choice she'd ever made. There was no freeing herself from them. She could only persevere.

She thought, as she closed the door to her family home, that she heard a keening—the first wretched sounds of a man breaking.

CHAPTER FORTY-TWO

PATRICK

Patrick and John followed Polly at a distance through Lavnonshire and back to the cliffs, where the antiques shop was perched. They found Mrs. Trunk dusting a collection of cherub figurines and nodded to her as they passed. She didn't look their way, but her mouth moved without emitting any sound. She shuffled away among her rows, as though wishing to disintegrate into them. The piano trilled something irritable-sounding. Patrick imagined their company was wearing on her.

Upstairs, Theo was sitting upright. Nina's hands were on his bare stomach, reapplying a clean bandage. Patrick felt something gnash at his insides.

Nina stood at their arrival. "Well?" she asked, her eyes on Polly's hands.

Polly sighed. "The cypher wasn't there."

Patrick thought she looked different. Sounded different. He wondered what had transpired in that house.

Nina's face fell. John cursed beneath his breath.

"But it isn't far," Polly continued, her eyes hard. She squared her shoulders with the same surety she'd possessed in Kenton Hill. "My father donated it to the library."

"What *library*?" asked John.

"There's a library in the Artisan quarters of Lavnonshire. The Geoffry Tanner Collection."

John practically spat at the sound of the name. "Sounds about fuckin' right."

Theo shrugged. "He *was* the one to build it."

"And name it after himself," John scoffed.

"Much like one would name a pub after themselves," Theo muttered.

John narrowed his eyes at Theo as though weighing the consequences of flogging him.

Patrick looked at Nina. "Do you know it?" he asked.

She nodded. "Theo and I studied there a fair few times."

"Then I'll go," Patrick said decisively. "The rest of you will stay here."

But Nina sighed. "You can't, Pat—"

"It can't be anyone else," he said, already turning away. "Polly will write me instructions on where to go, and what shelf—"

"No, I meant you can't get into the library, Patrick, not unless you're an . . ."

Patrick froze. "A swank?"

She pressed her lips together. Nodded. "They'll ask to see your Artisan brand at the door."

"I'll go myself," Polly announced. It seemed she'd already made the decision. "I have a brand, and enough anonymity that I shouldn't draw attention." She spoke with conviction. "Besides, I know what I'm looking for. It's quicker this way. Safer."

Patrick's eyes stuck to Polly, scrutinizing her.

"It'll be a big old building with more than a few ways out," John said. "She'll take off the second she's past the door."

"No," Patrick countered. "She wants to be on that ship." He would have laid a bet on it. Whatever it was behind her eyes, she wanted it very badly. "You'll go in and get the book," he instructed. "And you'll get out immediately."

But she shook her head. "It isn't that kind of library," she said. "It's a protected collection. They don't allow anyone to remove texts from the premises."

John groaned. "Lord, you swanks truly have naught in your heads but fumes. If they won't let you take it, Polly, you *steal* it."

"And put it where?" she asked him, holding out her arms to show her tight corset and waistcoat, the constricting waistline of her skirt. "Where do you suggest I hide a nine-hundred-page tome, Mr. Colson?"

"For all I care, you can hide it up your—"

"We can't smuggle it out without notice. The guards there are hawkeyed," said Theodore. Some color had returned to his face, the bluff working its magic.

"I'll have to complete the translation in the library itself," she said. "There isn't another way."

Patrick scrubbed his face. "It never fuckin' ends," he muttered to himself, so low no one heard.

"It'd only be a matter of hours," Polly said. "A single day, at most. And then you'd have your translation."

Oh, but it was tempting. The thought of having that fucking book decoded by this time tomorrow. He needed to be done with this. The sooner, the better.

"I can go with her," Theo said now. He pushed down on the arm of the settee and stood, albeit gingerly. "If it eases you."

Patrick looked at him with dry reprisal. "No, it doesn't fuckin' *ease* me, Teddy."

He rolled his eyes. "I've proven myself enough to warrant a little credit," he replied. "And I'm the only other person here with a brand and no wanted bulletins."

Nina seemed to assess Theo. "It might be the safest bet, Patrick."

Patrick shut his eyes and tried to suppress the pounding in his head.

"You could follow," Polly offered. "Stay out of sight while Theo and I are inside. I swear to you, Patrick, I'm not looking to run."

He was calculating the odds, banking on the notion that what Polly wanted most could only be given by him, and that what Theo wanted most was standing next to him. He wouldn't go anywhere without Nina.

"We'll go tomorrow," he said finally, a warning gong sounding in his chest now. And here was the miner's shiver. Lord, there was nothing to do but forge ahead now. "Theo will act as our go-between while John and I wait out of sight, watching the exits."

"And me," Nina added. Before he could protest, she crossed her arms over her chest and said, "I seem to remember you saying that I'd 'go where I wanted.' I won't stay behind all day waiting on the rest of you."

Patrick pressed the tips of his fingers into his forehead. Everyone in the room seemed to be waiting, perched on the edge.

John was noticeably quiet. Patrick wondered how long he'd hold his tongue.

"Fine," Patrick relented, feeling as though he'd lost his grip on the chains, the whole pulley tumbling free. "Fine."

Through the dust motes, Polly held herself tall. "I'll prove myself to you, Pat."

He gave her a dark look before turning away. "You've already proven yourself to me."

CHAPTER FORTY-THREE

DONNY

Dusk was swallowing Kenton Hill.

Donny imagined the jaws of the earth opening, cradling them in the hollows of its mouth. Light petered out of his mind. He could smell the night frost on the air, feel the collapse of the day. It was orange and pearlescent and then suddenly leaden.

Half of Kenton stood in Main Street, armed to holy hell in whatever they'd drudged from the drains and their wardrobes. A baker threw a bandolier of ammunition over his shoulder.

One of the miner boys, just sixteen, held only a pickaxe and the arrogance of youth. Steam bled from his nose like a horse behind the starting gate.

There were women in their housecoats, in their aprons and church wear alike. They'd run the last time Kenton had been invaded, and they were loath to do so again.

Briggs shifted at Donny's side, leaned in to speak into his ear. "Here they come," he said. "Armed."

"How many?"

"Six."

"Lord," Gunner sniggered. "Almost feel bad for 'em, don't you? It ain't hardly fair."

"Don't shoot unless you have to, boys," Donny reiterated, a silver bullet pinched between his fingers. The hum he felt at its touch was muted, as though the ink in his blood was dulling by the second.

Patrick, where are you? a near-constant refrain.

"Ah, where's the sport in it?" Gunner bit. Violence leaked out into the air.

"This ain't war," Tess said, subdued now. The brigade must be drawing close. "It's familial discord."

Gunner scoffed. "My family's here beside me," he said, and Donny heard the rack of the hammer.

"Please, Ma," Donny said to her. "Go inside."

But she wouldn't. She put a hand on his shoulder, there for a brief moment and then gone. "You speak, Donny," she said to him, her voice cracking. "Go on." She sounded to Donny these days as though she were vanishing.

Donny stepped forward and wondered if he looked the way Patrick looked, the way his father had looked. Behind him, a hundred or so chests inflated.

He heard the unsure footing come to a standstill ahead, the snow spraying off the toes of their boots.

"Comrades," Donny called in greeting. "Welcome to Kenton Hill."

The six had come, it seemed, in some last spasm of futility, with naught but one gun apiece, and Donny imagined the slow recoil of their bravado, chins just now, at the sight of Kenton Hill's response, beginning to quiver.

"We—we ain't here to fight," one said. He did a poor job at diplomacy with that voice, grated at its edges.

"Haven't you?" Donny turned the bullet over in his fingers. "Perhaps you came to return the guns, then? Union property, I presume." Bold of them, Donny thought, to come toting the weapons Kenton Hill had provided them with.

"Perhaps they came to see the sights," Gunner growled loudly, and the Kenton brigade laughed in their cruel way.

"No vacancy, I'm afraid," Donny said. "You should have sent a note. We could have saved you the walk."

"We came to . . . see," another voice said, this one female, no less trepid. "To see for ourselves."

"See what, darlin'?" asked Gunner.

"The bluff," the voice answered, stronger now. "We want to see it with our own eyes."

There was a damning, expounding silence.

"And from which sorry corner do you hail?" Donny asked, but not quick enough to absorb the disquiet, not quick enough to conceal their hand.

"We're representatives from Dunnitch, Dorser, and Scurry," said the gruff voice.

"Representatives, eh? Ambassadors. You got a name, O Ambassador?"

"Burgess. The surrounding parishes had a meeting, night afore last."

"Did they?" Donny sniffed, pulling a cigarette into his mouth.

"Everyone's scared. Seems like each way you look at it, the Union's finished. Only no one's sayin' so."

"Only ones who can say so are the Colsons," Gunner answered. "And we ain't sayin' so till the fight is won."

"Accordin' to the papers, there are two Colsons currently sittin' in the House of Lords, drinkin' fuckin' tea with the ministers and makin' their bargains on our behalf," said Burgess. "For all we know, they're sellin' us down the river as we speak."

Gunner's rifle clacked as it lifted, and Donny held his hand out in warning. "Put it down, brother."

"If Patrick Colson is makin' agreements with the House, we ought to know what they are," said Burgess. "We ought to have a fuckin' say!"

From Donny's side, Tess's voice rose. "You're a fool," she said, then after two stilted breaths, "You're more fool than you are a man. At this moment, my son and husband are in the brink, evadin' the fuckin' infantry, makin' their way back home. And you're sittin' in your parishes, warmed by the coal we send, readin' your fuckin' papers, and blowin' smoke up each other's arses!" The words turned ragged at their ends, and she struggled to catch her breath. A stream of wrenching coughs ensued. It was too cold out here, the air thin and difficult to breathe.

"Please, Ma," he murmured to her. "Go inside."

"How quick you are to shed your loyalty!" she continued. "Couple of lies from the House, and you're runnin' scared!"

The Kenton brigade hollered their agreement.

"Then show us the bluff," said the woman's voice. "You say you have it, but we ain't seen a pinch. And those of us in Dorser . . ." Here, her voice cracked. "Those of us in Dorser have someone at home who needs it. Husbands with limbs blown off, kids with burns . . . The Union is supposed to be about givin' to each other what the House won't. That's what it's always been about!"

"Aye," said Gunner. "And Kenton's given more than its fair share."

"And we've come to rely on it," said another man. "You Colsons made it that way. You made it so's we were beholden to you. Well, you can keep your fuckin' coal and your fuckin' tunnels. It don't mean squat if your Alchemist is gone, and the bluff with him!"

"Show us the bluff," the woman repeated. "We won't take none. We won't stir bad blood between our parishes if it's the truth. But we want to see it with our own eyes and know that we ain't fightin' a war already lost."

"And if we refuse?" Donny asked, it was a trial to keep his voice cocky. To grin around his cigarette as though it were all a lark.

"Then the Northeast parishes withdraw their oath to the Union," said Burgess, and it was said with a great heaviness. "We end our strikes, and you leave us at the mercy of the House, and the thin hope we'll find them forgivin'." This last came out slowly, as though the man could hardly believe he was uttering the words. "You'll leave us no choice. We have our own parishes to pull through this winter."

In Donny's center, a rupture widened, all his hope spilling into it, and he thought of his father speaking in the pub, in the marketplace, standing on the podium he'd built himself, out of wood and nails and sheer thought, preaching to his widening congregation about the walls of community, and how tall they could stand, how quickly they could fall. *One fissure . . . the smallest wavering, and the entire thing collapses. Like the walls of a mine, like mud sliding.*

Donny felt it coming now, the ripples growing quicker than he knew how to stop them. Soon it would be a wave, a great tidal breaker seething overhead.

He sighed seismically and said, "I'm afraid we can't have that."

One by one, Gunner and Briggs took the guns of those six men and women, the bullets trapping in the barrels before they could fire.

One by one, the ambassadors from Dorser, Dunnitch, and Scurry went to their knees.

Donny turned over the silver bullet, loaded it.

One by one, the six shots discharged, and he felt them as though he pointed the revolver to his own chest. Felt them, because he couldn't see them.

The sound thundered down the lanes and into the sky, loud enough to reach all of Kenton. High enough to reach the heavens, to make sure that even God, wherever he slumbered, looked down at Donny and saw the smoking barrel.

CHAPTER FORTY-FOUR

THEO

The bluff helped him heal with remarkable speed, of course.

The day after they had arrived in Lavnonshire, the wound was no longer red and flaming at the edges. It did not weep. Each time Nina came to nervously lift the bandages, the flesh seemed less mottled. Still, every couple of hours she came with her warm cloth to clean it, to replace the bandaging. She did it without looking directly at him, answering his attempts at conversation in monosyllables. She touched his skin as though it burned her.

Part of him hoped it did. Surely that was better than indifference?

In the night, she woke to check on him, illuminating the room briefly with a candelabra, and her in its nimbus. The most beautiful haunting Theo could think of.

The quieter, crueler part of his brain knew that she was acting out of guilt. He'd thrown himself into the path of a bullet meant for her. He knew Nina well enough to understand she wouldn't reconcile with it easily.

If he were honest, he was well enough now that he could change his own bandages. He could stand without too much pain, but he didn't. He waited for Nina to come to him, and he lay still and quiet, like a carnivorous plant.

Daylight clung still, and Theo found himself wishing for dark. The afternoon wouldn't bleed away.

The others were sauntering in lone corners after an early supper. It was difficult for each of them to tolerate one another's presence in close quarters.

Even Patrick and his own father seemed always on the precipice of coming to blows. John was downstairs, hunting through Mrs. Trunk's inventory. Patrick and Polly, he presumed, were in their rooms.

Theo finally stood. His muscles unfolded, the blood rushing to the soles of his feet. The window overlooked the ocean as though he were looking at the world from a mountaintop. The waves, aquamarine and foamy, shuddered against the ramparts. The wind howled its agonized lament. The last light stuck to the horizon, refusing to vanish.

Down on the path overlooking the cliffs, her elbows propped on the railing, was Nina.

The cold had emptied this thin vein of a street, and the spray from the ocean made it uncomfortable for strolling. But Nina stayed where she was, hair tucked inside Patrick's cap, a dusty oversize coat billowing out behind her.

Theo felt his heart hurtling toward an approaching end. He felt as though at any moment, a cliff would rear up before him, and he'd go hurtling off it before he could stop.

Without thinking on it too much, he left the window and took the stairs one slow step at a time, finally entering the shop. He smiled to Mrs. Trunk and skirted by John, who was at that moment upending an old cello with his back turned. Theo went out to the street quietly, carefully, his hand supporting his stomach as though he were keeping his intestines in place.

He limped across the lane to Nina, put his arms gingerly on the cold railings. He'd forgotten to don a coat, and the wind lashed at him.

He ignored all of it.

"It's beautiful, isn't it?" she said to him eventually, distantly.

He nodded, though he did not look to the sea. "You used to enjoy painting it."

"I found some canvas and brushes in the shop," she said absentmindedly, frowning at the rolling clouds. "I hardly remember what it feels like to paint."

Theo had rarely heard of a thing sadder than that—an artist who'd forgotten herself.

She finally looked over at him. "You seem improved."

He shrugged. He didn't want her nighttime visits to end. Instead of answering, he changed the subject. "You used to stand right here and watch the waves when we visited as apprentices," he commented.

She looked indifferent. "Did I?"

"Yes. You asked me to meet you in this very spot in the middle of the night. Have you forgotten?"

Her expression fixed itself. She was careful not to look at him.

Theo leaned on the guardrail and looked down into the wash. "Mrs. Trunk kept us in separate rooms and wouldn't let us so much as speak after nightfall. We had to be clever. You left a message in my pocket."

The column of her throat worked to swallow the memory. She kept her eyes on the view. "I don't recall."

"Really?" he asked casually. "You kissed me like crazy. Practically ravaged me."

"Stop it, Theo," she said emotionlessly, though heat flooded her cheeks. She turned and walked several paces down the lane.

But Theo was right behind her, close enough to murmur, "You haven't thought of it since? I myself revisit it frequently."

"Then I pity you," she hissed, turning on the spot. "If the only happy thing you can dredge from your memory was some kiss when you were eighteen."

"As I recall, we didn't stop at just a kiss." And he wasn't lying. Just thinking of it stirred Theo, enough that he could ignore the voice that told him to stop pushing her.

"Fuck's *sake*," she murmured, like a miner would. It didn't sound right in her voice, from her lips. "What are you doing?" she asked him then, coming much closer than Theo was prepared for. He was hit with a sudden rush of her. "What is this? Some sorry flirtation?"

He tried not to blink, as though doing so might result in a loss somehow. "Perhaps," he said. "That depends on whether it's working."

She seemed close to either laughter or tears. She cinched her eyes closed and opened them again. "This . . . *thing* you imagine still exists between us, Theo. It isn't real."

Theo shook his head. "It's real to me, Nina."

"Theo—"

"Please, just let me say this and then I'll say no more." Here was that cliff he was barreling toward, the fall inevitable. "I know your feelings for me can never go back to the way they were. I'm not so arrogant that I can't see that. But I prayed every night that you would be brought back to me, and I promised all sorts of desperate things to God and to the House to have those prayers answered. And then suddenly, you were there in Kenton Hill, and I felt as though every good thing I'd ever done counted for something. As though God had gifted me you." Theo heaved, his breath expanding in his chest. "Surely only *love* is worthy of that sort of miracle?"

"You're insane," Nina said, eyes widening.

He felt suddenly unmoored, like every thought he'd ever had was horribly singular. "I know." He swallowed. "But I can think of no better reason for a man to lose his mind."

He watched a dozen different emotions skitter across her face. Some he latched on to—sorrow, remorse, familiarity. They were better than the pity, the frustration. In the end, any reaction melted away and left her blank. Her lips thinned and the gold flecks in her eyes blinked out of existence, and she exhaled as though she were trying to expel him.

Over the cliff edge he went.

"Is that the last of it?" she asked.

"No, not nearly."

"Then journal the rest," she said. "And bury it." She closed her eyes. "If Polly finishes the translations quickly, we may be on our way to Hoaklin as early as tomorrow evening."

Theo felt the concussion of what she'd say before it hit.

"You shouldn't come with us, Theo," she said. "There's no sense in it."

He rocked backward on his heels, felt something cold and viciously sharp stab at his windpipe. But he looked out to the ocean as she did and pretended he wasn't falling. "I want to come anyway."

"You don't believe in this, Theo," she said bluntly. "And it's dangerous. You were almost killed. If you were to die in this undertaking, it would be—"

"I have my own undertakings," he said thickly.

Nina closed her eyes. "Me."

"Us."

"There is no *us*."

Another blow. Another hole to match the others. Soon he'd be riddled through.

He looked at her then, and surely the light shining at that moment wasn't a coincidence—the way it clung to her and brightened her skin, turning her ethereal, as though even the heavens were determined to keep his attention on her. "There is to me," Theo murmured, broken but true. "Everything you've ever said to me, everything you've ever done—it's still here." He pointed to his chest, where he felt her beating heart next to his own. "I can't simply tear it out."

Her jaw tightened. "You can."

"I've tried."

"Not hard enough," she said, turning to him. "It isn't easy. It takes time. You have to halt those thoughts in their tracks. Divert them, until you can't recall any of it. Not the touches or the laughter or the promises. Eventually you'll find that all of it, every single piece, is imaginary. Just a memory, a little more faded each time it's inspected, washed of whatever magic it had." There were no tears in her eyes, no shake to her lips. She spoke as though she read from a transcript. "Then other things will return. The ability to think without thinking of me, to hear another woman's voice and not compare the sound. Eventually, the pain won't exist at all. You'll be free of it."

The ocean blurred. He did not lift his fingers to wipe his eyes out of defiance—even that felt like a shedding of her.

"Was it truly as easy as that?" he asked. "To be rid of me?"

Something in her expression closed. "I've had more than enough practice."

He thought of whatever family she'd left in Scurry, her Aunt Francis, her mother . . . and him. Perhaps, that was the difference between them, that she was in flux, morphing to the shape of her confines, peeling off her home and her name and moving onward while he stayed as he was.

"Are you asking me not to follow you? Or are you telling me?" he said now, bracing himself.

He remembered her at a much younger age, dressed in Artisan navy and unable to meet his eye.

Now she looked at him unflinchingly. "I'm telling you."

He pressed his hand over his bullet wound, thinking for a moment that it had reopened and that he was spilling onto the ground. "Where do you propose I go?" he asked, and now it was he who could not stand to meet her eyes. "I thought—" he started, but couldn't finish. It sounded so incredibly stupid now. He'd thought they'd find each other again. He'd thought she'd love him. He'd thought all the problems in the world would become negligible if he had that.

"That's not for me to say, Theo," she said, looking out at the sea. Then she forced a painful sort of grin. "Maybe here. You'd have the whole ocean to command." Her hand touched his shoulder briefly, and still he felt changed by it, as though there was something tangible passing from her to him. Surely, she felt it, didn't she?

How many times had they walked along the cliff edge on their excursions to Lavnonshire, him making shapes out of the sea mist, her laughing at his cleverness? But she'd forgotten it all. Still, he could remind her—he would.

He leaned in and pressed his mouth to hers, and she flinched in surprise, then froze, her lips unmoving.

But there was a breath's moment when she didn't pull back, and his hands were holding her face again, and it felt like coming home.

Then he was stumbling back, the wind leaving his lungs, Nina's hands shoving him away.

A charge running wild over his skin. "Nina—"

She was breathing heavily, hair falling free from her cap and covering her eyes. "Are you insane?" she said, furious now. "Have you lost your mind?"

"Me?" he said, laughing without a hint of mirth. "No, Nina. I'm thinking clearly. One of us ought to."

She huffed out a breath of indignation, mouth agape. Then she stormed off across the lane, and slammed the door to Mrs. Trunk's shop.

Theo followed.

He watched the back of her vanish through the maze of the shop, ignored John's queries as he went after her, took the stairs two at a time, and ignored the flaring pain in his side.

He caught up to her in Mrs. Trunk's living room.

"Leave me alone, Theo," she said, ripping herself free of the oversize coat.

"You don't want me to leave, Nina."

She laughed. "Lord have mercy."

"Say it, then," he said. "Tell me that you want me to leave."

"It's better this way," she said. "For everyone."

"Better for Colson," he nodded knowingly. "Easier to lead you along without me in the way."

"He isn't *leading me along*, Theo!"

"No," came another voice, its tenor unmistakable. "Let him get it out."

Theo turned to see Patrick at the windowsill, his back against the wall, arms crossed over his chest. Mostly shrouded in the darkness of the evening, just now deciding to fall. He pushed off the ledge—the one with the perfect view down to the ramparts where Nina and Theo had stood not moments before.

Theo's face heated. Some instinct snarled to the surface.

Patrick stopped two paces away and waited, tilting his head at Theo. He gestured for Theo to speak. "Now's your chance, Teddy. Tell her how much better off she'd be with you instead."

"Patrick," Nina said warily. "We were speaking *privately*."

"And now you ain't."

He'd always spoken this way. Like a lord, in a sense. Unswervingly. The words already cocked on his tongue, every response measured ahead of time, shrinking men where they stood. Tying them up in their own words.

Theodore felt his hands shaking. He looked at Patrick but spoke to Nina. "He brought you to Kenton Hill with a sack over your head and your hands tied," he said slowly, wanting her to hear every syllable. "He tried to lock you up in a room."

Patrick didn't interrupt, nor did he lift his eyes from Theo. Instead, they seemed to bore further in, waiting for something.

"It's the same now," Theo continued. "He has you exactly as he wants you, Nina. Blinded, tied up in his mess—"

"Ah," Patrick said now, nodding slowly. "Yes. A dirty Craftsman, running off with his little Artisan hostage." He tsked. "And I suppose, she'd have to be stupid, wouldn't she? To fall for a trick like that? Defenseless, too. Or how would I overpower her?"

Patrick stalked closer, and Theo felt his fists clench. "That isn't what I said."

"But that's what you're implyin', Teddy. That's what she hears when you tell her I've got her eyes covered. That I'm the one pullin' her strings."

"I'm scared for *her*!" Theo shouted. "She was almost shot, not days ago! Have you yet considered her well-being on this *fucking* conquest? Or will you lead her into any snake pit if it means winning your bloody terranium?"

Patrick's expression blackened instantly. "I wasn't aware she'd made you her guardian, Teddy, or did you assume the position all on your own?"

Theo didn't balk, didn't turn from him. "Someone ought to look out for her."

"That's rich," Patrick nodded ominously, stepping forward into Theodore's space so it was obvious just how imposing Patrick's stature was in comparison. "That's bloody rich, since you would have left her bleedin' against the whippin' post, had your chivalry not awoken at just the right moment."

"Stop," Nina said, putting a hand on Patrick's chest.

"Let's hope *yours* awakens soon, Colson, before you've siphoned everything you can take from her," Theo spat.

"That's your problem, Teddy. You still think she's the sort of woman who can be managed. Have you met her? She ain't manageable."

Theo stood as tall as he could. "Yet she'll walk where you point. And you're not pointing her anywhere safe."

"I'll point you into a fuckin' grave, if you'd like." He looked as though he wished for nothing more than to obliterate Theo where he stood.

"*Enough!*" Nina called, a hand on each of their chests now.

Theo and Patrick had come almost nose to nose, breathing steam into each other's faces. Patrick's breath was laced with intention, like it would mean nothing to him at all to throw Theo over the cliffs.

"Theo," Nina said, straining to get his attention, her face red with anger. "When we leave this parish, you won't follow. I've made my choice."

Theo shook his head. "You'll never mean as much to him as idium does," he said to her, and he knew he was cruel to say it. He saw the flinch of pain cut across her face. "He'd forfeit your life to win this war."

Theodore found his head bouncing off the glass window, the pain momentarily blinding him.

Nina was shouting, Patrick's face looming an inch from his, ice in his eyes. The grip of his wide hand around Theo's throat, threatening its collapse.

"Wrong," Patrick growled, the tendons in his hand flexing. "Never met a man who was wrong so often."

Theo's hands went desperately to Patrick's, trying to peel it away. He couldn't breathe.

"You'll kill him, Patrick!"

"I would," Patrick agreed coldly. "Do you feel it, Teddy?" His hand tightened, sent Theodore onto his toes. "I'd do it without losin' a single night's sleep."

Black curtained Theo's sight, curling inward. But he still felt Patrick's steaming breath wash over his face.

And then he was on the floor, his legs numb, his side searing, his vision returning in spots of color.

"I told you, it ain't my place to say whether you stay or leave. She's the one who decides," Patrick said, somewhere above Theo. "And if she says leave, best you find that genteel nature of yours and listen to her. I'm only waitin' on a reason to beat the shit out of you."

Oxygen rushed into Theo's lungs, and he bent over on himself, his head down. He didn't want to see Nina's reaction, didn't want Patrick to see the tears that had sprung free. He felt Nina bend tentatively beside him, her breaths too fast, heard Patrick's footsteps recede.

He wanted to shout at Nina, point to Patrick's receding back and say, *See? That's the man you're following. That's what he becomes in the night.*

Theo gripped his throat and shrugged off embarrassment, and with Nina's wary hand on his shoulder, felt more resolve than he ever had.

CHAPTER FORTY-FIVE

NINA

Through the thin walls, I thought I could hear the other rooms thrumming, sleep evading us all.

I imagined Theo wrestling with himself on the settee, Patrick on the other side of the wall I was curled against, knuckles still pulsing. His father languishing on the mattress, strangely subdued since his foray into town.

I glanced over at Polly beside me on her own bed. Her eyes stuck on the ceiling, her lips moving in spell work, or prayer perhaps.

I simply dwelled. I knew I was right to cut the tie between Theo and me. He imagined a time and place where war wouldn't touch me. Where I could make choices that wouldn't impact all of Belavere. What he failed to understand was that I was a runaway train. The collision was imminent.

"He loves you, you know," Polly whispered to me. She was holding what looked to be letters to her chest. Her fingers moved over them. "Spoke about you nearly every hour we waited together in Kenton Hill." She went quiet for a time, and I prayed she would say no more. "I just thought it should be said, in case he hasn't yet found the courage to say it out loud."

She turned over then, and I was spared further barbs. I didn't sleep a wink, and when dawn came, I felt as though the sun taunted me, rising unhurriedly.

The rooms beyond the walls roused.

We met in the living room once properly dressed. Theo's brow was lined in deep thought, and his gaze met mine immediately. I shirked it. John leaned against a china cabinet. Polly clasped a cloak around her throat, and Patrick took the coin from his pocket and gripped it tightly.

"Every half hour, Theo will exit the library to the front steps. He will send the signal that all is well. If he comes out early, then something is wrong. If he's late . . ." Here Patrick glared at Theo. "Then we can assume they've been apprehended in some way." He looked to the book in Polly's hand. "If that happens, Polly is to try and leave the *Testament* behind somewhere, along with her translations, for us to find later. But above all, Theo, if someone comes for Polly or you, then you ought to fight your way out." He handed Theo a gun. There was a second as it traded hands, when Theo pulled and Patrick refused to let go.

But then it vanished into Theo's coat pocket, and neither traded another word.

"Will there be anyone at that library who recognizes you?" Patrick asked Polly.

She shrugged. "I doubt it. It's a big city, a big library. Easy enough to stay hidden in the stacks."

"Then you'll be quick," Patrick implored her. "Done by nightfall at the latest, or we're comin' in." It sounded more like a threat than a promise.

We departed Trunk Antiques gradually, and I gave the old woman a tight hug before I left in case we never returned. The piano played a somber farewell.

Patrick accompanied me into the lane a fair distance behind John and a bigger distance behind Theo and Polly. We each bled into the tide of Lavnonshire patrons, trying to look normal.

Shop doors opened and shut, the first wagons and horses pushed up the street, and streetlamps were snuffed out by hand. Gulls swooped in lazy circles overhead, and in all the activity, the ocean's roar was never quite drowned out.

I was dressed like an Artisan, and Patrick like a Crafter, and so we walked with a careful space between us. Anything closer might have drawn suspicion, even in Lavnonshire.

The Artisan quarters had already started to envelope the Craftsman precinct when Patrick finally spoke. "If you wanted to run away with him, I wouldn't stop you," he said. A horseless coach intersected us then, but even when it had passed, my face remained dumbstruck.

"What did you just say?"

"I said, if you feel safer runnin' off with Teddy," he spoke with a tick of his jaw, "then you should go."

I looked across the lane at Patrick like I'd never heard of anything more ridiculous and almost collided headlong with a wagon.

I shook my head and stomped around it, walking too quickly now. "If that's not the stupidest thing you've ever said to me—"

He drew a cigarette and wet the end on his lips. "Well, never claimed I was smart, did I?"

I made a scathing noise. "Maybe Theo and I will laugh about it one day with our many children."

His eyes flashed momentarily. "If that's what you want, then you should have it."

I scoffed. "Shut up, Patrick."

"He kissed you," he said now, flicking ash to the pavement.

I quickened my pace. It annoyed me that he didn't seem to have trouble keeping up. "And?"

He sighed. "And I flew off the handle. It wasn't my place. I'm tryin' to apologize for it." He looked up at the sky, at the roiling clouds. "Damn it if you don't make it fuckin' difficult."

"Me?" I growled, frustrated now. "No, Patrick. *You.* You make it difficult. My life grew exponentially more difficult the moment you arrived in it."

He pointed at me with his cigarette. "Now, ain't that the *bloody* truth of it?"

I laughed again, tempted to cross the space and shove him hard enough to make him stumble. "And I suppose I've made your life so completely unbearable?"

"Unequivocally," he said darkly.

"Then we're a pair. A more intolerable man I'll never meet." I spoke like I was spitting rocks. "Every night, every waking minute of the day, I think of *you*. And yet you think you know what I want? I'm so damn *tired* of men pretending they know what's best for me."

We walked silently after that, Patrick seething with something he did not voice, and me stomping down the Artisan quarters toward the library with fire on my heels.

The library was made of stone and ranked in high columns, a verse from the Book of Belavere etched into its cornices, pigeons spilling shit into the lettering. It sat along one side of a town square with a clock tower in its middle. There were Crafters selling newspapers, tea, charm trinkets that gave the beholder good luck, as though an Artisan ever grew short of it.

Theo and Polly were already ascending the stone steps to the library entrance in the distance. One last flash of Theo's dark hair, and they disappeared inside. A volley of other Artisans swallowed the space they left behind.

Patrick looked to the clock tower at the square's middle, its face cloudy with salt. "Top of the hour," he said. "Thirty minutes starts now."

CHAPTER FORTY-SIX

POLLY

When she first entered the library, Polly felt as though the walls were watching her.

They had passed a bored policeman at the front, checking Artisan brands with a cursory glance at each person's wrist, then shuffled through revolving glass doors into the foyer. The library was brimming with visitors, many of them Scribblers, but other scholars, too. Some seemed to have come to view Tanner's architecture. They stood with guides and gawked at the ceiling fresco, the statues, the passages from the Book of Belavere etched into the stone.

Polly and Theo didn't stop to admire these things with the rest. They walked on at a forced casual pace into the maze of stacks. Hundreds of thousands of books looming down over them.

"Well," said Theo, looking overwhelmed at the collection. "Where should we start?"

"Fiction," Polly said immediately. "Fantasy and mythology. Anything pertaining to Crafter folklore will be there."

Off they went, arm in arm. The shelves towering into the vaulted ceiling, great ladders rolling of their own accord with Artisans atop them. Balls of fire Charmer light floated without candelabra or sconce.

The fantasy and mythology collection, Polly knew, was extensive. It seemed to go on for row after row. They would lose an hour just searching for the cypher. Polly only remembered the color of the spine and the shape of the lettering. She let her eyes skim off the titles as they walked, as though simply perusing at her leisure.

Polly heard her name in every whisper, felt every pair of eyes on the back of her neck, and prepared her body to bolt. But the half hour depressed and no one approached. Theo left to reassure Patrick, then returned. The Artisans whispered their idle gossip. The Scribblers carried out their work peacefully. Their eyes passed over her and Theo just as they would any other. She remembered she wasn't a fugitive in the way Nina and Patrick were, only something discarded by the House. These Artisans might pass straight through her. Not a single one knew or cared for her name.

Finally, in the last row, the spine of the cypher leaned, waiting for her, against a book titled *Mr. Kipper's Clumsy Canary*. The cypher looked ludicrously oversize among a set of books for children.

She lurched forward and pulled it out on an exhale. "Here." She smiled, looking down at it. It bore no title. In the corner were initials—her grandfather's. "This is it."

Theo, too, seemed relieved. He had grown pale again, his hand clutching his side.

With the Stewards' book and her notes tucked into her coat, they found a table and lamp in a small study corner between classical poetry and music. She set out her things just like any other scholar—binding, parchment, and no quill or inkwell, of course. Polly even nodded politely to a few passing Artisans as she set down the cypher and sat.

"Top of the hour," Theo mumbled to her after a while. "I'll be back in a moment." He left, winding into the shelves.

Polly looked up at the ceiling fresco and sighed outwardly, flexing her fingers. The idium left in her throbbed like an overused muscle, the way it did just before another dose was due. She felt a thrill of disquiet at that—that after this, no more idium would run through her. She would use these final dregs to complete the translation, buy her ticket out of the Trench, and start anew on some continent that didn't harvest magic from the ground and consume it. She'd be no different, then, from any other.

Polly smiled wanly. A trade worth making, she thought. If it meant she could go where she pleased without her blood pounding in her ears, without looking over her shoulder wherever she went. To be without fear, there was nothing she wouldn't sell.

CHAPTER FORTY-SEVEN

NINA

The square was rabid with activity. It was easy enough to look purposeful. Busy. There were enough shadows between buildings in which to lurk.

John remained somewhere at the rear of the library by the servants' entrance, while Patrick and I kept our eyes on the library itself as each half hour gave way to the next. Theo appeared on the steps on time, not a second too late, pretending he was buying a pear, a newsprint, or else simply stretching his legs in the sunlight before returning inside. No one paid him any mind.

Patrick and I kept a careful distance from each other, but I felt his eyes on me as I wandered in aimless circles. Twice, I was approached by Artisan men, asking if I needed accompaniment somewhere, since a lady rarely traveled by herself. Each time I shook my head politely and pointed in any direction. "My father will only be a moment." For a woman without a ring, the mention of a father was the best way to dissuade an Artisan man. They nodded and carried on.

Theo came to the steps again, right when he should. He perused a nearby cart at the bottom of the steps with his hands in his pockets, then reentered among a large group of Artisans.

I sighed. Noon had passed. Four hours lapsed, then five, and still no Polly. My back ached from sitting proper on a wrought-iron café chair, listening to the Crafter buskers. Patrick moved from one shadow to the next, the light of his smoke flaring in the dark.

I narrowed my eyes in his direction, and he lifted an eyebrow in return.

Lord, it was difficult not to look at him. Impossible, even. Just now, several young Artisan women in a group were looking over their shoulders, whispering with their foreheads lowered toward one another, giggling. How scandalous it would be for one of them to break the pack and approach that daunting Craftsman who lurked in the alley. How shocking. Should they do it? *I dare you*, one of them would urge. *I dare you to ask him for a cigarette.*

The girls in the Artisan School had been the same, turning their noses up when it suited them but flushing at the idea of some sordid encounter with a miner, a welder, a miller. All that brawn was difficult to ignore. Too alluring by far. More than enough good Artisan girls had fallen victim to it. The perceived wickedness of it, was, at times, too tempting. There were devils all over the brink.

I scoffed. Maybe I ought to scandalize them myself. Walk right up to Patrick and pull his mouth down to mine. Push my body against his. Take the smile off their faces, off Patrick's. Maybe he'd forget for a second that he wasn't supposed to want me. Maybe he'd finally forget about those fucking lines.

I felt if he didn't soon, I might go mad.

The hour was closing. Two more minutes until Theo would appear. I reasserted my attention to those stone steps, the revolving doors. Maybe this time, Polly would appear at Theo's side, *The Stewards' Testament* tucked safely away.

The hands of the clock tower ticked.

One minute remaining.

A coach and its horses clopped into the square, halted before the library steps, and blocked my view.

I stood, annoyed, trying to see over it to the entrance. Theo would arrive any moment.

But a man alighted the coach, tall enough to garner attention. He was followed by four others, all of them uniformed in Artisan blue.

The tall man climbed the steps, long ministerial robes sweeping the stone behind him, and I lurched forward one step, then two. Patrick left his shadows to stare, eyes bulging at the man and his contingent.

Lord Terrence Shop went through the revolving doors and disappeared within.

The clock chimed.

Something cracked in my core.

Theo. Polly.

The Stewards' Testament.

Had they called the lord themselves? No, I couldn't believe that. Refused to. Just because I'd told Theo to leave didn't mean he would turn on me so quickly.

And Polly. I'd believed her when she said she was sorry.

But I'd believed her in Kenton Hill, too.

Another minute lapsed, and somewhere within that library, *The Stewards' Testament* and its translation were trading hands. Idia's Seam handed over to the Head of House himself. There'd be no resisting. His contingent were likely fire Charmers. Armed soldiers. And how many bullets were in Theo's gun?

I locked eyes with Patrick—he across the square, and me much closer to those steps. Too close for him to catch me. No hope of him making it past the doorman, not in his garb.

No, he seemed to beseech me, seeing the lean my body was already taking. *Don't do it.*

But I was a runaway train.

I went inside.

CHAPTER FORTY-EIGHT

POLLY

Polly held her finger to the parchment and watched ink bleed to the page. The pad of her index felt more connected to the parchment than to her.

The translating was swift with the aid of the cypher. She found herself languishing in the challenge of it—nose bent over parchment, ink bleeding from page to page, fingertips soon stained. She transcribed the strange glyphs from *The Stewards' Testament*, then methodically consulted the cypher. Verian Script was a jerry-rigged language of three origins melded into one. Polly pored through her grandfather's tome and fished out any lettering as though pushing together pieces of an ever-expanding puzzle. Each word was practically strangled from the book, like it was reluctant to give it up. Polly wondered if somewhere, deep in the earth, the three daughters turned in their graves, their stories torn from their skeletons against their will.

She was beginning to recognize the layers of glyphs that turned up more than once. *Beast*, for instance. *Witch* was another. Not for the first time, her mind wandered to that unnamed enemy. Presumably, the enemy referred to the foreign continents, the ones that Idia and her army defeated in the Battle of Belavere. Polly was sure this part of the story was about to unravel. Idia would lead her army of loyal Belaverians into a battle against this beast, and she would sacrifice herself to defend the land—leave her magic behind in the ground as a gift to those who served her, who defended her.

That was what the Book of Belavere had taught them.

But then she thought of Joan, then Dione. Where was their army? They'd died with little more than a small band of Stewards to defend them.

Theo remained nearby, pretending to peruse the shelves. Sometimes he sat by Polly and watched as she translated. He came and went twice with each passing hour, and Polly barely noticed.

The third daughter was named for her beauty. Of all three daughters, she seemed to harness the least power, preferring instead to perform the menial tasks of farming—tilling soil and crafting all manner of tools.

The *least* powerful? That didn't seem right.

Her work was solitary. Idia was not prone to the grandiose displays of her older sisters, and she thereby went quietly into the belly of the continent and stayed hidden for many years.

Polly huffed a quiet laugh. "Not all of us are so lucky," she murmured to herself.

She secluded to the deep hills and rarely surfaced. We Stewards hunted and lived simply alongside her contemplation. We recount her meditative practice, her connection to the country, to the earth, and her deep love for this soil on which she'd been born. Idia murmured to this land, and it sang to her, worshipping as we worshipped.

In those quiet days, we, her Stewards, grew devoted. She nourished the earth, and so the earth nourished us, who never knew a greater peace. We offered our lives to Idia, but the third daughter would not accept.

To us, she entreated instead, "The Stewards shall witness and live on long enough to scribe these stories."

Polly's head lifted from the parchment, her brow furrowed. High on the southern wall of the library were the carved words of the Scribblers' doctrine. WE WHOSE BLOOD IS INK WILL SCRIBE BELAVERE'S STORIES. The same credo she'd chanted in the Artisan school. The one written on her official fellowship diploma. She looked back at her splotched rendering of the Stewards' words and wondered if these men and women weren't the very first Scribblers.

The time for peace was not lasting, for across the lands, shepherds, thieves, and travelers wandered, and Idia's presence could be felt by even the daftest man. The beast came.

"No," Polly muttered. This was not how the story went. Where was Idia's army? The cavalry of horsemen and the foreign enemy in their armada, pillaging Belavere's sacred lands in search of its magic?

Outside the library walls, the sun was sinking into the sea. Daylight already slipping through her fingers. Polly turned on her lamp and ignored the ache in her back, in her head. The final page of the Stewards' book distended, and she worked in a frenzy now, growling when the ink bled wrong.

The beast came as it had for the first and second daughters. The beast was greed and envy. It was both laborer and conqueror. They were governors, priests, and farmers. They were the insidious arrogance of men who believe themselves a worthy custodian of power. They were Idia's own countrymen, who came to those soft hills of widow's lace and took Idia out into the night.

Polly breathed as though she were sprinting, not scribbling.

Idia did not fight as she was taken. Instead, she let her fingers whisper over the wildflowers and conversed with the moon. The murderers of her sisters carried burning torches and blades. They bared teeth stained red and seemed possessed of their intention. When Idia spoke to the sky, they called her witch. They screamed their convictions as though to make them true. "Evil," they screamed. "Wicked."

They cut and bled Idia as they had her sisters, and she made no sound, nor did she mount any defense. She went willingly into this slow death.

And when it seemed she would succumb without relinquishing her magic, Idia's enemy, as they had with her sisters, grew desperate in their inadequacy. They took Idia's Stewards to the knife, and when the blades touched their necks, Idia rose like a dark creature.

Theo came to tell her that the half hour had elapsed, and that he would be back momentarily. She waved him off, hair falling into her eyes, suddenly frantic.

Theo's footsteps withdrew.

Polly's hands shook.

She sent a shudder through the earth so mighty that the hills reformed, the slopes melding and splitting. The soil turned to liquid, shifting underfoot and swallowing men whole. The earth rose and fell to protect her, its loving mother. A crack appeared, cleaving the land in two, so deep the pit of hell was glimpsed. And Idia, ebbed of power and blood, greeted the black as though it were an old friend and went gladly into it.

The earth cradled her and closed its seam, so no man would reach her again.

But in coming years, the fields and meadows would grow abundantly, and the ones who witnessed the magic there would come to believe that beneath the surface, magic lurked.

Even after death, Idia's enemy would not relent, and the people of the Trench pillaged the earth . . .

"Almost done with that, are you?" came a voice.

Polly paused without looking up, her entire body convulsed in shivers. The very makeup of her existence, of every existence, shifting. "Another moment, please," she said hurriedly, praying she was mistaken.

"Take as many as you need" came the answer, only this time, the speaker pulled out the chair opposite, the wooden legs shrieking across the tiles. The man sat straight-backed, crossed one leg over the other, and leaned his cane against the desk.

Lord Shop looked back at Polly and seemed to settle in. Over Polly's shoulder, she noticed, for the first time, the outfit of Artisans, of policemen, shackles and batons in hand. Between two of these officers, Theo was detained, his lips white with fear, his eyes beseeching her.

"Go ahead, Miss Prescott," Lord Shop said, his eyes lowering to the glistening ink on the page. "I'm dying to see how it ends."

CHAPTER FORTY-NINE

NINA

I slipped through the doors as a surge of Artisans exited.

There was a scream, and it was difficult to tell which direction it came from. It seemed the Artisans were being shepherded out by Scribblers, all of whom wore stark expressions, their eyes wide and fearful. One called to me as I barreled past. I ignored them and fought my way through the confused horde.

And then, the stacks, the dim oppressive light, the close air and the smell of a thousand pages. Normally comforting, but now, an omen. Another scream—a woman's.

There were sounds of protests from behind, and I turned to see Patrick, so patently out of place, skirting around the sea of Artisans flooding the exit.

"Hey!" shouted an officer, trying to funnel toward him. "You can't be in here!"

The moment he got close, Patrick pulled a gun from his coat and held it to the man's gut. "You're gonna scare all the swanks, lad," he said. "Get out of here while you can."

The officer swallowed once, seemed to consider Patrick's size, then turned on his heel and left with the remaining visitors.

My back was pressed against the first row beside a rolling ladder, and Patrick met me there, his eyes icier than ever. "Well," he murmured, looking around the corner, down the empty aisle. "That was a fuckin' choice, wasn't it?"

My heart pounded. "We can't let him just take everything," I whispered, sweat beading over my forehead. "It can't all have been for nothing."

Patrick swore beneath his breath, then held his gun up to me. "Not a single bullet in the chamber," he breathed. "Do you understand that? Not a single fuckin' one."

"I'll rip the ground up around us if I have to," I told him.

"Lord almighty," he growled quietly, looking up to the ceiling. "We're outnumbered, Scurry girl."

But I hadn't lost everything only to lose this, too. I'd kill Lord Shop here, in this very library. It didn't matter who else I had to bury with him.

"Please," I said to Patrick, the void in me yawning wide. "Let me do this." He must have seen the desperation leaking through, the shake in my breath.

Seconds passed, and then he growled and looked away. He took my wrist in his hand and held it tightly. "Have mercy," he said. "Stay behind me."

Backs hunched, we slunk down the aisles, listening for voices. The vaulted ceiling only fed us the sounds of someone's whimpering. It was almost impossible to tell from which direction it came. Adrenaline swarmed me.

Patrick pulled me down the maze of aisles, stopping every so often to listen. To redirect. Eventually we could hear boots squeaking off the marble. The whimpers had turned to gasps. We stopped at a corner and looked around its edge.

There, down the end of the row. A study corner with desks and lamps built in among the shelves. Black-inked pages strewn across the floor. Two steel-eyed soldiers. Between them, Theo, their forearms encasing his.

Two fire Charmers stood with balls of light hovering above their palms. They stood before a woman with a flurry of unbound black curls and an expression so despondent, she might have had her neck on the edge of a sword. Polly.

A voice came. It was a voice I could have recognized in my sleep, or on the brink of death. I felt it like a long-fingered hand gripping my spine. Lord

Terrence Shop stepped out of the gloom, his cane glancing off the tiled floor, his expression somehow more severe now, the fire sharpening every angle of him. He bent to retrieve the pieces of parchment from the floor and perused them.

"You can come out, Miss Clarke and Mister Colson," he said easily. "Unless you'd rather retreat. In which case, I wouldn't fault you. There are far too many things in this building to set alight."

Patrick groaned in my ear, then gave me one pleading look.

We stepped out into the open.

Polly's chin trembled at the sight of us. Theo pulled against his restraints.

And I couldn't understand it, how Lord Shop could know to come to this exact city, to this building on this very day. "You brought them here?" I asked Polly. For who else could alert the House so quickly? Why would she stand unshackled and peaceful while Theo fought his captors?

A tear ran the course of her cheek. She made to speak.

"Her father, actually," said Lord Shop. "Mr. Prescott has an . . . understanding with the House." I noticed that he stood behind his fire Charmers.

"Welcome," he said genially, nodding like any good gentleman. "I assure you the Scribbler is not to blame." Shop continued, his sights now sliding over Polly. "In fact, she is much less cooperative than her father suggested."

It was only then that I noticed the shake of Polly's hands, the way she swayed where she stood. The skin of them looked strange in the dim light. When the firelight glinted off them, I saw that the skin had been melted away. Something horrid dripped from her fingertips.

Lord Shop held up the ruined pages in his hand. Each piece was sodden with ink, as though someone had overturned well after well over them. Just like the Artisan children had done so in school. The ink dripped from the pages onto the marble, blacker than they were white.

"I can just imagine the very important information you must have been trying to hide," the Lord said, grimacing at the parchment, and then discarding it. It slapped wetly off the marble. He went to the only desk with a lit lamp and picked up the two books upon it. One was *The Stewards' Testament,* still open to its last page. The other was a heavy tome—the cypher, I presumed.

"At the very least, all is not lost," Lord Shop mused. "We persuaded her to stop drowning the texts eventually. I was concerned she might let us burn her to ash." Indeed, it seemed as though the books themselves were unsullied. Polly hadn't gotten to them in time.

A sob escaped her then, and her head dropped down as though it had grown too heavy for her neck, and I imagined her Scribbler hands being incinerated by fire, while she bled every last drop of ink from herself, until she couldn't.

"I'm sorry," Polly moaned, and the misery was too much to bear.

Patrick pointed his revolver straight at Lord Shop, over the gap between his men's shoulders. I imagined his face splitting apart around a bullet we didn't have.

"Ah now," Shop tsked. "Fools rush in, Colson. And fool though you may be, even you can guess what happens next."

Patrick's eyes reflected fire. "If it involves a hole in your head, I'm all ears."

"You'll attack with poor results," he said calmly. "Our side will retaliate. John will arrive from wherever he is hiding—an alley, perhaps? It will end in bloodshed on both sides, Mr. Colson, and the whereabouts of the Seam lost somewhere in the middle. Neither of us wins then, do we?" Shop tucked his hands behind his back, his chest an open target. "I'd sooner make you a deal."

I spat on the floor like a miner, and Patrick gripped my wrist tighter. "I don't make deals with monsters."

"Then we'll call it . . . an offering," Shop reiterated. "Theodore and the Scribbler will come with me. And you'll leave here peacefully."

I scoffed, sounding deranged. "And how many of your army will we find waiting on those steps?"

"Not a single one," he said. "I've come on rather short notice, so you've found me woefully ill-prepared. You may slither away."

But there was something else in his expression. Some hidden strain beneath the surface.

Patrick clicked his tongue, considered Shop for a moment. "Nah," he said. "I'm thinkin' you're terrified Nina will tear the ground up and pitch you into hell at any moment, eh?"

A flicker of something passed over Shop's eyes.

"Yeah," Patrick said. The gun did not lower. "You've lost some sleep to it, I'll bet. Watchin' Tanner spit dirt and go under. She scares you." It made Patrick smile malevolently.

Lord Shop did not balk, but I thought I saw his lips thin. "So, then, it's an impasse, Mr. Colson, because you see, we both have too much to lose."

There was a scuffle from behind them, and two more men came into view. One was a fire Charmer, by the glowing red of his hands. The other was John, the side of his face badly burned. A rope of fire wrapped around his neck, not yet touching his skin, but slowly burning it. John's face was mottled red and suffused in sweat. It dripped into his eyes and stained his shirtfront. He sucked breath through his teeth. "Teddy," he heaved, lengthening his neck to keep his chin from the fire. "Don't suppose you got any water handy?"

The barrel of Patrick's gun swung instead to this new fire Charmer, an older man, his hand held lazily in front of him with the arrogance of skill and decades of practice. He did not flinch at the revolver pointed at him.

"Let him go," Patrick said evenly.

"In just a moment," Lord Shop said.

John panted, moaned in pain. The skin on his neck glowed.

"You'll be on your way," Lord Shop said. "The Scribbler and her books come with me. And I'm sure"—here he looked toward Polly and her ruined hands—"that she'll be amenable in rewriting the translations."

"You have no use for me," Theodore said, pulling uselessly at his arms. The officers tightened their grip. "And I won't go back."

"You're right, in one regard at least," Shop said. "I'd rather have the Alchemist instead, but I doubt Nina would make the trade." He was inquiring me now, his brow lifted. Waiting.

A trade? Patrick for Theo? My tongue stuck to the roof of my mouth. I said nothing.

John groaned. Polly wept.

Shop nodded knowingly. "I thought as much. I daresay, Theodore, that you've rather outstayed your welcome."

Theo looked at me for a moment, and something in my expression must have solidified this, because he stopped struggling. He looked down at the marble floor.

I felt suddenly subsumed by guilt. The walls distended.

John cursed loudly. "*Patty!*" he begged.

"Let him go," Patrick said. "And we'll be on our way."

Lord Shop nodded to the fire Charmer, who curled his fingers inward, and the rope of flames around John's neck vanished.

"I suspect we'll see each other again soon," Shop told Patrick, the ghost of a smile touching the corners of his mouth. "When the time is right."

Patrick pulled me back, and I resisted, my eyes latched on to the book and the cypher. "You won't reach the Seam," I said, teeth gritted. Idium undulated within me—thin but ravenous, stretching veins and expanding my mind. "Not without me."

"Perhaps," Lord Shop said, nodding, as though this were a meeting and he was examining the facts. "But I believe in innovation. In progress. Where one door refuses to open, another can be carved." He stepped around his officers, close enough to stand inches from Patrick's gun, as though he knew the chamber held no bullet. "In the meantime, I suggest you dig yourself a hole deep enough that even the worms cannot find you, or summon the courage to put his gun in your mouth and fire. Because there are plenty of ways to break ground, girl, and the day you outlive your usefulness to me will be the end of this war."

He looked faceless in that moment. He could have been a Crafter or Artisan, the devil himself. Futility descended, spirals of it circling my entire being until my fingers curled in and my rib cage folded.

He must have been stark raving mad if he thought I'd blow myself away and not bring him with me.

"Nina, we have to go."

In the square, the clock tolled, the hole in me widened, everything toppling into it.

Patrick had hooked his arm around my chest and was hauling me away. No matter how hard I fought, I couldn't seem to break free. Theo and Polly, the cypher and the translations, they were becoming further from reach.

"Don't do it, Nina," Patrick begged.

Shop had the audacity to smile from a distance. "Get my son out of here," he ordered his Charmers.

But not soon enough. In my veins, the idium exalted, and I felt the earth beneath all that marble awaken. The ground heaved. Marble cracking. A titanic groan shook my middle ear, and the great labyrinth of shelves teetered.

The first seemed to wobble and overcorrect, and Patrick froze in his bid to drag me out. They each stilled and watched in horror as the shelves swayed back and forth, and then, finally, they fell, crashing into the next row. Hundreds of books rained down.

"RUN!" John bellowed.

We escaped down the labyrinth, the party of us scattering in different directions, John, Patrick, and I one way, Theo and Polly dragged in another. The giant walls of shelves toppled at our backs, one into the other, gaining momentum, a landslide of books crashing and filling the corridors. The thunderous crunch of wood as it collided and splintered. A heavy volume struck my shoulder as we ran. John expelled pieces of broken timber falling overhead, just barely holding off the weight of them long enough for us to pass through, to turn the corners, to sprint down the aisles. Books crashed into my shoulders, my head, caught the backs of my legs. But Patrick had my arm, hadn't let it go once, and he pulled me onward faster than my legs could manage.

"Don't look back!" he shouted, and I ran harder than my lungs could tolerate.

We spilled out into the main foyer as the last shelf fell, buckling in an earsplitting crash, and we didn't stop. We rushed to the doors, feet pounding off the cracked marble.

We ran out into the briny air, a small crowd of Artisans in the square watching on in horror. Pieces of the clock tower were now strewn on the ground, the cobblestones cracked. Several members of the crowd approached as though they meant to offer help, faces stark in the approaching night.

We barreled through them all, past the limp coppers with their gaping mouths and half-raised batons, past the buckled coach and its frantic horses.

I tripped on my skirts, my legs failing me now, my heeled shoes slipping on the debris, and then Patrick's arm was around my torso, lifting me off my feet.

I was carried past the gawkers who were just now realizing they knew my face, and Patrick's. That fugitives, escaped war criminals, had been among them. My limbs went slack in Patrick's hold. The darkness of an alley closed in.

But my eyes stuck to the library doors until they were out of sight.

CHAPTER FIFTY

THEO

Theo walked as though sleep had taken hold of his limbs.

With two soldiers on his arms, he moved as one does in dreams, mindless and numb, their bones not their own. His father walked ahead of him with the Charmers flanking his sides. Polly was pulled along somewhere at Theo's back. He could not look at her without his eyes descending to her ruined hands.

They were escorted not to the coach, which had buckled beneath the fallen clock tower, but to the edge of the ramparts, a handful of soldiers awaiting them, looking reticent to have been called to duty this night. Theo noticed that there was a certain care to the way they marched him away, as though this were a rescue and not an arrest.

He blinked at the passing streetlamps and watched photons burst in the distortion of his sight. He felt stupid, dazed, his head rattling with the effects of shell shock. He couldn't be sure if the stars over the sea were rearranging their constellations or if he was finally succumbing to madness.

Perhaps it was best he let it come. Let sanity give way to something painless and quiet. Let him hope for less than love from this moment on.

Better that than this yawning awareness that he was utterly alone.

They were loaded hastily into a wagon under flickering lamplight while most of Lavnonshire hid itself away and the sea thrashed the cliffside. The horses were unadorned and matched the choleric officers who lifted Polly, Theo, and his father into the wagon bed.

There was no canopy, and so the braver residents watched from their high windows as the wagon was pulled away through Lavnonshire's maze. The Charmers and officers followed behind at a leisurely pace, scowling up at the fluttering curtains until Crafters scurried back from the glass.

Theo's father sighed tiredly. "We're a spectacle," he said, adjusting his gold-rimmed glasses on his nose—embarrassed, Theo imagined, to be seen on Crafter transport. "We'll be taken on a private train to the city."

Theo barely heard him. He leaned forward, let his face fall into his hands, and suppressed the urge to vomit.

"What you're feeling, Theodore, is shame," his father said bluntly. "You've brought every bit of it onto yourself."

Theo had never been surer that this was true, though not in the way Terrence Shop thought.

"If you're so ashamed of me, why not leave me in the brink?" he asked. "Why bring me back at all? Surely the House won't let you reinstate me after I deserted."

"But you didn't desert the House, Theodore. You were taken hostage, and this is your rescue." What he implied was clear. The newsprint would establish his father a hero by morning. Another win for the House.

"You can save your tantrum for the journey home, if you please. There are plenty of walls for you to thrash your head against. But you *will* return home with me and carry out your duty as you were meant to, whether willingly or by force."

"Because it spares you a scandal?"

"Because you are my *son*!" Lord Shop said, his voice rising for the first time. "And because I did not invest every ounce of leverage I had in you only for you to squander our family name on some *girl* from the brink!" He said it as though there were no greater insult to him.

Theo closed his eyes and felt the invisible pressure of ever-tightening binds cinching him inward. He said the only helpful thing he could hope to say. "If your Charmers burn Polly again, I'll drown them. There's plenty of water at hand."

"Interesting," Lord Shop said condescendingly. "Have your affections changed?"

Theo looked up to see him inspect Polly with no small measure of disgust. She was cradling her bleeding hands carefully against her chest, curling into herself like she was expecting another blow. His father shook his head, perplexed. "Truly, Theo, you are a simpleton when it comes to the female persuasion."

But of course his father wouldn't understand friendship. There were only ever alliances. "She needs a doctor," Theo said. "And bluff."

"Penance is a medicine of its own kind," his father answered, adjusting his cane so that his hands rested atop it. His eyes pierced Theo's. "As you'll soon learn."

Theo did not fear his words. In fact, he couldn't even bring himself to disagree with them. "Is that your great plan?" he asked boldly. "To have me lashed on the citadel steps and claim I've been saved? Do you think the Trench will believe I've been cured of my beliefs?"

"And what beliefs are those, Theodore?" his father asked, his tone darkening. He tilted his head to the side. "Are you a bleeding heart for the Crafters? A Union sympathizer?"

Theo's mouth popped open, then closed again. No, not only for the Union. There were those on both sides with whom he sympathized.

His father scoffed mirthlessly. "You have no idea of your own convictions, boy, do you?"

Theo boiled. He and his father had never come to blows. Their sparring was the verbal kind. Boxing was for Craftsmen. But Lord, how Theo wanted to belt him now.

"You let them go," Theo said in a voice that seethed. "Why?"

His father looked back at him drolly, as though even this disappointed him. "As punishing as it has been of late to be your father, I do not wish for us to be at odds. I know you care for the girl. You've made that abundantly clear to me."

"No. That isn't all of it," Theo pressed. "There's something else."

"There's always something else, Theodore," Lord Shop intoned.

"Decisions like these take time. Careful planning. My aim was simply to retrieve *The Stewards' Testament*, the translator, and of course, *you*. The Alchemist and the earth Charmer are desperate and young and rash. I didn't much want to incite the kind of gunslinging that would surely have ensued once the rats realized they were cornered."

Polly breathed through her nose like a bull, hands shaking.

It didn't make any sense, or perhaps the intricacies were now beyond Theo's capability. "You had enough fire Charmers to take them all hostage. Enough leverage to tip your hand. Why wouldn't you have them arrested?"

Lord Shop considered Theo as though he truly could not fathom what had become of his son. He crossed his legs and looked up into the expansive sky. "You know, the thing about rats is that they're entirely difficult to catch. One might set up a hundred traps with the most enticing bait, and they'll find a way to steal the bait and slip through the cracks. They're smarter than they seem. For though they might be vermin, they are . . . *determined* when properly motivated."

Theo tried to follow the words, tried to see what lay between them. This was how an Artisan spoke. In encryptions and mazes and tightening spirals.

Lord Shop spoke on. "One might drive themselves to insanity trying to eradicate an infestation for good. The better thing to do is wait. The rat in the walls soon runs out of bait to eat. It grows frantic, it eats its young, its own foot. Soon, the rat dies. It does the work for you."

Theo stood, despite the moving wagon, eyes wide and wild.

"We've arrived," his father announced suddenly, and the wagon came to an inelegant halt.

Theo staggered and nearly fell.

With that, Lord Shop gestured to the opening of the wagon, where the uniformed men waited with their sullen faces.

The train station was empty and still but for the steaming plume of a train engine, and the soldiers who waited on its small platform.

"Don't be stupid, Theodore," Lord Shop said, rebuttoning his coat. "Your moment of rebellion is over. Do you understand me?"

As though following some invisible summons, the soldiers waiting at the end of the wagon gripped the handles of their batons.

Theo clenched his teeth, tasting blood. He nodded stiffly.

The train, empty but for them and a contingent of soldiers who walked like wraiths between the compartments, labored full-tilt from the moors into marshlands. Wide stretches of water passed, and though it looked glassy and picturesque in the late light, Theo knew the depths were murky, full of eels and whiskered fish and beady-eyed mud-dwellers. Water was sometimes deceptive and sometimes not. Sometimes it rolled and crashed and warned a man of its true nature. But mostly, it reflected something far calmer than what waited beneath the surface.

Lord Shop poured him and Polly a cup of tea. He took up his own and looked out the window of their private compartment, apparently taken with the view. His cane rested beside him. He spoke as though Theo were accompanying him to the countryside for the weekend.

"I often wonder why our ancestors did not build a city further south. The winters are far more pleasant here. I'm afraid you'll be returning home to a freeze."

Theo ignored this. He watched his father's face for its tells. He knew something thrashed beneath the surface.

Polly, however, did not know to wade in carefully. "Where will you take us?" she said, her sobs giving way to something more fierce, as though she'd finally been divested of her fear.

"You'll speak when spoken to, Scribbler," Lord Shop said around the lip of the teacup, but in a voice that radiated danger. "Though I daresay you cannot help it, can you? Entitlement is such a scourge upon your generation."

Theo bid himself to stem his anger, to watch.

"My father would rap the back of my head with his cane when I spoke out of turn. This very cane in fact." The lord gestured to the cane in question.

"I chose a less tempestuous approach with my own son, though I've come to see that as an error in judgment." His eyes finally came to rest on Theo's. They were heavy-lidded, so as to be discreet. It was difficult to read a man who only showed you half his eyes.

This was what he wielded in lieu of a cane.

"*Where* are you taking us?" Polly repeated. She looked at Theo's father with the kind of flint Theo had never quite managed.

"I'm taking *you* nowhere, Scribbler," said Terrence. "You are a flea hitched to the back of donkey. You'll be at the mercy of the city authorities. They will sit you down in front of these texts and relay to me whatever they manage to choke from you. So heed my warning, young lady, cough it up quickly. It is the only thing that might save you from the gallows now."

"She has been punished enough," Theo said, stomach still roiling, the shake of the train wreaking havoc on him. "And she was forced to help us."

"Us?" Terrence Shop said, picking out that one word and spitting it back out. He looked out the window, contempt in the flicker of his eyelids. "Miss Prescott is an agent of the House, as are all Scribblers. They are mandated to report any crime to their superiors. To the *House*, if the crime necessitates, and yet not a single note of correspondence from Miss Prescott, when she could have called upon us at any time." He leveled Polly with a glare. "You are a traitor to your kind, Scribbler. And such a shame, after all you'd done for your country."

Theo thought of all she'd done—moving about the continent like a game piece, making trades for safety and never quite finding it.

There was a sizzle in the air of the compartment, the wick of a dynamite stick half-spent.

Polly kicked at her teacup and it shattered against the window, hot amber liquid sluicing the countryside. Her eyes shook in their sockets, tears brimming and spilling over. "My country stripped me of everything, including my fellowship, as a reward. I owe it no loyalty!"

The compartment door slid back into its recess, and a wide-eyed soldier appeared. "Sir?" he said, looking to the splintered china.

Terrence lifted a placating hand. "Close the door," he said. "All is well."

The door slid shut once more, the navy blue moving away beyond the stippled glass.

"Sit down, Scribbler," he said. "Or you'll go to the hounds sooner."

"*Polly*," Theo urged.

"Fuck you," Polly said, and it sounded odd coming from her. More offensive, somehow.

Terrence spoke as though he hadn't heard it. "I'll admit to you, Theodore, that I did not think you had this stupidity in you." It was cold, cutting. "When I'd found you'd not only left with the miners and Miss Harrow, but you'd *aided* their escape, I was confounded. I thought of your mother, lying on her deathbed, begging for reprieve from the pain. I wondered how any child could forget such an image, much less have it wiped away by the mere sight of another woman." He turned baleful eyes on Theo. "I will forgive you, Theo, for following that cunt out into the fray. I will forgive you your weakness, your stupidity, for the very last time."

Theo felt heat in his hands, at the back of his neck, in the empty pockets of his belly. He felt that familiar decline into boyhood, the same crippling hand on his shoulder pulverizing him into something smaller, lowering him to his father's feet.

This time, resistance was easy. Theo squared his shoulders. "She didn't beg."

A flicker of confusion crossed Terrence's face. "What?"

"Mother. She didn't beg before she died. She cried. She prayed. She said all kinds of nonsensical things once the fever took hold. She told me she loved me, right at the end. But she never begged. You would know that, had you been there."

Terrence's expression turned arctic.

"The begging came long before the influenza," Theo continued. "When she begged you for attention, for even the slightest show of affection. When she begged me not to accept my lordship. She was terrified, she said, that I'd grow cold, as you had grown cold."

"You disappoint me" was all his father said.

"And I must disappoint you again. I won't return to the House," Theo said, his voice harder now, his ears ringing. "Not unless you agree to my terms."

Terrence's lip curled. "Found those convictions, have you?"

Theo took his time answering, he looked at his father squarely, an older man than when he'd last seen him. Just as tall and severe, but wearier than he would ever admit. "The Lords' Army razed Trent," he said. "And Dorser, and likely a dozen other places."

Terrence's lips quirked in frustration.

"There were hundreds of bodies on the Trent riverbanks, frozen in the snow," he said. "Hundreds wounded inside a cold factory, some of them children. It was a slaughter."

His father showed no reaction. No outward display of any sort.

"When my mother died, it was in a warm bed with several pillows and a thick blanket. Nurses sponging the sweat from her forehead, the maid spoon-feeding her, laudanum keeping her in a trance. But these people? They were dying on a cold factory floor with their limbs blown off, Crafter women holding their mouths shut to keep their crying from waking the children."

"The spoils of war," Terrence said prosaically. "Arrive at your point, Theodore."

Theo did not dare drop his gaze. He wanted to see his father fully when he exposed himself. "If there is terranium to be found in Idia's Seam, it ought to be distributed to the people of Belavere who need it most. I want the original agreement you made with the Colsons upheld. I want you to call a ceasefire. I want Nina Harrow and Polly acquitted of their crimes. Put it in writing, Father. Release it to the print press, and I'll be the good son upholding our celebrated family name."

Terrence was unresponsive for a moment, and then he laughed. It was dry and painful-sounding, as though the muscles in his throat were unfamiliar with the movement. "So, you are a true convert now, Theodore," he said. It wasn't a question. "An ambassador for the toiling Crafters of Belavere."

Theodore didn't answer. He watched the veneer of his father slide back and reveal the callous shell of someone who'd shed themselves of humanity and its limitations.

"You place too much value on yourself, Theodore. There are only two paths ahead. The path of forgiveness, of *sanity*. Or you can continue to be an embarrassment to the name I gave you, and I could strip it from you."

Theo felt the ringing in his ears become a scream. "And even if it saved Artisan tradition, you wouldn't choose this, would you? You'd never sacrifice your precious fucking terranium for the Crafters, even if it meant an end to this war."

Lord Shop clicked his tongue. "You finally hit one squarely, son. The problem with giving a dog a bone, is that the dog then grows territorial. It snaps and barks at anyone who comes close. It's best to take it away before they grow familiar with the taste." He took a sip of tea from his cup and sat back in his seat.

"You know, even if I translate that book for you, you'll be no closer to finding Idia's Seam," Polly's voice shook, and she looked moments from collapse. Lord knew how she remained conscious with the pain of her hands. "All you'll have is the truth about how your ancestors murdered women for their own gain."

"Don't be so righteous, Miss Prescott. You, of all people, are familiar with sacrifice."

To her credit, she didn't cow this time. Didn't sink back into herself. "You have *nothing* without the Seam!"

"That's true," the lord allowed. "Though, the same can be said for your friends."

"Then you're not as smart as you believe yourself," Polly said, spittle collecting at the corners of her mouth, a sort of delirium taking over. "You should have bled me dry rather than simply burned me, *my lord*."

Lord Shop watched her over the top of his glasses. "Why?" he inquired. "To stop you from scribbling the translations to your rebel friends?"

Polly laughed in a way that suggested her mind was failing her. Her blinks lengthened. Words ran together. "Yes," she said. "And they'll find the Seam, long before you can. By now, they'll have already figured it out. They'll be on their way."

Theo watched with increasing dread as his father simply crossed one leg over the other, sipped at the rim of his cup, and watched Polly as though she were a curious insect he would soon squash. "Oh, but I'm counting on it," he said. "Officers?"

His call summoned three of them. They slid the compartment door aside and did not hesitate in their remit. Within a matter of moments, Polly's arm was pulled forth. A pocketknife was produced. The piercing sounds of Polly's screams rent the hollows of the train.

When the officers retreated, Polly's hand was clutched over her mottled forearm, blood seeping through her fingers and into her skirt. She slipped from her seat and onto the floor, Theo just barely catching her around her shoulders before she toppled forward, unconscious.

Theo clutched his own hands over the gaping wound, hot, viscous blood collecting in the beds of his nails, dripping off the tips of his fingers.

He turned his face toward his father with unveiled fury. And his father still looked to Polly as though she were a rat.

The rat in the walls soon runs out of bait to eat. It grows frantic, it eats its young, its own foot. Soon, the rat dies. It does the work for you.

"You don't intend to mine Idia's Seam yourself, do you?" Theo panted, feeling an acute sense of horror settle over him.

"Of course not," his father said from his place above, looming over him. "What outfit of miners would you have me use? In case you've missed the news, they're all currently on strike. The only person on this continent who has a hope of uncovering Idia's Seam is currently scampering across the countryside to do it for me.

"As I told you, son, rats are difficult to trap. It's far better to let them run free—or at least offer the *illusion* of freedom."

Theo felt bile rise up into his throat.

The train took a corner onto the bridge, the tea-colored marsh water below it stretching in all directions. The carriage swayed and sent Theo's stomach careening. A reckoning lashed at him. An irreversible choice rearing up.

His father replaced his cup to its saucer, then smoothed his fingers over his cane while Polly bled and bled.

"Nina Harrow and Patrick Colson are leading the way to the terranium. Their presence will make itself known to me. And at this very moment, the Miners Union are turning their guns upon each other. Soon, the order of things will right itself, just as nature intended, and years from now, people will call it God's work." He looked out the window at the water, silver in the night, and he sighed as though he were a tired angel delegated to earth, carrying out the necessary acts of the righteous. "You can't see it yet, son. But one day you will. One day, you'll see that this is the way of things, no matter how much you resist. Power was not meant for everyone."

Inside of Theo, a switch he did not know existed threw itself.

The water outside gleamed.

Theodore took Polly's torso into the circle of his arms and pulled her to standing, and with thoughts that perhaps this breath might be his last, Theo reached outward with his mind, throwing it as far as it would reach, to every molecule of water his medium could bend.

"Goodbye, Father," he said.

And a violent wall of water came rushing across the marsh, and the soldiers outside the compartment saw it coming too late. They only had enough time to slide back the door, to pull their Head of House into the aisle and bury him in their own bodies.

And when it hit, the train was barreled from its tracks. Windows buckled. Shouts were replaced by the titanic groan of water.

Theo and Polly tumbled and rolled with the momentum of the train.

But Theo did not let Polly slip from his grasp.

The water cradled them like a blanket.

CHAPTER FIFTY-ONE

PATRICK

Patrick carried Nina not to Trunk Antiques, but away from Lavnonshire. She was shivering by the time they reached the marsh. Larks soared overhead like demons, and the stars winked themselves out, not caring to witness them sludging through the wet taproots.

Tunnels were no good. No point trekking back the way they'd come. They would have to venture on until they found a boatman dumb enough or scared enough to hand over his vessel.

Here and there, Patrick stumbled in the bog under Nina's weight, John cursed and lit a cigarette from a seemingly endless supply, and Nina didn't speak. Patrick counted the seconds passing in silence and waited.

"You went in," John finally uttered, when it seemed he could remain silent no longer. He pulled forcefully at his own collar where it rubbed against the burnt ring around his neck. "Against all fuckin' reason, Patty. You went in."

Patrick ground his molars together. There wasn't a single mite of patience left in him. "Your thoughts on what I do no longer have much bearing on me."

"*I* went in," Nina said in a voice not quite present. Her face rested against Patrick's sternum.

John groaned, pulling a moth-eaten cap from his head and slapping his thigh in frustration. "Followin' her into the fuckin' fray again," he muttered to the sky. "You didn't think to *stop* her?"

He'd thought about it plenty. "No one stops her," he said, blood boiling. "No one takes her liberty away."

"God have *mercy*! She almost got us all fuckin' *killed*, Pat!"

Nina lifted her head suddenly, pushed away from him. "I can walk," she said.

He put her on her feet. She seemed unsteady, teetering. One gust of wind might carry her off. "I'm sorry," she said to them both. Her cheeks were tear-stained. Her fists balled, and she was trembling in the chill of the night.

Patrick felt murder come over him. "No," he said. "Don't apologize."

"You told me not to go," she said blankly, as though every ounce of energy had been wrung from her. "It was stupid."

"I don't care, darlin'."

"I didn't listen."

He put his hands on his hips and breathed out heavily, trying to warp his face into something that would calm her. "And when have you ever listened?"

She didn't smile. Didn't lift her eyes to his. She stayed swallowed by that which had gradually consumed her from the day her mother swung.

"They burned Polly's hands," she said, her lip trembling.

He nodded. The unraveling had arrived.

"They took the book."

"It's all right. We'll figure something out. There's a fix, I promise."

"They'll have the Seam," Nina said.

And we'll have nothing.

He needed to get back to Kenton Hill. He needed to *think*. He needed to get Nina into the safety of his own parish, where he wouldn't worry for her every fucking minute of the day. He'd walk all night if he had to. Walk all the way north. And while he walked, he'd think. He'd think of a way out of this new trouble. The Miners Union wouldn't surrender. Couldn't surrender.

He went to Nina and pulled her against his chest, lines be damned. He wrapped his arms around her back and felt her face press into the hollow of his throat. His shoes sank into the mud of half-tilled pasture.

Beetles swooped in the night, emitting their strange clicking, drawn to the warmth of the marshlands while the rest of the continent iced over, and Patrick thought at first that the itch he felt came from them. That the night bugs had burrowed into the sleeve of his shirt and were digging beneath his skin.

Then he halted.

The sound, though . . . the sound of the scratching reminding him of Polly's scribbles.

The skin of his forearm felt like it was being incised with the tip of a quill.

He drew away from Nina with a frown, looking down at his sleeve.

Something dark was seeping through the fabric. Like he'd been cut, and the night had turned his blood to ink.

He pulled the cuff down to the crook of his elbow.

On his forearm was a haphazard scrawl of words, badly smudged. Wet and stinging.

Too dark to read them. Too difficult to separate the bleeding letters.

"Dad!" he called over his shoulder. "I need a light."

Orange flame from a match caught the very last letter scratching itself into the crease of his wrist. Nina touched his skin with her chilled fingers and read Polly's scribble aloud.

"They were Idia's own countrymen, who came to those soft hills of widow's lace."

Nina looked up at him, her eyes seeing everything. "The translation," she said.

The one Polly had blotted to high heaven before Lord Shop had burned her.

The ones she could no longer trade for safe passage off the continent.

Yet here they were.

Patrick breathed. He held his arm still, as though the words would turn to sand and slip away. His eyes ran over them, again and again.

"There was no foreign enemy," Nina said, her eyes closing. She pushed at them with the heels of her hands. "It was her own people."

"They were Idia's own countrymen," Patrick read beneath his breath. He looked up at Nina, imagining her forearms bleeding again, the wounds ripped open. "Belaverians killed the three daughters?"

"And took the magic," Nina said, still in a far-off voice. "Those were the first Artisans."

They all stared at the sloped writing, shining wetly in the glow. Patrick imagined a woman who looked something like Nina. Not mounted on a horse and armored, riding off into battle, but a woman with soft skin and warm eyes. A woman whose blood was pulsing in the milk of her wrists, in the slope of her neck. He imagined a woman cornered by her own countrymen. The pieces of her harvested and bled and burned.

Polly, Rose Harrow, Nina.

Joan, Dione, Idia.

"It don't say *where*, though," John bleated, taking Patrick's wrist in his hands.

"It does," said a small voice. Nina swayed where she stood, bending slightly at the torso as though her middle was crumpling. She looked at Patrick as she spoke, the hazel of her eyes barely discernible in the dark. "Widow's lace," she said. "Only one place it grows on the continent."

Those soft hills of widow's lace.

Patrick's heart thundered.

Nina's eyes dulled. "Scurry," she said.

In the distance, the screech of metal rent the air in time with the fracturing of his mind, an uproarious crash of iron he couldn't place, sending larks into the night.

THE TRENCH TRIBUNE

HEAD OF HOUSE SURVIVES TRAIN CRASH

Startling reports from the National House confirm that a train derailed yesterday in the continent's South, with the newly appointed Head of House, Lord Terrence Shop, aboard.

In a statement scribbled to The Trench Tribune, *the House stated that Shop survived the accident with minimal injury, but that his son, Lord Theodore Shop, was killed. This, alongside a Scribbler, Polly Prescott, and several train workers and soldiers also aboard.*

The House and this tribune extend their deepest sympathies to their governing leader.

From his recovery bed, the Head of House extended assurances that, despite the tragedy, he was determined to remain a force of strength in these trying times.

Long live Belavere.

KENTON HILL SIGNS TRUCE PACT

Issued today to Belavere press was the announcement that Kenton Hill, the self-proclaimed rebellion capital, has today signed a treaty agreement with the House to cease strike action. A tremendous breath can be felt in the East this winter as the temperatures drop. Kenton Hill will deliver its coal quota to the capital, in hopes to encourage fellow parishes to continue their own labors for the greater good of the continent.

CHAPTER FIFTY-TWO

NINA

We arrived in Scurry in the same way my mother once left it.

Patrick helped me out of the bowels of a passenger boat, his cap pulled low over his brow, adjusting my own hat to keep my face in shadows. "Ready?" he asked.

But there is no readying for the assault of one's childhood. Particularly if one was a child in a town like Scurry.

John let the boat float away, and there was no one to pay us any mind as we made our way onto the sodden banks, slipping in the slush, skin already mottled with the cold.

John sniffed at the air and looked about the town. "Smells like home," he said.

"Horse shit and smoke?" Patrick muttered. But I thought he meant the bite in the air, less stinging than Kenton. Never cold enough to freeze the ground, but enough that snowfall melted as soon as it touched the earth, all of Scurry turning to mush underfoot. The roads were the color of molasses. The roofs dripped from their eaves in a perpetual rhythm, sagging under the burden of it.

Everything sagged in Scurry. Women lugged laundry and children and baskets that seemed intent on breaking bones. Men bowed in their miner's coats, shrinking inward from the chill, bent almost double before they turned thirty. By fifty, their noses skirted the puddles.

Most of Scurry was set atop a hill, cut off like an island between the river and its mines, so we had to walk the slope, slipping the entire way. I was hounded by sour memories, and some sweeter ones—Ma dragging me up the hill while I sat on a wide tin oven tray, then pretending I was too heavy and letting me slip back down the slope, right to the culvert next to the river. The days I'd spent on this slope, watching the river for boats mooring and pulling away, my mother not aboard, the boatmen watching on with obvious pity.

I thought of the resilient red flowers that dared to sprout heads among the dust in the spring. Widow's lace, only there for a short while. You had to be quick in the picking before they sagged, too. *No one but us has this,* Rose Harrow would say, twirling the flower before my eyes. *The city might have its own beauties. But no one else gets this.*

Midwinter, and the flowers had mostly decomposed. The hills were brown and sullen. But I wondered if perhaps, when Idia lived here, the land was beautiful. Before the hills were plundered and the flowers squashed.

Patrick's arm caught me as I stumbled, his fingers tightening around my forearm. "Easy," he said.

I tugged the heavy hem of my skirt away from the ground. Women in Scurry did not wear long skirts in the winter. They wore their husband's trousers, or their brother's. Practicality and warmth outweighed fashion.

Patrick took the folds of skirt from my hands and held it aside for me as I walked. He watched me warily. Likely he was noticing the strain taking hold of me as Scurry grew closer. I was trembling a little. Sickness spilled into my belly.

"Do you want to hear a story?"

I looked at him. "What?"

"A story. See if I can't take that pin out of your arse."

I grinned, though I didn't want to. "You're a pig. Have I ever told you that?"

He nodded. "Among other things. Now, when I returned home to Kenton after our siphonin', I promised myself I wouldn't mention your name, not even to my father," he looked up toward John, who was ten paces ahead.

"But I told Gunner. Couldn't help it. You were bangin' about my skull and I wanted to brag to someone about you, so I told him your name. I told him that I knew the earth Charmer was the same girl from that courtyard, and that I'd held her hand and kissed her stupid."

"You barely touched my cheek."

"Well, the way I told it, there was a lot of skillful tongue work."

I rolled my eyes, but I couldn't contain a chuckle.

"Now, Gunner don't look like he gossips, but trust me, he's worse than a widow in a tea shop. He told Donny, and Donny told our Ma, and the first thing she did was cuff me about the head and tell me that a man never kisses a girl so soon into courtship. I had to confess my lyin' so she wouldn't think her son was a tail-chasin' scoundrel."

A genuine laugh slipped free. I could picture him cowering beneath Tess Colson's scorn.

"She told me the next girl I kissed better ask for it first, or she'd find out and flog me." He twisted my skirt up in his hand.

I grinned. "And did you honor her?"

"I waited for you to ask me in Kenton Hill," he said. "Nearly killed me, but I waited."

I looked up at him, his hair more overgrown than I'd ever seen it, a thickening scruff of beard shadowing his jaw. But still the same boy underneath it. Still the man I loved, even if he tried to smother it.

"You're impossible to ignore, Nina Harrow," he told me. "You're cunning, and powerful. Grown men have to hide their fear around you." He said it softly, seriously. "Whatever lies in wait here, you've faced worse. Remember that. You're stronger now."

I nodded once, a tight soldier's nod, the kind that hid the quaking and cracking of one's chest.

We reached the summit of Scurry and ventured inward, and imbued as I was by Patrick's warmth, a chill slunk over my shoulders. Scurry was unchanged. Identical slate roofing conjoining one flat to the next. A sea of brick chimneys, soot-encrusted and coughing.

Scurry was twice the size of Kenton Hill, with triple the population stuffed inside its flats and all their waste dumped in the alleys. There were no hanging lanterns, no gleaming pipeworks, trolleys, canals, drains. No cobblestones or flower boxes. Just the flat exteriors of homes, and then, farther inward, the shop fronts, the trading post, the church, and the school in the westernmost part of Scurry.

We passed a bulletin board, its notices peeling away from the cork in reproach. Upon it, over and over again, was my face.

Did the House expect I'd return here after I'd disappeared seven years ago? I supposed most people's first thought in times of trouble was home.

And I had to admit, there had been those awful nights where I'd lain awake, suffocating in fear, and I'd thought of this town. Dreary as it was, there was comfort in the familiar. Still, I'd never returned.

"Never did get this far out, did we, Pat?" John said casually. "Ground's too fuckin' unstable for tunnels."

"Too many coppers, besides," Patrick replied. "Crawlin' with 'em. Always was. Too much terranium lyin' about for it to go unguarded, or at least there used to be."

"Reckon all those hats ain't got much to do nowadays," John muttered.

And indeed, the town did seem to have an air of complacency about it. There was an eerie silence. A hum of activity now missing, the miners short of terranium and the coppers short of remit.

A man passed on horseback, and a woman with three baskets stacked one on top of the other overtook them. A group of grubby-looking men stood clustered on a stoop, lighting three cigarettes with one match. They kept their noses down, their eyes never wandering, not even to the young boy who sat a few feet from them up against the bricks with his hat out for coins, his feet bare and his gloves bitten through. A skinny dog lay at his side, one stray warming himself against another.

"Poor bloody kid," John muttered too loudly, patting his pockets for coins he didn't have. "Ain't they got hearts in Scurry?"

Bleeding hearts bleed out, my father used to say, and he wasn't often right, but about this he might have been. There were too many hungry mouths in Scurry to feed. "We'll pass a dozen more yet," I muttered.

A few paces later, there were two more, then a whole family. "Bloody hell," John cursed, shaking his head. "Can't imagine a place that don't take care of their own."

I wanted to tell him that the people here were so troubled by their own poverty that it was dangerous to take on the burden of another's. The drowning often drowned their rescuers. But in truth, there wasn't much to be said in defense of Scurry. I had once knocked on doors that refused to open, pleaded with strangers who ignored me.

"We headed to a hotel?" he asked. "A pub?"

I shook my head. "They'll be full of police."

"Where then?" John insisted, rubbing his chapped hands together. "Wouldn't mind a nip."

I sighed, turning a corner I hadn't believed I'd ever take again. Past Mrs. Penhaligon's and my childhood neighbor's.

"Where are we headed?" Patrick asked warily, though I was sure he already knew. There was never another place to hide when I was a kid. Stood to reason it would be no different now.

"To call on my father," I said. "If he isn't yet dead."

The door to the attached town house, in an endless oblong row of town houses, now had its brass numbers missing. The faded impression of the number 348 remained. The doormat was missing. A rat fished scraps from an overturned bin beneath the window.

I swallowed. Knocked.

And Patrick, who perhaps sensed that my heart was lashing itself against my ribs in some last spasm of self-preservation, took my hand in his, enveloped my fingers with his own and pulled me just slightly behind his left shoulder. He took on that indecipherable expression, the one he used in moments of bad business.

There was a grunt from within, the sound of wood whining against tile, heavy discordant footfalls, a wracking cough.

The door opened, one hinge pulling free of the frame.

Fletcher Harrow, a man who was fifty but looked seventy, stood at the threshold, as though the past fourteen years hadn't gone by at all.

There was still the apparent sense that he flirted with death, as though he was already half gone. Leathery skin pulled down toward some grave he was destined for. The blond of his mustache, now stark white and untrimmed, covered his lips. The scruff of his beard was encrusted with what might have been decades of soot. Likely bluff, too.

The hair on his head was thinning, his eyelids impeding his pupils, the capillaries beneath threatening to burst.

When one opened the door on Fletcher Harrow, they opened it to one of two men. The first was sedated from top to toe, tongue still wagging, eyes rolling, the venom slow-moving. He slept in fits and spurts, never conscious long enough to be of any trouble.

The second was a possessed man. A frenetic one. The tips of his fingers pulling at the tangles of his beard, twisting the hair behind his ear until it broke off. Tongue darting out to wet his cracked lips, eyes moving over you, past you. Hardly seeing you at all.

"What d'you want?" he said, Eastern accent so thick it was barely understandable.

He didn't look at me long enough for recognition to dawn. But then, had it been so different at the age of twelve? How many times had he confused me for an intruder? For my mother, weeping to know why I'd left him?

I shivered back into that old skin, stung myself on a thousand thorns to do it. "It's Nina, Dad," I said loudly. Those who were closer to hell than earth didn't hear so well. I bent slightly to put my face in his line of sight. He was looking to the street, then down it, as though something beckoned him.

"He's strung out," John grunted unnecessarily, scowling. "Lord . . . he ain't got a gun in there, does he?"

"You coppers?" said my father, his eyes oscillating to Patrick's hands now, then John's, then mine, as though expecting shackles.

"Dad. It's me. Nina."

Finally, he looked at me. "Caranina," he mumbled. "Like the singer."

"Yes," I nodded heavily. "Like the singer."

Patrick pulled me farther back, as though he could drag me out of this pit and spare me.

"Do you remember me?" I asked.

My father's eyes narrowed, moving over my face too fast. "Nina?" he said, mouth gaping. Then again, as though he was trying out the sound. "Nina."

John stepped forward then, his patience apparently spent. He skirted Patrick and stood an inch from Fletcher's face, leaning down to accommodate the height difference. "All right now, lad? Mind if we come in for a nip?" John spoke loudly, too.

Fletcher Harrow startled, some reflex shrinking him. He blinked spasmodically. "Ain't got none."

"Not a beer? Or brandy?" John inquired, looking over his shoulder at Patrick. "Workin' man like you needs a pick-me-up." John pulled a bottle of whiskey from his coat. Shook it.

Fletcher's eyes fell to the bottle, and then he was backing away from the door, leading them inside.

My father was skeletal. His shoulder bones jutted outward, his waist was too narrow with a double-looped belt. When I passed him, his sunken eyes skirted over me, and I shivered.

"Just needs a little weight in the gut," John was saying conversationally, finding a mug on a shelf—the same shelf my mother had put up. He wiped the grime from the inside with his finger and poured in an ample amount.

Patrick took his hat from his head and looked around the single room.

It was smaller than I remembered. Dingier. It stank sweetly of rot. The counter was laden with every dish and utensil Fletcher seemed to own. Flies hovered lazily, as though even they were sobered by the mess.

I was ashamed to bring Patrick here. To have him see it.

"Here you are, lad." John pressed the mug into Fletcher's hands, and the man looked down at it the way I wanted him to look at me.

Patrick seemed to note the shake of his wrists as he drank, the tremble in his legs. He turned sympathetic eyes on me, and I hated it. "How long has he been on the bluff for?"

I shrugged. "Long before me."

Patrick nodded, then regarded the man sitting now on the one kitchen chair. With a heavy exhale, he stepped forward, leaned down on one knee. "Get that in you, man, eh?" he said. "You ain't got a shift today?"

"Ain't a shift to be had," said Fletcher from the depths of the mug. "Mines're barren." With every sip my father took, he seemed to come back into himself.

Patrick grimaced. "And what of the coppers? How many stayed?"

"They guardin' the pubs now. Guardin' the liquor an' sittin' on their arses. Fuckin' *dogs*."

Patrick watched the spittle leak out the side of Fletcher's mouth and descend into his beard. "You got any food in here, lad?"

Fletcher slugged the whiskey and winced, then he looked up and around, his eyes landing squarely on me.

They stuck, held. He seemed to stutter in a barrage of thought. "Rose?" he said, eyes narrowing and widening, as though I was expanding before him. "Is that my Rose?"

A tear came free. I let it wheedle its way down my face. I hated this house. I wished I were anywhere else. "It's Nina, Dad," I said yet again.

And like some wire had reattached, recognition struck him. He stood slowly, the way an old man gets to his feet. "Not *my* Nina?" he said.

I nodded once. "Yes."

"Nina's some fair Artisan now," he said disjointedly, waving a hand. "At school."

"I've come home," I said, trying to stand taller, to shake off the feeling I was regressing into a little girl. I was more afraid of being a child again than anything else.

He left the mug on the table and came toward me, hands out. And I thought, for one foolish moment, that he might take my hands in his and check they were real. That he might turn them over and view the lines gouged into them over time, the brand burned out of my forearm, the scars puckering the skin.

But he didn't do that. Instead, he kept them outward, proffered like a beggar. "You got any coin?" he asked with renewed fervency. "Anythin'?"

Another tear fell. I had feared he would be unrecognizable. I hadn't known to fear him being the same. "No," I said.

"Nah, you got *somethin'*," he said, hands at the lapels of my coat now, shaking it out for proof I carried nothing.

I didn't tear his hands away. Not yet. "I don't."

"Swank bitch" was what he muttered, his teeth baring themselves, his hand fishing the inside of a pocket, and then he was yanked away.

Patrick had the scruff of his neck in his hand the moment the words left his mouth, his expression having morphed into that of the devil. He pulled Fletcher Harrow back into his chair with the ease one dragged a dog to the back door.

"Patrick," I warned. "He doesn't know himself."

But Patrick was already standing over him, his body a barricade, a wall of bricks. "That ain't the way to speak to a lady," he said, hand pinned to Fletcher's shoulder, thumb digging into his collarbone, holding him there.

"Patty, he's off his rocker."

"Nevertheless," Patrick growled, eyes promising violence. "He'll mind his manners, or I'll mind 'em."

Fletcher's eyes rattled around his head, directionless.

"Get your wits about you, digger," Patrick said now, tapping Fletcher's cheek harder than he ought to.

John poured more liquor into the mug. "Here, lad," he said, passing it to my father. "Take the buzz out of your head."

That's how it once was. Killing the clang of his skull with the booze and the bluff until his head was swimming. If I could crack him open now, I'd find nothing but mush.

Fletcher drank and drank, and what came over him was a nimbus of deadening quiet. A boneless peace. He slumped further and further into his chair as though he might fuse himself to it, as though he hadn't known relief for days, weeks.

"Thank yeh," he said, his tongue too slow now. He panted like he'd reached the summit, finally resting after a long climb. He patted the air as though he were stroking the head of a dog. "Thank yeh kindly."

Patrick and John moved him to the cot in the corner before he slid off the chair, taking either arm in a practiced way. Fletcher's feet hardly moved. He let them lift him across his own kitchen, feet scraping the tiles, and collapsed gladly atop the foul mattress. His eyes shut immediately, a snore already escaping his open mouth.

"Lord almighty," John said, taking the cap from his head and swiping it through the air as though he could rid the room of its sour smell. "He's pickled. I hate to say it, darlin', but he ain't long for this world. Bluff well and truly has him. Men like him can't come off it once they're on."

No one knew it better than I. It was once *me* escorting him to the pub to load him up when the bluff ran out, me pouring liquor into a mug to keep his mind soft between doses. The only times I could remember him sober were the times my mother had tried to clean him up. She'd grit her teeth and block the door with her body. Sometimes he heeded her. More often she found herself knocked aside.

"He'll swallow his tongue," I said as though I was someone else. "Turn him over."

Whatever Patrick saw in me in that moment, it seemed to haunt him. He looked at me like he wanted to lift me into his arms and run off with me. Instead, he turned to the heap on the bed that was my flesh and blood and rolled him onto his side.

"We'll find a room somewhere else," he said decisively. "A miner's pub, maybe. Dad, can you find one that's friendly to Union members?"

"It's too risky," I argued, but already I wanted to turn for the door, launch myself over those steps. "We might be recognized."

"It's all right, darlin'. We'll find a room somewhere else." He said it with finality, turning me away from my father while I proceeded to fall apart. "Even if we have to climb in through the fuckin' window."

CHAPTER FIFTY-THREE

DONNY

Donny heard *The Trench Tribune* scrunch up in the ball of Gunner's hand.

"*Fuck*," Gunner yelled over and over. For the first time, Donny wished they had bluff on hand to knock his brother off his arse.

The sound of a copper frying pan falling told Donny his brother had broken into a rampage, something he would never risk in the presence of Patrick. Patrick would have him out in the cold, freezing his bollocks off. Tell him to cool his blood or stay out with the chickens in the yard.

"Bloody hell, Gun! Sit down before I'm forced to trounce you."

"By a blind man?" Otto asked. "Seems unlikely."

"It'll make it all the more embarrassin'," Donny insisted.

"Gunner," Tess warned. "You mess up my kitchen, I'll knock you flat myself."

"How old is the issue?" Donny asked Otto and Scottie. The two men had brought it down the tunnels just this afternoon, having dredged it out of some dust yard on the east coastline.

"Two days" came Scottie's grave voice. They all sounded this way now. Thick with increasing despondence. Their luck worsening by the day. Just this morning, they'd received a telegram from Dunnitch threatening retribution on Kenton Hill. The trades had choked altogether. Kenton Hill was marooned in the north on its own desolate island. Winter's end was still so far away.

"It ain't true," Gunner was fuming. Donny could practically feel the heat he was emitting, hear the turn of his heel as he paced. "Patty would never surrender to the House."

"Of *course* it ain't true!" Tess snarled, but at the notion of surrender rather than at Gunner. "But it'll be enough to disband the last of the members, and we ain't done a single thing to ease their minds."

No, Donny thought. *We've only worsened the tension.*

Tess was right. This would be the final straw that broke them. And it seemed horribly tragic, poetic even, that years of work, of fortification, could be dismantled with a few pieces of newsprint.

"What do we do?" Otto asked, throwing a rope out in hopes someone would snag it and reel it in, as the Colsons always did.

But the right Colsons weren't anywhere close, and Donny sat heavily in a chair, head in his hands, feeling the first waves of defeat finally crash over him. A terrible blankness washed in. It reminded him of deep water.

"What do we do, Donny?" Otto repeated, his voice so thin it might snap.

Suddenly, the door to the kitchen burst open. Sam appeared in an oversize coat his father used to wear, snow sticking to the fibers of his cap. "Someone's coming down the western line," he said, winded, chest heaving. In his hands he held a rifle, knuckles already white around the barrel.

"*Shit*," Gunner intoned. Another pot collided with the brick.

Donny heard the sound of feet shuffling in the snow before anyone spoke. Three sets.

By his estimate, they were outside the haberdashery in the old town, where the lane turned to dirt and led up to the very edge of the quarry.

Donny heard the click of Gunner's pistol, felt the chill of early morning cut into him.

"Briggs," Gunner called ahead, his voice swallowed some by the wind. "Who've we got?"

Dunnitch miners, Donny guessed. Lads who drank too hard in the night and got the notion they'd ease their boiling blood in Kenton, start their own uprising with naught but a couple of Union-issued guns.

These were fraught times indeed.

Soon, Kenton would wake. The early risers would pull back their curtains. Old Mrs. Earnest would open her haberdashery. Best they get this sorry business done before the whistle for first shift blew.

"You'll never believe it," Briggs replied, still a ways off. Donny thought the drag of their feet sounded labored. Surely the snow hadn't piled so high in the night?

"Holy shit," Scottie mumbled. Donny heard the clack of his rifle as it lifted to his shoulder. "You don't fuckin' say."

Gunner had taken two paces in front. Hostility crackled through the air and raised gooseflesh. "Now just what business do you two have, walkin' back in here, eh?" he growled, the words curled in fury.

Donny sighed. "If someone doesn't tell me who the fuck it is, it's a bullet apiece."

A heavy body crumpled to the ground like it had been shot, crunching into the snow.

"Don't shoot," said a broken voice, as though the bearer hadn't drawn a proper breath in days. "Please. Just listen to me."

It was a voice that sent a shock through Donny, momentarily paralyzing him.

He lifted his own gun.

"You'd better speak quick, swank," Gunner snarled. "I've been itchin' to cut someone, and the Scribbler is first on my list."

"Polly?" Otto said aloud, stumbling forward. "What happened to her?"

Theo. Polly. Here in Kenton Hill.

It couldn't mean anything good that they were here.

"She's been badly hurt—she needs bluff, please."

"Then you've come all this way for nothin'," Gunner said, no less menacing. "Don't have a drop. Wouldn't spare none on a traitor, either, now, would we?"

Beside Donny, Otto shuffled, as though battling the urge to go to Polly.

"She has a fever," Theo continued in that breathless voice. "She's been unconscious for hours now. Please. Help her."

"You don't look in no better shape," Scottie said. "Looks like you've been through a war, lad."

"Why should we help her?" Donny asked.

Gunner scoffed. "Over my dead body. Best we can do is put her down."

"*No*," said Otto. His breaths had shortened. "Please, Gun."

"She's the reason, Otto!" Gunner thundered, his mind already made. "She's the reason we're in this mess. They both are. These two and that *fuckin'* earth Charmer."

"I want to hear what she's got to say," Otto continued, his voice stronger now. "I don't ask you for hardly anythin', Gunner. Do I? But I'm askin' for this. I want—I *need* to hear her explain how she could . . ." Here, emotion took hold. "How she could do it," he finished.

Donny lifted his chin again. "Why should we help her?" he asked once more. He pictured the water Charmer reduced in the snow, the outline of him fading.

But Donny also remembered how he'd saved him and Patrick from the fire Charmers. How he'd washed out the entire square. They might all be dead if not for him.

"Because I know where your brother is headed," Theo said now. "And he's in danger."

A second body crunched into the snow.

It took some time for either Theo or Polly to wake. They took them to the hotel, to their old rooms, and lit fires. Their clothes were damp and freezing, but when Donny suggested to Tess that they change their clothes, his mother spit on the hardwood and walked out of the room, slamming the door behind her.

They were lucky she'd let them over the threshold at all.

It was Otto who cleaned and bandaged Polly's hands. "I can't look at her face," he said to Donny, as though he needed to justify his actions. "I just can't stand to look."

Donny doubted she'd have much use of those hands once the flesh healed. Some burns, some cuts—they went too deep, muddled all the feeling. Gunner said they were "hunks of meat," and they smelled to Donny like something fouled.

In number 14, Theo dragged his body upright as Donny and Gunner entered, sounding like he housed a reluctant skeleton that he dragged from place to place, like he was caved in by sleeplessness.

"Right," Gunner said with no preamble. "Tell us all of it."

And he did. He started with their escape from the National Artisan House, he, Patty, Nina, and somehow, their living father. He told them about Idia's Seam and Polly's translation of *The Stewards' Testament*.

"That's what Patty meant?" Donny said aloud. "When he said there was a lead on terranium?"

Theo described how they'd fled to Lavnonshire, and how Polly had been captured in the library by his father, the new presiding Head of House. How Polly had scribbled the translations to Patrick before she'd been bled of her ink.

"He played us," Theo said like he was spitting rocks. "And now Nina and Patrick are likely crossing the countryside toward the Seam, and the House will be right behind them, ready to take possession of it once she uncovers it. They can't reach the Seam without Nina." He looked to them pleadingly.

"And Patrick and Nina don't know it. They think this is a race. Them against the House to reach the Seam first, and there's no way to warn them. Nina can't uncover it. If she does, she becomes dispensable. You understand? She'll be shot like any other rebel." He pressed the heels of his palms to his eyes. "It might already be too late. I didn't know where else to go, who else to call on."

Donny felt his urgency. "Easy, Teddy. Tell us what the translation said. Where are they headed?"

"I don't know," Theodore said, panicked. "*I don't know!* I wasn't able to read it, and Polly has been unconscious. Whenever she wakes, she mumbles something about . . . about widow's lace?"

"Widow's lace, you say?" said Scottie, his tone curious. "You sure, lad?"

Theo inhaled. "Yes."

"Only one place it grows," Scottie said assuredly. "East central, right in the bloody middle. Scurry."

Something pulsed between them.

"You sure?" Gunner asked him.

"Been all over the place," Scottie said, and Donny pictured his great shoulders shrugging. "Every parish, whether by tunnel or boat. 'Bout the only remarkable thing about Scurry. Bloody red flowers everywhere in the spring. Fuckin' pollen makes my eyes water."

No sooner had he said it than Theo had demanded, "You should leave for Scurry now. Take all the fighters you have. Does Scurry have its own Union presence?"

Together, both Donny and Gunner deflated. Donny could practically hear his brother ripping hair from his own head. "There's hardly a Union presence there at all," Donny said in a voice that already screamed of defeat.

"What?" Theo said. The bedsprings groaned. "What do you mean? Scurry is a mining town."

"A mining town we never reached," Gunner said. "Never traded with. When we dug the tunnels, we couldn't chance the gas pockets in Scurry. The ground there is wrought with 'em. Ain't no better place for a gas explosion than a Scurry mine."

"Our only contacts there are now dead," Donny added. He didn't mention how their deaths came about, or how it would likely get Patrick killed if he announced himself on Scurry soil.

"Then call on the other parishes!" Theo said, frustration taking hold. "Whoever you can reach!"

The silence that followed this plea was so thick, it coated the walls of

Donny's throat, made it difficult to speak. "There ain't no one to call on, lad," Donny said. "No one but us."

"And it'll have to do," Gunner said, turning on his heel so that it squeaked on the hardwood. "Get your rest, swank. We're headed to Scurry before nightfall."

"We'll leave sooner," said a voice by the door. Donny imagined Tess standing with her hip pressed against the frame. Her expression would be grim. Her voice was too weak to belong to his mother. "I'll tell Otto that he and Briggs are to hold over until we return."

"Ma, you can't come with us," Donny said, but it was more pleading than authoritative. "It'll be a long journey, and you're already unwell—"

"That's my *son*, walkin' into an ambush," she growled. "And I've got quite a lot to say to your father, heaven forbid he's breathin' when we get there."

Donny frowned. "Ma?"

But she was gone, her feet already pounding down the stairwell, fading into the floors below.

CHAPTER FIFTY-FOUR

PATRICK

Nina led them to a grubby drinking hole with few patrons beyond the windows. He guessed there wasn't much coin to spare for a pint of late. Colson & Sons had been the same in the winter before the rebellion. Tess had given people a cup of tea and a stool anyway. They stayed for hours and played cards and didn't buy a single drink. Sometimes it was just the warmth and company they needed.

Something told Patrick this bar wouldn't be as hospitable.

John procured some coins from his pockets and flashed them before Patrick's and Nina's eyes, likely pinched from some sorry Artisan's pocket in Lavnonshire. He gave them a wink and disappeared inside the pub, only to give Patrick a nod through the window several moments later.

With their hats pulled low and noses down, they followed John inside. No music, no fire in the hearth. Just a handful of men at the bar. One other playing checkers alone by the window. The air was so full of tobacco smoke, he could hardly see their faces.

Up the rickety stairs they went, and into the first pair of rooms they came to. John gave a key to Nina, then used another on one of the doors, holding it ajar for Patrick to follow.

Patrick found himself shaking his head. "I'll be a moment."

John sighed knowingly, then shut the door.

Nina seemed in a trance. She tried the lock three times with no success. He had to take the key from her. "Here," he said. "Let me."

He let her into the room and watched as she drifted inside, her fingers already pulling at the men's cap she wore, letting her hair out. She pulled off her coat and left it on the skinny bed, its mattress sunken in the middle, the coverings on top wrinkled.

She said nothing, did nothing more. Just stared at the coat as though she couldn't recall whose it was.

Patrick stood at the threshold, feeling horribly unsure of himself. The cogs of his mind clanked an assault. No fix in sight. He ran his fingers through his hair and sighed so audibly he thought the building sighed with him.

He had watched Nina retreat into herself incrementally from the moment she stepped off the boat, disappearing into realms of memory. Now, beneath this roof, she resembled someone much smaller than he knew her to be.

At twelve, she'd come into that courtyard ten feet fall and stolen all his bravado. In Kenton Hill, she'd come down that tunnel spitting fire at him. But somewhere between the clutter of her childhood home and this hovel of a pub, she had faded into the gray of Scurry.

A voice told Patrick to take her away from this town, to shut her eyes and not let her open them again until they were long gone. He wanted to return her to Kenton Hill and walk her among the yellow hills and show her that there were still parts of the world not all bad.

He was swelling with premonition. An omen.

"Is there something I can bring you?" he asked, almost desperate for it.

She looked up, as though just now realizing that he stood there. She shook her head. "No. No, I'm all right," she said in a voice that barely held, each word breaking away from the last. "Really, Patrick."

She dusted her hands together as though concluding some sort of business, nodded in a perfunctory way at the wall, then went to the waiting basin bowl on the credenza, half filled. She took the pins out of her hair, one by one, her lovely face growing wetter with each.

There was something strange that happened to Patrick when Nina cried. Like God had grown tired of giving him chances and was demanding his toll.

How else to describe the rupture of his heart?

Or perhaps it was just evidence that she'd changed him irreparably. Made him a man possessed of something more than anger.

He went to her and took the towel from her hands. He turned her by her shoulders and gathered her in his arms until he felt her bones against his. He tried to absorb from her the pain.

There was no fix for this, but he thought he could ease something in them both, with her head beneath his chin, his fingers against her lower back. He pushed his brow into the crown of her head. Breathed in the scent of her for a moment.

He felt her cling to him. Shake.

"Just breathe, Scurry girl," he said.

They stood there like that for a long time. For as long as it took for her heart to break and piece itself together again. Patrick wiped the backs of his fingers over her freckles until the tears ceased.

"If you tell me you want to leave and never come back, I'll take you away," Patrick told her. "You only have to say it."

Nina took a moment to answer, armoring herself bit by bit. "The last time my mother really spoke to me was in that house, in this town," she said. "She left it to try and find a way to dig me out, and she died for it." Nina looked at Patrick with steely eyes. "There are people all over the continent with their last hope in our hands. What you saw . . ." she said, and he knew she was imagining her father, deteriorating into that cot. "It's not just in that house. It's everywhere. You and I, we can change it," she said. "It's about time I did something to change it."

He paused, not knowing if he should say what he was about to. "I need you to survive it," Patrick said. "I can't see you hurt." Though he feared she had already been hurt in all the ways a person could be.

"When I was under the Artisans' roof, they wanted to weaponize me," she said. "When I hid from them, they found me. What is there to do but fight back?" She squared her chin, pushed her shaking lips together, and Patrick felt relief overtake him at seeing this strength return to her.

"I'll do the fightin', darlin'," he promised her, looking from one hazel eye to the other. "But you'll be the one to change everythin' for good."

He pressed his lips to her forehead and held them there. Felt heat and hurt and a thousand other things transfer in that touch.

And then he backed away from her. Wishing, as he had innumerable times, that the two of them were any other pair.

"G'night, Nina."

"Would you stay if I asked?" she said. "Just to sleep." She paused. "I—I don't sleep well anymore. Not since . . ."

Since Kenton Hill, where they'd shared a bed.

He should deny her, but what man could bring themselves to?

He sat in an unforgiving wicker chair all night, pulled close to the bed, where Nina slept fretfully.

But when his hand rested against her forehead, she quieted. Her eyelids settled. Her lips parted and released a breath, like it had been trapped in the cage of her.

So he kept it there until his arm deadened, and until his own eyelids drooped shut, and he dreamed of yellow hills, yellow hair, and a girl who felt like the sun.

CHAPTER FIFTY-FIVE

NINA

I woke the next morning in a frigid and unfamiliar room.

I recalled tangles of nightmares all evening—holes opening up in the earth and me pinwheeling into them infinitely, bracing for a shattering end that never came.

There was mercy in the sunlight touching the little window.

I turned my head to find Patrick still in that chair, his head hinged back, his mouth slack, purple eyelids unmoving. He didn't flinch when I slipped out of bed.

I leaned down to touch a wave in his hair, to push it off his brow, and for a moment I was captured by how peaceful he looked in sleep. It was the only time there was no edge of tension on his face.

Someone had slipped a fresh newsprint beneath the door, or rather, jammed it beneath. I had to edge the door open to pry it free.

I held it up to the light, shook open the paper.

And froze at the headline.

My eyes sped over the rest, stopping at certain points, reading and rereading but not fully absorbing. *Lord Theodore Shop . . . killed . . . alongside one Ms. Polly Prescott.*

For an endless moment I looked down at the front page, trying to make sense of it. A train crash? Trains driven by Artisans didn't crash. Not unless they were blown up. Not unless—

Lavnonshire, surrounded by water and swamp, came rushing to mind. Then Theo aboard that train.

There was nothing about what had caused the accident. Only that Theo and Polly, not so long ago standing beside me, were now dead.

I dropped the newsprint to the floor and left the room.

I found myself slipping out of the now-empty pub into silent streets. I followed them down a familiar route. A strange sound was welling up inside me, spilling over. A keening. I pressed a hand against my mouth and bit down on it.

Theo. Dead. Theo and Polly.

There was an empty chicken cage strewn to the side of the road, and I kicked it hard. There was a roar, and it took several seconds to realize it had come from me.

I walked until I found myself somehow back at the front door of 348 Cobbler and Brum, Row 5.

The door opened without protest.

My father remained exactly as we'd left him, and I approached with caution.

Mornings had always been easiest. Dawn brought with it a naïve hope. The film over his eyes would be thinner. His mind pounding but clearer, the drink sitting stale in his gut. Not so far gone that it consumed his thoughts, not so fresh that it made him unreachable.

"Dad," I whispered, and shook him once, twice. He rolled over the third time I called to him, blinked like his eyelids were made of cement.

At one point, my mother must have been taken by those eyes.

"Rose?" he murmured, like he was praying.

I shook my head. "Nina," I said.

He looked struck for a moment, his eyes tracking over my face. And then he exhaled in a gust that I thought might cave in his chest. "Oh," he said. "Oh . . . love." He reached out to me, thin arms lifting on either side, tears shaking off the rims of his eyes.

I went into them. Like I was a girl again, savoring those only good minutes. His hands clasped over my back.

"You went and grew," he said into my shoulder. "You grew well and strong."

I let loose a sob that seemed to have come from my bones. I let him console me this one last time before his mind was stolen. I sat with this version of him while it lasted.

"I had to leave," I whispered, so softly I wasn't sure he'd hear it. Didn't much care if he did. "I had to." I was only twelve, and the cupboards were empty, and the wages went to the bluff, and I needed someone to look after me.

"You went and got big," he repeated, patting me over and over, his voice fading. "Big and lovely."

Moments later, he was asleep again, his breaths coiling into my hair, his arms slipping away to the mattress. But my forehead remained pressed to his shoulder, and I gripped the front of his shirt in my hands like I could draw sustenance from it.

I found Patrick awake when I arrived back at the pub.

I already had my boots on. I'd found a hat my mother used to wear that covered most of my hair and could be pulled low over my face. I'd changed into her clothes, too—trousers and a coat and scarf.

Patrick was standing expectantly, like he'd been awaiting the moment I walked back in. Discarded on the chair he'd vacated was the newsprint, its headline now facing down.

He took one look at me and grimaced. "I'm sorry, Scurry girl."

I had the vague sensation that I wasn't really there, that I was wax all the way through. I wouldn't feel a knife if it plunged into my stomach. "You shouldn't be," I said. I was surprised to find that I was, once more, crying. "There was . . . bad blood."

Patrick came and tipped my chin up to his. "They were allies in the end, however reluctant," he said. "And you cared about them."

"I—I didn't—"

"You cared about them," Patrick said again simply. "You don't need to try and understand any more than that. You cared for them, and now they're gone. Of course you should mourn them."

This gentle permission was enough to unbolt the grief. The confusion. The guilt. How did one reconcile the deaths of those who weren't always friends, but weren't quite enemies?

I cried silently while Patrick simply sat there with me, waiting. Until the well seemed to empty itself and fill with something else. A restlessness. A need to do something.

"Do you want to eat?" Patrick asked me quietly around the snores of his father one room over.

"No," I said. "I want to find the Seam."

"It can wait a moment—"

"I want to find the Seam," I said with finality.

Moments later, John was struggling down off the stoop while we waited in the street. He pulled his coat around him and groaned. "Too fuckin' early," he said, squinting into the weak light. "Where're we headed?"

"To the hillside," Patrick said, rubbing the cold out of his hands. "We'll see what there is to see."

The rest of Scurry was slow to wake. We hardly passed a single soul as we left the town limits, back to the slope, and down into the soot-filled gullies by the crumbling hillside. It was black and pockmarked, as though it had been decimated by giant vermin eating at its sides. The exposed seams were empty now, long ago quarried by hand. Pickers, we'd called them. Those daring enough—or daft enough—to steal little specks of terranium out from under the coppers' noses. When I was a child, I could see the glinting specks of terranium all the way from the schoolyard fence. It reflected the light in the afternoon, like the incline was made of diamond. Russel Stacker had his arm broken by a copper who'd caught him picking. Another classmate had been found with her feet sticking out of the dirt after the small cavern collapsed on top of her. Even in my most desperate moments, the idea of picking never took my fancy. The coppers were too brutal, the risk too high. I wouldn't have even known who to sell the terranium to.

Now, the hills were dull and ugly. The coppers didn't bother to watch them for pickers. We walked through the deep gully, with the face of the hill leering over us, throwing us into shadow.

"Lord," John said. "Chewed up the entire hill." He looked into the burrows and caverns with intense interest. "Bloody hell. They've got some big bullocks in Scurry. Wouldn't catch me wormin' my way into any of these."

But this wasn't half the danger. The real test was fathoms below them, where the shafts led to the deep seams.

It didn't take long before the gullies became wooden tracks, abandoned terranium carts still sitting upon them. Shovels and picks left to rust.

The main pit entrance was twice the size of any they had in Kenton Hill. I used to think of it as a kind of monster, men walking willingly into its jaws.

A chill descended that had little to do with the weather. I watched as Patrick and John grew rigid, weary, as though donning some cloak that allowed them to keep moving forward when they wanted to turn back.

The pit diverted into several different tunnels, and we took one at random. There were no lamps in the pit, no strange hats like they'd fashioned in Kenton. We moved forward with only the flame from John's lighter.

The shaft lift groaned as though disturbed from its deep slumber, the lantern within just barely flickering to life when John touched his flame to it. It seemed to take an age to reach the bottom. Patrick and I kept our sights on each other, anchoring ourselves to something. When it seemed the shaft might be taking us into hell itself, it finally met with the bottom.

We walked the first tunnel with Patrick's hand pressed to the walls, John and I trailing behind him.

"Well?" John said.

"Nothin'," Patrick answered. "Not a single fuckin' thing."

It went on like that in the other tunnels, each shaft taking us deeper than the last, each tunnel barren and pitch-black, but yielding not a single nod from Patrick. No indication that any terranium lingered here. For the first time since arriving in Scurry, I began to fear that Theo had been right. That Idia's Seam was a hopeless endeavor. Perhaps it had already been harvested without anyone realizing what it was. These mines were surely as deep as a person could reach.

By the last tunnel, dejection came swarming in. There was no terranium here. This was a fool's errand. A treasure hunt, just as Theo had tried to tell us. And who did I think I was, that I'd be the one to uncover such a thing?

We had sunk to the deepest fathom, then taken a hand-cranked mine cart down the tunnel, where the air was horribly torrid and thick. We were in unstable earth, and I felt the warning of it all around, bearing down on me.

"Patrick, we should turn back," I said. The fear was overwhelming now, beating in my ears. "Patrick?"

"Shh," he said in the dark, and I couldn't see him, but I could feel the heat of his breath. I could hear the sudden tension in his voice.

Another moment passed without word.

"Patrick?"

"There's something here," he said. I heard him move from one wall to the next, traveling farther in. "Something big."

John held up the lighter, and it threw into relief the shadow of Patrick pressing his ear to the wall as though he could hear something on the other side.

"It's distant," Patrick said, his voice energized, refueled by something unseen. He pointed a finger to a spot on the wall as though he were placing a pin on a map "But I can feel it," a laugh of exasperation left him. "Oh, it's big all right," he murmured again, hand sweeping over the earth wall.

John hooted, laughed along with him. His hand came clapping down over my shoulder. "Ha ha! Ain't nothin' to it then, eh? These bloody Scurry miners stopped diggin' too soon."

"We'll need a canary," Patrick was saying, pulling his arms free of his coat as though he meant to start digging right this moment. "Find someone who can listen for the gas pockets."

"There ought to be a few good men left in this sodden town," John said spiritedly. "How far in, Patty?"

"I couldn't say," Patrick mused, pulling the cap from his head, looking at the wall like it was the gate to heaven. "But it's here, Dad. Never felt anythin' else like it." He seemed to come alive, his hands trembling. I knew the feeling well. I was suffused in it that very moment, the idium in my blood drumming in my veins.

"We'll need to round up a crew, even with Nina here," John said.

Patrick nodded. "It'll have to be Union boys, assuming Scurry's got some left."

John scoffed. "The payoff will make believers out of 'em. They'll be sworn in by sundown."

Patrick nodded. "Let's find a foreman," he said. "If anyone can corral a team, it'll be their foreman."

"Twelve diggers, I reckon?" John looked around in a knowing way. "Twelve who can keep their mouths shut. Ain't no way we're gettin' that ore out of the parish otherwise."

"We'll have to go about it carefully," Patrick continued. "Make sure none of 'em are friendly with the coppers."

"Shouldn't be difficult," John said and clapped his hand over my shoulder again. Already celebrating.

All around me, the walls spoke.

CHAPTER FIFTY-SIX

PATRICK

They walked back to the pub in broad daylight.

A risk, certainly, though they'd not yet passed a copper. A blessing. He supposed with the terranium in such short supply, there wasn't much need for them. Likely they were holed up somewhere, waiting out the winter and keeping their boots clean.

Scurry moved with a sort of lethargy not found in Kenton Hill. The Crafters went about their business with invisible millstones tied to their ankles, kicking through the slush.

A church bell rang. In Kenton, they'd repurposed them. It must be Sunday.

Nina's eyes lifted to the steeple in the distance and held. He wanted to ask why she was smiling but thought better of it.

Back to the hovel and its bar, past a skeletal dog tied to a standpipe growling at them as they went by. John would charm the bartender into giving over names. They'd make their careful plans from there.

They would have to tread lightly, send notes of an ambiguous nature while they felt out the potential in these Scurry miners. Likely, it would take days to confirm a decent crew. Their one good fortune was that Shop was miles behind. No signs yet of his approach.

But that window was closing. Any day, a train would come clattering through the hills.

For now, though, there were no coppers, no infantry, and the townspeople kept their heads down and minded their own. Patrick thought it all seemed rather too easy.

John opened the door to the pub ahead of them and stepped inside. Patrick let Nina in before him, then he followed, pulling his cap off and shaking out his wet hair.

The door was pushed closed behind him. A lock slid into place.

A miner's shiver, arriving too late.

He looked up slowly.

The bar wasn't as vacant as it had been the night before. Now, there was a man on every stool. A weapon on every man. All of them turned in the direction of Patrick, Nina, and John.

Spitting tobacco hit the pots, barely touched lager turned stale. A man larger than the rest sat closest, his legs resting on the table, boots clad with mud. He had a bulbous forehead, two missing teeth, and a thick brown mustache. The others sat back from him as though they guarded his flanks, like a resting pack.

Patrick's chest tightened. An ambush.

He pulled a cigarette from his pocket as he stepped forward. Made it look like he only meant to approach John for a light as he stepped in front of Nina.

He held his hand out, and his father slapped a matchbox into it.

Patrick lit the stub, then shook out the flame.

"Boys," he said, releasing a cloud of smoke to the ceiling. "To what do we owe the pleasure?"

The pack leader let loose a groan and pulled his feet off the table. "Now that's funny, ain't it?" he asked his men. "'Cause we was waitin' to ask you the very same." He stood, and Patrick saw that he was taller than even him, than Gunner.

Patrick clicked his tongue. It wasn't clear yet if he recognized any of them. "Visitin'," he said simply.

"Seein' the sights, eh?" the man said. "Strollin' through the mines, I hear."

So then, the mines *were* guarded. Just not by the coppers. He recalled the glint he'd seen on the hill. "Scurry mines are famed," he said. "Thought we'd take a gander."

"I'll bet," the man said darkly. He had a voice like gravel. "Lookin' for some stray terranium, were you?" he said.

"Somethin' of the sort."

The man glanced over his shoulder. "Search 'em."

Two men came to shove hands into their pockets and feel along their sleeves. "Ah, this one's got a tender touch," John said, chuckling. The miner with his hand entrenched in John's back pocket withdrew quickly, grimacing.

Patrick balanced the cigarette between his teeth and held his hands out to the side. "Pulls out too quick, though."

John barked a laugh. This was a performance they'd perfected.

When they got to Nina, Patrick resisted the urge to knock them flat.

But it wouldn't serve to show his hand like that, so he grit his teeth.

"Nothin'," one of the young lads mumbled, then retreated.

"You're as unlucky as the rest of us, then," said the man Patrick wagered was once a foreman. He'd fit the shoes proper—imposing, head full of gas, stature like a block of flats. A puffed up, cock-swinging boor of a man, strong-arming the pack. Gunner would have him on his arse in the space between two breaths.

"You can hop the next train back to your own parish, now," he said to Patrick. "Stick to your own holes. Don't see none of us bent over to welcome you into ours, do ya?"

So then, he didn't recognize them. Patrick grinned. "What's your name?" he asked.

He lifted his chin. "Kicker."

"That ain't your real name."

"It's the only one you're gettin'."

"His name is Harland Seymore," Nina said, clear as a bell. Patrick groaned internally.

Patrick felt her step to his side so that her face was visible, and he felt the stern exteriors of several men buckle. They shifted in their seats. Chuckled low.

There was a slow whistle from the man named Harland Seymore. "Well, well," he leered. "And who's that there? Hard to see your face in the dark, darlin'. I didn't father no bastards by yeh, did I?"

It was met by snorts and hoots.

Nina stepped farther into the glow.

Harland's face turned from mocking to incredulous.

A name formed on the man's lips, the rounding of the letters all wrong. "Rose?" he murmured, brow pinched.

No putting the genie back in the bottle now. And no point, if this man was in fact the foreman they sought. "Close," Patrick said. "Have another go."

Harland's eyes swept warily to Patrick and away. "Not the kid?" His eyes widened at Nina.

Nina inhaled deeply. "Hello, Uncle," she said.

Harland Seymour flinched like he'd been stung by a hornet. For several moments, he simply sealed his great jaw back together, considering Nina from afar while his men grew wary. "Your pa says you went off to swank city," he said.

"I did," Nina replied.

Harland chewed on that a little longer. "Never believed him, if I'm honest. Thought he probably gave you to some orphanage in the west."

It was Nina's turn to sneer now. "Would've been the only good thing he ever did."

"She looks right like her, Kicker, don't she?" said some faceless miner. He shut up immediately with one look from Harland.

He addressed Nina with a guarded expression. "Thought yourself too good for the likes of us, eh? Just like your ma."

Nina started forward like she might slug him. Patrick took her wrist in his hand as she passed. *"What choice did she have?"* Nina spat at him. "What help did you lend her?"

Nina's uncle grunted good-naturedly. "We all got our problems, missy. The moment she married Fletcher, she became someone else's."

Nina stared furiously at him for several moments. Then she turned to Patrick and said under her breath, "You can't trust him."

"Wait a minute," John interceded, stepping forward. "Perhaps we ought to let the men talk, eh? Temper all this hot blood?"

Patrick took his gun from his coat and checked the barrel. "Say that again for me, Dad."

His eyes slid to his father, whose hands came up. "All right, Pat," he said. "You know what I meant."

But Patrick's attention was already on Nina's long-lost uncle. "You're a foreman, I presume?"

"And you're trespassin'," said Harland.

"I'm acquirin'," Patrick corrected.

"Oh, are ya?" Harland chortled and his men followed—a flock of mockingbirds. "A man here on business, then?"

Patrick nodded once. "Of a sensitive nature."

Harland shook his head in amusement. "Go on then, give us your pitch. Must be no good if it's brought you all the way out here."

Patrick sighed and brought the gun into view. It remained clutched at his side, but the effect was immediate. Harland's face morphed into something menacing. Two of his men stood.

"Haven't decided yet if I should bother. The lady here says I can't trust you." He watched Harland's eyes flicker to her. "And she ain't hardly ever wrong."

"Don't even know yet what it is you're trustin' me with, do I?" Harland said. "You got a swingin' dick on you, kid. Pullin' guns in this parish?" He tsked, pulling a bent cigarette from his pocket and straightening it with his fingers. "Sizin' me up like I'm some fuckin' tart."

Three of his men suddenly produced their own handguns. They pointed them directly at Patrick.

Predictable, Patrick thought. Gas heads were always the predictable sort.

"Why don't you tell us what's brought you to old Scurry," Harland continued. "I'm certain it ain't the family reunion."

Patrick felt Nina watching him, silently pleading, and he hoped she understood that this was only a game. Only the flex and jostle of business, nothing more.

"My name is Patrick Colson," he said. "This is my father, John, chairman of the Miners Union."

There was a beat of silence, and then a bark of laughter from Harland. He nodded at John. "Don't seem like it," he said.

John shrugged. "These old bones ain't gonna hold out forever," he said. "Gotta let the young lads take their place."

Harland shook his head. "Colson, eh?" he said. "Heard about you in the paper."

"Don't believe everythin' you hear," Patrick said. "Tell your men to put their fuckin' guns away. Lord knows they ain't got a single bullet between 'em."

The men balked, confirming his suspicions. They looked to Harland for instruction.

A deadly smile slid onto their foreman's face. "Put 'em down, then," he said, and the guns lowered. "You ain't daft, boy. I'll give you that."

"Are you men sworn to the good cause?" Patrick asked.

Harland lifted his arms. "We're diggers, ain't we?"

"Don't make you Union."

Harland's smile slipped. "You heard of a man named Jericho Burgess?"

Patrick faltered. He couldn't fathom the question. "Can't say I have."

"Ah, well, young Jericho were a devoted Union man. A good miner, too," Harland said, something rearing up between the words.

Harland didn't say more, and Patrick knew better than to try and fill the silence. Better to let the oaf turn the cards over himself.

But Harland didn't offer an explanation. Instead, he took a swig of his lager, then tried a different route. "Union ain't rendered much help to us in these parts," he said with no small amount of bitterness. "But we certainly ain't bendin' the knee to the coppers."

"Speakin' of which," Patrick noted. "Haven't seen a single one."

"They've been kept busy and content," Harland grinned. "They've left Scurry in my capable hands."

And Patrick wondered what it was that kept them content. Only so many good things a man could use before he resorted to the bad. "At dusk, our work is done."

"At dawn we fight," Harland intoned. "Though the fight out here ain't been so successful. As you've pointed out, we're short on bullets."

"And what if I was to promise a loaded rifle for every man and woman in the parish?" Patrick asked, seeing the flicker of interest in Harland's watery eyes.

The man chewed his tongue for a moment, then said, "I'd call you a ruddy swinder. We hear the whispers, Colson. The Union's gone belly-up."

"Whispers tend to be just that," Patrick countered. "Nothin' more."

"Heard other things, too," he said. "Like how you're workin' for the House now," he said. "Made some kind of truce pact."

Patrick clicked his tongue. "The House grows more desperate by the day," he said. "They'll say anythin' to cause division. They can always rely on the least intelligent to fall for the scam."

"Are you sayin' you ain't the Alchemist, then?"

"Oh, that I am," Patrick said, nodding. "I'm sayin' I'll be *your* Alchemist, if, indeed, you're a man to be trusted."

Harland laughed, but there was a shiver of something passing over him, too—greed. "So his lordship falls off a train, and now you want to be *my* Alchemist, eh?" he said. "You hopin' to find some terranium here, boy?"

"Already found it," he said. "Just need a few miners to help us bring it up."

Another man shook his head, backed away a step. "We've mined every crevice of this fuckin' place," he said.

"Not *every* crevice," Patrick countered. "The far east tunnel. If we mine down and due east, I believe we'll find more terranium than you've ever seen."

But the men were already shaking their heads. Harland grunted. "We don't mine no further in, boy."

"Why?" John asked, his brow furrowed.

"'Cause we'd be minin' beneath town proper," he said. "And if there's an explosion—which there surely will be—then the whole bloody parish caves in."

This explained, at least, why Idia's Seam had never been found. It was buried beneath Scurry itself.

"And what if there was a way to mine it around the gas?"

Harland frowned. "You got a way to sniff the gas from the other side of a dirt wall?"

"No," Patrick said. "I got a way to break through the rock without dynamite."

When no recognition dawned, and one confused face turned to the other, Patrick nodded to Nina. "This is Nina Harrow, boys," he said. "Formerly known as Nina Clarke. The earth Charmer."

Disbelief abounded. Patrick could almost see the cogs of Harland's mind shifting, piecing the bulletins together with the kid-turned-woman before him. His eyes narrowed. "Prove it," he said simply, but his posture had already changed, his frame leaning forward just slightly, his fingertips rubbing together as though they itched.

Nina shook her head and sighed heavily, then looked up as the surface dust at their feet rose, circling slowly overhead, then moving more rapidly as more particles joined. She waited until each of those men were gawking up at the ceiling before she let it all come raining down, dusting their skulls and getting in their eyes.

They shook their heads like wet dogs and cursed their wonderment.

"No diggin' required, lads," Patrick told them as they blinked the grit away. "All I need from you is an export operation. You'll get your cut once I'm sure you ain't full of shit." Here, Patrick looked directly at Harland. "The guns in Kenton have bullets to spare," he said. "In for a penny, in for a pound. You understand?"

Harland broadened his chest. "I want me own idium, for me and my men here," he said. "And twenty-five percent of the bluff."

"Don't, Patrick," Nina said now, her face having grown sallow. She didn't lift her eyes from her uncle. "He's a hawker," she said. "He'll only water it down and sell it sullied."

Patrick thought of her father, so far gone he was a shadow, and it was enough to once more trigger a violence within him.

"Patty," John warned.

But Patrick didn't lift his gun, but a coin, tarnished black. "Tell you what, Kicker," Patrick said. "I'll play you for the bluff, eh? Heads, and I'll give you *fifty* percent. Tails, and you get the scant offerings I'm willing to part with."

Harland grew tempestuous. "No deal."

"Seventy-five, then," Patrick offered genially. "But if it's tails, you'll get naught but the bluff your parish needs, and I'll come visitin' once in a while to make sure it's not bein' fucked up with your hawker's shit."

Harland rolled his jaw. Men like him were easy to read. They never turned down a gamble, never saw past the win to the possibility of a loss. He jutted his chin upward in acceptance.

Patrick tossed the coin.

It turned over on itself, rising, but never falling. Instead, it hovered for an eternity, flipping over on itself incessantly, never slowing.

The men watched it with mouths agape, Harland blinking stupidly.

"I'll come visitin' with those guns and bullets, Kicker," Patrick said. "You work for the Union now."

The coin fell to the ground and rolled, all the way over the warped floorboards to Harland's feet, where it tapped against his boot and finally fell. The canary looked back at the man, black as terranium ore.

John laughed once. "Welcome to the new world, lads," he said. "Kicker, you've got some arrangements to make, sharpish."

"And in the meantime," Patrick added. "If you hear word of anyone in Scurry recognizin' an earth Charmer or an Alchemist, make sure they're quick to forget it."

To this, Harland smiled. "That won't be a problem." He pulled his trousers up by the belt. "A drink, then. To celebrate."

Never mind that it wasn't yet noon, and that Patrick would rather drink from the puddles of the town than with the likes of this man.

But this was the business—pints with thugs and handshakes with criminals. When you wanted something kept hidden, you trusted those with something of their own to hide.

The other miners were in fine spirits, by Patrick's estimation. Bumping shoulders and laughing like they'd placed a two-way bet on a winning horse. The bartender poured drinks like it was a forgone conclusion and didn't bother asking for coin.

"I don't like this," Nina said at his shoulder.

Patrick sighed and turned to find those fists balled up, thumb tucked in. He reached for the hand closest and pulled the thumb free. "It's just business," he said in an undertone. He held her gaze. "All will be well, Scurry girl."

"You told Polly about the miner's shiver," she said now, imploring him with her gaze. "Back in Morland, you said you'd know if the walls were prepped to cave in. Well, I feel it now, Patrick, I'm tellin' you. Something isn't right."

Patrick put his hand on top of hers and let her head fall briefly onto his chest. Behind them, John was indulging Kicker in a spirited toast. When Patrick lifted his head, he'd fashioned a grin of sorts. "None of it's right, Scurry girl," he admitted. "But it's as good a hand as we'll get."

"I'm asking you," she said now, her eyes going to her uncle, at the black circles beneath his eyes. "And I know you don't trust me, Patrick. I *know* that. But I—"

"This is the only shot we have, Nina."

"I know that."

"And if it's not that man, then it's another just the same. Some bastard with dirty hands and a trail of sin to his name. If he's got the coppers under his belt like he says he does, then we need him."

Nina shook her head, perhaps in disbelief at Patrick, perhaps at the inevitability of the disaster she was sure would come. "Fine," she said, quietly seething. "Fine."

CHAPTER FIFTY-SEVEN

NINA

The men drank into the afternoon, and then the evening, in a nauseating display of masculinity. There seemed to be a contest to see who could outdrink the other—the men from Kenton Hill, or the ones in Scurry. By nightfall, most of them were falling off their stools. More unneeded, restless miners had come to fill the empty spaces, and Harland demanded free beer for them all.

I could have retreated upstairs and spared myself this scene. This was the same drinking hole my father had sat in. These faces were the same gnarled second-shift men, stomping and seething and seeking out bluff. They slurped at their free lager and threw vitriol at the barman when he lagged—a man who himself seemed moments away from knotting his noose.

I stayed and endured it, because there was no sleep to be found on the floor above while Harland lurked below. I would stir and pace and imagine what words were being exchanged between him and Patrick. What deals were being made. I couldn't stand to think of Harland banding his arm over Patrick's shoulder, of Patrick shaking his hand in camaraderie.

Harland Seymour had fed my father every dose of bluff. He'd pocketed our coin, watching his own sister try to fill the gaps with sewing and laundering. He'd see my mother in church with bruises on her jaw and still take her husband's money on the next shift.

Patrick seemed strangely balanced for the amount of pints he'd pulled.

John, too. I wondered if they'd found a way to water it down. Careful observation led me to believe they were tipping half their drinks into the Scurry men's undefended glasses. It was quick-handed. Blink and you'd miss it. Anyone glancing would see a couple of drunks, sloshing liquor over their rims. But their eyes were too steady, while Harland's turned glassy and reeling. Patrick and John affected the posture and talk of the inebriated quite convincingly. The Scurry men wilted, but Patrick and John kept their seats. They traded covert glances with one another and took stock of these men who would soon delve into the earth with them.

Patrick looked at me most often, though. And he grew more and more agitated with each passing hour. Twice, he'd urged me to go upstairs, and twice I'd denied him. "I'll leave when you do," I said.

I'd succumbed to my own drinks. The beer was tasteless. I had a mouth coated in venom and it dulled the flavor. With every sip I grew more tempestuous. What right did Harland have, remaining fit and well in Scurry while my mother rotted in an unmarked grave, and my father faded between his four walls? A witless, overgrown bastard, flouncing through this town as though he were its ruler. He barked laughter into the air and shoved one of his men off a stool, puce-faced and pulsing with barely suppressed violence. Lord, but I wanted Patrick to take out his legs.

But Patrick only laughed at his jokes, warned me away with silent glances. Harland crowed and scratched his balls and beat his chest. He spat on the floor and asked the barman for a woman good for cleaning it. He mimed, crudely, what he would do to such a woman if she were to materialize.

I downed the last dregs of my pint and stood from my corner, feeling full and lopsided. Equal parts hate and beer, just like a miner. I let all that blood and loathing in my head tip me forward in Harland's direction.

I didn't see Patrick stand as well.

He intercepted my warpath before I could collide with Harland, and I bounced off the wall of his chest. *"Uh, uh,"* he said, blocking my view. I blinked stupidly at the buttons of his shirt. He took the glass from my hand,

and until then, I hadn't been aware I was clutching it like a weapon. "And just what are you gonna do with that, eh?"

I glared up at him. "I think I could get in a few good hits."

Patrick's frown faded into bemusement. "You think?"

"I *know*."

"Three beers, and she thinks she can take on a pub full of miners," Patrick scrubbed his face. "Nina, please. Go to bed."

"Don't fuckin' tell me what to do." I tried to skirt around him.

"Woman, I'm *beggin'* you—"

"Hey!" I shouted to Harland's back. He was singing uproariously with the rest of his crew. A Scurry limerick about a beggar and a prostitute. He didn't notice my braying. "Harland! You hawkin' piece of scum—"

Patrick's arm closed around my waist like a vise, and I was immediately lifted off my feet. The room blurred, faces passing, my feet kicking. Seconds later, I was in the stairwell. The noise had dulled.

"Always promised I'd throw you over my shoulder, didn't I?" Patrick said, and without further warning he hefted me just so, my view now upside-down, his arm banded around the backs of my thighs. I kicked to no avail, pushed at his back. "Put me down!"

"So you can scamper off and pick a fight?" he asked.

"Someone ought to," I spat. "He has it fuckin' comin'."

"He does, but didn't I tell you I'd do the fightin'?" I heard him kick open a door. "You can put that Scurry tongue away."

I found myself flopping gracelessly atop a bed. The springs squeaked.

"You're defendin' *him*?" I spat, trying to get up. The room was distending. Beer retraced its path from gut to throat.

Patrick caged me in, kneeling on the floor at my feet, an arm either side of me. His chest pressed against my kneecaps. No escape. "He don't need defendin'," Patrick said. "But if you slug him and he retaliates, I'll be defendin' *you*, and a brawl ain't what we need." He was far closer than I'd bargained for. Blue eyes, fans of lashes, the sharp line of his brow.

I tried to look menacing. "I don't need you to *defend me*." I swiped at his arm, but with startling speed, he caught my wrist. "Don't mean I won't do it anyway," he said. "I'd cave in his head, and we'd be run out of town. We've got to keep the peace."

"Why?"

His pupils flexed. "There ain't another choice."

"That's not what I meant," I said, freeing my wrist from his grasp and pushing at his chest. I might as well have resisted a brick wall. "Why would you defend me?" My hands turned to fists in his shirtfront.

He frowned at me, seemingly oblivious to his proximity.

Or perhaps not. The tendons in his neck were visible. He seemed to be taking pains not to look at my mouth, not to touch my thighs. His hands fisted the bed linens. "Why wouldn't I?"

"Because I broke your heart."

He exhaled heavily. "Yes," he said slowly. "You did."

My chest was on the verge of splitting. I twisted his shirt in my hand, hardly aware I was doing so. "You should hate me."

"No one should hate you." He said it so forcefully, I was taken aback. My breath stalled.

He closed his eyes as though he were banishing something, a thought. He untangled my hands from his shirt and stood upright.

"No more talkin'. You're goin' to sleep."

I blinked a few times. The ceiling and its water-damaged paint loomed above me. "I'm not at all tired." In fact, I was thrumming with something no longer violent, but urgent all the same.

Patrick sighed. I sat upright to see him collapse back into the same chair he'd attended the night before. "Well, I am." He groaned. He turned the chair to the door, and settled back into it. "And the longer you resist sleep, the longer you keep me from my own. Do us both a favor, Scurry girl."

I crossed my arms over my chest. "You're my warden now?"

He closed his eyes and tilted his head back, resting. "You're entitled to your fantasies."

I huffed. "*You're* the one who insists on watching me sleep."

"Right now, I'm watchin' you prattle." He slitted his eyes open. He must have seen the heat in my cheeks, because a grin found its way onto his face. "You need a lullaby?"

I groaned. "I need another fucking drink."

"That, I cannot accommodate," he said. "You're a violent drunk."

I let out a noise of frustration and threw myself back onto the bed. Better than seeing his smug, handsome, infuriating face.

"Handsome, eh?" he murmured. "Yeah, well. At least there's that."

I threw my forearm over my eyes. *Did I say that aloud?*

"You did," Patrick answered. As though he weren't just in my chest, but in my head, too. "You're also a ramblin' drunk."

"You could always leave."

"I could, but I'd need to put a bell round your neck," he said. "And somethin' tells me you wouldn't be willin'."

I was fuming. I made a break for the door.

He caught up to me, of course, closing his hand around the doorknob before I could, once more caging me with his body without taking hold of me. I whirled around, my back pressing into the door, and was immediately overwhelmed by the nearness of him.

"Nina—"

But I was hitting him now. Blows that didn't make a dent. I pushed and shoved and growled at him, that void in me yawning wider and wider. And I was as much taken by the anger as I was the comfort of him. I wanted to fall into something, to find some kind of cliff I could throw myself off. When he trapped both my hands against his chest, having finally grown weary of the assault, I pressed my mouth to his.

There was a moment of shock, his lips unmoving beneath mine, and then he disengaged. He pulled away as though he'd been stung.

He cursed beneath his breath and looked up at the ceiling as though summoning restraint from it. "Now, Nina," he muttered slowly, closing his eyes. "Don't do that."

"Why?" I asked, my voice too loud and too urgent.

He was tortured now. Praying. "I've told you why."

"Because you're afraid?" I asked. "Of falling in love with me again."

He laughed, exasperated. *"Again,"* he murmured as though he were tasting the word. Inspecting it. "Nina, it's lookin' like all the men who love you once are cursed with it for the rest of their lives."

I went slowly to him and took his jaw in my hand, pulled his gaze down from that ceiling and back to me. "Is that so?" I asked.

The cerulean of his eyes whirled and whirled. "Aye."

I swallowed. "Then you might as well surrender now—"

"Nina."

"—because I'm cursed, too. I love you, Patrick Colson."

He seemed to quake, that shield of his cracking. "You're drunk."

"Then I'm drunk, and I love you."

His chest deflated beneath my hand—a yielding. I was somewhere in the deepest blue of his eyes, already under. He said nothing, just stood with my hand running over the rasp of his stubble, the last of his restraint twitching in his jaw.

My fingers went unbidden to my own shirt, unbuttoning the front, my fingers sliding down to my belly.

The tendons in his neck tensed, but he didn't stop me.

I pulled my arms free of the sleeves and let the blouse fall between us. Then, I tugged the strings of my bra loose, and with deliberate slowness, I pulled the material down over the hills of my breasts, inhaling as it caught on my pebbled nipples. It was a disciplined thing. Measured. I wanted to see the shadows descend over his eyes when he saw me baring myself to him. I wanted to see the familiarity in his eyes, the memories of my body imprinted in his irises, in his hands when they clenched. And as that hunger washed over him, something in my chest exulted.

He stepped forward, perhaps without meaning to; it was difficult to tell which part of him ruled the rest. I felt the door against my back once more, but still, he didn't touch me. He only watched, warring with himself.

I didn't take my eyes off his. I wouldn't be the one to break.

I pulled at the ugly trousers, let them bundle at my ankles. I stepped out of them in the little room I had, my knee sliding between his legs. I revealed that I had no underwear beneath.

His tongue ran over his bottom lip, the muscles of his shoulders contracted. I was melting into the door behind me, my body sinking into it. Candlelight flickered along the edge of his cheekbone, the rim of his ear, the column of his neck.

And I was losing whatever battle we were trapped in. Unraveling. Something thrashed in my core and bid my fingers to slip over my pelvis, to touch the space at the apex of my thighs, to cup the ache. I rubbed the pads of two fingers over that tight bundle of nerves and still, I didn't look away. I was awash in him. A moan escaped me.

He watched, hypnotized it seemed. Tormented and enraptured all at once. His hands flattened to the door either side of my face, and he watched my fingers slide in and out and over, slowly at first, then faster. It was too much—the expression he wore, the reverence in it. The pleasure and pain coalescing. My hand moved of its own accord, quite apart from my mind.

I whimpered, and he watched the sound leave my lips. *"Patrick,"* I whispered desperately.

He exhaled, and it was more a growl than a breath. "Fuck it."

He took my mouth, and he was not gentle.

CHAPTER FIFTY-EIGHT

PATRICK

She met him with teeth and nails. His tongue swept over the points of her canines and she groaned, dug her fingers into him, tried desperately, desperately to find purchase on something.

And his own hands? They were finally free of shackles. He set them loose, and they fled from him, sprinting over the land of her, starved. He let his thumbs weigh the underside of her breasts, let his fingertips trace ribs, felt the breath collecting in her sternum, the heat of her thighs, the swell of her hips. All of this, he mapped again, as though recounting favored haunts, relieved to have arrived. Relieved to languish there, a weary traveler. He collected her gasps and stored them away in his lungs, and he thought, *This is what greed is, what hunger is.* He felt as though he could drink those sounds of hers until they drowned him. Only when he could no longer bear it did he let his hands venture down her body, over the soft planes of her stomach, the breath filling there, and expending, and finally, finally, into the valleys of her, the slick, hot center of her sex. He made sure his mouth had closed over hers, so that he drank that whimper, too.

Her spine arched under the persuasion of his hand curved into her lower back. Their foreheads jammed together, and her hands pulled at his clothes, wrestling buttons away as though disconnected from thought.

"You'd better tell me to stop." He thought he might die if she did.

"Don't," she said, with an urgency that bordered on madness. "Please. Please."

And he was helpless to her, had been from the beginning. He was too drugged by her proximity to know if it was right or honorable or if he was merely sating a need, and afterward he'd feel like she owned yet another piece of him that he'd never retrieve, and he a piece of her.

But he was just a man like any other, and not a very good one, had never pretended to be.

He flipped her around so that her hands were pressed against the door, her arse to the aching ridge of his cock. He groaned without restraint.

He leaned down to her ear, and she whimpered. "Don't beg, darlin'," he said, and his hands ran over her backside. "Hard to stay gentlemanly when you beg like that."

"I don't want a gentleman," she growled.

"No?" he said, playing with her clit now. Her head tipped back. A keening sound came from her chest, and he exploited it for a moment. "Do you want me to fuck you like this, then?"

"Yes," she said immediately, trying to turn her mouth around to his.

He could have taken her against that door. Lord, but she looked like heaven. Arching back, her bare arse already rubbing, seeking. Her breasts flattening against the door.

But it wasn't what either of them needed.

He withdrew his touch. "Get on the bed."

She moaned in sufferance, but she went. She only ever listened to him when he had her like this—wound tight, thrumming, balanced on the tip of a blade.

He watched her perch herself on the mattress edge with that straight Artisan posture, that defiant Scurry chin, the blush betraying her courage, creeping up her breast to her throat.

He strolled languidly toward her, and it tormented them both.

He undressed as she had, without hurry, undoing his cuffs first, then one shirt button at a time. The suspenders next. Impatient, she reached forward and took hold of his belt, pulling it free from the buckle, and he chuckled.

Eager. She was always too fucking eager. Always testing the bounds of his control.

But those bounds were obliterated when she freed his cock from his trousers and pulled it past her lips. He gripped the back of her head on instinct and sucked air through his teeth. "Fuck," he snarled. The sound seemed to break through the cage of his chest.

She pulled him further, her mouth too hot, too wet, her cheeks hollowing, and he felt it in every nerve ending of his body. The muscles of his stomach contracted. Her wild curls freed themselves from their pins as his fingers delved into her hair. She had the tenacity to look up at him, her tongue running over the underside of his length. It was almost his undoing. He groaned. "When you look up at me like that, darlin'," he said in warning, "it's like darin' me to *ruin* you. You understand?"

She pulled him deep then, so that he could feel the moan in the back of her throat.

And he could take it no longer. He pulled himself free of her mouth and fell to his knees, spread her thighs apart before she could stop him.

Her legs were already shaking, her lips glistening. Before he pushed his mouth to the inside of her thigh, she was already falling back onto the bed. "Please," she was murmuring again. Always fucking begging. Lord, but she'd be the death of him.

Then he closed his mouth over her clit and sucked, tasted her again, finally. Every moment until now, he'd been deprived. He understood that now, how he'd only ever been fighting a losing battle.

Nina exhaled his name, and it was the sweetest song he'd ever heard. Before long she was trembling, her legs clenching. He felt her thighs contract beneath his hands as he held them apart.

"Patrick! I—"

She broke beneath him, pulsing against his tongue. Her fingers in her own hair. He waited for the waves to subside before he stood.

Patrick thought it wouldn't matter if he saw her like this another hundred times, another thousand. The wonder of it would never dim. She was so beautiful, so utterly perfect that it sent pain through his chest and into his stomach. His cock ached unbearably.

He feasted on the small eruptions of desire in her eyes, need returning with every passing second. Desire doubling. He'd never be strong enough to resist her again.

"You need to work some of that anger out, darlin?" he asked, and she nodded. "Then you work it out with me."

She made to back away then, slide herself farther up the bed. Lay herself out for him like a goddess. "Ah, no you don't, Scurry girl," he said, and he scooped her up easily, felt her soft body slide against his, and he carried her to the windowsill, the lip just the right height, its position opposite the mirror, where she could watch him fuck her over his shoulder.

He planned on doing so until she was mindless, until she was slivers of herself. He planned on showing her just how ungentlemanly a miner could be.

Her back pressed to the glass of the window, and he rubbed the head of his arousal down her slit.

"What if someone sees?" she whispered, tits heaving with each breath, nipples so delectably rosy he could hardly keep from devouring them.

"Let them see," he said, and he pushed himself inside her, watched her eyes widen and glass over. He pushed his hips up, and she gasped a curse, clawed for purchase on his back.

He groaned at the feel of it, deep within her again. All of her surrounding him.

"Lord, I'm a weak man when it comes to you." He pulled out slowly, to the edge, then rammed in again, right to the hilt. Her legs squeezed at either side of his abdomen.

"Fuck," she cursed, her head falling back to the glass.

Patrick pulled her chin down, so that she could see where they were reflected in the mirror, his whole body at her disposal, bending to her will.

"You'll keep your eyes open," he said. "And watch what you do to me."

He took her without apology then, pounding into her over and over without mercy, her mouth hinged open in that breathless O, her moans growing louder and louder each time he pushed inside. "Patrick," she said, her cheeks reddening, scandalized. But moments later, she murmured, "More." Then it came louder, something awakening inside her. *"More."*

He pushed her thighs back, angled her to his advantage, growled in her ear all the ways she drove him to madness with nothing more than her presence. He told her she was the strongest person he'd ever known, ever would know, and that he promised . . . he *promised* they'd find what they were owed. He'd restore what was taken.

In answer, she kissed him, unrestrained, pulling him closer, her body undulating and meeting his with every thrust.

The window rattled, their pace increased, and he drove inside her like a man possessed, felt the walls of her sex compress around him in response.

And he exalted in the knowledge that this intensity between them had not been taken with everything else. That some of what they'd built in Kenton had remained. He imagined a time and place where the tethers of their souls had somehow restored. Coalesced in the heat of her, it did not seem like such a wild fantasy.

Time became meaningless. Beyond the window, the sun was toppling over roofs. Somewhere in the Trench, the infantry were circling, closing in.

Patrick had forgotten it all.

"Patrick, I need to—" Her body was keening, rising.

"Just a little longer, darlin'," he told her. "You can take it."

Her thighs squeezed around him once more, her moans increasing in volume.

He felt heat burst in his lower abdomen, his own climax swelling in response to her, back arched, hips rolling, completely detached from reality.

He reached down to where they were joined and pressed the pad of his thumb to her clit. She became frantic, her eyes pinning to his. *"Patrick!"*

His mouth came over hers so that he could swallow her release, taste all that fire she was now made of, just like him.

She was burning alive, the walls of her cinching tighter, tighter, until she exploded, every muscle in her body taut with pleasure, his name a prayer on her lips. Unable to stand the rapture of it, Patrick allowed his own release to follow.

They came back to themselves slowly, but fused, their limbs still wrapped tightly. He did not allow her feet to touch the floor again, as though she might descend through it and disappear, and she didn't try to detach herself. She only wrapped her arms around him, shaking slightly. Puffs of breath fanned over his shoulder. "I love you," she said again, then pressed her lips against his collarbone and stayed there.

Eventually, Patrick took her tenderly back to the bed and laid her down. He covered them both with a blanket as though he could hold the rest of the world at bay with it.

Their mouths stayed connected for a long while after, neither willing to allow the havoc of the night to rush in. With their lips sealed, nothing that ought to be said could escape.

In his mind, whirring like a siren, Nina told him again and again that she loved him. And it felt like a salve, a drug.

A trap and a liberation.

In her sleep, she said his name.

Wide awake, he whispered that he loved her.

CHAPTER FIFTY-NINE

NINA

Harland took a day to secure whatever boat passage could be found between Scurry and the surrounds of Kenton Hill. In the interim, I pretended I was in some other room with Patrick, perhaps the cherry blossom room in Colson & Sons, my face pressed to Patrick's chest for most of the day, and neither of us willing to leave the realm we'd carved. Every so often, the need would eclipse me again, and he sated it as though helpless to resist. Sometime near midday, he laid his ear to my bare sternum and said, "It never slows." I could feel it, too, the pounding of my heart. "One day it's gonna break out and make a run for it."

"It goes where you go," I told him simply.

Patrick listened, enraptured, waiting for the tempo to come back down. But I didn't have that kind of heart. I had the kind that stampeded onward, always vigilant. Bracing for the next blow. The blood surplus might have been armor. It took hours for my heart to think itself safe. When I was a child, it never did. The blood raced and raced, and I was perpetually shielded. Children like that had hearts that grew accustomed to the quickening. They became adults who would will let any fool in, mistaking the racing of their heart for love instead of danger.

How to consolidate that with the way Patrick made me feel safer than I'd ever been?

"Do you think there's still a chance?" I asked him. It had taken half the day to build the courage.

"A chance at what?" he asked, his fingers skimming down my spine, back up again.

"At a life together," I said. "At happiness."

He sighed, his breath skittering over my skin. Why must his body fit so perfectly around mine? "I don't know," he said sadly. "Couldn't say."

"You'll go back to Kenton Hill soon, after this business is settled?"

"I will."

"And that'll be it," I said, chancing a look at him. He was looking over the crown of my head, frowning at the walls. "We'll part ways."

He grimaced, but didn't argue it, either. "I need to think," he said. "I need to talk to my brothers. To my mother."

I shook my head. "They'd never take me back," I said softly.

Patrick was quiet for a few moments, then said, "they might have to."

The following day, rain sifted through a platinum-colored sky, carving networks of rivers through the slush and down into gulleys. Patrick, John, and I walked back to the rails between hills and followed the tracks into the pit.

John looked energetic. He was coaching Patrick through the personalities of each of the miners. It seemed he'd spent much of the previous day with them.

"Now Kelsey, he's got not a single thought between the eyes and his family's long gone. Died years ago. He's dependent on the bluff, in any case. Ain't gonna stick his neck out and risk Kicker chopping off his head. Now, Tripp? He's another story. Young lad, can't get a solid read on him. He's listenin' to everythin', though. Clockin' it. Don't know if it's for Kicker's benefit or his own. But someone's got his ear, you can be sure of it."

Patrick pulled his collar up to keep the rain off his neck. He'd given me his coat to hold over my head. Trickles of water were running off his hair and down the sides of his face. He seemed unperturbed by it, like his skin was made of something hardier. "I'll keep an eye on him" was all he said.

The other men were waiting in the pit in their work collars and peaked caps and mud-caked boots. They had a cart already laden with pickaxes and shovels. Two were pushing it down toward the tunnel entrance.

Harland Seymour stood smoking, leaning against an overturned cart with the rest of his men. Each stood straighter when they laid eyes on Patrick and John. All except Harland.

"Mornin'," he said on an exhale. "You Kenton boys don't wake on the whistle?"

Patrick tsked. "We Kenton boys've repurposed the whistles back home."

John lit his own cigarette. "We let the kids kick 'em round the dirt." He chuckled at himself.

"If you're all caught up on your beauty sleep," Harland grunted. "Then how about a little wake-up, eh?" He pulled from his coat a flask.

"That'd better be whiskey, Kicker," Patrick said. "'Cause if it's junk you've cooked in the same pot you piss in, you can put it away. No dope."

Some of the men looked suddenly stricken. "No dope?" one of them voiced.

"None," John reiterated. "You're goin' down with a clear head, boys, and comin' up just the same."

A shiver seemed to pass through them.

"Some'd call that cruel," Harland said with no small amount of agitation. "Puttin' men in a hole with naught to distract 'em. You must've repurposed the miners in Kenton, too."

"Some," Patrick agreed. "Repurposed the hawkers, as well. We put 'em in the pig troughs as feed now. Thrown their vials of shit into the canals."

Harland gazed at Patrick as though he were gazing upon a competitor in the ring. His eyes sparked with the challenge. "All right then, big man," he said, tucking the flask back in his coat. "Don't gotta get hysterical, if it offends you." He gestured to the mouths of the tunnels. "Down we go."

The shaft sank, and we jostled like swine in a stockyard, too close together. The lantern was dim enough to cast shadows over every face. Thirteen ghosts in a box.

Patrick had made sure to corral me into a corner, then stood in front of me with his hands hooked through the top of the cage. His positioning didn't seem to go unnoticed by my uncle.

"Ain't ever had a lady in the pit," he said conversationally. A few of the men snickered. "She ain't gonna faint, is she?"

The shaft clattered to its stop, and the men swayed with the shudder, their bodies long used to these mechanisms, while I stumbled into Patrick's back.

Harland laughed.

"You'd better hope not, Kicker," Patrick told him. "She's your only chance of gettin' out of here alive."

That sobered the man instantly.

Patrick led the party down the tunnels, the path wide at first but closing as it continued. The cart had been abandoned at the end of its tracks, the tunnel too narrow to push it farther. They stopped when Patrick stopped, and I couldn't tell if it was the same place he had determined before. The walls were still bracketed by the same timber, the tunnel curved at the same angle. Every inch looked the same to me as the last.

But Patrick stood with his fingers pressed to the dark rock as though something beyond it were whispering to him. He cocked his head at it and concentrated, the back of his neck suffused in gooseflesh.

He tapped the wall with his knuckle. "Here," he said. Knocking at it as one knocked on a door. "Here is where we start."

"It's a straight shot beneath town," said one of the men, the youngest of the group and the scrawniest by far. He had golden-ginger hair and wore a miner's bandanna round his neck, a smattering of freckles over his nose and green eyes. He was considering the wall shrewdly. "A fork in any direction, and you'll pass right under."

"Aye, well, that's what my dear niece is here for, ain't she?" said Harland. "We ain't usin' bangers." Dynamite would blow the rock but ignite the gas pockets.

But those gas pockets could still erupt if a pickaxe struck flint, or if one of the idiots before me decided to light a smoke. The gas, if not avoided, could still suffocate us all.

"Off you go, swank," Harland said, shooing me along. "Work your magic." He rubbed his hands together—maybe to stave off the cold or his own greed—a thief at the vault's door.

The miners stepped aside as I passed them, trepidation slowing my steps. Patrick still remained engrossed by that black rock wall and whatever he felt on the other side.

I stood as close to him as I could. "Please don't give him any idium," I whispered.

Patrick looked down at me, his trance broken. He grimaced. I felt Harland rearing up over my shoulder, as though he could feel his name in my mouth.

"Now, you wouldn't be tryin' to underhand me, would you, Nina?" he asked.

I didn't turn. Didn't trust my self-control. I hated the man, relation or not.

"A deal's a deal," Harland continued, speaking to Patrick now. "And that little boat to Kenton ain't leavin' the docks unless I say's so."

"You'll get your dose," said Patrick. "And then you'll keep your end of the deal." Patrick nodded to me, pointed to a spot on the wall, and backed away from it.

"Slow and steady, Scurry girl," he said into my ear. "If Idia's restin' somewhere in here, we don't want to wake her."

Harland crossed his arms expectantly.

I blinked grit out of my eyes and stared ahead. I could feel the density of the earth here, trillions of particles compacted to stone. I suspected dynamite wouldn't have rendered much of a dent.

The idium prodded at it, testing, feeling its weight in invisible hands. Feeling how unwilling it was to move. But my mind was expanding to several times its size. It could shift this weight no matter how reluctant it was. No matter how fiercely Idia guarded it.

The rock cracked, and I felt Harland flinch at my back.

Then I crumbled it to dust.

It collected in mounds at my feet and filled the air with soot. I had to lift Patrick's coat to my mouth to keep from breathing it in. There was no hope for my eyes. They began burning immediately.

The wall opened. The smell of methane gas assaulted me. I stopped when Patrick took my shoulder. "Whoa, there," he said.

I was already swaying.

The men, some ways behind in the main tunnel, were swearing. Spitting. A canary tittered lethargically.

"God almighty," someone said. "Gas, lads!"

"Stay here!" Harland barked. "A single one of you tries to scamper away, and I'll be comin' to find you!"

"She's gonna get us fuckin' *killed*, Kicker!"

I looked at the progress I'd made. Twenty feet, perhaps.

"We have to let the gas find its way out," Patrick said now, breathing like there wasn't enough oxygen to harvest. And he was right.

We breathed though the fabric of our shirts for long moments until our heads cleared some, until the air became tolerable.

"Get to work, boys," Patrick called once our chests stopped fighting for each breath. "Kicker, get your strutters in here."

It went on like that for some time. The men shoveled out the debris with increasing listlessness and carted it back up the shaft. Others, including John, framed the tunnel, strutting the ceiling, moving as though through molasses. They marveled as John held the beams with his mind while they were nailed into place.

I charmed the earth aside at Patrick's instruction, burrowing deeper and deeper inward.

"We're close," Patrick said, hours and hours later, sweat dripping off his chin, down the column of his throat. "You got one more push left in you, Nina?"

I swallowed thickly, feeling like I was halfway filled with soot. My nostrils and eyes stung with it. I could hardly remember what the point of it all was. For what did we toil?

I resorted to pushing my hands against the rock, thinking, in a detached way, that I'd scratch a hole through it with my fingernails. My mind slackened.

The rock gave way dispassionately. My energy waned. A cloud of gas seemed to swarm me.

But when I looked up, it was not a wall of ash that bore down on me.

It was studded with something jagged and glistening. Black as ink.

The tunnel reeled. I stumbled back and crouched down, my neck sagging.

A hand came to my back—hot and familiar. Patrick. I felt his mouth suddenly on mine.

I blinked slowly, and his face swam. His eyes were sparkling. "You've done it!" he was saying, perhaps shaking me. I felt it moments after the fact.

A great glittering wall of black.

We looked at it, all of us, almost serenely.

Every man in the tunnel was still, silent.

A miner's shiver. Starbursts erupting, blinding me. That hole in my chest sang, triumphant. A breathless laugh broke free. "Terranium," I said.

"Idia's Seam," Patrick said.

Behind us, the canary fell off its perch and went silent forever.

CHAPTER SIXTY

PATRICK

They came topside victorious.

Patrick held a bag of terranium ore, the other miners singing their songs up the shaft until the light came. By the time they funneled out into the mouth of the pit, the men were soot-painted and red-eyed. Their throats bobbed in laughter—they were drunk already on the triumph, heads full of gas.

Nina looked ill, soot hiding the blood in her cheeks. But she was smiling, too. She looked at Patrick every so often and shook her head in wonderment.

Even Harland had lost his menace. He took one of his men in a headlock and mussed his hair.

Patrick set the coal bag down and pulled forth the first piece of terranium. A substantial size. Bigger than he'd ever seen. He went out into the day, where the sun fought valiantly through cloud cover for just this moment, and held it high.

The terranium devoured light and revealed its true color: blue, like the deepest parts of the sea. A slow-falling night.

"Idium," Patrick said with a grin.

The miners whooped and cheered. John came to take Patrick's shoulders from behind and shook them. "We did it, son!" he brayed.

They had indeed.

Patrick took the rock between his hands and felt for the hollow inside. "Get your flask ready, Kicker," he said.

The man emptied the flask of whatever garbage he'd been storing there and offered it to Patrick.

The terranium ore left his hand and hovered there in the sun, glinting blue-black. Patrick held up the flask beneath it.

The rock split down its middle slowly, as though the tip of a blade were tracing its equator. Separating cleanly, the idium within trickled out. It collected on the lip of the flask and plinked off its sides. Specks of it colored the dirt below.

But the flask was left with enough mouthfuls of ink for all of them.

Patrick stared at it for a moment, his mind already ahead of himself, picturing more victories in a long line. Dominos falling, one after the other.

He screwed the flask shut and threw it to Harland. "Your payment," he said, and he didn't miss the lust flashing in the man's eyes, to be holding that which Crafters rarely did. "Hold up your end of the deal, Kicker," Patrick said, pointing a finger at him. "Or you'll see no more of it."

There was still work to do, of course. More of the Seam to expose, and these men didn't have a hope of getting to it without Nina's help.

Patrick figured they'd return in the morning, dig out what they could and strut the tunnel—make it sound. With Nina tunneling miles in a day, they'd uncover enough to last them a few years or more. It would be up to the Scurry men, then, to harvest what they'd found. Tons upon tons of terranium ore to be picked from the walls and ceiling and shipped to Kenton Hill.

They dragged their weary bodies back over the tracks and up the hill, the Scurry miners pulling ahead. Patrick let them. There seemed little need to hurry now. All urgency had fled him. He wrapped his arm around Nina's waist and took most of her weight. She looked up at him, covered from head to toe in dirt, golden hair turned ashy, and he wanted to kiss her like that, covered in grit and sweat. He had plans on bathing her from head to toe, of massaging every sore muscle in her body.

Scurry in twilight had never looked so charming.

He felt, for the first time since Kenton Hill, like he might be strangling some good from the world after all.

And it was upon this thought that he heard it.

Before they could make it past the first houses, there was a bang.

In the distance, some disturbance sent people running. Kicker and his crew hurried down the lane. A fountain of water spurted into the sky like a geyser.

"Now just what the bloody hell do you think that's about?" John asked, coming up behind them. "Burst standpipe?"

Another went off farther in distance, matching the first, plumes of water in the air. And Patrick's blood went cold.

"No," he said. "Artisans."

CHAPTER SIXTY-ONE

DONNY

They arrived in Scurry after days aboard an overfull longboat, driven alternately by both Sam and Theo, the latter of whom stayed standing by sheer force of will.

In an unspoken agreement, Donny and Gunner minded Theo like wardens, but the boy seemed single-minded, determined only to reach Scurry as quickly as possible.

Donny shared his urgency. He'd picked the skin around his nails to shreds. The canals curved and turned inefficiently, rounding hills and mountains and other parishes. Pure torture. Tunnels, he thought, were far quicker.

But finally, on the third day, Gunner crowed as the empty docks of Scurry emerged. Scottie groaned in relief and cracked his neck. "May I never see a fuckin' boat again," he said, rubbing his eyes. "Can't stand the rockin, Don."

"It's a long walk home," Donny answered. "Unless you plan on becomin' a Scurry lad?"

"God, no," Scottie grumbled. "You seein' this shithole?"

"I'm blind, cockhead."

"Kenton weren't much better," Tess intoned, having risen from the cabin. "Before your father took it over."

Donny couldn't see it, rearing up beyond the river, but he could smell it. Smoke and fumes and despondency. Even the river turned sluggishly, as though it, too, were weighed down by the smog.

"Anyone about, Gun?"

"Not a one," he replied. Lighting a cigarette and passing Donny one. "What's the plan?"

"Ain't got one, truth be told," Donny replied. "Scottie?"

"You don't pay me for my thoughts."

"Nor your looks," Donny nodded.

"Lord," Tess intoned. "Ain't a single wit between you." Her boots clopped over the deck, and she hammered on the cabin door. "*Charmer*," she beckoned, voice full of splinters and something else. Something desperate. "Get out here."

Theo came on lead feet. His was moving the way soldiers marched on their last legs.

"Rise and shine, gorgeous," Gunner said.

"You're gonna create a diversion," Tess told him.

Theo's voice was brittle. "Why?"

There was the sound of someone's hand—Tess's, most likely—cuffing a skull. "*Wake up*, boy. Use your head. A ragtag bunch of strangers creepin' through in the middle of the bloody afternoon. We've got no idea where we're goin', and we need time to look around. You can put your swank bullshit to good use."

"How?" Theo asked, relenting quickly. There wasn't any point arguing when it came to Tess Colson.

"There'll be a standpipe somewhere, probably a few, with a town this size," Tess said. "The river will pump water to 'em. Burst the tops off 'em. Let 'em flood."

"How do you know they'll have standpipes?" Scottie asked curiously.

"This ain't Kenton," Tess responded. "No runnin' water. Just a river and some wells."

The boat bounced off the sandbags and ground along the pier. They each stumbled dangerously over the deck.

"Fuck me, Sam!" Donny near shouted.

"Missed it by an inch," the kid said.

"I thought you called yourself a practiced driver?"

"Had plenty of practice," Sam said defensively. "Me Dad taught me himself—'round the Kenton canals, at least."

"Just throw us the rope," Gunner grumbled. "And stay with the boat, you hear me? Anyone comes knockin', you scamper off without us."

The slope to Scurry was covered in sludge, and they stayed low to it, Donny holding on to Gunner's belt loop like they were kids, sneaking through the streets after dark, looking for trouble. Scottie had taken Tess's arm, and still, she seemed to struggle to keep up. Her breaths were too harsh, too labored. She coughed often.

Donny felt a shudder of fear pass through him with every rattle of her chest.

At the edge of town, Gunner turned. "Right, swank," he said to Theo. "You see that pipe in the middle of the lane?"

"Yes?"

A silence, and then, "You need an invitation, Teddy? Fire in the hole."

Theo sighed, but there was a loud crack, and the spray of water, volumes of it shooting skyward.

Within moments, they heard the pounding of feet. Donny heard the shouts as those nearest tried to temper the geyser, calling for a wrench, a spanner.

"That ought to do it," Gunner said. "Fine work, Teddy."

They traveled quickly through the parish, over sodden ground that moved underfoot. When they passed a standpipe, Theo blew it up, and they moved on as the residents came from their houses, suspicion in their shouts.

"Where the fuck are we goin'?" Donny asked, once it seemed they'd made a dozen turns, blown a dozen standpipes. "We ain't got a single fuckin' clue where Patty'd be."

"Shit," Gunner said, and he struck Donny in the chest, hurtling him backward into a brick wall.

"Coppers?" Donny asked.

"A fleet of 'em," said Scottie. They remained still and silent as feet thundered by, and Donny felt a familiar panic rise. He didn't know this place, didn't know if he faced east or west. If the walls of this alley were an arm's-width apart or closing in. He had the sensation that the world was turning too fast, that soon he'd find himself hanging upside down, falling.

Feet approached.

They each turned toward the threat.

"Patty?" Scottie said.

"Goddamn," a gut-deep voice replied. A voice Donny thought he'd recognize with his head in a canal. A voice that immediately righted the world and held back the walls.

And he thought he might buckle right there, let his knees hit the filthy ground.

Instead, he clawed toward the supernova of gold now erupting, that shining specter. "Pat?" he said. Arms caught his shoulders firmly, shook him.

"Fuck me," Patrick breathed.

And then he pulled Donny to his chest so tightly that their ribs rebounded off each other, and Patrick's hands pounded at shoulder blades.

Donny laughed. Felt relief seep from his eyes.

Patrick held him at arm's length again, mussed up his hair and slapped his cheek. "You fuckin' cryin', Donny?"

Donny took Patrick's coat lapels in his hands and shook him. "You ruddy *bastard*," he laughed. "We thought those swanks must've put your head on a pike!"

"Worse," Patrick said. "They put me in the House."

Patrick released him, but Donny only dropped his hand to Patrick's elbow, pinching his sleeve like he had when he was a kid. He only let go of Patrick as he caught Gunner up in another back-slapping hug. "Good to see you alive, Gun."

"Stealin' my words, brother," Gunner grunted, the emotion clear in his voice. "Fuckin' hell, it's *good* to see you."

There hadn't been another time in life when they three had been apart so long. Donny felt something that had been constricting his chest pull free.

"Ma?" Patrick said next. The sound of two bodies colliding again, their mother's breath escaping in a whimper. "What the hell are you doin' out here?"

"Standin' in a fuckin' alley with coppers a few feet away," Tess said tearily. "Take us to the hole you've been hidin' in, son. Before we're shot, if you please."

Patrick sighed. "Don't cry, Ma."

There was a sniff and the swipe of a hand, and then Tess said, "Where's your father and the girl?"

"Waitin' round the corner," Patrick said. "We thought you might be swanks."

Donny registered the sort of grim silence only his mother could exude. "Let's get some walls around us," she said. "There's a few things we need to discuss."

Donny didn't release Patrick's sleeve. He let his brother guide him down the alley and around a corner, where their footsteps echoed off the tight brick walls and water dripped from eaves discordantly.

There came a voice he hadn't heard in more than two years. A voice he revered more than God's.

"Donny boy" it said fondly.

Donny remembered a thousand mornings greeted just like that, a warm voice beckoning, making him promises for a future that hadn't yet arrived and screwing together broken parts.

"Dad?" he said, shakily.

CHAPTER SIXTY-TWO

NINA

John was as bold and encompassing as ever, thrusting himself into Donny's midst and heaving him off his feet, colliding with a wide-eyed Gunner like he was returning from a trip. "My boys!" he said over and over. "Pick your jaw up, lad. You haven't forgotten me, have you?"

I wondered if the Colsons had ever been apart for longer than a day in their lives, or if the spirals of their genes were so intertwined they were not many people, but one. They came crushing back together like thunderclaps.

Around the corner came Scottie, looking nervous, and a quiet Theo, three shades paler than I remembered him and gaunt with exhaustion.

My mind reeled. "Theo?" I said, more surprised to see him than I was to see any of them. For the third time in my life, I'd believed we had parted ways for good.

And I knew that I'd told him to leave, and that there were things severed between us that couldn't be fixed, but without thinking, I went to him and embraced him.

His arms encircled me just as fiercely.

"Lord," I said wetly, some well of emotion I couldn't identify leaking through. "Just can't shake you, can I?"

"I'm persistent," he said weakly, his whole frame leaning into me. "You've got to give me that, at least?"

Gunner shook his head, incredulity giving way to a smile so wide his beard crackled like burning paper. "Can't hardly believe it," he laughed, eyes traveling over his father like he was a mirage. "Patty sent that scribble, but we didn't dare hope it were true."

John laughed and locked Gunner's neck in the crook of his arm. The two of them seemed so alike. Reflections. "Didn't I tell you I'd be back, eh?"

"You're a fair bit *late*," said Tess, who was standing apart from the reunions. Her face was more thunderous than I'd ever seen it.

She looked between me and John as though she couldn't decide which of us she found more detestable, and I realized that Theo's hand still rested on my shoulder. I disentangled myself quickly.

John smiled toward his wife, but I thought there was something strained about it. Something wary. "Hello, darlin'," he said tentatively.

Her eyebrows lifted. "You fuckin' *dare*?" she asked, shrapnel in it.

The Colson brothers grew still and quiet, confusion brewing. Patrick, however, only sighed and sagged.

Scottie smacked his lips together and cleared his throat. "Well," he interjected, just as it seemed tensions would snap. "As much as I don't mind standin' with the rats in the gutters, we oughta find some sort of cover, eh? Before we're pinched."

Patrick was looking between his parents as though watching an approaching disaster. "We've got a place," he said. "A couple of rooms above the pub."

"It needs to be somewhere private, Pat," Tess pressed. "Away from anyone who might be listenin'."

And what other place was there to retreat to in Scurry, with ears that had long ago stopped listening?

Patrick and John took my father upstairs and put him away like a coat, tucking him into the bedroom and shutting the door behind him. He'd hardly lifted his head when we arrived. Someone had left him with a bottle of liquor while we were away—John, I suspected.

In the kitchen, animosity thickened. Tess had been given a chair to sit in, but she'd refused it, opting instead to lean against the counter. She watched me with a contempt I could not fault her for.

"I warned you, girl," she said to me, finally. "I warned you I would pull the trigger myself, didn't I?"

I was grateful she'd said anything at all. Better than the silent contemplation. Better than the group of us, standing in the too-small space and choking on unspoken wrath.

I nodded.

She tsked bitterly. "If you were smarter, you'd have scarpered while you could." She eyed me with open loathing. Gunner and Donny did the same.

Hot shame flooded me, but I knew better than to let my chin droop. "If it helps," I told her, "I love your son."

"Then he's cursed," Tess said coldly. "And I'll be aggrieved enough for the both of us."

I didn't much blame her.

Patrick and John returned to a tension so fraught it crackled in the air. Patrick seemed to ready himself for something. "Right," he said. "Tell me the trouble."

Scottie straightened and adjusted his belt. "There's been some developments, Pat—"

"Not you," Patrick said blankly. His eyes were on Theo. "I got a feelin' this story comes from the dead man." It was said with no malice, no heat.

Theodore exhaled in a gust. "Did you find the Seam?" he asked, eyes turning from Patrick to me.

I hesitated. Nodded.

Theodore inhaled sharply. "And is it now exposed?"

Patrick carefully watched the emotions playing across Theo's face. "Yes."

The room seemed to withdraw, shrink.

"Idia save us," Theodore said, the stalk of his neck falling. He ran a hand through his hair and closed his eyes. "You have to bury it," he said. "As soon as you can. Tonight!"

"What?" I blurted, frowning at the fear in his face, the dread pulsing from him. "Why?"

"Because any moment, my father is coming on a train," said Theodore urgently. "He'll be bringing an army with him."

Patrick's expression was neutral. "We're well aware," he said. "But he's too late. By the time he figures out where to go, we'll have already taken control of the Seam. If Polly is dead, then—"

"She's alive, Pat," Donny said. "She's banged up, but she'll live. Teddy brought her to Kenton."

I let out a breath of relief I couldn't make sense of. I turned my eyes to Theo. "She's all right?"

He nodded. And what were the odds, that they'd both made it out? That the train had crashed at all? "You derailed it," I guessed. "Over the marsh?"

He nodded again, slower this time.

His father could have died in that crash. He and Polly might have, too. My throat tightened. "Does your father know where we are?"

He shook his head. "I can't know for sure, but he seemed confident that he'd soon learn, Nina. It was like he meant it to play out this way exactly. He wanted you to find the Seam. He wanted you to dig it up. That's why he let you and Patrick go back at the library. He's only waiting to hear word of your whereabouts. The way he was talking, he's got ears and eyes everywhere." Theo looked to Patrick. "For all we know, his army is sitting on a stalled train in the next parish, waiting to funnel in and take control of the Seam."

"It ain't a fight we're ready for, Patty," Gunner interjected. "We'd lose. Badly."

Patrick didn't look away. Not even to me, who stood with my heart lodged in my throat, feeling as though a wire had been tripped, the seconds ticking down.

"It was a swindle, Pat," Gunner said somberly, grasping his brother's shoulder. "That bastard needed an earth Charmer to dig up the terranium for him. After that, Nina becomes expendable. And the House will string you up and take you back to the city."

Patrick looked at his brother darkly. Then he went to retrieve the coal bag he'd left by the door. He hefted it up and set it down on my father's kitchen table, making the timber legs groan. Terranium ore tumbled out.

A breath shuddered through the house.

"There's enough for every man and woman in the brink down there," Patrick muttered. "Enough in here for every Crafter in Scurry." He looked more violent than he ever had. *"Let them come."*

"Patty, it won't be enough!"

"Then we'll call on our comrades from Dunnitch and Dorser. Put out the call all the way to Baymouth if we have to!" Patrick looked to each of them. To his father, who said nothing. "The revolution is *here*. Everything we've prepared for. It's *now*."

Donny looked stricken, eyes shaking in their sockets. He spoke with apology. "Patty . . . we've lost the comrades in Dunnitch and Dorser."

"In Hesson, too," Gunner added. "And Trent."

John swore softly.

My breath abated.

"What?" Patrick uttered, stepping forward, swelling to twice his size. "How?"

"It's winter, Pat," Donny pleaded. "And we had no bluff to trade with—"

"We give 'em coal when we can't give 'em bluff," Patrick gritted out.

"There weren't enough coal by half with the eastern mine buried and half the miners dead or injured. We tried to hold 'em at bay, Patty, I swear it! But they were insistent that you owed them. They kept mentionin' debts to be repaid."

Patrick ran his fingers tightly through his hair, lips moving as they did when he was consulting with himself. "Fuck," he said once. Then he kicked a chair. *"Fuck!"*

"The newspapers haven't helped, son," Tess said. "There's been doubt. Discord."

"I've got the bloody rock here in my *hands*," Patrick said to himself, his voice reduced to cinders and smoke. "We've got the *fuckin' Seam* beneath us. *I feel it!"*

"It was a good shot, Pat," Donny said, voice paper-thin. "But we can't win."

"That train ain't here yet," Patrick muttered. "They ain't here *yet*." He looked out the window as though he expected to see the enemy thundering down the lane.

"But they *will be*, Pat!" Theo reiterated, trying to break through his reverie. He put a hand on Patrick's shoulder, but he was shoved aside. Theo set his jaw and tried again. "They're *coming*, Pat. At any moment. And if the Seam is uncovered, there won't be enough Crafters in Scurry to fend them off. Our only hope is to bury it again!"

Patrick paced the kitchen. John stayed mysteriously quiet, watching the conversation unfold.

"I'll siphon all night," Patrick said through his teeth. "We'll distribute to every willin' Crafter in Scurry by morning."

"That train could arrive at any moment, Pat—"

"Gunner and Donny will go to the Seam. They'll bring up as much rock as they can carry—"

"Enough." It was his mother whose voice seemed to reach him when no other could. The word was spoken softly, sadly, eyes glossing over, connecting with Patrick's and communicating something no one else could read. "Enough, son," she said. "I'm not askin' you this time. I'm tellin' you."

Patrick locked onto his mother's gaze, something devastating falling over him.

"I'll be *fine*," Tess said, so gently, it felt like the rest of us were intruding.

"You won't," Patrick argued, and his face broke slightly.

I couldn't make sense of the torture in his expression, or what the winning of terranium should mean for his mother, in particular.

"What're you talkin' about?" Gunner said, eyes sweeping over his mother, who stood colorless, then to Patrick, who looked like he'd been asked to point a gun at Tess and fire.

"Ma? What's he sayin'?"

Finally, John shuffled in from his corner, hands deep in his coat pockets. "It's her lungs, son. You know they ain't right."

Gunner looked at his mother uncomprehendingly.

But Donny had turned alabaster.

"She's tough," Gunner said. "She always pulls through."

"With a dose of bluff every other day," Patrick said then, bracing himself on the back of a chair, turning himself away from his mother while she stared after him, sorrow written all over her. "Sometimes more." Something no system of rations would provide, unless it were run by him.

Gunner turned slowly wretched, realization first reaching his limbs, which froze in place, then his jaw, his eyes.

Donny put his hands on his hips. Scottie rubbed his jaw and murmured, "Have mercy."

And I watched Patrick Colson with new understanding. The man who said it was all just business. The man who had taken on the burden his father had left him and gave work to fatherless boys and hawkers and delivered bluff to the raided parishes. The man who blew up schools for his father's war, who led his brother around on his shirtsleeve and kept an old dog at his heel.

A man who would do what was necessary to keep his mother alive.

He was—and had always been—a constant battle of scales that wouldn't balance. The cost of need outweighing the cost of failure. Bad deals and bullets and me, digging out terranium with a guillotine hanging above. Saving his mother at the mercy of an approaching ambush.

I looked at Patrick. Inhaled deeply. "I can do it," I told him.

Patrick turned to face me. He only seemed further pained.

"*No*," Tess said, pushing herself off the counter.

"Ma," Patrick said, his knuckles white. "Please."

"This is exactly why I came here myself, Pat," she said, pulling her cardigan closer around her. "To talk some fuckin' sense into you. If I hadn't, you'd forge ahead no matter the cost, and your brothers would let you. Your *father* would let you." She looked to her husband then. "Not a damn thing is worth the cost of my sons," she said, nailing John to the wall with her eyes.

He looked unwilling to face up to her. "Sometimes a risk has to be taken," he said warily. "You were never able to see that."

"And you were never able to see past your own ambition," she said in return, barely withholding her temper. "Even if it meant tradin' in your loyalty!"

Gunner looked to his father. "What's she talkin' about, Dad?"

"He told you lot that he'd go to Belavere City and capture their Alchemist, Domelius Becker. But that ain't all he was there to do."

My heartbeat doubled. I heard Patrick's voice in my head, telling me the story. *Something went wrong*, he'd said, never able to pinpoint what that something was.

"You went to the House," Tess said, a tear sliding down her cheek. "And you offered them a book. *The Stewards' Testament.*"

Patrick went eerily still. So still that I went to him, touched his hand, and felt how cold it had become. In the lines of his stark face, I thought I saw him fracture at his core.

"That book came from the archives," I said.

"It came from the brink," Tess retorted. "Where the Stewards always intended it to be. Safely in the hands of a Craftsman named Sullivan Prescott."

Another blow. "Polly," Theo realized aloud, eyes bulging.

"Polly." Tess nodded. "Girl should have shut her mouth. But she came to Kenton Hill homesick, and she told stories about her grandfather. The second my husband learned of the book's existence, he went hunting for it. He killed Sullivan Prescott in his home, and he dug out that damned *book*." Tess spoke of it like it were a curse. "Brought it back to Kenton Hill and told me it were a map to the biggest seam of terranium that had ever existed. Only he couldn't read a fuckin' thing it said, and he was too much a coward to ask Polly, to admit to how he'd come by it." Tess laughed mirthlessly. "*Need to keep her in our good graces*, he said. But he figured there were a bunch of scholars in the city who could translate it."

"So, you took it to the Artisan capital," Patrick said, closing his eyes. "And tried to sell it to the House."

"Dad?" Donny said, something dark in his voice. "Tell her she's got it wrong."

John was silent. He expelled a breath and braced himself against the wall, shaking his head.

"*Tell her*, Dad," Gunner said, his voice breaking on its way out. He rocked where he stood. "Say somethin'!"

Patrick seemed frozen in stasis, his eyes on his father.

"I tried to find a solution," John said. "For the Union."

"No," Patrick argued, the pieces finally falling into place. "No, you tried to find a solution for yourself."

Donny and Gunner looked stunned. "What do you mean?" Gunner asked.

"I mean Dad promised those parishes more bluff than we could give 'em, found his head on the choppin' block, and he ran off to the House to save himself. Traded one evil for the lesser, and left behind a mountain of debt." Something new reared its head in Patrick. "A debt I became well aware of when he didn't return from the city. A debt I've been repayin' ever since, to keep the Union members compliant."

Donny took off his cap and screwed it into a ball. Gunner simply looked dumbstruck. "God, Patty," his older brother said. "You never said nothin'."

I looked at John, detesting every part of him. Upstairs, my father faded into the mattress by degrees, but I thought there'd never been a sorrier excuse for a father than John Colson.

He stared back at us all like we were all mirrors, reflecting the ugliest sides of him.

"You boys never understood," he said to Gunner now, to Donny. "Never had any idea how delicate the balance is." All the levity in him winked out of existence. There was no spark in his eye, no flash of teeth. Only shadows. "Rebellions need fighters, and fighters need incentive. Somethin' more than their own anger and frustration. Otherwise, they're content to keep *whinin'* over their booze." He scratched fingers through his own beard like he might rip it right from his neck. "Kenton Hill was full of 'em. Lumps of men moanin' in your mother's pub. Not a single pair of bullocks between 'em! You want men to march?" He pointed a meaty finger at his sons. "You've gotta give 'em somethin' they *can't live without*. And you've gotta make sure you're the only one who can give it to 'em!"

"You left your son with a target on his back," Tess spat. "With the rest of the Union breathin' down his neck, threatenin' to cut off their trades and end their strikes."

"Why do you think I went to get that fuckin' book, eh?" John shouted. "Why do you think I took it, hat in hand, to the fuckin' House? I meant to find a truce for us!"

"And turn your back on the Union," Patrick added in a deadened voice. "To give up the fight."

John looked at Patrick as though he were an insolent child. "You think this was all for the workers, son? For the miners and the factory tinkers and the orphans?" He straightened, and there was no shame there. Only cold conviction. "Everythin' I did, the travelin' and the tunnels and the fuckin' *rebellion*—it was all for *us*." His arms lifted to gesture to his sons and slapped down on the table, the wood audibly cracking. "To give us a better life than the one every brink man and woman suffers. To keep you boys out of the fuckin' mines!"

"And look at 'em, John," Tess growled. "Look at 'em! Belowground every fuckin' day."

"Yeah," John nodded manically. "So I took their Alchemist, didn't I? And I made my son into the only fuckin' Artisan that matters!"

"You never asked him," Tess responded acidly. "You never asked Patrick *once* what he wanted. You only ever did what you decided was best, and you let your sons fall in behind you."

"Tanner couldn't translate the book," Patrick murmured, frowning, still untangling the pieces.

John's expression darkened. "No. Didn't much believe in it, either. He was more interested in where I'd put Domelius Becker. I had to let him think the man was still alive, and bein' held hostage somewhere, or he'd go tearin' into Kenton Hill to find him. He didn't understand the book's worth. Short-sighted *bastard*."

"But Shop did," Patrick finished. "He was willin' to make a deal."

John's silence was confirmation enough. "I thought you'd understand the sense in it," he said. "In what he was willin' to give us. He came to me when the terranium crisis peaked and proposed a plan. A way for us both to move up in the world. It were only a matter of time before the bluff ran out altogether. He was offerin' us a fair chance."

"And all you had to do was give up the Alchemist," Patrick said. "Only Domelius Becker was dead."

"*You* gave up Patrick's name?" Donny asked, his foundations visibly crumbling.

John opened his mouth to speak, then closed it again, reconsidering. He looked to Tess, and with a strange intensity, said, "There weren't nothin' else left to do."

Tess pressed her lips together, her eyes filming over. A line of tension spun between her and her husband.

"The terranium mines were empty," John continued, "your ma needed bluff, and sooner or later, the House was comin' for Kenton Hill to put a stop to the Union. Patrick would have died fightin' while they looked for Domelius Becker. They had to know who he was. Bein' an Alchemist guaranteed him protection." To Donny, he said, "There's always a bad and a worse decision to make in this business, son. I chose the one that protected my family."

I recalled the scribbles Polly had received before the attack on Kenton Hill. *The House moves to strike. Provide safest routes to the heart . . .*

"You chose to dig graves for our fighters back home," Patrick said. "You're a traitor." He sounded hollow. It frightened me.

John swallowed, averted his eyes. "It ain't how I wanted it, son," he said.

Gunner suddenly advanced, pulling a gun from his coat. But when he waved it, he waved it at the walls and the ceiling and everywhere but his father. Scottie wrapped his arms around his torso while he brayed and shouted at John. "YOU FUCKIN' BASTARD!" he screamed. "WE DID EVERYTHIN' YOU ASKED US TO DO! EVERYTHIN'!"

Donny had walked backward until he hit a wall, sliding down it so that his knees bent up around his shoulders. He cradled his hands in his lap like a child in hiding.

"Put the gun away, brother," Patrick said, his voice sounding disconnected. Gunner went still and looked at Patrick with utter despair.

John shook his head once more. "Patty. *Listen to me!* We're so close now, son. The House will see sense in bargaining with us. They need you—"

"You'll walk out of here," Patrick said to his father without looking at him. "And you'll keep walkin' in any direction that ain't home."

John mashed his lips together as though he held the truth of the world and we were too naïve to hear it.

"We're almost there, Patty!" he implored, as though these revelations could all be left in the dust. "I was wrong, I know it now. I have you to thank for that. But there's still hope left, son—"

"Walk away," Patrick said again. "And don't ever again entertain thoughts that I'm your son."

In the silence that followed, John hitched up his trousers. He looked at his sons, his wife, like they were statues that might come to life at any moment.

"You don't know it all, Patty. I raised you—"

"*Go*," Patrick said with finality.

John swallowed, and slowly seemed to see that there was nothing more he could say. No words to fix it. "I'm sorry," he said to all of them.

Before he made it to the door, Gunner had freed himself from Scottie's hold and fired a bullet into the wall, if only to let off a sliver of his rage. Donny sat there with his face pushed into his hands. And Tess started forward, reaching for Patrick.

Without another glance back, John Colson was gone.

"He wouldn't talk of home," Patrick said in a disconnected way, his eyes filming over in the wreckage. "Like it didn't matter to him."

Tess gripped Patrick's forearm in both hands, like she could stop him falling over this cliff.

"Pat, let's go home," she begged. "*Please*, son."

He closed his eyes, and one stray tear fell down the valley of his nose and over the ledge of his mouth.

CHAPTER SIXTY-THREE

PATRICK

It was decided that they would leave at first light, after the flooding in the streets had subsided and emptied some. After Tess had had time to rest and eat. The journey to Scurry had wearied her, and she coughed soundly until she was bent double. It hurt to look at her—she had deteriorated so much in the time he'd spent away.

How long? he thought. How long could she hang on before that gray fever returned and stole what was left of her?

Nina moved like she was made of engine parts, collecting blankets and making a pallet for his mother on the kitchen floor. She brewed tea and passed each of them a cup, found bread for sandwiches, and did what she could. They took her offerings without a word, the shell shock of loss still ringing.

The men would go back to the boat docked in the river and sleep in its cabin. It was more comfortable than the floor of the Harrow house. They left with leaden limbs. Gunner and Donny looked at Patrick as they passed as though they wished to say something but couldn't find the words.

If they had any, Patrick couldn't bear to hear them.

There was only a handful of hours left in the night. Not enough to find sleep, not enough to piece together the wreckage of the day in his mind. Dawn would soon hunt him down. A million new problems for which he had no solution.

He'd failed his family. Kenton Hill. The Union.

He sat at the kitchen table and kept so still, he might have been turning to stone. He could hardly find it within him to lift a hand. To lift his eyes from the half-eaten sandwich on its cracked plate.

"Patrick?" Nina said to him in that melodic way. He couldn't bring himself to rise even to this.

"I have to bury the Seam," she said. "We could go now and take whatever we can carry first."

Patrick nodded. He could feel his failure crowding in from every corner, threatening to suffocate him. Best to retreat before he made any more mistakes.

He'd been fooled countless times. By Shop. By his own damn father.

"Goddamn it," he muttered quietly, and he leaned forward, head hanging. "I've fucked it all up, Scurry girl."

"Look at me," she said. And when he couldn't, she went to the floor between his legs, placed her hands on his thighs. "Not you," she said. *"Them."*

He pushed the hair away from her lovely face. A face that didn't belong in a place like this, in a life like this one. "I promised you I'd fix it all," he said. "I'm sorry."

She shook her head, cradled his hand to her face. Tears were falling. "I think you and I . . . we're meant to carry on as we are. Broken parts and all."

"What do we do now?"

She shrugged as though he were asking her to hold his hand in a courtyard, to come home with him on a train to Kenton. "We keep going," she said.

"I could put you on a ship out of Hoaklin," he told her, and it sounded offhanded, but the offer was real. "If you asked."

She tsked. "I've got a miner in the north," she said. "He'd be forlorn if I left."

Patrick placed his other hand against her cheek, whispered his fingertips across her soft skin. "Pretty girl like you? With a miner? Such a waste."

She grinned sadly, then kissed him.

And he melted against her, wondering if there was a place inside her where he could stay and never resurface.

THE TRENCH TRIBUNE

NEW TERRANIUM FOUND IN BRINK

The Head of House, Lord Terrence Shop, urged Belaverians in every parish to celebrate this morning as a rich new terranium mine has come to light.

It was discovered by none other than the former rebellion leader and hidden Alchemist, Patrick Colson, who informed the House late last evening that a seam was uncovered deep in the brink, in the mining town of Scurry. This, as Miners Union strikes fall in the North and East.

Lord Shop promised that this was just the first victory to come from his new alliance with Colson. He assured this print press that the earth Charmer, Nina Clarke, will carry out her sentence under the watchful eye of the Lords' Army, exhuming that which Idia left for us to find.

"Surely," Lord Shop said, "God has heard our prayers. Long live Belavere."

BULLETIN

TO THE ATTENTION OF: SCURRY

The parish of Scurry is hereby held under occupation by the National House and the Lords' Army of Belavere.

The House thereby orders all residents of Scurry to vacate to open country.

CHAPTER SIXTY-FOUR

PATRICK

At the worker's whistle, Nina and Patrick left the town house, Tess red-eyed and gripping a mug of tea as though the plate of the town was tipping and she would go sliding off with it. After they buried the Seam they had just yesterday etched from the belly of the earth, Patrick would take his mother home to Kenton Hill.

They entered a quiet lane, most of Scurry not yet waking to the cold, gray light. Newsprint was left in bundled stacks on the stoops of flats, slowly soaking in the frost. The only ones awake were the night soil man returning from his shift, a skin and bones goat tied to an iron gate, the paperboy and his satchel, pinning a new bulletin to the board in the distance. Patrick couldn't make the headline out from here.

Nina pulled her collar more tightly around her neck and nodded to him.

He took her freezing hand in his, buried them both in his coat pocket.

Back down into the black they'd go. Undo all they'd done.

"Pat?" said a voice.

It was John. He stood at the edge of an alley, cigarette glowing red between his lips. He pulled his hat from his head as though he were stepping into a church. Instead, he only stepped into the street.

Patrick looked away from him and kept walking. "You ought to be halfway to the tracks," he said. Something wretched swelled in him again. Something he'd hoped to keep buried until he was home and he had a room he recognized surrounding him, so he could bring war to the walls and windows and bellow all of it out.

"Train don't leave for another hour," he said. "I wanted to give my apology now, before I left, Pat. Please."

Patrick came to a slow, reluctant stop, his breath fogging as his head tipped back.

"Let's keep going, Patrick," Nina murmured quietly from his side. "Come on."

"You gonna make me beg, son?" John said. "A moment, and then I'm gone."

And Patrick realized how desperate he was to hear some remorse from the man he'd followed into every dark corner of the world. A single redeemable thing. He could spare a minute.

Patrick looked down at Nina. "I won't be long," he said.

She looked like she might argue, but the night had been fraught enough. "Come back soon."

"Always do."

He left Nina at the corner, chickens pecking at her feet, an empty milk crate overturned and stacked high with broken flowerpots. She leaned against the wall there and watched him go. Hems of light fought through the gutters to find her.

Patrick looked back at her once more before he followed his father down the alley. They didn't trail far—just around the corner and out of sight, where John lit another cigarette and passed it to Patrick.

Patrick relented. He dragged smoke into his lungs, felt the irresistible burn of it. "Lord," he muttered, closing his eyes. It felt rapturous.

John lit his own. "I didn't mean for any of this to take the turn it has," he started.

"I don't much care for what you meant," Patrick replied. "Only what you did."

John looked to the blanket sky. Swallows flying south. Even the birds shied away from Scurry. "I'm hopin' that one day, you'll understand. You'll see that I'd do anythin' for you boys. For your ma. I always promised you that, didn't I? That one day we'd have everythin'."

"You promised more than just us. You promised the Union. You promised every Crafter man and woman."

His father said nothing to that, only flicked the ash of his cigarette to the ground. "The thing is though, Patty. All those people? They ain't my kin. A man takes care of his own lot first."

"Gunner nearly died in that fight in the square," Patrick said coldly. "Should have seen them all, Dad. Hundreds of navy blue dogs, all of 'em armed. Fire Charmers and Smiths. So many of our own throwin' themselves on the blades to stop them from breaking out into the lanes." Patrick closed his eyes on the memory. "If he'd died. It would have been your doin'."

John grimaced and hung his head, finally contrite. "Walk with me," he said.

They rounded chicken coops and garden stakes and overflowing tomato bushels. The grass here crunched underfoot, the frost setting in but not holding. The very last wilted stems of widow's lace lay flat to the ground, red petals still somehow attached.

"That girl of yours," John said, his breath puffing out in small clouds. "She truly is somethin' else."

Patrick did not show any outward reaction. He watched John pull on his cigarette.

"Will you marry her?"

"Don't know if there's much choice in it."

John nodded. "Well, marriage ain't for the faint of heart, let me tell you. Your ma? She got under my skin early on, when we were hardly grown, and she never left, you know? Not a thing I could do about it. When that fever took her—"

"That fever took her while you were venturin' around the countryside, rallyin' troops in a war you insisted upon," Patrick said in a deadened way. "You should have been there."

John looked at him with more remorse than Patrick thought him capable of. "The thing is, Pat, I ain't all powerful. And I made the mistake of thinkin' I was. Of thinkin' I could fix anythin', so long as I was willin' to do what other men wouldn't, to accept what other men would never, never accept. So long as I was willin' to cross the line as many times as I had to."

"Now you've crossed so many, you can't see straight," Patrick said.

"Wouldn't you do the same?" John said. "Ask yourself, what wouldn't you do for someone you loved?"

Patrick didn't answer. In truth, he wasn't sure he could. He'd already done things, crossed so many of his own lines. But none of that mattered against the promises he'd made to Nina, to his mother. Promises to take care of them. What sort of man was he, if he couldn't keep his word?

"That girl," John was shaking his head now. "I couldn't have foreseen it. When you arrived at the House with Nina, you and her undid everythin'," John wouldn't meet Patrick's eye now. "You and the Charmer, boy. Neither of you were willin' to let sense prevail when it came to her. So, you see? You and I have made the same mistakes, son."

Patrick felt his blood heat, but he said nothing. He only waited. He sensed his father hanging over a cliff.

"That fuckin' Charmer boy," John said again. "He went and broke us out. Stole that damned book. And I knew I wouldn't talk you out of rescuin' her. You were too far gone already. You would've burned down any bridge I tried to build. It wasn't meant to go like this, Pat."

"What are you talkin' about?" Patrick said, dread bubbling up in his chest. His father wouldn't look at him.

"Two years I spent holed up in that city," John spat bitterly. "Two years of buildin' somethin' more than we'd ever dreamed of, and we only needed the key. We needed Nina. But you'd gone and fallen in love with her. Squandered it all for the sake of a girl." He shook his head. "But there's still time to right it all, Patty. The army were always gonna march in. They were always goin' to take control of the Seam. But they don't have an Alchemist, son. They don't have *you*."

Patrick pulled his gun from his pocket and pointed it at his father's head. He was shaking. "What did you do?"

"*I've salvaged us a victory,*" John spat, looking maddened, like the years in captivity had finally caught up to him. "And it was *my* call to make, son. You ain't the chairman. You *ain't* the head of this family."

Patrick cocked the gun. "Tell me," he said. "Or I shoot you here, where you stand. That'll be the line *I* cross."

John rocked on his feet, the capillaries in his eyes straining. He looked once more to the sky. "You won't, Patty. I know you won't. Your bullets are spent. And I can't let you bury that Seam," he said. "One way or another, that terranium is comin' up."

"And you plan on forcin' Nina's hand?" Patrick said. "You think I'd *let* you?"

John shook his head manically. "I'm sorry, son. I had to do it, you understand? They *need* her, and we're the ones who can deliver her to them." Tears now, streaking into his beard.

The gun shook in Patrick's hand. "No," he whispered desperately.

John looked at his son as though he was seeing his own reckoning. "It's too late, Pat," he said. "They're already on their way. One day, you'll thank me."

"You fuckin' bastard." Patrick lowered the gun. He meant to turn, to run back the way he'd come, back to Nina.

But John grabbed his collar in both hands, the action pleading, manic, rather than confrontational. He clapped a hand around the back of Patrick's neck, and Patrick fought against him. "You know the funny thing, Pat?"

"Get *off* me!"

"No, listen! The funny thing is, your ma . . . *she ain't perfect, neither.* She's crossed her own lines, Patty. And I've looked the other way. She—"

But there was the click of a gun hammer pulling back, a shadow emerging from an alley. A figure Patrick knew like the back of his hand.

"Ma," he muttered.

But the sound of a gunshot rent the air. Smoke blew from the muzzle of the rifle she held.

And John toppled to the ground, blood seeping from a hole in his neck. A terrible sound expelled from him. He blinked slowly, once, twice, then went completely still but for the blood gurgling out.

Somewhere overhead, birds took flight.

A siren, wrenched from the depths of Patrick's nightmares, permeating muscle and sinew. Shaking his rib cage.

The siren wailed and wailed.

His father bled.

Tess Colson, shotgun still in her hand, looked upon her husband and did not utter a sound.

CHAPTER SIXTY-FIVE

NINA

The shop across the way had once been a confectionary. The lady who owned it would spare me a butterscotch toffee every so often, if I looked forlorn enough.

Now the windows were barred and the lettering read FULTON BROKERS. A kid slept beneath it, back pressed against the coal bin, which had no doubt gone cold in the night.

I crossed to her.

She was maybe twelve. A twelve-year-old who wouldn't board a train to the city and attend her siphoning ceremony. What did the boys and girls of the brink hope for now, if not the scratch of a Scribbler's letter? If not the prospect of magic?

The girl slept with her ruddy face half hidden in blanket. I took off my coat and laid it over her.

Scurry was waking around me. Doors opening, reluctant feet dragging. I backed away from the girl and stumbled over the pile of newspapers, still bound in twine at the stoop of the brokers.

"Shit," I mumbled, righting myself before I fell. I looked down at them.

The headline blared back at me.

NEW TERRANIUM FOUND IN THE BRINK

And there was something about the energy in the air. Some change in

Scurry. The doors that opened snapped back on their hinges. Voices called loudly down the lane. Feet ran, bolted.

A siren wailed.

"RAID!" called a far away voice. "RAID!"

My stomach fell away. *No*, I thought.

And I could picture that train rattling down its tracks, thundering into the station, the platform teeming with soldiers, just as the square in Kenton Hill had.

"Raid!" more screamed, bashing their fists on doors. "Raid!"

And I ran. I ran and collided with bodies, everyone scrambling in the opposite direction, some half dressed, still in housecoats, feet bare. When the sirens blared here, all of Scurry ran for the river.

I ran for the alley, for where I'd last seen Patrick, tearing through the stream of people, but as its mouth reared up, another body met with mine, this one shoving me sideways.

I fell, my head hitting the icy ground.

"Got her, Kicker!" A shout. Something heavy pressing into my back, pinning me down. *"She's here, Kicker!"*

All the air squeezed from my lungs. I tried to cry out and couldn't.

The siren heightened, growing louder, more insistent.

The lane was full of pounding feet, none of them stopping for me. I tried to free myself, my fingernails digging into the dirt.

Then the weight was gone, replaced by a hand on the scruff of my neck, a vise on my hair and collar, pulling me off the ground. I cried out, and it was drowned in the chaos.

Harland stood before me, his face so close I could see the flecks of color in his irises. Smell the fury on him. "Now, where're you goin'?" he growled, teeth bared. Years of drinking showed in the veins of his cheeks, rivers of them. He looked rabid. "Fuckin' worthless swank!" He struck me. I didn't see from which direction it came, only felt the slosh of my brain collide with my skull, saw the light burst in my vision, felt the pain moments later.

"*Where's Colson?*" Harland yelled. "Eh? Where the *fuck* is he?"

My lips sealed themselves shut. I wouldn't give him another fucking thing. I pulled at his arm uselessly, but he held me too close. I reached outward, visualized dirt rising up and funneling into his eyes and nose and mouth. But he struck me again, and I lost my hold on it.

"Little birdie John Colson told us you sent a little scribble to the House. Bringin' the *fuckin' army* into my parish!" he said, spit flying over my mouth, into my eyes. He pulled a blade from his pocket and held it against my neck. "Told us you were plannin' to cut us out. But I'm thinkin' the House will make some nice concessions in exchange for their earth Charmer. You ain't cuttin' me out, Harrow!"

He turned his head to someone out of sight. "Find John Colson," he growled. "He'll have Patrick in hand by now."

There were hands at my legs picking me up, men on my arms, taking me away. Away from the alley and Patrick.

They dragged me down the middle of the lane one foot at a time as I struggled to remain awake. I fought against the rising black tide threatening to swallow me.

My hair was yanked back wrenching my neck painfully. A blow hit my side. I blinked, panted.

Residents came to their doors to peer at the commotion.

"Please," I called weakly. "Help me."

But there had never been any help in Scurry. They locked their jaws and averted their eyes the moment they saw Kicker. The sirens churned on.

And I was ten years old again, knocking at each house and begging for scraps. I was eleven and fishing through their garbage bins. My own uncle dragged me on limp legs as my doped father faded away in the same house my mother had left me in, and there was no help in this world. You didn't get what you deserved, you got whatever was handed down by those more powerful. You lost what you weren't willing to take.

They carried me all the way to the church, the only statue in Scurry standing before it, encrusted and blackened with mold and soot. Impossible to tell who the statue depicted. Desecrated now and left to erode, just like everything else here in Scurry.

But there was enough of it left that they could tie me to it. They could wrap rope around my ankles and stomach and bind my hands at the back of it. I heaved and screamed and felt the blackness encroach, waiting for me to fall into it, my fingers clinging to the ledge of consciousness.

Harland drew monstrous breaths from the air, possessed by something I couldn't hope to fight. "Those fuckers can try," he declared, foaming with rage, "but they can't run us out of our own fuckin' town!"

Idium was suddenly there in my veins, awakening while the rest of me went under.

"And I'm bettin' they can't lose the key to their fuckin' vault, can they?"

Me. I was the key.

Then something sharp sliced through, something horribly familiar: the feeling that I had been stripped away to raw materials, that I was a tool. A piece of machinery. A weapon.

In another lifetime, hundreds of years ago, a woman not so different from me stood here, tied as I was, when this place was still full of wildflowers. And she let the ground devour the men who came to take her.

The church loomed. The same one my mother dragged me to every week to pray to Idia, to beg her for something more.

We're meant for bigger things, Ma whispered.

"Fuckin' *witch*!" my uncle spat.

Hide, hide the witches . . .

Then, one last voice. Patrick's.

Bury them all.

There was no part of me that hadn't been stripped and cut and picked to the bone.

Wet lips at my ear now, panting into it. "I'll set you on *fuckin' fire* if I've got to."

I laughed. "Then let me be fire."

I closed my eyes.

At first, it started as it always did. A tremble in the earth that might have passed as a figment of imagination. But it grew.

It grew until my mind expanded beyond its bounds, frequencies ringing to holy hell. My blood screaming, rejoicing.

It grew until my captors' voices became distant, the rot of their breath dissipating.

I heard the screams rise, and it intertwined with the ringing. A symphony.

The earth shook and feet pounded as though we were all the contents of a jar, picked up and rattled, and in my mind, or perhaps in reality, I saw them run from me, looking over their shoulders as the first cracks split the earth beneath that cursed church, then through the lane.

The fissure spread down the street, dividing the houses, then branched off in new directions, weaving through the town like tributaries of a giant river.

The sound was monstrous, cataclysmic, the tearing of the town so violent even the buildings screamed. The church toppled in on itself like it was made of paper.

Then, silence.

The ground stilled, Scurry now cleaved in two.

And I let out a scream that had long been trapped in my lungs, gave flight to it. I looked down at the crevasse in the earth before my feet. And I thought of how cruel it was that I couldn't simply step into it and let the ground swallow me, no matter how hard I pulled at my bindings.

But then came the only voice that might bring me back from the edge.

"Nina!" it called.

And finally, finally, I crumbled.

CHAPTER SIXTY-SIX

PATRICK

Tess dropped the rifle as though it burned her, her breaths sharp.

Her hand went to her chest, where her heart was.

And the ground shook in a way that had become familiar to Patrick.

He looked at his mother. "Ma?" he said.

Her eyes were pinned to the man on the ground behind Patrick. "Better that I do it," she gasped, tears slipping down over her cheeks. "Better it be me."

Patrick looked down at his shaking hands. A pool of blood sank into the earth. He covered his face and sank to his knees. "Lord almighty, Ma. What did you do?"

"Had to," she murmured, her lips trailing on senselessly. "Had to be done."

Patrick shook harder now. His father, dead. His mother with a rifle at her feet.

"Why?" Patrick asked, eyes cinched shut.

"Had to," she said again. Tess fell to her knees, pushed her face into her hands. "Lord," she moaned. "Your brothers . . ."

Patrick felt a wave of nausea come over him.

"Look at me," he said, hauling her against him for support. She coughed in a stream, panted for air in a way that frightened him.

"Just—just listen. I can fix this."

"Lord, I didn't mean . . . *I had to*."

A wrenching sob left Patrick's chest. He gripped his mother's frame and rocked her. The ground shook. Pebbles danced around them.

Nina.

"Listen to me," he said, though his heart had shaken free of his chest and sunk to his stomach. "Go down to the docks. Right now. You hear me? One foot in front of the other."

She seemed to shrink in his arms. A low keening sound was coming from her. "Don't think," Patrick told her. "Don't think of anything else. Just one foot in front of the other. Come on."

He lifted both of them off the ground. He shouted the names of his brothers as loud as he could, hoping the sound would carry down those hills to the river. "Go," Patrick told Tess, placing a hand between her shoulder blades and leading her away from the body. "Don't think. Say nothin'. You hear me?"

She nodded continuously, like her head was trapped in the motion. With her fists clenched to her chest she moved forward, momentum carrying her, as though she was very slowly falling.

Patrick left at a sprint.

Back down the alley to the street.

But Nina was nowhere. All around, Scurry was alive and running through the street. The siren chased them onto the hills beyond. Sallow-faced mothers with wide-eyed children at their hands. Men hauling suitcases.

No Nina among them.

"Fuck," Patrick intoned, turning in circles to catch a glimpse of her. Perhaps she'd retreated to her father's house. Or to the hills with everyone else.

The tremble beneath his feet became a quake that shook buildings. No telling where it was coming from. But it meant she was in trouble.

"Nina!" he yelled, running toward the main square as though she was calling directly to him. People were suddenly screaming, running in the opposite direction. Then he saw what they were all running from.

The ground cleaved, separating, toppling the townspeople left in Scurry.

They screamed and fled. Facades cracked and the clay tiles shook free, falling in cascades and exploding on the frost-hardened ground.

He ran like there were walls caving in around him, like the crumbling earth chased his heels and the light was just ahead. And then the ground stilled, quieted. The houses settled back on their foundations. Ahead, a cloud of dust plumed where the church had been.

He heard her cry before he saw her, tied to a post. Nina. Her head was down, hair sticking to the soot and sweat on her face.

"Nina!" he shouted. He moved faster still.

There were tear tracks over her cheeks, a tremble to her chin.

He finally reached her, ripped at the bindings around her. "Come on," he said to his own hands, begging them to hurry.

There it was: the miner's shiver. No canary in sight, but he could already smell the gas.

When the last binding was freed, Nina fell into his arms, barely conscious.

"We have to run," he told her, already lifting her arm over his neck. "Listen to me, the ground is full of gas, we have to—"

Thunder roared.

Not from the sky, but from the ground as it began to break beneath them.

"Let's go, Scurry girl," he said, pushing her ahead of him. *"Run!"*

She ran and fell as the earth shifted off its axis, as the town's buildings broke and crumbled, Idia rising from her grave. Gas explosions sent the ground cratering inward, morphing the hills around them. Sending rock crumbling down the hillside. Patrick picked her up, shoved her onward. "Go!" he yelled as they left her birthplace for good.

They passed the town limits, over a fallen fence and into the hills, the earth still rearranging. Patrick felt fire at his neck, the heat of it blistering his skin. He didn't turn to see Scurry cave in on itself. Idia swallowing the parish whole.

The dirt and debris reared up behind them, spilling over the sunken hill, and they couldn't outrun it. Couldn't hope to make it all the way to the river.

Nina turned to grab his collar, to pull him down as the dust clouded around them, swallowing everything in sight.

They went to the ground together, his arm around her waist, hers over his head. And Patrick held his breath, waited for that wall of dirt to barrel into him, to bury them both.

But it didn't come. He felt the rock and dirt slide by, but it never touched them. When the ground finally settled and the roar died, Patrick lifted his head.

All around them a curtain of dirt and dust hung in the air, refusing to fall, and Patrick could see nothing but her. Nina was panting, shaking, one hand outstretched to the nimbus of dirt. With a gasp, she let her hand fall, and the wave of earth flew sideways, and tumbled down the hill. It did not touch them.

Nina blinked like she was waking from a nightmare, her lips waxen and shaking. She finally returned his gaze.

Patrick felt a titanic breath leave him. His forehead fell to hers.

"I'm sorry," she whispered.

But Patrick shook his head, already absolving her.

And she faded out of consciousness, her breaths mingling with his.

He carried her the rest of the way down the slope, now filled with the former inhabitants of Scurry, who looked back at their town with gaping mouths and horror in their eyes. He walked past them like a ghost.

At the dock, Gunner paced. He called out to Patrick the moment he and Nina came into view.

"Ma," Patrick panted. "Where's Ma?"

"She's here," Gunner grunted, running up the hill to meet Patrick.

He nodded to the smoke and fire of Scurry on the hill.

"Was it her?" he asked, awe in his voice. He looked down at the sleeping form in Patrick's arms.

"Yeah," Patrick answered. "It was her." He tried to draw breath. "We have to leave," he panted. "Now."

Theo, Sam, and Scottie were waiting on the deck, their caps in hand, jaws limp at the sight of the sunken town.

Theo's attention drew to Nina as Patrick came aboard with her. "Is she hurt?" Theo asked Patrick, going to them. "Nina?" he said softly, trying to rouse her.

Patrick felt like he might collapse where he stood. "In more ways than you could imagine," he said. He looked right at Theo. "I need you to get us out of here," he said.

Something passed between them. A truce of sorts. Theo glanced down one last time at Nina, then nodded. He went to the till.

"We're goin' home," Patrick said.

"Pat . . . Ma said Dad was . . . was shot. She said he—"

"I shot him" was Patrick's reply. He kept his eyes down. "I shot him myself. He's dead."

He felt the repercussions met out slowly, first to Gunner, then to Donny. They seemed unable to voice any response.

Calamity was all that remained now. They each swayed amongst it, barely keeping their feet, their breath.They glided upriver against the pull of the water, Theo charming it to part at the stern.

The morning around them finally relieved and turned ashy, then ice-blue. Behind them, a whistle blew thinly. The call for first-shift miners in Scurry, its relentless mechanism somehow having survived the dust.

And another whistle that Patrick thought might only exist in his mind. This one from a train, rattling into the brink from the city.

EPILOGUE

TRIPP

When Tripp was a child, he'd been allowed to sleep in the church.

Not always, and not on Saturdays, but Pastor David had found it in his heart to let him in from the cold—he and the other Scurry orphans.

On Saturdays, Tripp had to break in through a door in the back of the nave. The wood was so rotted it bent under pressure. Enough for a skinny hand to fit through, just enough to slip the bolt. He thought God probably didn't mind. He never stopped him, in any case, and as for Sunday mornings . . . well there weren't many in Scurry who worshipped. In the winter, there were none.

Except the Harrows; the mother and the girl, Nina.

Tripp watched them often. The church was full of shadows, full of places to hide. He found there was no need to go out into the cold if he was still and quiet. They would come, sit, pray, talk, then leave.

Tripp thought they must have been the good, devout sort. Which explained his immediate trust in Harland, the mother's brother. These things—religion and goodness—they ran in families.

Harland Seymour had been a saving grace when Tripp was a kid. He'd employed him in the mines, given him somewhere better to sleep. He found he liked the tunnels more than the other lads. He'd spent his formative years out in the open. Close spaces, he'd found, were a welcome change.

He didn't need the bluff the way the other men did. This had been the only point of contention between himself and Harland. "This here," he'd said to Tripp, smearing ink on his gums, "is the best cut you'll find anywhere." He was an easily insulted man, but his cuts made Tripp feel ill, like his insides were eroding. He stayed clear of them. He kept his mind. He learned how to be a good miner for Harland. How to be quiet and still and watchful. Harland's shadow was a close space to occupy. Tripp was safer there.

The trouble was, of course, that boys—even orphaned Scurry boys—outgrew their shadows.

Tripp lined up with the rest of crew, Harland at the spearhead, and they faced the church. Strange, Tripp thought, to see it sunken in and burning. To have seen that same Harrow girl destroy it.

"Good evening, gentlemen," said the Lord before them, and who'd ever thought they would see a lord in Scurry? It was a strange way to address twelve Craftsmen, all with their hands bound, rifles pointed at them, two navy-robed Artisans at the Lord's side, presumably fire Charmers. "My name is Lord Terrence Shop."

Harland spat at the ground. His face was slashed by the most twisted snarl Tripp had yet seen. "This is *our* fuckin' parish!" he growled. "You ain't got no right!"

Tripp kept his gaze on the Lord, saw the bored look in the man's eyes. Lord Shop watched them in the manner a man would watch a roving herd. The only intelligent creature among small-brained beasts. "Believe me," he said, apathetically. "I don't intend to stay longer than is necessary. My generals tell me that you are fighting men? That you tried, *valiantly*," he said with a slight sneer, "to stop the infantry's procession from the station platform?"

"That's right," Harland said defiantly, veins protruding in his neck. "That's fuckin' right!"

"They also tell me that you were seen using some very curious tactics to divert the infantry," Shop continued, his tone unperturbed by the force of Harland's. "Levitating garden stakes, for example."

"Aye!" said Harland, his breath fogging in a great cloud. "And now you find yourself evenly matched."

"Oh, I doubt that," Shop said calmly. "It'll take quite a bit of practice before that idium you stole can be put to any use."

"It ain't stolen," Harland said, viciously. "We took what was ours! Every bit of terranium here is *ours*!"

"I don't disagree."

This brought Harland up short. He seemed to cease his rampage, eyes narrowing, the cloud of his breath evaporating.

"I'm here to discuss a business arrangement," Lord Shop said. "One that I think will benefit us both greatly." Lord Shop seemed to wait for Harland to speak, which he didn't.

But Tripp did. He lifted his head and said, very carefully, "You need miners."

Shop turned to him and nodded with the air of polite surprise, as though Tripp were a dog who had just performed a trick. "Well done," he said, nodding. "I do indeed need miners." He turned to the group at large, all of them on their knees beneath him. "I presume you've each helped yourself to a dose of idium. By now, I daresay you've already felt the zeal course through you, that sense of potential. The vibrance and promise of it."

None of them contested this. Even as the Lord spoke, Tripp felt his blood thrum, felt the world sharpen.

"If you want more," Shop said slowly, precisely, as though he were speaking to simpletons. "The ore will need to be exhumed. Now that the concern of unstable ground has been . . . neutralized," he perused the burning, crumbled ruins of Scurry. "There should be nothing to inhibit you from doing so. And you will need to tell me where Mr. Colson is hiding, I'm afraid. There's no need to harbor him any longer. I assure you, no harm will come to him."

"Fled, hasn't he?" Harland grunted. The muscles of his latticed arms flexed. "Fuckin' *coward*."

At this, Lord Shop's face transformed into a glower. "For your sake, I hope you're mistaken."

Harland only fumed and pulled at his restraints.

Tripp felt a reluctant resolve swell in him. "And what if you don't need him?"

Lord Shop turned to Tripp. His eyes masked themselves once more. "There can be no idium without an Alchemist," he said impatiently.

Tripp steeled himself. Once it was done, it could not be undone.

He felt the restraints at his back, and in his pocket, the hard-edged lump of terranium ore. He felt it as though it were an extension of his hand. Felt his fingers close around it in his mind.

Slowly, unsteadily, the rock lifted from his pocket. It rose, dropped, rose again. It turned in place before his eyes, before finally wavering and falling to the dirt.

He could have sworn he saw something rabid in the Lord's expression.

"That'd be me, then," Tripp said, "wouldn't it?"

ACKNOWLEDGMENTS

This book far exceeded my plans.

Sometimes a story comes fully fleshed and I'm the vessel plagued to, somehow, honor it on the page. Other times, the story comes in tiny pieces. I sit here at my desk patiently waiting for the whole picture to occur to me. Its at these times that I doubt myself most.

A Forsaken Prophecy was saved and entitled on my computer as: "A Fucking Pain in my Arse" for a long, long time. By far, it has been my most challenging book. I kept losing the threads of the story. I'd wake up in the night and think, "I've got it! This is how I'm going to tell it!" and two days later, I'd detest the entire thing. I'd start over.

I deleted (and believe me, I kept count) sixty thousand words from the first and second drafts. I was so sick of myself that I couldn't bear to sludge through the word soup and try to salvage it. It felt cleaner, and more honest, somehow, to simply cut my losses and try again.

A Forsaken Prophecy is my favorite piece of work. I toiled and toiled until I could stand the sound of it. It isn't perfect—no book of mine ever will be, but I'm so proud of this story, of its trajectory, of its messaging. Book three is waiting (impatiently) to be written, and its so loud in my mind that I'm afraid there can be no breaks for me. It can't be put off. The canaries are screaming.

First thanks must go to the readers, who have been dragged all across the Trench without a single peace offering: *I know.* I know, okay? Hang in there! Shhhhh. I'm so grateful to you for being here.

This book would not have been possible without a brilliant team of industry professionals, who were always patient, kind, and encouraging. You helped guide me when I needed it, and insisted that I knew what I was doing when I felt like a hack: Amara Hoshijo, the shrewdest of editors, the kindest human, I write in the comfort of knowing you won't let this story waste its potential. Amy Collins, of Talcott Notch Agency, thank you for going above and beyond the call of an agent. You truly are one of a kind. The team at Saga Press: Karintha, Christine, Jéla, Cameron, Theresa, Ali, and Savannah (How could I possibly leave you out?), and their fearless leader Joe, thank you for championing my stories and giving me every chance to be successful in this industry. Authorship can feel isolating for some, but among this team I feel constantly supported. To the team at Atria Books Australia: Anthea, Jasmine, Kelly, Tiana, and Bec. The experiences I've had with you all have been an author's dream! Thank you for giving me opportunities I wouldn't have dared ask for. Thank you for the visits and the social media antics and the hot wings! Your enthusiasm and ideas never fail to amaze me. I'm honored to work with you all. To the team at Solstice Books in the UK, and in particular, Gemma Creffield, I'm so excited to see what we can accomplish together, and I'm thrilled to join the party!

Now, to the heroes in my life: the wine pourers and shit talkers and the most loyal guard dogs: Julie, Andrew, Alycia, and Teagan. Thank you for being nothing like the families I write about. Thank you for keeping my feet on the ground, and for cheering the loudest at every event.

To my Found Family in the USA and my friends here at home, I love you all. I hope we never ever part.

Lastly, to my husband and children: Michael, Zoe, and Dean. Words cannot express how fiercely I love you.

READ ON FOR AN
EXCLUSIVE BONUS CHAPTER . . .

The best thing to be said for Scurry was its lack of Artisans. This was also its biggest fault, because a town full of tradespeople need someone to pay them for their trade. Say what they might about rich folk, the Crafters would still line up to wash a swank's clothes, cook their meals, raise their children, polish their shoes. A lesser pay by far than the mines and factories, but one tended to keep their minds and limbs intact far longer for it.

Before she left Scurry forever, my mother laundered and mended clothing for rich folk, which is to say, she found herself continuously jobless with her limbs and senses in perfect working condition. Scurry pockets were shallow all over. They always had been. If you had something to sell to your fellow parishioners, it ought to be something they couldn't live without. Scurry folk only wanted what they needed. Swanks only wanted everything

It was enough to push nearly every inhabitant of Scurry beneath the thumb of the House—but not Rose Harrow. With Dad in the mines, Ma seemed determined to keep all of her whole. I'd like to presume it was for my sake. Everything I remember of my mother leading up to abandonment indicated she had loved me. Everything I'd learnt of her since indicated that she'd left for that same love.

But children don't know why their parents leave. They just wait for them to come back.

There are other things I remember: drawings, embroideries, flower pressings, painted china. She and I going door to door with these wares, trying to sell rich things to poor folk, Ma's smile waning between doors. Every so often, there would be a widower with his soles peeling away from his boots and a coat with popped stitching and bed linen that hadn't been seen to in months. From them, Ma found remit. The other times were grim indeed.

Say what you like about swanks, but a poor town needs a few rich folk.

There were times so desperate that days seemed to pass in which Ma never stopped crying. My father is absent from my memory on these days. Perhaps they'd fought, and he'd taken refuge in the pub. Perhaps he was just working a shift. But it was usually on these days that Rose's brother came knocking, and when Harland Seymour knocked, one had no choice but to open the door.

I knew very little about my uncle before my mother left Scurry, but when your mother is scared of something, you know to be scared too.

"Upstairs," she'd say when the knock came, and it was so imploring that I never argued. I sat on the topmost step, where I could hear but not be seen.

"Sister," Harland would say, and she'd try to block the door. To head him off.

"He ain't here," Ma would tell him. "I don't know where he is." Sometimes, this was enough to send him away.

On one occasion, perhaps the very last, it wasn't.

"That ain't any way to greet your kin, now is it?" Harland said, and I heard him push his way inside, heard the floorboards creak beneath his feet. Another pair of boots followed, then another. Everywhere Kicker went, his crew followed.

"What do you want?" Ma said. She had a way of flattening her voice, her body, as though to shrink the target. "Nina's sleepin'. I don't want her wakin' up."

"Aye? She alive, then? Ain't seen her round."

"By design," Rose said shortly. "What d'you want?"

A grunt of laughter from Harland. "Ol' Fletcher finds himself in arrears again, Rosie."

"And I've told you not to sell to him more times than I can count," Ma said in reply, her voice still in that carefully neutral tone. It did not rise in anger or accusation. I thought that if I could have seen her in that moment, her eyes would have been firmly planted somewhere out a window, or over Harland's shoulder.

"And send the poor bloke into the ground with naught to help him fight the shakes?" Harland admonished. "Wouldn't dream of it, sister. What I'm doin' for him is humane. Charitable—"

"What do you want?" Ma repeated in her deadened way.

"Well, that's just the thing," Harland said slowly, and I heard the creak of his boots as he moved. "I doubt I'll find anythin' here worth what Fletcher owes, will I? Bloody hell." He picked up something, perhaps a dish, then dropped it noisily. "He's fuckin' lowly, Rosie. You sure can pick 'em. Look at this place, eh?"

"I've told you, Nina's sleepin—"

"Then you'll come with me quietly," Harland said then, "and be back by mornin'."

Silence from the room below. A pounding in my small chest.

"I can't leave her alone," Rose said. "She—she wakes in the night."

"Ah, she'll be fine! What's one night, eh? One night, and we're square. I've got a nice chap from Baymouth who wants to make your acquaintance, and between you and me, his business is worth more than any debt Fletcher could incur in his lifetime."

I thought this chap from Baymouth must have clothes in desperate need of repair. If you wanted to sell something to a Crafter, it had to be something they couldn't live without.

There was a padding of boots. A door closing. Silence.

I slept on that topmost step, waiting for morning.

Children don't know why their parents leave.

They just wait for them to come back.

BELAVERE

Belavere City
Gilmore
Morland
Fenway
Gyser River
Brimshire
Sommerland
Baymouth